THE PROPERTY OF RAIN

Also by Angela Lambert

LOVE AMONG THE SINGLE CLASSES
NO TALKING AFTER LIGHTS
A RATHER ENGLISH MARRIAGE
THE CONSTANT MISTRESS
KISS AND KIN
GOLDEN LADS AND GIRLS

non-fiction

UNQUIET SOULS: THE INDIAN SUMMER OF THE BRITISH ARISTOCRACY
1939: THE LAST SEASON OF PEACE

ANGELA LAMBERT

THE PROPERTY OF RAIN

CORIN: . . . *the property of rain is to wet, and fire to burn;*
Shakespeare, *As You Like It*, Act 3, Scene 2

BANTAM PRESS

LONDON · NEW YORK · TORONTO · SYDNEY · AUCKLAND

TRANSWORLD PUBLISHERS
61–63 Uxbridge Road, London W5 5SA
a division of The Random House Group Ltd

RANDOM HOUSE AUSTRALIA (PTY) LTD
20 Alfred Street, Milsons Point, Sydney
New South Wales 2061, Australia

RANDOM HOUSE NEW ZEALAND
18 Poland Road, Glenfield, Auckland 10, New Zealand

RANDOM HOUSE SOUTH AFRICA (PTY) LTD
Endulini, 5a Jubilee Road, Parktown 2193, South Africa

Published 2001 by Bantam Press
a division of Transworld Publishers

Typeset in 12½/15½pt Ehrhardt by Falcon Oast Graphic Art

Printed in Great Britain
by Clays Ltd, St Ives plc, Bungay, Suffolk

1 3 5 7 9 10 8 6 4 2

For Tony Price
who went so far and did so much for this book,
with the same old love

DRAMATIS PERSONAE
SUFFOLK

Sam's Family
Old Abel, Sam's grandfather (1856–1928)
Abel Savage (1882–1946/7) m. 1905 **Flora**, née Hopton (1887–1957)
Little Abel, b. and d. 1905
Tom, b. 1906
Joseph (1907–20)
(1908 one stillborn child: Jude)
Joan, b. 1909, m. 1947, twins: Flora and Giorgio
Matilda (Matty), b. 1911, m. 1932 Jim Collett; 2 s., 2 d.
Davie (1912–28)
Ezra, b. 1914, m. (1) Audrey Winterton (d. 1953), 3 s. (2) 1958 Pauline Neale, 1 s., 1 d.
Sam, b. 27 March 1921

Marjorie Savage, b. 1961

Sam at School
Matthias (Matt) Spring nicknamed **Beddy, Isaac Winterton, John Moulton** (all b. 1921)
Edith Satterthwaite, b. 20 May 1921; Sam's friend, then sweetheart, later wife
Mary, b. 1910, and **Victoria**, b. 1912, Edith's older sisters

7

Mrs Satterthwaite, her mother, b. 1882, washerwoman, m. Peter Satterthwaite 1910; he abandoned the family in 1924
Jake Roberts, b. 10 May 1918; nicknamed Ox, Sam's enemy

Jake's Family
Maggie Roberts, Jake's mother, née Wright (1885–1952) m. 1909 **John Roberts** (1883–1918)
Lizzie, b. 1910, and **Rose**, b. 1913, their two daughters (Lizzie m. 1929, 2 d.; Rose m. 1931, 2 s., 3 d.)
Billy Debney, b. 1897, Maggie Roberts's second husband, m. July 1920

In the Village
The Hon. Marjorie Jamieson (1898–1978), teacher, comes to Lower Flexham 1919
Mr and Mrs Persimmons, vicar and wife, childless
Lord and Lady Manning, local grandees, landowner, school governor
Mrs Neale, the district nurse

Sam's Army Friends
Albert Fitch, Sidney Hale, Ivor Wordley (all b. 1918)

BUDHERA, INDIA

Lakshmi's Family

Matin, b. 1879, village midwife, and **Dada**, b. 1875, former sweeper;
Lakshmi's grandparents
Their sons, **Bakha**, b. 1893, and **Prem**
Prem, b. 1895, m. 1911 **Sukhia**, b. 1899
Preeti, b. 1915, 1st daughter, m. 1926, 4 children
Mithania, b. 1916, 2nd daughter, m. sweeper's son in 1930, 3 children
(1917 a stillbirth)
Ghashitia (1918–29), 3rd daughter
(1920 a stillborn son)
Lakshmi, b. 1921, 4th daughter
Shivram (1923–9), 1st son
(1925 a stillbirth)
Hari, b. 1927, 2nd son
Kubri, b. 1929, 5th daughter
Davadin, b. 1931, 6th daughter
(1933 a miscarriage)

In the Village

(All these belong to the sweeper caste, *mehtar* or *bhangi*, one of the
lowest among the Untouchables or Pariahs, nowadays known as Dalits)
Bakha, Prem's elder brother, Lakshmi's paternal uncle, sweeper in the
cantonment
Parvati, his wife; two daughters
Moti (1897–1926), Parvati's brother
Maya, b. 1902, Moti's wife
Ramu, their son, b. 1919
Sidda, a village sweeper
Lalla, another sweeper
Davadin, beautiful young village girl
Kempa, son of a well-to-do sweeper in next village, m. Davadin in 1926
Beera, b. 1896, Sukhia's elder brother, m. 1915, widowed 1934, 6
children

GLOSSARY

bhangi – sweeper (an insulting word referring to their low caste)
bidi – acrid small cigarette, hand-rolled in a leaf and filled with cheap tobacco
chapatti – a flat Indian bread made from coarse flour
chaudhury – caste leader in a village
devas – goddesses
dhanuk – midwife, a function reserved for the wives of sweepers
dharma – the universal law as applied to various aspects of life: the cosmic, moral, social, etc. For the individual, *dharma* is the moral code relating to his or her status in the world at each stage of life.
dhoti – length of cotton wrapped round the body and knotted into the waist to form loose baggy trousers, worn by men
ghat – a landing place beside a river
gully danda – a favourite boys' game, a kind of aerial cricket
harijan – a word introduced by Gandhi meaning children of God and used as an acceptable description of those castes previously designated Untouchables
kabaddi – a game played by boys
karma – action, work or deeds and their influence on the level of rebirth in the next life
kurta – a loose shirt or tunic
mehtar – sweeper

paraiyars or Pariahs – lowest of the four main ranks of Indian caste, each of which breaks into hundreds if not thousands of sub-divisions, arranged according to their designated area of work

pukka – proper, well-made, solid

PROLOGUE

Autumn 1999

THERE IS A MODEST SCATTER OF APPLAUSE AS THE SPEAKER rises to her feet. She smiles confidently at the audience and begins:

'The first good thing that's happened to me in putting together this book – it's going to be called *Good Morning, Miss Jamieson!* – is that it's reconciled me to my *name*. When I was growing up in the Sixties, most girls had names out of Jane Austen – like Emma and Sophie – or else rather old-fashioned biblical names like Rebecca and Sarah. *Marjorie* sounded uncool, as they say these days. But now that I've done some research into the life of Marjorie Jamieson, I'm proud to be called after her. She was a remarkable woman, though not unusual for her generation, and I'm here this evening not only to remind you about her but in the hope that you'll be able to tell me something about the school in which she taught for the whole of her working life. OK: first picture.'

Someone dims the lights and on the screen an old photograph of a young woman with bobbed dark hair wobbles into focus. One or two members of the audience draw breath sharply, as if in recognition.

'That's Marjorie Jamieson. We don't know who took it or even when, but at a guess it was in the late Twenties, which was about her age at the time. Some of you obviously recognize her. Was anyone here taught by her?'

A few timid hands are raised.

'I wor taught by her till I wor fourteen an' left school,' one old man says. 'Knew your parents, too, miss. We wor all chillun together.'

'So did I,' says another voice. 'She wor a wholly marvellous teacher, Miss Jamieson. *Marvellous*. T'hear her reading poetry, or out of th'Bible – Oi've niver forgotten it!'

Next slide.

'So you'll recognize this . . . Lower Flexham School, where she remained until it was closed in 1954.'

Another sharp intake of breath, then people begin to laugh and murmur and point at the screen.

'The epidiascope on which these pictures are being projected – quite a rare optical instrument nowadays, or so the Science Museum tells me – is the very one she used. She probably bought it for the school with her own money. The vicar's wife also used it, I believe, in her Sunday School classes. It was found in the attic when the school building was sold in the early Seventies. Next picture.'

A class of about twenty children, mostly thin and tousled, wearing drooping frocks or trousers and over-large boots, is lined up in front of the school. Marjorie Jamieson sits in the centre of the group.

'We don't know exactly when this was taken but again it must have been in the late Twenties, early Thirties . . .'

'Miss! Miss! There be Oi!' a man calls out excitedly. 'It wor taken – *Oi* remember – 1935, musta bin, year that Sam Savage an' Jake Roberts went off to join army.'

'There you are, I'm learning things already! So that's 1935 – and there they are . . .' – she waves her pointer at two swarthy faces, one small and pinched, the other large and moonlike, sitting at opposite ends of the row, as far apart as possible. 'They must've been enemies even then, yet they went off to India together. I've always thought that was odd.'

One or two people in the audience nod agreement.

'I'm getting off the point,' the speaker says. 'Let's stick to the Honourable Marjorie Jamieson.'

The Woodbridge Historical Society settles back on wooden chairs in the hall of the school that replaced the one they've just been looking at. Its members hear that their former teacher was born into one of the county's great families but became a teacher after the deaths of her brother and her fiancé in the First World War. Thereafter she devoted her entire working life to the children of Lower Flexham. In the phrase often applied to dedicated teachers of that era, 'she never married'. When she retired at the end of the Fifties, she wrote a book called *Three Men Went to War*: the story of three people from the village whom she had encountered as a teacher; how soldiering had affected them, their lives and their families. The book was not published till after her death in 1978 but its compassion, humanity, insight – and anger – made it a minor classic.

'I'm here this evening because I'm writing a biography of Marjorie Jamieson, and I hope some of you will be able to help with my research. I'm the first person from my family to have made it to university and I got the idea for this book because I wanted to celebrate not only Marjorie Jamieson but also the place and the people I come from. OK: more pictures to prompt your memories . . . next, please?'

Onto the screen flash a number of black and white photographs. Men harvesting, a horse-drawn wagon piled high with sheaves of corn. Women and children gleaning. The village inn with its painted sign and a scatter of men outside, wearing waistcoats and breeches.

'That be my ol' man's father!' one of the women calls out excitedly. 'Owd Bart!'

'Aye,' chimes in another voice, 'Oi remember 'im!'

A forge, in front of which stands a pair of huge Suffolk Punches waiting to be shod, their reins held by a small boy barely higher than their fetlocks. A magnificent kitchen garden surrounded by old brick walls; in the foreground, the gardener and his three lads gaze respectfully into the camera, caps in hand. The squire and his wife, he short and extremely stout, she lofty both in height and manner, the height emphasized by a large feathered hat.

'Lord and Lady Manning of course . . .'

'My grandparents,' says a clear voice from the hall. Thank God I didn't say anything dismissive, Marjorie Savage thinks.

'Oh, really? How *interesting*. Perhaps you can vouch for the story about the grapes, then?'

'Grapes? No, I don't think I ever heard that one.'

Moving forward in time: the Coronation – 1937 – the village hall decked in patriotic bunting. The British Legion Hall, late Forties perhaps, a group of men assembled outside it. The show ends with a last picture of Marjorie Jamieson, by then quite an old lady, seated in her dappled garden, a cane table beside her, writing in an exercise book. The lights come up. People settle back and clap.

'Right. Those are the pictures. But for once you, the audience, are not going to ask the questions: I am. Because although both my parents were born in Lower Flexham, by the beginning of the Sixties, when I came along, the old dialect was already starting to disappear – maybe due to the influence of television – and I keep hearing words that puzzle me. *Mawther* I know, of course – teenage girl – and I still sometimes catch myself saying *wholly* when I mean very . . . but what's *duzzy*?'

'Duzzy be stupid, miss,' says someone.

'Oh, stupid . . . like dizzy?'

'Aye, chance.'

'Same as *shanny*?'

'Shanny be more loike flighty, spirited.'

'Uh-huh. And *blore*? My mother used to say to me, "Stop yer blorin', choild!"'

'Blore be bellow, like li'l ol' cow!'

'Good, now that's another one . . .'

The audience starts calling out words . . . '*Tunky* be stout,' – 'Loike Lord Mannin'!', and the two laugh reminiscently. '*Putter* wor the woife's naggin'.'

'Aye, an' *heeler* wor that worthless feller, 'er 'usband!' an old lady whips back.

'Dew you say that to 'im and 'e'll *ding* yar!'

'Ding meant to clip around the ear?' Marjorie Savage asks.

'Aye, 'twor that!'

'Aye – or *clapper-claw* . . .'

'Same thing.'

The audience is beginning to buzz with remembered words. They call out several more and Marjorie writes them in a note-book. Finally she stands up and claps her hands.

'This is wonderful – I'm so grateful to you all. It's just what I need. Makes me feel like a foreigner – *furriner* – to be so ignorant of the speech my parents and grandparents used every day. I'd very much like you to write down any others you can think of and perhaps let me have them afterwards, or send them to me – I've got some stamped addressed envelopes here – along with anything else you may remember about Marjorie Jamieson, her school and the boys who went off to fight. The two that particularly interest me, of course, are Ezra Savage and his younger brother, Sam . . .'

PART ONE

CHAPTER ONE

March 1921

To every thing there is a season, and a time to every purpose under the heaven: A time to be born, and a time to die . . . A time to love, and a time to hate; a time of war and a time of peace.
Ecclesiastes, 3:1

I HUNGER AND THIRST AFTER RIGHTEOUSNESS, THOUGHT Flora Savage. Mostly I thirst. I'm a-going to get a hot cup of tea to soothe my churning belly. It mustn't be dawn yet; only the little old owl is hoo-hooing, too early for cockcrow. She yawned and stretched her arms to get rid of the stiff feeling in the joints, then cracked her swollen knuckles. Hoisting herself out of the high bedstead she caught her breath quietly, so as not to wake her husband. Oof! Could this be it? I need my tea first. Leaning on the creaking banisters, she heaved her swollen body down the stairs, not bothering to light the Tilley lamp since after sixteen years in this house her hands and feet knew every step and surface of it by heart. Thank God! The fire had stayed in. She blew gently on the embers till they glowed orange, put more wood on, hung the blackened kettle over the hearth and sat down to wait for it to boil. In the chair on the other side of the fireplace her father-in-law, Old Abel, was snoring, his breath whistling past the gaps in his teeth. In Flora's belly a dull ache quickened and tugged. *That it may please thee to preserve all women labouring of child, all sick persons and young children, we beseech thee to hear us, good Lord*, prayed Flora, the familiar words easier than original thought. Outside the dawn was coming up, stealthy as a stalking cat. Pains griped in regular spasms. The ninth labour is quick for a woman thirty-four years old.

A village is a good place to be born and coming into the world under your own roof is best. All Flora's children were born at home and three had already died there. Her babies' first gulp of oxygen was the air they breathed throughout their childhood, sometimes stained with the tang of the sea if the wind blew hard from the east. It was not easy to break away from Lower Flexham. People often told the story about an old neighbour who left the parish just once in his life with a tumbril and two horses to take a load of corn to the mill six miles away. Returning safely to his own side of the parish boundary he lit his pipe and said, 'Thank goodness I'm back in good owd England! Oi'll niver go abroad again.' Even those driven by poverty, scandal or hope to distant places like Newmarket or Australia felt compelled to return to their birthplace before they died, to sniff the smell of belonging, the last gasp of their first breath. Joseph, Flora's gentle second son, had breathed his last hardly more than a year ago in the bed he used to share with his brother Tom, dying in the last miasma of the flu epidemic. He sank, poor boy, from life to death in less than a week, the doctor too busy to come even if they could have afforded him.

Abel Savage, Flora's husband, had been called up in May 1916 to replenish the losses in France, although farm-workers were supposed to be exempt. Before he went off to fight, Young Abel had been known for his swarthy good looks but also, as local people put it, for being 'a straight man up and down'. When the Great War ended he came back to his family and his native village alive and in one piece, or so it seemed. But his mind was twisted by what he had witnessed and endured – though he never talked about it, not a word. People said he was lucky that his physical injuries were slight but Flora knew better. His resilient spirit and simple kindness had gone. In the first months back home he took her with angry, tight-lipped lust, desperate for the smell and touch of a woman after months clogged up among cold, wet, broken and sometimes dead men. He never did find comfort again, but he fathered a late child; a boy.

The last member of the family came into the world on 27 March 1921. This was the infant about to be born, here, now, downstairs, just before sunrise. Two of the older ones were sick and Flora, afraid of infecting the new baby, had improvised a bed in the parlour and now lit a fire with bits of kindling propped on dried lumps of turf. It was the fourth week in March but the unused air of the room was cold. When her delivery was imminent she climbed the wooden staircase to wake her elder daughter, Joan, and the twelve-year-old slipped into the chill dawn to fetch the midwife. Too late; the child was forcing its way out. Flora stood by the fire, one hand leaning heavily on the mantelpiece, the other supporting her labouring belly. She heaved and strained by herself, legs braced, groaning and panting in short shallow breaths like a dog on a hot day, until the baby slithered between her cupped hands. Then she crouched down exhausted, the infant lying limp and silent on her knees. The neighbour hurried in, a shawl thrown over her flannel nightgown, cut the cord, snatched up the baby and thumped his back, forcing him to inhale. He gasped, emitted a gargling wail and at once his bluish-purple body was suffused with a healthy, glowing pink. The midwife heaved a snort of satisfaction.

''E'll live! Let's 'ope 'e dunna regret it.'

Mrs Hulse's forty years of practical experience were complemented by a host of old beliefs and customs to welcome new arrivals and speed the newly departed. Using the tongs, she picked a glowing shard from the fire, dropped it into a bowl of water and, with her fingers, moistened the baby's pursed lips.

'There!' she said. 'Cinder-water. That'll drive devil out of 'im.'

Suffolk superstition decrees that a newborn child's first movement should be upwards, in the belief that if life starts on an upward path it will go on that way. Flora knew this and she whispered from the bed, 'Stand on a chair, lift him up!'

'He has risen already,' Mrs Hulse reassured her.

'Be he whole?' his mother asked.

'A fine, healthy boy,' the midwife soothed, and she put the baby in his mother's arms.

Flora looked at his matted hair, tightly closed eyes and contorted features. Shall I call 'ee Joseph? she thought. No, I won't. He's not come into the world to replace my gentle Joey, he's a li'l ol' boy with his own immortal invisible future. *May he honour his father and mother, and be pure in thought, word and deed. Renounce the devil and all his works and allus do as it says in the Holy Bible. Amen.* She became aware of her daughter.

'What be 'ee gawpin' at, Joan? Can't thee homage thy brother? Gi'im a kiss.'

The girl looked at the puny scrap of flesh, its wrinkled skin streaked with what looked like white paste.

'I'll not,' she said. 'What be that stuff?'

'I dunno. Axe him thyself. Th'art a stubborn mawther. Now go'n, move those legs of yourn and fetch his clo'es warmin' in kitchen. Wake thy father and tell 'im 'e's got anither son. I 'ope it pleases 'im . . . though God knows,' she said to herself, ''ow we'll feed 'im. Yer dad'll need 'is drink too, before he goes abroad in cold.'

The midwife washed the child's face and hands in an enamel bowl of water warmed by the fire and sponged his waxy body. She handed him back.

'What shall 'ee name li'l ol' boy?'

'Sam, for poor Samuel Merrilees over t'way that was killed in France. To comfort 'is grieving mother. And Henry for my brother Harry, that died also.'

'Samuel Henry Savage. A fine name. With a name like that wor'n't be narthen he cudd'n do when he grow up.'

'Show 'im to they upstairs. Hold 'im up at the door. They must know their own brother,' Flora said, her voice weak.

'Gie me some clothes to cover his nakedness. Are his tail-clouts ready?'

'In the basket: there . . .' Joan answered.

The midwife cleaned and bandaged the end of the umbilical cord and tied a scrap of material round the baby's shrivelled bottom, folding and knotting it like a loincloth over his engorged genitals. She wrapped him in a ragged shirt outworn by the older children and, cradling him firmly, carried him upstairs to his brothers and sisters. Tom, one of three boys who normally shared the iron-framed double bed, lifted his head towards the doorway while Ezra, seven years old and still only half awake, murmured sleepily. The other two, nine-year-old Davie and his sister Matty, huddled together under crumpled bedclothes in the far corner of the room. They were both poorly, with the drooping eyes, bluish cheeks and running noses of perpetual cold and hunger.

'Wake up, sleepyheads, and homage your new brother!' the midwife said. 'Your mother has named him Samuel Henry, so he be Sam. Ain't he a fine boy?'

'Oh!' said Matty, struggling to sit up. 'Oh look, our new-laid Sam! In't 'e a foony colour? Jus' loike a li'l ol' piglet!'

Sam's grandfather, Old Abel Savage, was a bent figure in his mid-sixties with one eye half out of its bloodshot socket.

Crippled by arthritis, he ate slops and slept in the rocking chair by the kitchen fire most of the day and night, sometimes with a hen on his knee or a hatful of chicks keeping warm in his lap. His son, Sam's father, was known as Young Abel. Both men wanted the new child to take their name but in a flash of spirit Flora refused. She had already lost one Abel – her first-born, who had died after a few weeks of mewling, struggling life – and besides, she didn't want him to be known for ever as Young Abel's Son. She preferred to honour the cheerful lad across the lane whose body and soul had been shattered in the mud of northern France. She got her way and her sixth son was christened Samuel Henry – *wherein he was made a member of Christ, the child of God, and an inheritor of the Kingdom of Heaven* – though everyone called him Sam and forgot about the Henry.

Old and Young Abel, Flora and their six children shared the timbered cottage with its privy at the bottom of the garden; cold and stinking in the winter, hot and stinking in summer. Tom, the oldest, had been working in the fields since the age of eight – during the war when men were scarce – earning sixpence a week at harvest-time. By the time Sam was born Tom was fifteen and could bring home as much as three and ninepence in a good week. Since his father's wage after deduction of rent was thirty-eight shillings and sixpence, the extra money was crucial. After Tom came the two girls, Joan and Matilda, twelve and ten, one dark, one fair, like night and day. Then two more boys: Davie and Ezra. They'd been called the Lill'uns up till now but with Sam's arrival they were promoted to They Boys. The Savages were a swarthy nest of East Anglian rooks, all black-haired and dark-eyed except Matilda. A throwback to Nordic stock, she was tall and fair-haired, her skin as pale and clear as water.

Sam was the youngest in the family by seven years. The war had interrupted Flora's run of births. By the time she was twenty-seven she'd borne six living children and another who died before being weaned. Only a year ago young Joseph, just thirteen, had been carried away by the flu. She suppressed the thought that always came to mind . . . why couldn't it have been her father-in-law, Old Abel; why her little Joe?

After Sam's birth, her husband's desperate ploughing of Flora's skinny body became less frequent. He could not afford to feed another mouth – could not afford to feed the mouths he already had. Before sitting down to their usual supper of beer, bread and salt and (with luck) a twist of fat bacon to moisten it, he sometimes muttered the poor man's grace:

> *Oh Heavenly Father, bless us*
> *And keep us all alive;*
> *There are ten of us to dinner*
> *And food for only five.*

Abel took little notice of his latest child but Sam was not short of attention. His every move was admired; his first smiles met by a circle of answering smiles. As he was one of the first boys to be born in the village after the war – a new life, when so many had been lost – everyone welcomed him, chortling at his toothless grin and starfish fingers. 'Ain't 'e a li'l ol' boy?' doting neighbours would chorus, and Flora would croon, ''E be that all right – a fine babby!' Matty spent the first weeks of the baby's life recovering from the feverish cold that half killed her, struggling back to health almost unnoticed. Her brother Davie, the runt of the family, became skinnier and more listless than ever. But they both survived and Sam flourished. Matty sometimes pinched him in secret with her long white fingers but no more than her big brothers had pinched her when she was little. Why should he have all the attention? Joan, however, deft and proud, was like a second mother.

Sam changed from a swaddled horizontal bundle into a squat

upright one. His brothers, out in the fields with their father, were a dour, unspeaking trio; stunted by bad food and hard work, grey figures against the dark earth. Ezra and Davie went stone-picking for an hour every day before school, collecting the stones and flints that grew in the fields like weeds and piling them in heaps to be picked up later by a cart and dumped beside the road for the roadman. The boys often filled two or three buckets, earning a halfpenny per bucket, which paid for their hobnailed boots. At other times they gathered potatoes, or acorns in October for the farmer's pigs at sixpence a sack. After that they spent the rest of the morning sullenly behind desks in the schoolroom; then wolfed a cold baked potato or a hunk of bread and cheese and trudged back to their father and brother. Tom, who had finished school, no longer counted as a boy. He was a *lad* and in a year or two would get half a man's pay. Young Abel bitterly resented the law that made his boys stay at school till they were fourteen. Their wages were sorely missed. Only just literate himself, he saw no point in education. It was their hands that needed educating, not their heads.

He was not the man he had been, not as father or husband. His head roared with a tinnitus of terror that became even more vivid in his sleep. He dreamed of earth hurled skywards by exploding shells, trees stripped of greenery in midsummer, fields plundered by marching boots, nothing growing, no order of the seasons, no sense, no safety. He turned up a hag-stone one day in the field – a jagged flint pierced by a hole – stuck it in his pocket, scrubbed it clean of earth under the pump and hung it from his bedpost to ward off the Evil Eye; but even this didn't keep the nightmares away. Wild unsaddled horses exploded across the earth with demented eyes and foam-flecked mouths. Their sharp hooves thundered over his soft body as he lay in a shell-hole, exposed and screaming, screaming for rescue. His comrades sprawled around, dead or dying . . . 'Hist, Abel! 'Tis only a bad dream,' his wife would say. 'Hush, or thou'lt wake the young'uns . . . thou be home, all's well. Here, take my hand. See, I be here.' He wouldn't let her comfort him but gradually his heart slowed its desperate pace, the sweat dried on his forehead and he would wait for sleep or dawn, whichever came first.

The girls stayed at school all day, struggling towards literacy, learning to be pious and industrious and not get above themselves. They were squashed in six to every desk, sitting with arms folded so as to take up the least possible space. Each desk had six cracked inkwells and a deep groove to hold six wooden pen-holders, their tips pitted with the marks of sharp teeth. Pupils were issued with new steel nibs once a week but their clumsy hands splattered the clean pages with ink blots. The girls embellished these into decorative flowers, suns, cats or the little round faces of babies until the teacher called out, 'Stop daydreaming!'

Forty children were packed into one schoolroom, chanting psalms and tables and capital cities; poems and spelling bees, kings and queens of England, dates and battles. The flaunting, incomparable seventeenth-century words of the Bible took root in their minds like seedlings in the earth, filling their heads with half-understood glory: '*Who coverest thyself with light as with a garment: who stretchest out the heavens like a curtain . . . who maketh the clouds his chariot: who walketh upon the wings of the wind.*' Many a child stared out of the window at the high East Anglian clouds that bestrode the sky, inflating their pomp against the sun, until its reverie was abruptly shattered by the teacher's voice.

'Mary Debney, what have I just said?'

'. . . *Maketh the clouds his chariot*, miss?'

'That was five minutes ago. You've been dreaming again. Which psalm does it come from?'

'I dunno, miss. Sorry, miss.'

'Who knows?'

A few wobbly hands.

'Yes: Felix Austin?'

'Psalm one hunnerd and four, miss?'

'*Good*, Felix. Psalm one hundred and four.'

The girls were told off for mistakes and misdemeanours (lateness, giggling, asking to go to the toilet during a lesson). Once Matty couldn't wait. She peed in her knickers and it soaked through and trickled down her legs. Spiteful Dot Croker who sat next to her put up her hand and said, 'Miss, miss, there's a foony smell and it's cooming from Matilda Savage!' In the playground afterwards Matty's brother Davie clapper-clawed Dot good and proper, pulling her stupid plaits until she cried. Davie got the cane but honour was restored. *An eye for an eye and a tooth for a tooth.*

The girls came home at teatime to help their mother and memorize their lessons, chanting them aloud for each other's benefit, watched by Sam. When they were busy his sisters put him down on a patch of floor, and ten minutes later he would still be there, motionless, absorbed in some inner vision of his own. He was quite happy to watch a shaft of sunlight flickering against the wall, bringing indoors the dancing shadow of leaves on a branch, or the geometry of the small square window panes that stretched light and shade like a cats' cradle across the uneven stone floor. 'Sam be dreamin' again,' they would say. Sitting outdoors in the home-made wooden pram, a contraption with iron wheels that had done duty for six already, Sam wondered why the distant strip of land that stopped the sky falling down was greyish blue and not brown like the ground under his pram. When the pram was moving he would lean over and watch the high springy wheels pick up leaves and whirl them round, then lean back again to look at the birds floating through the air. Once everyone forgot about him and he was left out until dark. When Flora came to find him he was staring at the night sky, indifferent to the cold.

'Look at you, sittin' up like rabbit in whatefield! Let's get 'ee inside afore the fox gets thee.'

'Wha' tha'?' he asked, pointing upwards.

'That be *moon*,' his mother told him as she wheeled him indoors. 'It be big 'n' full tonight.' Sam burst out crying.

'What be cryin' fer?' she said irritably.

'*Wantit moon!*' he said, howling for the moon at two and a half.

He imbibed unconsciously the spirit of the place into which he was born. He grew accustomed to its trees long before he knew their names – the elder by the door of the house, to ward off evil spirits; the holly that must never be cut; the hawthorn and whitethorn that must never be brought into the house except on the first of May. He became familiar with the song of many different birds – the woodpecker drilling for insects and grubs with a rapid *drrrr* like a snarling dog, the nuthatch's beak ticking like a clock at the bark of a tree; the monotonous two notes of the cuckoo in spring, the sweet carolling of the female blackbird and the harsh chatter of the magpie. He learned to recognize their silhouettes and their flight; the shrieking swifts that looped and sped after moths at dusk and the slow soft owls that wafted and hooted through his sleep. He knew all their patterns, his mouth twisting into whistles and grimaces as he tried to imitate them. He struggled to decipher the barking of dogs, a chorus of baritone and counter-tenor, to and fro, in twos and threes; then a silence, then a single howl; the chorus resuming till halted by an angry human shout. He caught the briefer, higher yelp of a fox. In the summer when they had finished threshing the traction engines would be used for steam sawing, and then the sooty smell of coal smoke mixed with sawdust thickened the air. At slack times, when the contractors were cleaning and overhauling their machines, it was the sweet scent of lubricating oil that teased his nostrils. Best of all, Sam liked the peal of bells as they wound through Sundays, holy days, christenings, weddings and funerals. Like everyone else he would stop to count the solemn notes that marked a villager's death: two peals of three for a woman, three times three for a man, before solitary muffled tolling reckoned up the age of the departed.

Sam was a thoughtful child who lived inside his head (as none of the others ever had time to do), fitting together from scraps of family talk a mosaic of Lower Flexham past and present. At first the words and phrases he heard – *Suffolk Punch* – *Plough Monday* – *Miss Jamieson says* – were just grown-up noises, sparkling and incomprehensible as dust in sunlight. Gradually he learned to associate them with the barrel-like chestnut horses that hauled huge cartloads of hay or stones, or the turning circle of festivals, All Hallows' Eve and Plough Monday in winter, the Harvest Frolic in summer. He watched the village rituals like Crying the Mare and Beating the Bounds – ordinary, familiar events, no different from the ritual of going to church every Sunday, the family on parade. Most exciting of all was the rousing cacophony of the Rough Band, when men paraded round the village banging noisy implements and instruments, tins and old pails, to show their disapproval of bad behaviour. 'T'men'll give yew th'Rough Band!' his mother would threaten if ever he misbehaved, and at once he would be good.

Until he was three, Sam had slept in a wooden crib beside his parents' bed. As he grew bigger it became increasingly uncomfortable until finally he could scarcely move, his limbs rigidly enclosed as if by a coffin. After that he was laid crosswise at their feet, occasionally kicked by his mother's sharp toenails or buffeted by his father's convulsions as he cried out and struggled with his nightmares. 'Hush 'ee, Abel, hush, hush, 'tis only I and . . . thy babes,' she would soothe and Sam would mutter to himself before falling asleep again.

The after-effects of the war became more marked in Abel's

behaviour and character. In the past he had always been quiet, his modesty all the more attractive for being allied to springy black hair, heavy-lidded dark eyes, rich tawny skin and a self-contained energy that never wasted time showing off but got on steadily with every task and most people. As a young bachelor these qualities, above all the looks, meant he was coveted by every girl in the village. Gentle, eighteen-year-old Flora – devout and diligent but by no means the village beauty – was radiant with pride when he asked her to be his wife. Their first few years of marriage, marked by the arrival of a son every year for the first three years, then Joan and Matty, and then another son, Davie, had been joyful. But after witnessing the fighting in France, Abel had turned belligerent and quick to take offence. Once the quiet listener in a corner of the taproom, he became aggressive, even predatory. He started eyeing other women and, remembering how ardently they had once competed for his attention, young widows and even wives sometimes met his eye. He could take his pick of half the women in the village, if he chose; and sometimes he did choose. This did not settle his rage, however. He was impatient with animals, booting dogs out of his way until they cringed and ran at the sight of him. A moment's carelessness by one of his children would bring the anger boiling up and his hard hand would deal instant retribution.

'Stay, Joan, wha' didst do to thy father?' Flora would ask when the fifteen-year-old came in crying, her cheek red from a slap. The answer was always a resentful 'Narthen.'

'Why didst clip 'er hid, Abel?'

'Shanny mawkin. 'Er be no use bar eatin' table bare.'

It was true that Joan was a big, raw-boned girl and always hungry, Flora thought, but no wonder; there was little enough on the table for anyone to eat. Every bowl was wiped clean in moments.

'Thou'lt hev all thy children feared o' thee?'

'Aye, why not? Larn 'em to watch their ways. An' thine!' he added bitterly. 'Axin' questions, allus putterin' away at me. I'll give thee what for next time, be done wi'it.'

Man that is born of woman hath but a short time to live, and is full of misery, but if y'axe me, Lord, the woman gits worse misery. Flora stopped trying to intervene. Instead, she and the girls looked out for his approach, warning one another, trying to gauge his mood. It was often, eventually always, bad. The boys knew their father had begun to beat their mother because they heard her cries and saw the marks next day, but they were afraid to protect her, knowing he'd have the breeches round their ankles and give them a thrashing.

Abel's nightmares grew worse. He often found himself struggling to protect the soft bodies of his children from attack. The girls might be running across a field, kicking up their heels, spinning and laughing – as they never did in real life – and he would be pounding after them, trying to warn them of imminent shell-fire. Just as he caught up, grabbed their skirts and dragged them to the ground, the earth would explode in a heavenward parabola of dirt and roots and tender flesh. He would throw back his head and howl, howl that he had done his best and wake in a muck sweat, panting. Flora would try to gentle him back to consciousness, stroking his shoulder, his hand, venturing to touch his face. Nothing soothed him. He no longer wanted tenderness. He wanted oblivion. He began to drink.

The older children slept in the next room, three boys sharing one bed under inadequate bedclothes, their sisters the other. They kept each other warm in winter and all slept the sleep of exhaustion, their bodies worn out by hard work and the perpetual fear of a beating. Although Tom and Joan, at nineteen and sixteen, were well into sexual maturity, nothing went on under cover of night. If Tom had clambered into bed with his sisters and tried to fumble them he would have been the butt of indignant curses and ridicule: 'Git away, thou great lummox! What be doing? Don't yew niver touch us or I'll tell our mother!' Sometimes in the middle of the night, if his father's nightmares were bad, Sam would climb out of his parents' bed and blunder into the other room, burrowing under blankets that smelled of sweat, hair and snot. Never urine, for nobody pissed in the bed. The first time you pissed in the bed you got such a hiding that you never did it again, but stumbled drowsily to the pot in a corner of the room. Little Sam could cuddle up to any of the five without being pushed away. Even Matty, chill and virginal as an ice maiden, would curl a protective arm around him in her sleep and murmur endearments.

The two girls taught Sam his letters. By the time he was three and a half he knew the ABC and could recite nursery rhymes, providing someone showed him the picture first to remind him which of Mother Goose's verses that page held. He loved rag books and calendars, building imaginary worlds on a vast scale from the flimsiest evidence. He had seen giraffes, buffalo and zebra in his sisters' school books and evoked them in his mind's eye: huge, hulking beasts, giraffes with high sloping shoulders as long and steep as a staircase, buffaloes whose udders drooped and billowed like newly washed sheets, zebra striped like the cloud shadows over the fields. He would have been amazed to know that none was very much bigger than the cows that passed along the back lane behind the privy every day: leisurely, sway-backed beasts with dappled flanks, legs as muddy as his boots and a warm privy smell.

As confirmation time approached Flora began to test the older ones, making sure they had the words of the Catechism by heart. '*To keep my hands from picking and stealing and my tongue from evil-speaking, lying and slandering,*' the girls chanted laboriously and the words swung in Sam's head as rhythmically as bells. He learned unawares, not knowing that he learned . . . the Collect for the Day; for Stir-Up Sunday, Rogation Sunday and the Lenten Sundays, the prayers and readings marking out the year as it moved from Lent to Easter, progressed towards the harvest, and declined towards *the deep midwinter*, when *frosty wind made moan, earth stood hard as iron, water like a stone.* That hymn made perfect sense, though others did not. *Blest are the poor in heart, for they shall see our God* – but what was poor in heart? On Good Friday his sisters warbled, '*There is a green hill far away, without a city wall . . .*' But why should a green hill need a city wall? They'd all subside into the pew to hear the sermon, glancing under their eyelashes to see who had new shoes or was trying to hide a swelling belly. When there were storms off the East Anglian coast his brothers rumbled, '*Eternal Father strong to save*' and at the school carol service Sam lifted his chin and sang, '*Away in a manger*' into their proud, smiling faces.

He believed in the Eternal Father and Baby Jesus just as he believed in amulets for warding off the Evil Eye – why else did the hag-stone hang above his parents' bed? He kept hoping to find the Fairy Loaf, luckiest of all, a fossilized shell that was occasionally turned up in freshly tilled earth. This lucky dip of pagan rites and Christian goodness stamped him a Suffolk boy from those particular few acres of soil. Like a watermark, their patterns marked him for life: *Sam Savage of Lower Flexham.*

CHAPTER TWO

1925–1926

THE MEN WHO HAD FOUGHT IN THE WAR AND SURVIVED ITS
horrors by conjuring up their home and village, turning both
into a lost paradise, came back to find life was still harsh and
poor. The war had ended eight years ago – they had *won*, hadn't
they? – yet they still had no money and no food for their children.
The land and its owners demanded too much from their under-
nourished bodies, and gave too little back. The Savages, like most
people, took hunger for granted. Sometimes in winter there was
nothing in the larder except a gristly lump of cold, fatty pork,
eaten by Abel and Tom with a potato and boiled mangel-wurzels
– since the workers must always be fed. Nearly everyone stole
vegetables from the fields and every other man was a poacher.
Even so, the children often had to make do with a hunk of bread
soaked in hot salt water – 'kittle-broth', their mother called it,
adding, 'Jack Frost hev frorne the cupboard doors shut.' They
never complained, but grew up hard and silent like their parents.
Flora fed Old Abel and tried to make sure that portions were
fairly divided between the rest but Davie, who had always been
scrawny and feeble, became thinner still while Matty, with her
height and pallor, looked like a climbing beanstalk.

Young Abel developed two deep fleshy ridges above his eye-brows from frowning and by the time he was forty his good looks had quite gone. His father at sixty-eight was very old. Querulous and demanding, he swallowed whatever was spooned into his toothless mouth and scrabbled in his lap when he needed to be cleaned up again. These services were rendered by Flora and the girls. *The days of our age are three-score years and ten*, he can't have much longer to go, she thought – and then reproached herself, remembering, *Honour thy father and mother*. The Holy Bible is my solace, she thought. It speaks to my sorrow and comforts my misery; it gives me hope, yea, and hope for my children, too.

The girls chewed bacon rinds as they walked to school in the mornings, to make the saliva run and give them the feeling that they had eaten breakfast. Joan at sixteen no longer sat down to lessons. Instead she was now a school monitor, responsible for cleaning the school and looking after the youngest children. For this she got two shillings and sixpence a week and a nourishing lunch every day. In the afternoons she went to the big house and did whatever Lady Manning's cook told her – churning butter until her strong wrists and forearms ached, or ironing sheets. The pillowcases were left to the maids of the house – smoothing their embroidered edges was too delicate a task for a hulking girl who might burn holes in them or tear the lace. This work earned her another shilling as well as providing endless gossip for Matty as they trudged the two miles to school.

'Be she all high and mighty, squire's wife? Be she botty and la-di-da?'

'Lork, I wudden hardly know. Cook's hoity-toity enow . . . I be too afeard of milady. I durn't dare look at her.'

'What do *she* do, then, in kitchen?'

Joan laughed. 'Thou be too innocent to live, Matty! *She* don't come into kitchen – kitchen goes to *her*!'

'Niver!'

'It do. Cook or Mrs Sparrow be called to drawin' room. Then

it's *yea* milady, *nay* milady, and they comes back and tells *us* what to do.'

'And 'is lordship?'

'He be all muddy boots and dirty dogs – an' 'is weskit be round as a barrel o' beer – or a lass that's bin up to no good!'

'Do 'e eat all day long then?'

'Drink, more loike.'

They laughed at the absurdities of rich men and their lazy wives.

Sam, being the youngest, escaped the worst hardships of a bad time. The framework of his life was determined by his mother's strict routine. Every Monday she washed. A cauldron would be hung from a hook and water warmed over the fire. Working clothes were soaked in carbolic solution while Flora ground the wet sheets and pillowcases against a washboard outside at the pump, to and fro, up and down, rubbing the heavy fabric until her hands were raw. The bedlinen – not linen at all but rough calico drill, woven to last a hundred years or more – was rinsed under running water and spread over the grass to dry in summer, or in winter hung over a washing line or a high pulley in the kitchen if it rained. No extremes of weather could make her change the inflexible order of her working week. On Tuesdays she mended and darned and ironed and folded and laid away the sheets and clothes. On Wednesdays, Sam's 'best day', she prepared sweet-smelling yeasty dough and baked bread for the coming week. In the autumn she bottled fruit or pickled vegetables to supplement the winter monotony of potato pie and onion dumplings. Sam wiped his finger greedily round the saucepan after she had made crab–apple preserve but there were no treats for the older ones.

In the evenings his sisters would come upstairs and one would tell him a story while the other mended by the late summer light from their parents' window or candlelight in winter. Sam loved fairy tales.

'Well now, once upon a time, long long ago in a land far, far away . . .' the lulling voice would begin, 'there wor a beautiful princess. Her hair wor *that* long, it was so long, and her eyes sparkled like the stars at night.' Sam would snuggle under the blankets and sigh with pleasure as his mind filled with pictures. 'One day she thought up mischief upon hersel'. She decided to go where her mother had forbidden her niver iver *iver* to go and off she set to find the Forbidden Place.'

'Where be that then, Matty?' Sam said from the bed.

'It be the place where even princesses dare not go. It be the dark place. It be the place of secrets.'

'Yes,' said Sam fearfully.

'So she mun walk and walk till her feet were that sore and then she walked an' walked some more and suddenly, whoosht!' – Sam jumped – 'There were a great high wall an' behind it were the Forbidden Place.'

'Will she go back now?' pleaded Sam.

'An' she walked round it once. And she walked round it twice. An' she cuddna see no doorway. An' then she walken roun' it a thrice time, sayin' to hersel', "Arter this I be goin' hoom."'

'She be a good mawther,' Sam said hopefully and Matty frowned.

'But as she were comin' to the end of the great high wall, she saw, sudden like, a door she'd missed. Quick as a flash, in she went, *whisht!*'

Sam jumped again, and Joan pricked herself.

'Inside this wall were dizens an' dizens of little snarly things, an' they snarled at her like this . . .' – Matty bared her teeth – 'an' like *that*' – Joan and Matty both leaned towards Sam and bared their glimmering teeth – 'an' when they 'ad all stopped snarlin' they says to she, "It be no good on 'ee, Princess, that 'ee found the door in our wall, for now we are a-goin' to do 'ee *mischief*! If 'ee come into our Forbidden Place, kewrious like, we'll do 'ee *trouble*. We will, aye, an 'ee'll get more than 'ee came lookin' for!" But she wor well-happed. For just as they githered and gathered around she, flurrin' an' frolickin' like moths at a candle or dogs on a rat, in a twinkle came a noise of clatterin' horseshoes and runnin' feet and there stood a fine, handsome young prince . . .'

'*Me!*' Sam said proudly.

'Thee cuddna be no prince!' Matty said scornfully.

'I be a knight of old,' he insisted.

'There stood,' Matty conceded, 'a fine handsome knight and what dost 'ee think he did?'

'Saved she! Saved she from all the liddel, snappy snarly things!'

''E did. Right as rain, thet's what 'e done for 'er . . . saved she! And they both lived happily ever after and she niver saw none of 'em no moor.'

'Now do 'ee snuggle down in bed and mind thou hev sweet dreams!' Joan said.

Sam, like his father, suffered from nightmares.

CHAPTER THREE

1926–1928

SAM'S IDYLL ENDED WHEN HE BEGAN AT LOWER FLEXHAM Infants' School. He was five and a half. Here, on the first day, he met his enemy. His sisters had marched him there between them, uttering warnings ('Do'ee keep quiet now. 'Ee munt not talk wi' teacher, not unless she be talken' to 'ee, Sam! 'Ee munt ask all 'em questions, like dost at 'ome,') twitching his clothes in an attempt to make his outsized shirt stay tucked into his out-sized trousers. After a rough kiss they shooed him through the school gates into the littl'uns' playground towards a group of boys, some of whom he knew from Sunday School and most of whom he recognized. Sam turned back and saw Joan and Matty standing there waving at him. Reassured, he walked on.

A bigger boy came up to him; so big it didn't seem possible he was still in the Infants'. His large, full mouth hung half open, he had sloe-black eyes, pouched, ruminating cheeks and a fine head of wiry black hair. This was Jake Roberts. Jake Roberts was eight years and four months old. Resenting Sam for having two grown-up sisters to kiss him goodbye, one tall and pretty, the other plump and comfortable, Jake shoved him hard in the chest. Sam staggered, recovered his balance and smiled to show he knew it must have been a mistake. Jake pushed again, harder. Sam nearly fell over.

'What be doin' that fer?' he asked in surprise.

'Th'art sissy,' said Jake.

'I b'ain't.'

'Thou be an' all,' repeated Jake woodenly. 'Sissy. Thee *and* thy mawthers.'

Sensibly, Sam turned away. He felt a thump on his back and fell over, scraping his nose and cheek against the flagstones of the playground and grazing the tender palms of his hands. He started to cry.

'Sissy!' shouted Jake in triumph. 'Sissy! Sissy! 'Ee be a babby! Cry-babby!' Quickly other children gathered round, thankful not to be the victim. They pointed at Sam. 'Sissy! Cry-babby!'

Sam picked himself up and started to run towards the gate of the playground where his sisters had been standing a few moments ago. Barring his way, stolid as tree trunks, loomed the lisle-stockinged legs of an adult. Sam stumbled, stopped and tipped his head back to see who it was.

'Where do you think you're going?' she asked.

'Home,' said Sam. 'Oi want me mam.'

'You can't do that. You're a big boy now. You have to go to school. What's your name?'

Sam had been prepared for this. 'Samuel Henry Savage,' he said. 'I be called Sam.'

'Well then, Samuel Henry Savage, I am your teacher and *my* name is Miss Jamieson. You may call me that, or if you can't remember it all at once, you may call me *miss*. Have you brought a handkerchief?'

'Yes,' said Sam, glad to have got something right. 'Miss.'

'Good boy. Take it out of your pocket, blow your nose, put it back and follow me.'

Sam did as he was told. He looked up at her again, brushing his sore palms together to get rid of the dirt.

'Now then, Samuel Henry Savage: you have come to school to learn your lessons and be a brave boy, not to run blabbering home to your mother. Don't you want to know how to read and write your name?'

'I cun read, miss,' Sam said, but his snivelling had almost stopped.

'You *can*? My goodness. Come along with me then and let's hear you.' She raised her head and her voice. 'Time, children! Everyone indoors!'

In her right hand she had a bell which she began to clang with tremendous vigour so that it racketed to and fro, louder than the church bells. Sam followed safely in her wake.

Marjorie Jamieson's fiancé had been killed in the last months of the war. Her only brother had been one of the sixty thousand casualties of the first day of the Somme. She left home two years later in flight from her father's laconic, unbending grief at the loss of his son, heir to a four-hundred-year-old title, and her mother's ceaseless demands. Her exasperation had reached a point when, if she heard the words, 'You forget, Marjorie dear, I *am* his *mother*,' once more she would say: '*I know* – and *I* am his sister and I lost him too, as well as my beloved Hugh, and you *couldn't care less*.' She fled by travelling forty miles across the county in answer to an advertisement in the *Lady*. 'No experience needed', it had said; 'must like children and rural life'. Well, she thought, since there doesn't seem to be anyone for me to marry, that's better than being a governess, a lady's companion or a typist. Her new life as a teacher had begun eight years ago and she did not suppose it would ever change. Once she would have cringed at the very thought of becoming a dedicated spinster schoolmistress. Now, she loved it: the Victorian buildings, the teaching, the dog-eared textbooks and laborious exercise books; above all, her pupils. *They* never reproached her for being alive but gloried in their own energetic – even if half-starved – young bodies. She loved the way they never stood still and square. One foot was always dangling behind the other, ankles crossed, or both feet would be tapping out a miniature hopscotch for sheer exuberance.

When Sam and Miss Jamieson reached the classroom she sat him down at a double desk in the front row. Sam poked about, exploring the hole gouged out of the desktop for an inkwell and running his finger along the smooth channel for a pen. She looked round the class and called out, 'Jake! Jake Roberts! Don't you go skulking at the back! This term I want you here in front where I can see you! Sit beside Sam, he's new. You can look after him and show him the ropes. He says he can read, so let's see if he's as good as you are. Come on, Jake, on your feet. Hurry!'

There was a sullen rumble of hobnailed boots on the floor of the classroom and a smell of serge as Jake slid into the double bench next to Sam. A pair of sharp fingers pinched his thigh. Miss Jamieson stood in front of the class.

'Good morning, children!' she announced clearly.

Forty voices chanted seven regular syllables.

'Good morning, Miss Jamieson!'

'*Register.*' She began to call out their names and by the time she got to S for Savage Sam knew he must answer 'Present!' After Peter Westrop and Isaac Winterton, the last names on the list, Miss Jamieson closed her eyes, folded her hands and said: '*Prayers.* Almighty God . . .'

Jake Roberts was almost three years older than Sam, at an age when three years is an eternity. He was also several inches taller and a good stone heavier. His father had been one of the last men to die in northern France in the closing weeks of the war, just as the Allied advance was making its final triumphant surge all along the Western Front. John Roberts never saw his son and apart from a studio portrait of a rigidly posed soldier in uniform, hardly distinguishable from half a million others, little John Jacob never laid eyes on his father. Jake's muddy brain had no memory of the man whose surname he carried, though it may be that his mother did him a favour when she gave it to him since the genes bequeathed him nothing; not his father's shrewd intelligence, or his gentleness with children and animals, or his wiry frame or blue eyes. The name they shared was Jake's only legacy from John Roberts.

Less than two years after her husband's death, just before the harvest, his mother married again. A farmer's widow with eighty acres was an attractive proposition and she was much courted. Maggie Roberts chose a younger man for her second husband, Billy Debney; young enough to have missed most of the war and keen enough to get his hands on the Roberts land to accept a woman older than himself; older – as he thought – by six or seven years, though the truth was more like twelve. He also took on Lizzie and Rose, two girls on the verge of their teens, and a strapping toddler, none of his making. Billy laid down one condition for the marriage:

'I'll not have the boy called Young John in my 'ouse. I'm that spooked, it's like the ghost of his father 'auntin' me. Either 'e gets anither name or I'm off!'

''E's got one ither name an' that's Jacob, after my John's old dad.'

'Jacob it'll hev to be, then. An' what's mine, eh?'

'Thou be my Billy now . . .'

Li'l John Jacob Roberts, just over two years old, was renamed Jacob and in no time at all Jake: the name by which he was known for the rest of his life. He never took Debney as his surname. His mother preferred him to remain Jake Roberts of Roberts Farm House.

Billy Debney laboured nightly to plant his own seed in his new wife, who had assured him before the wedding that she was of child-bearing age. It was his misfortune that, although Maggie conceived twice, she twice miscarried. Billy was denied a child of his own loins and forced to watch his predecessor's brood grow up, though he felt no need to love them.

The first Jake knew of his changed circumstances came when he was evicted from his mother's warm bed to make way for the intruder. He was put to sleep in an uncomfortable cradle that rocked when he tried to clamber out of it and get back to his mother. From this narrow bed he was often woken by the sound of Billy's grunts and his mother's cries. The breathing grew harsher and her cries, as time went on, turned from pleasure to pain. Jake saw the sheets hunch and judder against the moonlit walls of the bedroom but didn't understand at first what was happening. When, aged about four, he saw farm animals mate and heard his sisters snigger, and asked what was going on and was told, the meaning of his mother's frenzied movements dawned upon him. From the start Jake felt supplanted and rejected, not that he would have used those words. One of those upon whom he inflicted revenge was the newly arrived Sam.

At the start of the first lesson on Sam's first morning at school, Miss Jamieson asked Jake to read from the green reading book, the one for new readers. Jake stumbled through the simple words: '*The dog has a ball. Run, dog, run! The chil-dren call.*' Amazed that a big boy was having to struggle, Sam – who had taken in the page at a glance – looked up at his teacher and said, ''E dunnt know owt, do 'e, miss?'

Miss Jamieson saw Jake flinch and corrected Sam: 'You must speak more clearly, Sam. You should say, "He *doesn't* know *any-thing*."'

Sam smiled at her apparent agreement. 'No, 'e dunnt!'

'Sam, listen to me: "He *does not* know *anything*." Now you say it.'

''E *dusna* know *narthen*.'

Miss Jamieson sighed. 'Well then, let's hear you read; see if you can do better.'

Jake thought the correction meant that Miss Jamieson agreed with Sam. He felt that he had been ridiculed in front of the whole class by a new boy and by his teacher. The insult lodged deep in his memory. Moments later, Sam had forgotten ever saying it. But the artless, repeated words – ''E dunnt know owt' – 'He *doesn't* know *anything*' – became the seething basis for Jake's hostility.

Sam drew the book towards himself and, running his finger under the lines, read aloud without hesitation: '*The dog has a ball. Run, dog, run! The children call. The dog runs after the ball. The children run too. Look, they all chase the ball!*'

Sam would have been top of the class if he had not been made to share a desk in the front row with Jake Roberts. Jake never knew the answer to any of the teacher's questions and refused to be shown up by Sam, so if she called out an easy question and Sam's hand shot up, Jake would pinch him hard under the desk until the hand unwillingly subsided. Either that or he had to whisper the answer to Jake.

'What is the capital city of France?' Miss Jamieson might ask in Geography.

'Paris,' Sam would mouth through almost unmoving lips, without turning his head.

'Parish, mum!' Jake would say, if his frantically waving hand were selected.

'Paris, yes. *Good*, Jake! Now then, another one. Italy?'

But Jake, conscious that her eyes were upon him and Sam dare not whisper again, had to relapse into sullen silence.

She would address the class. 'Does anyone else know the answer?' Usually one of the girls would semaphore an eager hand, 'Me, miss, oh, miss: me-ee-ee!'

'All right then, Edith?'

'Rome, Miss Jamieson.'

'Good girl. That's right. *Rome*, Jake. Say Rome, everyone.'

At the end of the lesson the class would chant in unison the names of Europe's capital cities. '*Rome* is the *cap*ital of *It*aly. *Paris* is the capital of France; *Ma*drid is the capital of Spain;

Athens is the capital of Greece; *Lisbon* is the capital of Por-tu-gal.' They signalled contempt for the defeated enemy by chanting last of all, 'An' *cap*ital of *Germany*'s B'lin.'

Jake Roberts hated anyone possessed of that elusive quality, cleverness. In its place he developed cunning, patience, the ability to bear a grudge and plot revenge – for years, a decade or more, if need be. He nurtured his grievance with care, like a man blowing on embers to keep the fire going. Every day he found some new reason to hate Sam. Thanks to a good memory, Sam soon knew the answers to Miss Jamieson's questions but he could only murmur in his throat while Jake was sitting next to him, mutely threatening, waiting for lessons to end. When school was over, Jake would go down to the village pond to catch frogs, which he blew up with a straw until they burst. He would laugh raucously and fish about in the mud at the edge of the water until he found another frantically palpitating creature to scoop out with his huge paw. Sam did not care for this blowing up of frogs, nor did he like it when fragments of rubbery green flesh, so recently alive, landed on his bare skin or splattered his worn hobnailed boots, but he knew better than to intervene. When Jake tired of frogs he might go after birds with his cata-pult, knocking them off their perches in the trees to fall stunned to the ground. He would capture the victim, preferably alive, and either torment it himself or give it to one of the farm cats. While the cat was distracted he might grab a kitten. This he slowly strangled until the baby-blue eyes popped desperately from its skull, whereupon Jake might allow it another few moments of mewling life before squeezing its skinny throat. Cruelty was sport to Jake; the only sport he was good at. More often he would be summoned to help his stepfather, perhaps to catch rabbits at the end of the harvest and wring their necks; or to scrape out a pig's bladder with a sharp knife or jagged stone to make sausage skins. Cruelty in Jake was hardly a vice but a tool for survival. Lacking any quality except physical strength, he used this one advantage to stay on top. He was given the nickname of Ox, though never in his hearing, and called an iron-sided dog, meaning he was not to be trusted. Jake swaggered through his childhood flanked by a gang of bullies and cowards, with Sam as his chief target.

Sam was not without friends. Matt (for Matthias) Spring, whom everyone called Beddy, was his best friend and the two of them, along with Isaac Winterton and John Moulton, formed a gang that stuck close together for safety. After school the four went fishing for sticklebacks or in the autumn hunted for mushrooms. In winter they skated on the village pond; in summer they waited beside the road for an infrequent car to pass, jumping and yelling as it went by in a scatter of dust. They played Stone, Scissors, Paper so often that in the end they could anticipate one another's choices. In the playground they would crouch over a game of marbles or a handful of fivestones and if Jake kicked the stones away they would gather them up silently and resume the game later. Nobody thought of complaining to Miss Jamieson – what would be the point? They already knew from experience that the strong terrorized the weak. Sam's father beat his mother; Jake's stepfather beat him; Jake beat Sam; it was the way things were. Sam found safety in numbers. If Jake attacked one of the gang the others would come to his rescue, pulling his hair and kicking until Jake slouched away. When not fighting Jake they often fought one another, and made friends again, and swore the gang oath:

> *'Beddy, Isaac, Sam and John,*
> *Be the best the whole day long.*
> *Isaac, Beddy, Sam and John,*
> *One for All and All for One!'*

Once the shooting season began they were employed as beaters – *brushers*, they were called – at threepence a day, beating the undergrowth with sticks to drive partridges and pheasants towards the guns. They agreed to pool their savings until they had enough for a bicycle. They drew up a rota of who could use it and on what days of the week, arguing about whether Sunday counted double and rattling the jar that held two shillings and ninepence farthing.

If it hadn't been for Jake, Sam's childhood, despite its poverty, might have seemed a continuing idyll. But bad dreams assailed him once or twice a week, dreams in which he was snatched up by the Mares of the Night – great galloping horses quite unlike the sturdy Suffolk Punches of daytime. They sliced through the air and he clung frantically to a whipping mane that stung his face. Sometimes he would lose his grip and fall through a vast dark-blue sky, spinning towards the rising earth whose fields and trees grew larger every second. Just as he was about to be hurled against the ground he would wake with a yell and hear Tom's voice: 'Do 'ee shut thy gob and let a man get 'is sleep.'

'It be the horses I wor afeard of . . . mek the horses go away . . . I dun wanter ride 'em!' and Joan would murmur, 'It be only thy nightmares, li'l old Sam. Go to sleep.'

The winter of 1928 was unusually severe. In January the coast was inundated by floodwater when gale-force winds created a surge that gathered pace in the North Sea and whipped down the eastern side of the country, tearing huge holes in the flimsy sea-wall defences. Overnight, the sea flooded the fields for five miles inland and several weeks later, just as the breaches had been repaired and the water drained away, another high tide flooded the land all over again.

Bitterly cold blizzards continued to sweep across East Anglia. The frozen ground was rock hard. Nothing could be put into it and nothing hacked out of it, except with grinding effort. Right up to mid-March the temperature remained below freezing at night and, despite the stigma of being taken for a pauper, Flora was forced to go to the Poor Relief. They supplied enough food to keep her family alive, but although the givers were well-meaning the giving was done grudgingly. Thin vegetable broth was ladled out of a communal cauldron only after the names and number of people in the household had been verified. Flora banged it down onto the table at night, saying, 'Eat it in humility and give thanks, for I had to bow me hid in humility to git it fer ye!'

The winter brought another relief. Old Abel died. His wits had been addled for years. One morning, woken by a cold draught through the bedroom, Flora came down to the kitchen to find his chair empty and the back door open to a blast of freezing air. Abel was lying in the yard. Perhaps he had been trying to get to the privy and slipped on the icy ground. His bloodless hands and feet were cold as snow; the bones visible through tissue-paper skin; yet somehow he was still breathing.

'No use spendin' money fer doctor,' Young Abel said. ''E be's good's dead. 'E dun 'is threescore-'n'-ten. Let him allun.'

His father never warmed up, despite being put to thaw in front of the kitchen fire and covered with blankets. He never spoke again either. For two days he inched towards death, already corpse-cold, until his imperceptible last breath. The church bell tolled for him, three times three and his age: eighty-one separate slow chimes. He was buried in Lower Flexham churchyard beside his late wife. On the day of his funeral the first morning mist became a chill drizzle that would soon turn into snow and the yews in the churchyard were wreathed in frost like bridesmaids. Flora, listening to the sonorous words for the burial of the dead, saw angels and devils, cherubim and seraphim, corpses and the legions of the damned. They swooped and soared through her mind like rooks and seagulls over the fields at harvest-time. She yearned for *those unspeakable joys* and feared *those everlasting torments*.

Diligently, in her daily life, she tried to practise stoicism and resignation. Her misery grew with her husband's increasing brutality; her self-reproach with the knowledge that she could not care properly for her children. Sometimes she could not even master her anger and frustration and would hit them, especially tall, proud Matty or Davie, the runt of her litter, skinny and bleached as a flower grown in the dark. He would cringe as he did from his father's approach, wailing, 'Dunna ding Oi, Mam, dunna ding Oi,' which irritated her still more. Only Tom, dour and scowling as his father, and Sam, her favourite, never felt her stinging slaps. To escape from her sorrow and guilt she prayed constantly, *with the angels and archangels and all the company of heaven, lauding and magnifying His glorious name.* She became a zealot, exhorting her children to read, mark, learn and inwardly digest the holy word of the Lord, as if it were spiritual nourishment they craved.

''Tis not *righteousness* we 'unger an' thirst after, it be vittles!' Joan said.

'Or summ'un to keep comp'ny with,' added Matty.

'*Keep thy tongue from evil, and thy lips, that they speak no guile,*' Flora reproached.

'But there *is* no evil in us,' Joan countered.

'Shame on ye, mawther, for blasphemy! We be all evil sinners in His sight.'

'*Oi* be no evil sinner – though I wud an' all, if Oi hed the chance . . .' Matty whispered, and she and her sister leaned against each other and rolled their eyes.

When Sam was seven years old the school was struck by an epidemic of diphtheria. He and Davie both caught it. The vicar prayed in church for the children's recovery but five pupils died and the school was closed for the rest of term. Davie was sixteen but a poor constitution and poor diet meant he had never been strong. Surrendering passively to the fever and the sweats, he lay on one side of the high bed, eyes closed, while Flora sponged his forehead muttering incoherent apologies for her past ill-treatment and praying fervently for his recovery. After three days his shallow breathing spiralled suddenly into a gurgle, he choked a few times, and his breath stopped. Again the family put on its best clothes for the procession to the churchyard. They could not afford a headstone; just a plain wooden cross on which the village carpenter carved his name and lifespan: *David Walter Savage 1912–1928 R.I.P.*

After this Sam lay alone in the big cold bed, watched anxiously by his mother and visited twice in three weeks by the doctor. The two shillings and sixpence attendance fee was more than his father – now Abel in his own right – could afford, but Flora was determined not to give up another son without a struggle. Sam's brothers and sisters had been forbidden to go near him in case they caught diphtheria too. For the same reason his friends – Beddy, Isaac and John – were not allowed to visit. Sam lay alone in the upstairs room, his mind and body feverish, watching the tender colours of the early spring sky. At last the weather grew warmer and at last, between sweating and dozing, slowly and with infinite boredom, he began to get better.

During his interminable convalescence Sam was visited by the vicar's wife, Mrs Persimmons, the Sunday School teacher. In his own house there were no books except the family Bible, too big and heavy to read in bed. Mrs Persimmons brought a rich broth and an orange 'to build you up again', along with several shiny booklets called *Old Testament Stories for Boys and Girls*. He gazed avidly at the illustrations, in which the cloudless turquoise sky became a rich yellow as it approached the horizon – quite different from the pale fluffy skies of his own countryside – then orange and finally a brilliant sunset pink. When he peered closely at the page it broke up into thousands of tiny coloured circles that spun before his eyes. Swarthy men with shawls draped over their heads and shoulders rode on camels across a rock-strewn landscape; fishermen launched rowing boats into an azure lake; women in colourful garments clustered round a white-robed figure with upraised hand, modest yet commanding, his face framed by dark ringlets. When Sam had scrutinized the pictures and read the stories he borrowed his mother's mending scissors and carefully cut round the brightly clad characters, arranging them across his bed, inventing more thrilling adventures for them and making the flimsy paper figures collapse on top of one another in a heap to signify defeat in battle or climb rockingly up his steepled knees for exploration and victory.

Nothing could have confirmed his passion for reading or fired his imagination more than those weeks in bed. He spent hours disentangling the long words on the page until he could read them fluently. When he had mastered the simplified Old Testament stories, Mrs Persimmons gave him his own copy of the Bible, smaller and easier to handle than the family one, its frail India-paper pages crackling between his fingers. From this he learned to decipher even the most complicated words and names. '*Shadrach, Meshach and Abednego*,' he would murmur rhythmically to himself. In the end he was able to pronounce the full genealogical line of the house of David, to his mother's satisfaction.

Mrs Persimmons praised him. 'Well *done*, Samuel! You *are* a fluent reader now! You'll be the best in your class when you start back at school: mark my words! Everything will be easy for you.'

'Aye, madam, our li'l ol' Sam be a child of God and an inheritor of the kingdom of heaven – 'e be that, all right!' said Flora.

Mrs Persimmons lent him 'proper boys' books' as a reward; more exciting and less familiar than the Bible stories. Rudyard Kipling's two *Jungle Books* became Sam's greatest joy. He read and reread the stories until he knew them almost by heart. In his imagination he was no longer a bored convalescent but Mowgli, lithe brown leader of the young wolves, running with Bagheera the black panther, learning with Baloo, the old brown bear, being cradled by Kaa, the massively coiled python. Soon he felt himself more Mowgli than Sam and, like him, more wolf than boy. With an imagination as vivid as his mother's, Sam became one of the lean young wolves from the pack that called itself the Free People, loping fearlessly through the jungle on swift, stretched legs or listening with the other jungle creatures to the tales told by Hathi the elephant:

'Ye know, children,' he began, 'that of all things ye most fear Man;' and there was a mutter of agreement.

'This tale touches thee, Little Brother,' said Bagheera to Mowgli.

'I? I am of the Pack – a hunter of the Free People,' Mowgli answered. 'What have I to do with Man?'

His body returned to health, although his strength was never the same afterwards. His limbs were stick-like, his ribcage narrow. But from then on he had only to hear in his head, like an incantation, the words, *'It was seven o'clock of a very warm evening in the Seeonee Hills when Father Wolf woke up from his day's rest . . .'* to be transported to the magical land of India.

Meanwhile, unnoticed by her husband or children, Flora was saved one day, doomed the next, looking towards another world in an attempt to ignore the tribulations of this. Every action was performed to an appropriate tag from the Bible or prayer book. If she or one of her children washed their hands, she would murmur – or declaim – *'I will wash my hands in innocency, oh Lord.'* If a horse passed the window jerking its head against an uncomfortable bit, she would say, *'Be ye not like to horse and mule, whose mouths must be held with bit and bridle.'* Sluicing out the copper in which she had rinsed the week's wash: *'I am poured out like water.'* She rarely uttered her own natural, native, stunted speech; instead she would find some biblical approximation which the family had to interpret. When Abel returned drunk from the taproom and thrashed her, the frightened children would hear their mother cry, *'Let not man have the upper hand!'* Infuriated by these exhortations, Abel would rage at her – 'Hold thy peace, cunn't thee? Shut thy bloody Bible!' and Flora would respond as though to a priest, *'Oh Lord, hear our prayer, and let our cry come unto thee!'*

The cadences of this majestic language filled Sam's ears and lodged in his brain for ever. The Flood and the burning fiery furnace, the ten plagues of Egypt and the tortures of the damned were as much a part of his daily life as the games of marbles – Round Toy and Long Toy – that he and his friends played. His mother's pious words and apocalyptic visions became the stuff of his nightmares. The simian shrieking of the Bandar-log as they tore through the treetops was muddled up with the headlong fall of the damned into Satan's smoky pit. In his dreams Sam was always one of their number, leaping monkey or doomed soul.

CHAPTER FOUR

1929–1932

SCHOOL RESUMED IN THE AUTUMN. IF SAM HAD BEEN PUT NEXT to clever, bright-eyed Edith Satterthwaite or his attentive, serious friend John Moulton, his schooldays might have been very different. Instead, Miss Jamieson locked him and Jake Roberts into an ill-matched partnership. Jake had escaped diphtheria and after a summer in the fields he was ruddy with health and sun. Their rivalry continued, David and Goliath, circling and wary; Sam light, quick and good at anticipating his enemy's next move, Jake the Ox big and slow, but cunning. Sam was the faster runner and could leg it out of trouble, unless he was ambushed. Then he would rush at Jake, head down, an enraged little goat. Once he managed to butt him in the solar plexus, winding Jake so painfully that he hopped and staggered about the lane bent double and groaning while Sam made his escape, but that was a rare triumph. Sam nearly always got the worst of it in the end. He was taunted for being a field worker's son while the strapping, well-nourished Jake came from a farmer's household with eighty acres of land.

'Look yew here, my dad wudn't take thy dad on 'is fields, no niver, not if thy dad did pay 'im! Thy dad be *duzzy* . . .' Jake

58

twisted his fingers against his forehead and rolled his eyes.

Sam replied, 'Aye, an' *thy* dad be *dead*! Thee dunn't know *narthen* of thy father!' It was the one lethal, unanswerable truth.

By the time Sam was ten, his enemy – at thirteen – was almost the size of a grown man. Jake's pockets bulged with conkers, stones and a catapult, with which he was deadly accurate. He could knock birds out of the trees or kill a rabbit at fifty yards – and often did, for the fun of it. When Isaac, John and Beddy had been kept in school, or were needed in the fields for crow-scaring or stone-picking, Sam was at his most vulnerable.

Then he had to walk home alone, knowing that behind any hedge, round every corner, in the invisible stretch of lane ahead, Jake and his posse might be lurking, ready to leap out and hold him captive. He would hear the steady tramp of their footsteps, left right, left right, their boots thumping down on the hard road. If he tried to run, they were faster. They would overtake and surround him, and offer him the choice of a Chinese burn (two strong hands clutched around his arm and twisted in opposite directions) or the hobble (being forced to walk home with his boots dangling from bootlaces gripped between his teeth, wrists lashed painfully behind his back and his ankles tied together with string) or having a grasshopper stuffed into his mouth, which he had to chew and swallow before the eyes of his tormentors. Each journey was an exercise in terror. Sam would come home with a bloodied nose or bulging eyes and sluice his ringing head at the pump. His mother, singing hymns or absorbed in her Bible, barely looked up.

Once he managed to persuade his brother Tom to follow him at a discreet distance, to give Jake a good hiding. Sam felt a surge of secret joy as he walked home from school that day, but nothing happened. Perhaps Jake had noticed Sam's jaunty step and deduced that this time he would meet a larger opponent. Sam begged Tom to follow him a second time and, grumbling and scornful, Tom did so. Again, no Jake. Tom lost patience. 'Thee canst fight th'own battles. Thou be'st imaginin' things!' he mocked. 'Thee and thy *wolves* an' *tigers*! It be all in thy addled ol' head!'

Sam confided his troubles to Matty, but although she was sympathetic she could not protect him either.

'Why dunn't 'ee tell teacher?' she urged, as he gulped and whimpered against her flannel nightgown one evening. 'Tell Miss Jamieson!' But Sam knew this would only make matters worse. Instead he told himself stories of Mowgli's bravery, as though to imbibe his courage. He pictured himself surrounded by his four wolf brothers.

'Now,' said Mowgli, 'of us five, which is leader?'

'Thou art leader, Little Brother,' said Gray Brother, and he licked Mowgli's foot.

'Follow, then,' said Mowgli, and the four followed at his heels with their tails between their legs.

Occasionally one or both his sisters fetched him home from school and then he would hear about their chosen suitors. Joan was twenty, Matty eighteen. By now Joan had been under-kitchenmaid at Lady Manning's for five years, learning to prepare vegetables and make bread puddings for the staff, but mostly up to her elbows in carbolic water and dirty dishes. She was a chunky, greasy, healthy young woman who cheerfully gave all but a shilling of her wages to her mother. Flora passed most of it on to Abel, trying to keep back one and sixpence each week as a nest egg for when Joan married. Joan nurtured a hopeless passion for Jim Collett, the handsomest groom, and would lurk round the stables whenever she could escape Cook, watching the muscles in his forearms bunch and ripple as he rubbed down the horses till they shone or swung a saddle high onto their backs, ready for the squire to ride round his property. Jim was more interested in her tall fair sister.

'Thet Matty,' he asked once, 'be she walkin' out?'

'Why be thou axin'?'

'It lay kind o' uppermost on my tongue,' he answered evasively.

'*Why* be thou *axin'*?' she insisted.

'Whoolly fer curiosity. *Be* she wi' summun?'

'She be hard to please. Why, hev thee got thy mind set on 'er?'

'Oi dunno, do I? – ain't niver talked wi' 'er yet.'

'Nay, she be'ent,' Joan conceded reluctantly. 'An' Oi be'ent neither.'

'Luke Spicer, coalman's mate, did say as 'e fancied t'kitchen girl . . . munna meant *thee*.'

'Oi've got no edge for 'im . . . Oi wudna be no *coalman*'s sweet'art!' she protested; but she looked out for Luke, a strapping lad whose face was hidden under a black layer of coal dust. She caught his white, gleaming eye, blushed and tried to avoid it. Next time the coalman came Luke had gone to the trouble of washing his face and Joan saw that a harelip was the cause of his halting, whistling speech. After that she never met his eyes again.

Jim Collett tried once more a week later.

'Thy Matilda, wud she cum' steppin' with me at Harvest Frolic? Will't axe 'er fer me?'

'Axe 'er thiself! But you may depind upon it, she wud niver be bad,' Joan said, suddenly seized with jealousy. 'She be not *shanny*.'

'I didna say narthen about *bad*. Gie 'er this—' and he thrust a letter at her. Joan pushed it deep into the pocket of her apron and turned away.

'*If* I remember . . .'

'Thou'lt remember.'

'Dew you sit in 'er lap yew'll hev to pay the rent!' Joan said coarsely; but she gave Matty the letter and Matty accepted. The long, slow courtship began.

'Cudna thee pick a man to suit *me*?' Joan asked some weeks

later, jealous of Jim's attachment to her sister. 'Willum ain't got no sweet'art an' he'll be butler here one day. I cud larn to fancy Willum . . . Tell 'im to dance wi' me at Yuletide Frolic!'

'Thou hest a proper conceit,' Jim told her, grinning. Now that he was Matty's official sweetheart he was allowed to tease. 'Do yew first larn to fancy 'im and mebbe thou'lt catch 'im thiself.'

Sam was coming up to eleven. He worked harder than any other boy that year, sometimes as an excuse to linger behind but mostly because he had the best brains in the class. He knew that Jake knew, and he knew that Jake minded. His intelligence attracted the attention of Edith Satterthwaite, the brightest as well as the prettiest of the girls, and he knew Jake minded that, too. Sam learned by rote and never forgot his multiplication tables, the kings and queens of England, the capitals of the world, the mill towns of Lancashire ('Bolton-Bury-Rochdale-*Old*ham') and the chief exports of India ('tea, cotton, spices, precious jewels'). He knew the names of its viceroys and its great cities. In Sunday School he scrutinized the familiar New Testament pictures that Mrs Persimmons showed them through the epidiascope, blown up from book size to fill a white cotton screen, every detail brilliantly clear. He imagined India looking very like that; a country of brown-skinned people in long robes and sandals. India, jewel of the Empire, and Israel, the Holy Land, became one and the same place, except that to him India was sacred.

Lower Flexham was poor and getting poorer. Old people suffered most. Many a grandfather past his usefulness was shoved into a corner, sometimes even inside a cupboard, half starved and half forgotten, fed and cleaned by a child if a parent nagged or the child happened to remember. The Depression years dragged everyone down; the government wrestled with financial crises and so, more acutely, did the Savage family. The deaths of Davie and Old Abel had left fewer mouths to feed but their absence was outweighed by ever greater poverty. The hard-pressed farmers cut the workers' wages by a third. Abel earned only twenty-seven shillings and sixpence – less than when Sam was born, and they had been poor enough then. That winter was again harsh and cold; again Flora had to swallow her pride and apply to the parish for Poor Relief, knowing that their need would become a matter of public knowledge. Abel, from being brutal occasionally, when he was drunk, became brutal all the time. His sons cowered from him and the girls shrank into corners to avoid the blazing anger that anything might spark – a glance, a word, above all, the noises in his head. He still suffered, though none of them knew it and he could not have named it, from tinnitus. It roared in his head like the guns of the Somme, day and night, a deafening cacophony of fear. Abel Savage struck out futilely against it, not caring who he struck. Flora took the brunt of his violence, knowing there was no escape for her; they were one flesh. *It is not good that the man should be alone.* They had once loved each other fiercely, and even if the love had gone and only the fierceness remained, she would be his wife until death them did part, until the day she buried him and marked the spot with a tombstone incised with his name: *Abel Thomas Savage, beloved husband of Flora, dear father of Abel, Thomas, Joseph, Jude, Joan, Matilda, David, Ezra and Samuel* . . . Nine born, five left. *In sorrow shalt thou bring forth children.*

Soon after Sam's eleventh birthday in March, his oldest brother Tom had a fight with his father. It happened after Sunday lunch (an illicit rabbit in a steaming pot of potatoes and onion) when the whole family was gathered together. Tom, by now twenty-six, stood up from the kitchen table and declared gruffly that, having waited four years for his father's permission to marry his sweetheart, he would not wait any longer. His father, mad at the prospect of losing his strongest son's labour, to say nothing of his badly needed shillings, rose to his feet and knocked Tom to the floor. Tom was half his father's age; Abel the more experienced fighter. Their weight and reach were about equal, but so was their determination. Tom was fighting for escape and his girl; Abel to prove – or lose – his absolute authority.

'Don't, Abel! Ye'll kill him!' Flora begged, as her son struggled to his feet while his father loomed over him. Tom was braced to return the blow but his mother shoved him through the scullery door into the back yard. 'Fight outside then, if ye must!' Pushing Abel in the small of his back she propelled him after his son. Outside, momentarily blinded by the bright spring sunshine, Abel staggered and glanced round to recover his bearings, but in that moment off-balance Tom drove a clenched, rock-hard fist into his father's jaw. Abel recoiled and struck out wildly, missing his target. Fury upset his accuracy or he would have beaten his son in half a dozen blows. Sam crouched in the kitchen doorway, eyes round as an owl's, while behind him his trembling sisters clung together.

The two men feinted awkwardly, weaving round the yard, grimacing at each other. Tom's young face was flushed with excitement. The veins stood out on Abel's forehead and the knotted lumps of flesh over his eyebrows bulged. They danced and struck, struck and bobbed apart. Blood spurted from a gash over Tom's eye where his father's horny thumbnail had caught it, ripping a deep red line across his brow.

'Abel, stop, I beg yew in the name of God!' cried his wife futilely.

Abel began to aim blows remorselessly while Tom tried inexpertly to parry them. His head began to droop, his fists lowered, and he landed fewer, weaker blows in return. Already his father was shouting in triumph.

'Hev I got a coward son, huh? *Hah*, thet'll teach yew! Ha ha, come on, call yisself a man? Like this – *hah!* – and this – *hah!* – and this – *hah, hah, hah!*' as each blow thudded into his son's flesh.

Behind him, Sam heard Matty's fearful voice, 'He'll kill 'im! He'll murther our Tom!'

'Shut your noise!' muttered Joan.

'I'm going to get Elsie!' Matilda said. Dodging the two panting men, she ran out of the back gate towards the cottage where Tom's sweetheart lived. Behind him, Sam felt Joan settle into a more comfortable angle, leaning against the doorpost.

'Abel!' sobbed Flora. 'Tom! Will ye give over now? Will ye stop, afore ye both end up dead?' and she began gabbling to herself, '. . . *whoso sheddeth man's blood, by man shall his blood be shed*,' keening incoherently, hardly knowing what she said – '*Job, three: three* . . .' Her family, intent on the fight, took no notice.

Tom stopped trying to land blows and concentrated on moving out of reach, using his greater stamina to bide his time. At last his father began to tire. His face took on the primitive rigidity of a man bent on survival. Tom, now that he had the advantage, circled lightly, his breathing sweeter and freer than the rasping sighs fetched up from his father's damaged lungs. He raised his head, jutting his face defiantly towards his father, and swore:

'I'll *marry* her, afore—'

For a critical moment his concentration wavered. Abel drew back his elbow, measured his aim and with all his strength drove his fist against his son's uplifted chin. Tom's head tipped right back, further back than seemed possible without snapping his spine, and lolled sideways as he dropped to the ground. Abel's boot was ready to smash Tom's ribcage, but Flora fell across the prone body.

'Have ye no mercy? Wouldst kill him as well? *The increase of thy house* . . .!'

Her husband staggered backwards, coughing and retching, and lurched past Sam, still crouching in the kitchen doorway. Bending over the sink, Abel splashed handfuls of cold water into his stinging, boiling face. Matty burst through the back gate, followed by Tom's sweetheart. Elsie looked at her young man lying in a bloodied heap, almost unconscious. She stared in silence for half a minute, her face expressionless, then turned away and, stiffly upright, set off towards her own home.

'Elsie!' called Matty after her. 'Elsie! Will ye niver comfort Tom? He fought for ye, dun' he?'

'I'll not,' the girl said without turning or pausing. 'He lost.'

Sam sighed deeply and got to his feet. It had not occurred to him before to question the protection of his home. Now he realized he would never leave with his father's blessing.

Tom recovered physically, although for the rest of his life he carried a crescent-shaped white scar across his forehead to remind him of the fight. All the youthful pride had been beaten out of him, like a young horse broken into submission. He developed an uncontrollable tremor, first of the hands, then later his arms and legs as well. 'Poor Tom', as his sisters began to call him, dwindled into a mere appendage to his father, subservient in manner, fearful, silent. He never married, but spent the rest of his life under his parents' roof.

CHAPTER FIVE

1932–1934

MATILDA MARRIED AND LEFT HOME THAT YEAR, AGED TWENTY-one; a tall, shimmering girl in white, her flaxen hair crowned with flowers. Joan, being older, should have been the first to marry, but Joan was a jolly, fat kitchenmaid with rough hands that smelled of bacon fat and greasy hair that smelled of smoke while her sister, at least for a summer or two, was a young corn goddess. Matty and Jim moved into one of the cottages attached to the Manning stables, barely half a mile down the road from the cramped cottage in which she had grown up. Sam saw her every few days but now she belonged to her husband, had a different name and was part of another family. There was a new aura about her; an aura that transformed her into a mysterious, secret creature. It was, though Sam did not know it, the brief bloom of happiness.

The following year Sam found solace in a new and unexpected passion: bell-ringing. He had always been musical, though no-one had ever told him so and the school had no instruments for him to learn. He loved hearing the church bells as they pealed and swung over summer fields above the reapers' singing or carried across crisp winter stubble, and he had already begun to work out for himself the patterns of change-ringing that made the bells sound inevitable and satisfying. One day the vicar, Mr Persimmons, beckoned him aside as he was leaving the vestry after Sunday School.

'Sam Savage. Collect for the day? Got it off by heart? Good lad. My wife says you're quick to learn. I wonder if your arms are strong, too?'

Sam, mystified, flexed his muscles under his best black jacket.

'Think they might be strong enough to pull a bell-rope? We'll be needing a new ringer soon. Poor Seton Bradley – you know old Mr Bradley, don't you? – has been taken ill. Let's hope he'll be spared for a few more years, but I don't think he'll be ringing the bells again.'

Sam's eyes lit up and he clenched his shoulders with excitement. The vicar smiled.

'Your teacher says you've a good ear. Only problem is, you're a bit young still. Serious matter, ringing the bells. How old did you say you were?'

'I be twelve gone three month! I ain't young!' protested Sam eagerly. 'An' I be strong as my brother! Almost . . .' he added truthfully, since he was talking to the vicar.

'Come to the rectory after lunch next Sunday – Mrs Persimmons will let you off Sunday School – and I'll get one of our ringers to show you the bells and give you a try with a rope. We'll soon see if you have any aptitude. People either take to it or they don't. No half measures with the bells.'

A week later Sam, walking a respectful pace or two behind, followed the vicar and Hamill, one of the regular ringers, up the stone staircase of the church's squat Norman tower, then up a flight of wooden steps and finally mounted a ladder into the belfry. There he heard for the first time the resounding names given to each bell, some of them centuries old. The very names sounded like a sonorous peal.

'Here's Darcy, here's Stedman's Own, here's Chenery. Then Sweet Mary, then Young Tom, then Mercy and Blythe. This big one here's Old Tom. That's the tenor bell. She's the biggest and last. Ours weighs fifteen hundredweight. Most ordinary village churches like ours only have six bells, not many have eight, Sam: you can be proud of that – can't he, Hamill?'

Hamill grinned and clapped Sam lightly on the back. 'Eight, see?'

'Do you want to touch one?' the vicar went on, and Sam nodded. Mr Persimmons grasped the waistband of his shorts, his knuckles hard against Sam's spine. 'Lean over – don't worry, I've got you – and stroke her with your hand.'

Sam leaned into the vacant space around the silent bells and stroked a chill metal curve.

'What's it made of?' he whispered.

'*She*,' said the vicar. 'Bells are always called "she", just like ships. A mixture of copper and tin – more copper than tin – called bell metal.'

Sam tapped the bell; then danced his fingers on it; then fished in his pocket for his penknife and tapped the bell with it. A tinny note pattered into the high calm of the belfry. He could hear the vicar breathing in and out and the bronchial rhythm of Hamill's lungs. He turned his head. Through the louvred window he glimpsed narrow slats of sky, pale blue and very still. A bird swooped and he could hear the flutter of its wings as it settled on the spire a few feet above his head. One day he would fill that sky with bell noise, frightening the birds!

'*Can* I learn, sir, please, reverend? I s'll do me best.'

'Very good, young feller-me-lad. I think you will, Sam. What do you say, Hamill? I think he'll make a fine ringer.'

Hamill grinned at them both and Sam knew he'd been accepted. He smiled hugely.

Hamill tied the clapper to silence the bell. They climbed down the steps to the ringing chamber where Mr Persimmons showed him how to hold the rope end and pull evenly, steadily, with a firm caressing stroke, keeping his hands down until the rope itself lifted them up again, after Mr Persimmons had caught and pulled the sally: the furry grip at the end of the rope. The downward pull felt sluggish, as though the old bell were resisting his inexperienced hands. After a while the vicar said, 'You mustn't be discouraged. It takes a bit of practice. You don't need strength so much as timing and concentration. Now, will your father let you come to the practice night? Five o'clock on Thursdays. Takes an hour or two. Can you be spared?'

'Cud 'ee ask 'im for me, reverend?' Sam pleaded. 'Likely 'e'll find it harder to say *thee* nay.'

'Let's walk back now and ask him together.'

'Do I get paid?' Sam said, ashamed that he had to ask. ''E'll more willingly agree if I bring 'im some pennies for it.'

'Shall we say sixpence a week to begin with and an extra thruppence for weddings and funerals? At funerals, as you know, the bells are half muffled; otherwise it's the same.'

'Lork, that be grand!' Sam said and grinned from ear to ear.

'Don't go telling the others, mind you!'

From then on, one afternoon a week Sam had a reason good enough to keep Jake Roberts at bay, for even Jake dared not stop him attending bell-ringing practice.

A solemn friendship grew up silently, delicately, between Sam and Edith Satterthwaite. They rarely spoke and never risked the mockery of the class by walking home together or seeking each other out in the noisy schoolyard, but their aptitude in lessons was a secret bond. Edith's memory, as tidy and well organized as her mother's larder, stored away the simple mathematics that Miss Jamieson inscribed on the board with blunt chalk, whereas most children were mesmerized by the white dust falling softly to the floor at her feet. Edith found it easy to remember everything in their school textbooks – maps and diagrams, the subcontinent of Asia, an ox-bow loop, the rain-shadow area. She wrote and read ardently, as Sam did, cramming down the simple knowledge that the school governors considered sufficient for country children – peasants' children – who must not be given lofty ideas. They were lucky that Marjorie Jamieson was perceptive enough to recognize in them – two ordinary children – the seeds of the extraordinary, and dedicated enough to care about cultivating them. Edith was specially receptive. She was always ready with questions.

'*Why* do we want precious stones from India, miss?' she would ask. 'Why can't we use ourn?'

'England doesn't produce rubies and pearls and diamonds, Edith.'

'I know, but why can't we take stones from the fields and cut 'em into nice shapes? Why cudn't grand folk wear those?'

'I don't know, dear,' the teacher would sigh. 'That's enough questions now. You're holding up the class.' She looked round at the others, dreaming in the afternoon sun. 'In any case, we do take flintstones with holes in them from the fields, don't we? What for? Who knows?'

'Me, miss, I do!' Sam said eagerly. 'It be to keep nightmares away.'

'And does it work?' she smiled.

'Not allus.'

The hag-stone could not ward off Sam's nightmares, in which nowadays he often relived the fight. His grim-faced father would bear down upon him and batter him with his fist, one blow after another, the other hand gripping his coat so he couldn't escape. Then, as he lay sprawled on the earth with smashed face and blood in his eyes, Jake would appear and say, 'Why, *Sam Savage*: I've waited a long time fer this! On yer feet.' But Sam could not, dared not get up. He would seem to hear Edith saying, 'Come on, li'l ol' Sam, thou'rt no coward, be thou?' and the voices of his friends turning from encouragement to derision, until he was surrounded by a jeering circle of people saying, '*Now* let's see if he's a man!' When he failed to rise to the challenge, Jake would gloat, 'Got yer, Sam Savage! Yew'll niver live that down!'

He would wake to find himself curled up tightly, hugging his knees, protecting his privates, making incoherent animal noises of terror and sobbing, *No, no, no!*

Edith's wiry black hair was dragged back into tight plaits. She had tawny skin, nut-brown limbs and a square face lit up by unusually dark blue eyes, glowing with the reflected intensity of her brain. Two months younger than Sam, she was at the end of childhood, her chest still narrow and flat; fingernails bitten and legs scratched and scabby. Like him she was a post-war afterthought. Called after Edith Cavell, the popular heroine and martyr, she had been petted and spoiled as a baby and then left to fend for herself while her sisters grappled with the seasonal necessities of seed-time and harvest, their own and on the land. Her father had abandoned the family when she was three and Edith hardly remembered him, unless he was the jolly figure who had once carried her on his shoulders, high above everyone else. He vanished one day, unaccountably, and never came back. After this her mother was forced to become a washerwoman and Edith or one of her older sisters often had to help with the back-breaking job of mangling the heavy wet sheets, lugging them outside and pegging them over washing lines in the back garden. When it rained they were suspended from pulleys in the ceiling to dry in the warmth of the stove. Edith sat at her homework beneath them, the humid kitchen smelling of bleach and damp linen. It still had to be ironed, folded, piled in baskets and delivered to the few people in the village who could afford to get their sheets laundered at threepence a pair, pillowcases extra . . . the doctor and his wife, the vicar, the publican, Miss Jamieson; all those who lived in houses that were big, but not big enough to employ their own laundrymaids.

One evening, as Mrs Satterthwaite stood waiting meekly at the back door while Miss Jamieson hunted in her purse, the teacher said, 'She's clever, your little Edith. She ought to go to school in Stowmarket or maybe even Ipswich. If I could find someone to take her as a weekly boarder would you agree to that?'

'Oh no, thank 'ee, miss. That's not for Edith, nowt like that. She b'aint happy abroad. She's niver been fer from hoom.'

'It wouldn't cost money, apart from her bed and board. She'd get a scholarship.'

'She's but a *mawther*,' Mrs Satterthwaite said. 'She doan' need no eddication. Not above what you be givin' 'er. It wor good enow for her sisters and *you* can larn her all she need, miss. You may depind upon it, she warn't niver miss it.' There was a pause. 'That'll be sixpence, beggin' yer pardon, twopence for the pillows and thruppence yoor blouses an' apron makes . . .'

Miss Jamieson tried once more. 'The parish funds would buy her school uniform. I could drive her back and forth each week. It would be an opportunity. It could be the making of her.'

Mrs Satterthwaite searched for a compromise.

'I tell 'ee, miss: next time travelling library comes round, do 'ee choose a book fer Edith. She's that fond of readin'.'

'But she doesn't need just *one* book, Mrs Satterthwaite. She's got an enquiring mind. She needs lots of books.'

'Best be gettin' back. I'm obliged to ye, ma'am.'

Miss Jamieson was powerless in the face of the suspicion and mistrust of anything that might single Edith out, especially if it lifted her above the level of her labouring family. Cleverness, like money, belonged to grand folk. There was nothing to be done about it except ask the child to tea occasionally and lend her books . . . First the William books, which made her laugh and marvel at children with so much time to play; then Arthur Ransome's *Swallows and Amazons*, eventually moving on to

E. Nesbit ('What be a phoneyix, please, miss?') and H. Rider Haggard. In the end, like Sam – because of Sam – Edith preferred Rudyard Kipling's *Kim* and *The Jungle Books*. Middle-class English families seemed as distant as the village dwellers of India – with whom, in fact, the children of Lower Flexham had more in common.

By the time they were thirteen, Sam and his friends Beddy, Johnnie and Isaac had only one more year at school. After that, although most children left school barely literate, they would be released into the adult world. Sam devoured books avidly and wrote a neat hand, but the other three hardly bothered to concentrate. Once school was behind them they would seldom read more than a seed merchant's catalogue or write more than their own names – in church after their wedding, at the bottom of a petition, perhaps, when joining the army or a farmworkers' union. Their futures were already mapped out. Isaac, a horseman's son, would become a horseman in turn. His voice had already broken, a deep slow rumble that could reassure a skittish foal or a frightened mare. His big hands would gentle any animal into compliance. Horses were fewer than they had been but his father was sure it would not last. The fad for cars must soon die out, for how could man exist without horses? John Moulton, slow-footed, serious, a lad of few words, was ill-suited to life as an innkeeper but that was what his father did so he would do it too; there was no avoiding it except by running away and John was not the sort to duck responsibility. Cheerful, optimistic Beddy with his thatch of black hair and explosive laugh wanted to be a blacksmith, but blacksmiths were few and getting fewer. He had to be content with spending as long as he could at the forge, watching the hammer strike sparks from the anvil and the smith lifting the horses' feet by their long feathery ankle hair, hammering new horseshoes into their hooves. But for the moment all four were knockabout boys who squabbled and made up, kicked a ball around, followed the fortunes of

Grimsby Town Football Club, huddled over secrets and borrowed John's big brother's bike to bowl along the lanes, one leaning forward pedalling hard, one hanging on behind and the other two running to keep up. Sam was keeper of the bicycle jar and the list of footballers and scores, the teller of stories. They all closed ranks when Jake and his cronies threatened and they managed to stave off most attacks, but occasionally there would be an unavoidable challenge and an ugly fight. Having learned speed and cunning in evading his father's blows, Sam did not come off too badly. At least he no longer had to eat grass-hoppers or endure the Chinese burn, though in response to Jake's insults he would often taunt him in return: 'Thee dunnt know thy father!' Sam never told his friends about his night-mares or his father's beatings. Those were private; shut behind the back door of his home, along with his mother's holy mutterings and Tom's convulsive shaking.

In winter when the schoolroom was warm the boys dozed in the fug of the pot-bellied stove, bundled up in two flannel shirts, a jacket and a muffler against the bitter wind. Once spring came they spent most afternoons in the fields, singing as they worked, imbibing the old veneration for earth and growth. Their boots covered with soil, dirt under their fingernails, the smell of kicked-up clods in their nostrils, squatting to relieve themselves under a hedge, they became physically linked to the land. Their muscles hardened, their backs grew broader and their hands tougher to the point where farmers would pay a shilling a day for their labour, buying youthful energy if not the strength of a man. None of the village lads sat through an entire day of classes in June. They stayed long enough only to bolt the bread and cheese the school provided before heading away to join their fathers and older brothers. The time for play came later, after eight o'clock, when they had done five or six hours' work. During the long dusk and sunset, while the grass still held the day's heat and birds bickered over their night-time perches, they played Kick the Can or Peep Behind the Curtain. Sometimes the girls would join in, if they could escape the work demanded by their mothers. They were forever being told, 'Cleanliness is next to godliness.' Younger children, clothes, vegetables, pots and pans, plates, tables, floors and windows, doors and doorsteps, pathways and privy – all needed constant scouring and scrubbing until their hands stung. By comparison the men's grooming of the horses at the end of each day, rubbing them down with slow, rhythmical strokes until their hide shone, seemed a positive pleasure.

Sam found bell-ringing an escape and a delight. His co-ordination and aptitude made him a quick learner. He was proud to be one of eight ringers, in a village of more than four hundred souls, privileged to toll for the dead, ring out the summons to a wedding or christening and mark the Sunday services. In time he learned the intricate patterns of change-ringing, their logic and inevitability.

'You have to respect and love the art of the bells,' Mr Persimmons told Sam. *Love* was not a word Sam often heard and he was amazed to hear that he must not just manipulate but also *love* the bells. He took ringing books home and pored over the various methods, learning in advance what he practised in the bell-tower.

He began on the treble bell: the lightest and highest, the one whose ringer gave the signal to start. He would stand motionless in the circle of bell-ringers, holding the sally, tense with expectation in the last seconds of silence. Then he would call out, 'Look to, treble's going, she's gone—' and one by one they would reach for the tufted sally. Obedient to the fixed order of the change, each ringer in turn pulled strongly downward, followed (after a pause) by the sound of clapper on metal overhead, until belfry, church and acres of arching sky resounded to the clangour of the bells. Sam felt them in the tingling soles of his feet, they reverberated round his ribcage, he heard them in his skull. In time he progressed from rounds to call-changes to plain hunting.

His prowess won him respect in the village but increased Jake Roberts's hostility. 'Vicar ast *me* to ring,' he taunted, daring Sam to deny it. 'I told 'im, I'd better ways to busy my hands . . .' His cronies sniggered and made obscene gestures that Sam did not understand until later, when by imitating their rhythmic pressure against his own crotch, he realized for the first time why Tom and Ezra sometimes shuddered and groaned in bed at night.

Edith, too, was growing up; suddenly filling out, on the way to being what her mother called 'a well-built lass'. Her older sisters were involved in the rituals of courtship and Edith often had to take their place when they weren't at home to help wring and fold the sheets. At night she heard them whispering in their shared bed.

'An' then 'e . . .' The voice fell to a sibilant, giggling murmur.

'Yew niver let 'im!' Outrage.

Smugly: 'It wor ever so nice.'

'Tell me—'

'Not now. Our Edith cud 'ear.'

'She be sleepin'.'

'No she ain't – be thou, Edie? I'll tell 'ee termorrer.'

Hitherto Edith and Sam had simply shared a liking for things that didn't interest other children. Reading Miss Jamieson's latest books – Lamb's *Tales from Shakespeare* and *Morte d'Arthur* – their stories of high romance among lords and ladies or country bumpkins put precocious thoughts into her head. Late one Thursday afternoon she caught Sam walking home alone. Jumping out from the hedge, terrifying him for a moment, she took him to a deep hollow overgrown with meadow grass beside a blossom-laden, all-concealing hawthorn bush whose white flowers filled his nostrils with their rank scent. She pulled him down, reached for one of his hands – still flushed and tingling from the bell-rope – and stroked his palm. Sam shivered.

'What hast been doin', Sam?'

'I bin ringing bells,' he said proudly, thinking: but she *knows* that.

'Ringin' for a wedding, Sam Savage?'

'Nobbut bell practice.' A silence fell. He gathered his feet under him as though to get up. She put her other hand firmly over his.

'Doan' 'ee be goin', Sam,' she coaxed. 'Be thou needed? Ain't nobuddy expectin' thee?'

'No,' he admitted. They sat a while longer in silence, a silence that vibrated like the blood pounding in Sam's ears. He could hear a grasshopper. On either side the meadow stretched to an unbroken horizon. The sunken roadway was hidden behind the hedge. They were as invisible as if they had been Adam and Eve. Clouds banked hugely above the square church tower inside which, hardly fifteen minutes ago, he had been pealing the treble bell. That had been simple compared to this.

'Shall thee an' me be sweethearts, Sa-am?' she said at last, after waiting in case the idea might dawn on him. 'Wouldst like that, eh?'

'I dunno . . .' he mumbled, feeling his face begin to burn like his hands. 'Me sisters call me their li'l ol' boy. Me father dunnot like it if us goes courtin'. He wudna let me brother Tom wed.'

She laughed. 'Oi be not askin' fer to *wed*!' she said, peering at him sidelong. Sam, unable to meet her shining dark blue eyes, dropped his head. 'I be sayin',' Edith went on, 'wouldst like it if I were thy *secret* sweetheart? Nobuddy'll know, 'ceptin' only us!' Sam's heart leaped and thudded, making his ribcage reverberate as if the sky were filled with thunder. He felt an emotion as strong as his fear of Jake or his father, yet quite different.

'Why, Edith? Why *me*?'

Her eyes blazed. 'Thee ain't no *clodhopper*, thee ain't no great *lunk*, thou b'ain't a bullyin' shoutin' unkind sort of fellow. Thou'rt gentle, Sam Savage, an' good, which thet brute Jake Roberts'll niver be. If 'e lives fer a hunnerd years 'e'll always be a mad bull!'

'Aye,' he said with feeling. 'Thet be true orl right.'

She went on, hardly aware that she was speaking in the language of *Morte d'Arthur*, 'Some things be and some things pass. Thou'lt always have a good and honourable heart and thy arm sh'll protect the weak and stand up for right.'

Sam risked a compliment. 'Reckon thou'd protect thy cubs like Mother Wolf, if sumthen roiled thee.' A thrilling moment in one of the Mowgli stories came into his mind; the moment when '*Mother Wolf shook herself clear of the cubs and sprang forward, her eyes, like two green moons in the darkness, facing the blazing eyes of Shere Khan.*'

He grinned at Edith. 'Thou be good too, aye.'

'Be I?' she asked teasingly. 'Be thou *my* li'l owd boy, then? My special sweetheart?'

At that moment Sam would have been relieved to hear the cheerful straightforward shouts of Beddy and the others from the lane, giving him an excuse to leap up and run away from her insistent, beguiling pressure. But the afternoon remained silent. The small hand holding his own flexed and relaxed.

'Give us a kiss,' she said.

Sam had not been kissed since he was a little boy being comforted by Matty yet now he realized he would very much like to kiss Edith Satterthwaite.

'Us mun't,' he said. She had been very bold.

She laughed. 'Why not?'

At last he turned his head and looked at her with wonder. She was a girl from his class, the clever girl, the quick one: yet she had the power to make his hands and face burn and the imp in his shorts quiver with anticipation.

'Oi dunno why not . . .' he mumbled. No answer. Sam leaned across the chasm between them, shut his eyes and briefly kissed Edith's nut-brown cheek.

She sighed. '*Now* us be sweethearts!'

CHAPTER SIX

March–July 1935

There's a whisper down the field where the year has shot her yield,
And the ricks stand grey to the sun,
Singing:–'Over then, come over, for the bee has quit the clover,
And your English summer's done.'
Rudyard Kipling, 'The Long Trail'

BY THE TIME HE WAS FOURTEEN SAM AND HIS FRIENDS WERE
hard at work whenever there was work to be had, although they
were paid little enough. Smaller children searched the
hedgerows to fill their griping bellies since the day's ration of
food was seldom more than two hunks of bread and a mess of
potatoes, supplemented by the occasional rabbit – all the better
for having been poached under the nose of Lord Manning's
gamekeeper. The fact that many people were nearly starving
was no excuse: if caught, they would be punished. Only a few,
like Jake's mother, produced enough eggs and meat to nourish
their family. Jake, almost seventeen, was the very image of a
strapping young countryman, ruddy with health and sunshine,
brimming with physical vigour, but inwardly he was seething.

Billy Debney, his stepfather, no longer cuffed or walloped him since Jake now outstripped him in height and weight; instead he drove him mad by calling him 'Ox'. Jake retaliated by calling him 'yer man' to his mother and, with sullen malevolence, 'farmer Bill' to his face. Billy knew his stepson would take on the farm and its acres when Maggie died, since neither kisses nor curses had begotten a child. With no son of his own, hers would inherit the land into which he had poured his sweat for fifteen years.

Jake continued to intimidate Sam whenever he had the chance and began to prey upon the village girls, who also avoided and feared him. Only Edith, with her quick, sharp tongue, won his respect. Strength came easily to Jake. He wanted to be admired for his wits, as she was. School had not taught him much – after nine years he was hardly literate – but he had learned that some qualities were admired more than brute force, and might take a man further. His mind was slow to retain information or grasp new ideas. He comprehended only the elemental facts of life: the seasons, weather, cycle of crops, the breeding, birth and death of cattle; the hierarchy of man and beast, the strong lording it over the weak. Had he lived a few centuries earlier he would have been a bowman in the army of some feudal baron where his keen eye, strong arm and ruthless urge to kill would have earned the praise and glory he craved. As it was, he kept the upper hand only by making himself feared. He did not know how to talk to girls except by swaggering and boasting, so despite his clumsy attempts at courtship he had not found a sweetheart. Mothers warned their daughters to steer clear of Jake Roberts. 'I seen 'im watchin' thee loike an untried bullock next to field full o' cows. Mind yew let 'im alone. 'E'd do a mischief, if yew let him get close.' They could not bring themselves to say out loud the words *rape*, *pregnancy*, *shame* but the older women made sure their girls kept their distance.

Sam kept his distance too, from both Jake and his father. Abel

Savage spent his meagre pay on beer, leaving hardly enough money for his wife. Had it not been for the wages Tom and Ezra brought home and the pittance from Sam's bell-ringing, Flora could not have fed them or herself. Not yet fifty, she already had the lined, parchment skin and rheumy eyes of an old woman, worn out by fear and overwork. She cowered from her husband and barely spoke above a whisper. She was hardly on speaking terms with her neighbours, who felt sorry for her but had come to dread the litany of prayers and exhortation with which she responded to small talk. She became more and more isolated, lacking even the company of 'th'wulless' since Abel would not spare the five shillings and sixpence needed to buy a wireless. In his cups he could be so violent that it was a miracle he had not yet killed anybody. One evening he broke Flora's arm. The pain and, above all, the arm's uselessness forced her to call on Mrs Neale, the capable district nurse, next morning.

'How did you come by this, my dear?' she asked.

'I fell on it, awkward like . . .' said Flora, thinking, Lord forgive me the sin of lying.

The nurse said nothing.

'I musta dun, munt I? I be that clumsy, allus fallin' over.'

'Well, there *are* other ways . . .'

Flora Savage reflected on the consequences of disclosure. Shame, disloyalty, a stranger breaching the privacy of domestic secrets. And for what? The doctor might want to talk to Abel. And then? Another, worse beating. She said nothing.

'How are your children?' the nurse continued, probing gently. 'Your youngest?'

'Sam be a good lad,' his mother said. She gritted her teeth and tried not to wince as Mrs Neale splinted her forearm, bandaging it tightly. ''E do ring bells in church. Right addled over the bells, 'e be.'

'There! Six weeks like that, I'm afraid. Lucky it's your left arm.'

He *chose* my left arm, Flora thought. He needs the right to clean the house and cook his dinner.

'Can you spare a minute, Mrs Savage? There's no-one waiting at home, is there? Look, if someone in the family has . . . problems, perhaps, with drink or even . . . their *mind* . . . you can seek help, you know. It's not uncommon. There's no shame in it.'

'Jesus Christ my Saviour be an ever-present help in time of trouble,' Flora said.

'Yes, my dear, of course, I am glad your faith is a consolation to you, but . . .'

Flora shook and began to sway. Her half-closed eyes rolled upwards in her head and she rocked to and fro, uttering an inaudible mixture of incantation and prayer. '*Blessed are the poor in spirit . . . Blessed are the meek, for they shall inherit the earth . . . and let my cry come unto Thee . . .*' She worked herself into a frenzy, drumming her feet on the ground, banging her one good fist on her knees, rocking her head back and forth. Mrs Neale recognized a fit of what might once have been called demonic possession and was now described as religious mania. The only difference was that her patient wouldn't be ducked as a witch. Caught between pity and professional interest, she watched as the fit subsided.

Flora opened her eyes, looked at her and said, 'Beggin' yer pardon, Mrs Neale, madam, I be whoolly sorry. Sometimes I slip away, like, and then I hev a cup of tea and get back to misself.'

She was calm and tranquil, apparently unaware of what had happened. Could it have been an epileptic fit? The nurse knew she should investigate and knew too that the Savage family could not afford to pay for medical treatment. Best to say nothing.

'I must be on my way,' said Flora formally. She indicated the rigid arm. 'Six weeks' toime, Oi'll be back.'

'Don't go just yet. Tell me, how old is Sam now?'

'Fourteen. 'E be a good boy.'

'Does he – growing boys, you know – does he get on well with his father?'

'Oh aye, apple of 'is eye, is our li'l owd Sam. What be I owin'?'

'Two shillings and ninepence; that's two shillings for me and ninepence for the ointment, splint and bandage. Try and rest as much as possible, give the arm a chance to mend.'

'Oi will that. Thank you, Mrs Neale, madam.'

'And if ever you . . .'

'May the Lord go with thee in all thy ways. Seek ye first the kingdom of God and his righteousness; and all these things shall be added unto yew. Would you join me on yer knees in a liddul prayer, Mrs Neale?'

'I must be on my way now – lots of visits to make . . .'

With everyone earning less, Edith's mother was short of work. People kept the same sheets on their beds for a month or more and preferred to boil them at home rather than pay to have them laundered. Mary and Victoria, the older Satterthwaite girls, each handed over a few shillings a week from their wages and without this their mother could hardly have survived. Edith – like Sam, just fourteen – earned four shillings and sixpence for helping out as a pupil-teacher with the little ones, whom she supervised at the far end of the cream-and-green-painted class-room. In winter they found it hard to concentrate since fumes from the stove made the closely crammed children sleepy. On warm summer days they stared absently through the high windows at soaring illiterate birds while Edith tried to turn their minds from blackbird to blackboard, showing them how the curve of an 'n' joined the rising hill of an 'a' or the arching bridge of an 'o'. Her skill and sympathy won her the approval of their parents as well as respect and status among her companions.

For many families, the shortage of food became acute. Already pinched, the poorest children began to show the symptoms of rickets. One midsummer evening Miss Jamieson put on her good clothes and her upper-class accent and set off to visit the Mannings. Lord Manning was a governor and benefactor of the school, if at a distance; his wife a benevolent presence at the annual prize-giving and special occasions. The children knew them both by sight and greeted them with an awed deference that Miss Jamieson felt the couple had done little to deserve. She chose her moment carefully, timing it so as to arrive directly after the Mannings would have dined – assuming the upper classes still sat down to dinner sharp at eight and expected to rise from the table forty minutes later. She clanged the bell-pull under the stone entrance porch punctually at eight forty. The butler showed her into a bay-windowed room over which the day's last light fell softly, emphasizing the curves of hand-painted china and old glass. Streaks of oil paint glittered like cobwebs after rain on a portrait of the first Lord Manning, a rubicund Victorian who, to judge by his air of profound self-importance, was contemplating his own entry in *Debrett's*.

'I will inform his lordship of your arrival,' the butler murmured. 'What name shall I announce?'

'Miss Jamieson. No: the *Honourable* Marjorie Jamieson,' she answered, matching his condescension.

When the butler had disappeared she stood up and walked over to the open doorway giving an oblique view across the hall into the dining room. The Mannings were invisible at the far end but she could see the central section of a highly polished table. On it stood an ample selection of cheese, bread and biscuits, as well as a large crystal bowl of fruit in which reposed a magnificent bunch of grapes, each peridot sphere reflecting a dot of candlelight. Across the hallway she heard her name and the Mannings' surprised voices. They sounded just like her parents and she could interpret their bland responses perfectly.

'The Honourable Marjorie *Jamieson*? My dear, do we *know* her?' (Lord M., slow, baffled.)

'There is a Miss Jamieson in the village but she's the *schoolteacher*.' (Lady M., tinkling, irritated.)

'Ah, you may be right, yes, the young woman who teaches. What an inconvenient time to call. The Honourable *schoolteacher*. A high-minded spinster; no doubt a most worthy young woman. What can she want?' (How tiresome to be interrupted just as one is about to make the nightly choice between brandy and port.) 'I expect it's one of those educational things. I can't *think* why she needs to come to our *house*. Ask her to be good enough to wait, Davies.' (*Noblesse oblige*.)

'Yes, my lord.'

Silently, Marjorie Jamieson returned to her seat, folding her hands decorously as the butler entered.

'Her ladyship asks you to wait.'

Ten minutes later (port had been the choice) the Mannings processed across the hall to the drawing room and Marjorie Jamieson was summoned. They occupied matching seats on either side of the fireplace, his winged and brocaded Queen Anne chair a little taller and wider than hers, the spot behind his head a good deal greasier.

'Ah, Miss Jamieson, good evening. Yes, how good of you to pay us this visit. And how are the children? Behaving themselves, I hope?' (Proper concern for their welfare.)

'Working hard?' asked Lady Manning. 'Learning their seven times table?' (Archly.) '*I* always found that one the most difficult.'

'Forgive me for having interrupted your dinner . . .'

'Not at all. We had finished. We shall take coffee, Davies, in a moment.' (When you've gone.)

Forced to stand before them like a supplicant, her hands dangling passively, Marjorie Jamieson spoke more firmly and straightforwardly than she had intended. I am, she thought, their equal, or I was once; I will not be patronized.

'I have come about the children of the village, the children whom I teach,' she began. 'As you must be aware, they are very poor.'

'We are all suffering the effects of the Depression,' Lord Manning said lugubriously.

'No doubt. But *they* are *hungry*. In some cases, practically starving. There are children living not a mile from the end of your drive who go to bed hungry and wake up hungry. Their health is affected. Some are tubercular and others are beginning to develop rickets, a disease barely seen in England since the end of the last century. They live in poor conditions that are reflected in their personal cleanliness . . .' She glanced at Lady Manning and decided not to go into detail about the nits and lice, boils and eczema from which many children suffered.

'Ah, Miss Jamieson, as you know, it was ever thus,' Lord Manning said complacently. 'The standard of hygiene among the lower classes has always been lamentable.'

'Domestic science might be an idea?' Lady Manning put in. 'Teaching the older girls the principles of good home management?'

'The older girls already learn domestic science,' Marjorie Jamieson said firmly, determined not to let them take the easy way out. 'Also needlework and cookery. The latter, un-fortunately, is largely theoretical since we cannot afford the ingredients for practical demonstrations.'

'A great pity . . .' sighed Lady Manning, losing interest.

'At the moment their diet is inadequate. They are pitifully thin. Few of them ever sit down to a hot meal. Few sit down to table at all. They eat the leftovers from their fathers' and brothers' plates, if any. Other than that they live on bread, potatoes and, when they get older, home-brewed beer. To put it bluntly, the children need better nourishment if they are to grow up with strong, healthy bodies. Milk.' She thought of the grapes. 'Fresh fruit.'

She had said what she could to awaken their consciences. She stopped. The butler stood a little way apart to one side of the fireplace, rigid and deaf as a statue. There was a silence, which she did not fill. Let one of them speak. Eventually Manning said, 'What have you come to ask for, Miss Jamieson?' and she thought, so I *have* got through to him!

'You have a large dairy herd, Lord Manning. You must send hundreds of gallons of milk down to London every day. If you could spare just a few gallons, it would enable the children to have milk at school once a day. That would be a start . . .'

'What do you think, my dear?' he said, as though consulting his wife. 'One or two gallons could be spared, I suppose?'

Miss Jamieson turned her gaze towards Lady Manning in case she might be moved to offer some vegetables from their extensive kitchen garden.

'Just as you wish. A couple of gallons will not be missed, I dare say.'

'There are forty children . . .' Miss Jamieson reminded him.

'I shall give orders in the morning. Milk will be delivered to the school starting the day after tomorrow. I am sure you will keep me informed as to when terms begin and end. Waste not, want not.'

'I am extremely grateful to you, Lord Manning. I shall make sure that the children know who their benefactor is.'

He waved a deprecating hand. 'Not at all, not at all.' The moment had passed. 'Thank you for bringing the matter to my attention.'

'To *our* attention.'

'Ours. Goodbye, Miss Jamieson. Do call again. Davies will see you out.'

As she crossed the hall in his wake, Marjorie Jamieson glanced into the dining room and said in a low voice, 'How beautiful those grapes look!'

'Yes, miss,' the butler said uneasily.

'I don't suppose any of my children have ever tasted a grape in their lives, and most of them never will.'

The butler stopped, slipped into the dining room, scooped up the grapes and handed her the bunch. It was, she knew, an act of extraordinary rebellion. They would surely be missed. Questions would be asked and he would have to tell a lie, invent some excuse. She smiled radiantly as he swung the front door open.

'Good night, Mr Davies,' she said. 'Yours is the greater act of kindness. *Thank* you.'

The oak door thudded behind her as she placed the grapes in her saddlebag, mounted her bicycle and pedalled away.

Next morning in school she asked the infants: 'Who knows what grapes are?'

A puzzled silence. 'Be they fruits, miss?' asked one bright little girl. 'B'ain't they in Bible, like milk an' honey?'

'*Good*, Helen! Yes, grapes are a kind of fruit. Now, who knows what they look like?' Nobody knew.

'*These* are grapes,' she said, dangling the bunch like a rabbit from a hat. 'Aren't they luscious? That colour is – what?'

'Green!' shouted several children. 'No, it be yaller!' others insisted.

'You're *all* right. It's light green, a sort of greeny-yellow colour like – what? Who can tell me what it looks like?'

'Leaves in spring!'

'Anything else?'

'New corn jes' cummin' up!'

'Yes, it's that colour as well. Any more?'

'Like owd woodpecker's wings. Or a bluetit unnerneath.'

'*Excellent* observation, Derek. I didn't know you were a bird-watcher. *Just* the colour of a bluetit's breast. Now a hard question: what is it called, when we say something is *like* something else?'

Silence. The children looked around, shrugged their shoulders, waited.

'It's called a *simile*. "Grapes like spring leaves" is a simile. Poets often use similes to make their poems clearer and more beautiful. *My love* is like *a red, red rose*.'

Sniggers.

'All right, let's get back to our grapes.'

She had already extracted half a lesson from the Mannings' bunch of grapes. Pity they couldn't see and hear what these hungry, bright-eyed children made of the glorious tumble of grapes. She explained how grapes grew ('on a sort of bush, like gooseberries, only it's called a *vine* . . .') and how they ripened, ending, 'Now I'm going to walk round all the class so you can all have a proper look at them, and each pull off one to taste. Will there be enough on the bunch?'

'No!' they answered, knowing there was never enough to go round.

Miss Jamieson had counted in advance and knew there would be three left over. She watched their puzzled faces as they chewed one of the sweet, tart grapes and spat out the pips. While they did so she explained about Lord Manning's offer of milk. Thereafter the children brought tin mugs to school every day, dipping them thirstily into the fresh milk during the morning interval. Thanks to this, no more children developed rickets, though the boundary between health and want was still narrow.

Sam and the boys who had been his friends and conspirators, now in their last term at school and on the verge of manhood, had abandoned their old games and tribal rites. They still ribbed and teased each other when they met but no-one bothered to give the gang handshake any more, or chant '*One for All and All for One!*' John Moulton helped his father at the inn after school, learning to unlock his tongue and banter with customers. Isaac, whose father had taught him to stop a horse in its tracks so effectively that nothing could induce it to move until he gave the word – Isaac would be the last to possess these almost pagan secrets. He had been accepted into the Manning household as groom and apprentice chauffeur. Beddy would soon go to work for a prosperous local farmer as back-house boy. The gang was wound up when the contents of the bicycle jar were shared out, amounting to six shillings and sevenpence each.

Only the three brothers, Sam, Ezra and poor Tom, still lived at home. Soon after Matty's marriage Joan had also left, preferring to live under the Mannings' roof – literally, sleeping on an iron bed in a tiny attic – than suffer her father's rages and her mother's lamentations. The day Ezra reached the age of twenty-one, he left home as well. Forewarned by Tom's experience, he did not announce his departure but put a note on top of the family Bible which he placed on the kitchen table. It said: *I hev gon and I aint cumming back, I be 21 and a free man. Ezra Savage.*

Sam knew that he too must go soon. He feared his father terribly; feared having to defend himself or his skinny mother against the murderous rush that engorged Abel Savage's face with blood, made his red-veined eyes start from his head and the words thicken in his throat. Sam was puny for his age and if his strong brother Tom at twenty-six had been no match for their father, what hope had he, Sam, at fourteen? It did not occur to him to ask for help from his teacher or the vicar, but he confided in Edith.

They had been walking out for nearly a year, unobserved by anyone except the local Peeping Tom, who got little reward for his stealthy patience. Everyone else assumed they were too young to be courting seriously.

'I mun get away from 'ere. From me dad. He bin gettin' more 'n' more mad at I. He mun kill I one day soon,' Sam told her one evening, his voice heavy with foreboding.

'Where canst go? Can I come too?' asked Edith, already bereft.

'I dunno. Woodbridge ain't far enough – better be Needham Market. Mebbe I s'll get work there.'

'What canst thou *do*, Sam?' she enquired gently. She took his hand and rested her cheek against the back of it while she pondered. 'Thou'rt sharp an' can reckon well and quickly in thy head. Mebbe doin' sales in market?'

Sam shook his head. His voice was only just beginning to break. He could never command the attention of a jostling audience against a background of men shouting, cows and calves lowing, pigs squealing and general laughter. At fourteen, he still looked and sounded like a child. With grown men unable to find paid work, they both knew his chances were remote.

'Talk to Miss Jamieson,' she urged him finally. '*She*'d give thee a good character. Thou couldst do as I be doin', teachin'?'

'Teaching's work for lasses,' Sam said dismissively. 'Best talk to vicar, I reckon.'

'I dun' want thee to leave,' Edith said. 'What sh'll I do without my sweetheart? Who'll give me kisses then and tell me I hev eyes like . . . what didst say, Sam, my dear?'

'Sometimes they be the colour of forget-me-nots an' sometimes violets but mostly they be just thy eyes. An' that's enough, Edith Satterthwaite, or thy head'll not fit thy Sunday bonnet!'

'Thou'rt my dear good sweetheart, Sam, an' howsoiver far away thou be I'll hev no other!'

He knelt beside her and, running his hands down her slim brown legs, encircled her ankles between finger and thumb. She had made her declaration and he did not know how to answer. At last he lifted his eyes and looked directly into hers.

'Wherever I go, I s'll come back and marry thee, Edith. Thou'rt Edith Satterthwaite now but thou shalt be Edith Savage hereafter. I solemnly swear it – upon . . . upon . . .'

He looked round for a token of fidelity and spotted a tall foxglove growing in the clearing. Scrambling to his feet, he pulled off one of the freckled pink bells and set it upon her ring finger like a thimble.

'On this *foxglove* I promise: one day I'll come back with

money in my purse and then I s'll ask for thy hand from thy mother and by her leave – or without it – I'll take thee as thy wedded *husband*, to be my lawful wedded wife!'

'And so thou shalt; and I s'll wait and if squire's own son came courtin' me I'd tell him nay, for I'm bound to Sam Savage.'

It began to rain, scarcely more than a fine mist at first, then more heavily. Raindrops filtered through the dense branches of the oak tree above their heads, making its leaves shine and wetting their hair and faces. They moved closer and sheltered with their backs against its broad trunk, waiting for the rain to lessen and the storm to pass. It fell steadily and, still unseen, the Peeping Tom gave up his vigil and went damply home to his unmarried sister. Sam and Edith nestled together listening to the sound of each other's breathing. His brown hands touched the bodice of her dress. He stroked her breasts, soft and hard at the same time, making her inhale sharply and murmur, 'Oh Sam . . .' and then, 'Sam, we shudn't!' and finally, 'Oh, thou'rt my dear sweetheart!' Soaked by the rainstorm, they touched each other for the first time. He pushed his other hand under her skirt, groping through the mysterious layers that covered her bare skin, impeding him. Their caresses became bolder, their breathing faster, their kissing deeper. Sam felt the imp harden in his trousers, a fierce impatient mannikin such as he never knew he possessed. Reaching for Edith, gasping urgently for release, he was about to roll on top of her but she held his wrist and said, 'Sam! Sam! Oh my dear love, I want what thou wants, but t'would be shame on us. Most of all, me. Stop, Sam. Listen, I'm beggin' thee, stop.'

His searching hand became passive. The foxglove had dropped from her finger and lay crushed in the deep grass. Edith pulled Sam's hand from beneath her skirt, brought it to her lips and kissed it, breathing a hot familiar smell that had seeped out of her own body. Sam's head lolled backwards, his eyes closed and his shoulders slumped. Gradually, their breathing slowed to normal.

After a while he got to his feet and moved a few yards away. Modestly turning his back to her, he pissed on the rain-soaked grass at his feet. He plucked another spotted foxglove bell and, going back to where Edith sat, placed it on her ring finger to seal their wordless betrothal.

By the time they reached their separate homes they were both sodden. Edith's mother scolded her and fetched dry clothes but Flora said wonderingly, 'Why, li'l owd Sam, thou be'st all wet with the rain of Heaven. *He sendeth rain into the little valleys, He makes it soft with the drops of rain and blesses the increase of it.*'

'Yes, Mam,' Sam said. 'Oi be very wet.'

CHAPTER SEVEN

August–September 1935

THE FOLLOWING THURSDAY AFTER BELL PRACTICE, SAM tugged at the vicar's jacket as he was preparing to leave.

'Reverend, Mr Persimmons?' he said. 'I got summat t' ask thee, please, sir.'

'Hold on then. Let me tidy this away in the vestry and we can walk across the fields together. I don't suppose you've brought an umbrella?'

'I don't hev no brolly, vicar!'

'I thought as much. You know the old verse:

> *The rain it raineth every day*
> *Upon the just and unjust fella,*
> *But mainly on the just, because*
> *The unjust hath the just's umbrella!*

'Come on then, you'd better share mine!'

Hooking Sam's arm into the crook of his elbow and holding the black brolly over their heads, the vicar set off briskly down the churchyard path through an avenue of squat dark yew trees.

'My wife would never forgive me if I didn't bring you in to taste her cherry cake,' he said. 'Why don't you explain your question while we walk back to the rectory?'

Sam did not find it easy to talk to an outsider about his father. He imagined that what he had to tell the vicar would bring shame upon the family. He did not know that half the men in the village who had survived the Great War were similarly afflicted; they, too, drank and raged and beat their families in secret; nor did he know that the vicar had heard several such confidences, knew he could do nothing and was ashamed of his powerlessness. They walked in silence for several minutes before Mr Persimmons said, 'I hear your mother had an accident. Hope her arm is mending?'

'Aye,' said Sam; and then, in a desperate gabble of words: ''Tworn't no accident, vicar, sir. Nay, 'twas my dad wor beatin' me mam. I can't do narthen agin' him. Lork, when he gets that bate we *all* hide from 'im – even me brother Tom, an' 'e be nigh thirty year old! Me brother that wor Ezra, he run away and ain't niver coming back and m'dad wor that mad, we was all afeard o' him. 'E flogged me an' Tom instead.'

'Your father was in the war, Sam, was he not?'

Sam nodded. Rain pattered on top of the sheltering umbrella.

'He will have endured dreadful things. Sights and sounds that are not easily forgotten. Many people's minds were affected by that war. Your father is not the only one to behave wickedly, although he is not himself a wicked man. Can you understand that?'

'Nay,' said Sam truthfully.

The vicar began again. 'You've watched animals being killed, I dare say? You've seen pigs slaughtered before Christmas?'

Sam grinned. 'Aye, sir. That be summat we all go 'n' watch, to 'ear 'im squeal!'

'And can you remember how you feel afterwards?'

'We all be laughin'. We do lark about. An' after we 'elp farmer singe ol' pig's bristles an' scrape out 'is innards fer sausage skins.'

'But do you ever feel sorry for the pig, Sam?'

'Why, no, sir! 'E be just a li'l ol' *pig*, b'ain't 'e?'

'Does the pig feel pain, do you suppose? Is the pig afraid, when the farmer comes to cut his throat?'

'Oh aye, sir; that be why 'e squeal so loud.'

'Listen, Sam. This isn't easy to explain, but you're a clever lad so I want you to try and understand it for yourself. You aren't cruel, but you enjoy watching the pig suffer. It appeals to your baser instincts. It brings out something bad in you, even though you know the pig is in pain. Now then, your father wasn't a cruel man before he went off to fight. He *became* cruel because of the war. He saw so many men die, heard such frightful things, so much beastliness, that he lost his kindly nature: his innocence, you might say. He became like Adam after the Fall. He has looked on Evil, and now he cannot go back. *That* is why he flies into rages and beats you and your mother.'

'Will 'e iver stop?'

The vicar, compelled to honesty, shook his head. 'Probably not.'

'I hev to git away!' Sam said desperately. 'Doan' 'ee see, vicar, 'e'll *kill* me. I tell 'ee, next time 'im gets that bate 'e *will*, if 'e can catch I.'

'Sam, Sam – you're not yet a man. What could you do if you ran away from home?'

'That's it, reverend: that be my very question! Thou'st hit on it. Where cud I go?'

Nowhere, thought Mr Persimmons. You have the brain but not the money for a good education. You lack the strength and size to be a farmhand. Poor lad, what *have* you got?

'What have you to offer?' he said aloud. 'Let's see, what do you like doing best?'

'The bells. Bell-ringin' be grand. And sums, in school. I be best in all class – better than Edith Satterthwaite' – he blushed – 'at workin' out figures in my head.'

'So you have an aptitude for music and mathematics. Let me think.'

They walked on in silence, rain pattering on the Gothic curves of the umbrella, until the vicarage came in sight. Then Mr Persimmons said, his voice bright with energy, 'I think I've got it! *Here*'s an idea: the army might take you on as a band boy! How old are you, Sam? Fourteen yet?'

'Aye, vicar. I wor fourteen in March gone.'

'Have you paid attention in class? Do you think Miss Jamieson would give a good account of you?'

'Oh aye!'

'Have a word with her then, after school one day, and ask her to recommend you. Then I'll take you in my car to the Army Recruiting Centre in Ipswich and we'll see what they say. Time enough to talk to your parents after that. No point in getting them agitated before we know if the army will accept you.'

'Oh sir, vicar, I be ever so thankful!'

It is ironic, Mr Persimmons reflected, that I have just been attempting to make this lad see that his father was corrupted by the war and now the only future I can see for *him* lies in the army. But there is not now nor will there be another war in our lifetime, please God, so he should escape that same corruption. He is a sensitive boy with a finer nature than most country lads. The army might make him into a musician – as long as he isn't bullied and his life made a misery. Briefly, the vicar dwelt on his own days of purgatory at public school. Sam would be worse off than at home if *that* happened to him. With his diminutive size and raw country ways he would need an ally, someone strong to protect him.

'It's only an idea but I wonder if one of your friends might enlist too, as company for you? Who do you run around with?'

'Mostly Beddy an' Isaac an' John – but they be hevin' work to do an' wages to earn.'

'What about one of the bigger lads: Jake Roberts, for instance?'

'I sat wi' 'im at same desk, Jake Roberts. But he b'ain't what you cud call a *friend* . . .'

'Never mind, Sam: look, here we are. Now, I'd like your verdict on that cherry cake!'

A week later, Sam sat in the front seat of the vicar's black Austin Ten clutching an envelope containing his reference from Miss Jamieson. She had written:

Samuel Savage is a bright lad with an aptitude for mathematics, advanced reading ability and an alert, enquiring mind. He is obedient, enthusiastic and popular with his classmates. I have never had to apply corporal punishment, for he is biddable and attentive. His work was singled out for special praise in the Diocesan Report on the school. Sam's parents are decent folk of good character. His father is employed as a farmhand. Although small for his age, Sam's health appears good, apart from a childhood attack of diphtheria. In Physical Training he responds well to commands and has a keen team spirit.
(Signed) Marjorie Jamieson, teacher
23 July 1935

Miss Jamieson had bicycled over to the rectory to show this to the vicar before sealing it.

'Will they take him, do you think?'

'I don't see why not. Given your recommendation, and mine.'

'If he goes it will break the heart of young Edith Satterthwaite,' she said.

The vicar sighed. 'I didn't know. They mature so early. You don't think there have been any . . . goings-on . . . between them? He isn't escaping his responsibilities?'

'I very much doubt it. He's no Jake Roberts, thank goodness! One strapping young scoundrel like that is more than enough. Perfect menace. Never stops pestering the girls. Years ago I put him at a desk with Sam to try and keep him quiet, but it made no difference. I saw him this morning and thought *he* ought to be going into the army, not Sam Savage. That might lower his fine opinion of himself.'

'I was planning to have a word with young Jake, now you mention it . . .'

'He needs taking down a peg or two before he gets up to real mischief. The other children call him "an iron-sided dog".'

But the vicar, not a Suffolk man by birth, was unfamiliar with the phrase.

Now Sam was on his way to Ipswich in his best funeral bell-ringing suit. When they reached the Army Recruiting Centre Mr Persimmons went ahead to have a few words with the officer in charge. He summoned Sam, who watched nervously while the straight-backed recruiting sergeant read his teacher's reference. He looked up at Sam and asked heartily:

'So: fancy yourself as a trumpeter, young feller-me-lad?'

'Aye, I do, sir,' said Sam with lowered head.

'Look me straight in the eye when you answer a question and don't call me *sir*, I'm not an officer. See these three stripes? They make me a sergeant and that's what you call me: *sergeant*. You want to join the 1st East Anglian Light Regiment, is that it?'

'Aye, sir, I do, sergeant,' said Sam, looking directly at him.

'How old are you?'

'Fourteen – sergeant. And a half.'

'You look more like twelve.'

Mr Persimmons interrupted. 'I christened him. Sam Savage is fourteen all right.'

'Now then, Sam Savage: your teacher speaks well of you. The vicar has been good enough to bring you here personally. What have you got to say for yourself?'

'I s'd like to join the army, sir. I can do figgers in me 'ead and I knows the bells and I cun read music and I sh'd like to play in a regimental band . . . sergeant.'

'Very good. You're small. Reckon you'll grow?'

'His father's several inches taller,' the vicar interposed. 'It's in the blood.'

'Have to feed you up, eh, boy?'

'Yes, sergeant!'

'If you pass your medical we'd send you for six weeks' basic training. After that, the regiment's stationed in India, near Cawnpore. Might post you out there with the next draft to join the regimental band. Eh?'

'India . . .' breathed Sam incredulously. '*India*, sir?'

'*Sergeant!* India, yes. Do you know where India is? Mmm? Geography up to it?'

'Oh yes, I do, sergeant. It be east of the Suez Canal and that Arab bit an' north of Ceylon an'—'

'That'll do. Not a promise, mind, India. Have to wait till the monsoon ends. Arrive in the middle of that and you'd turn tail and come straight back. Another month here, behave yourself, help your parents, and come the autumn we'll get you square-bashing. Off you go. Come back in two days' time for a medical. You can take the bus. Here' – he opened a small red and black tin box in the top drawer of his desk and extracted three six-pences – 'the money for your fare. If the doctor doesn't like the look of you, you'll be back home the same day. If he passes you, tell your mother you might be away two years; maybe three.'

'That I s'll, sergeant.'

'No. Say, "Very good, sergeant."'

'Very good, sergeant!'

On the return journey he sat in the front seat of the vicar's car unable to speak. The vicar, glancing sideways at his set face, thought the boy was scared by the momentous step he had just taken. Instead, Sam was remembering:

This is the hour of pride and power,
Talon and tush and claw,
Oh, hear the call! – Good hunting all
That keep the Jungle Law!

His brain rang to the mighty word In-di-a.

Before returning to the recruiting office Sam had to tell his parents and – a greater ordeal – Edith.

His father merely snarled. 'Th'art a fool, boy! Army! *Thee?* Thou'lt niver last a week. But go, an' welcome. One less mouth. Dunna bother cummin' back.' His mother covered her face with her good forearm and her lips moved silently: *Man that is born of woman hath but a short time to live, and is full of misery.* His brother Tom muttered, 'I'll come with 'ee, Sam!' His father's head jerked round. 'Thou'lt *not. And*,' he added scowlingly to Sam, 'dunna think if thou goes, tha' canst come back wheniver it suits! Thou'n' Ezra b'ain't sons of mine no more. No labour, no roof.'

Before it was quite dark Sam ran round to Fir Tree Cottage where Edith lived and knocked on the door. Mrs Satterthwaite opened it.

'What's up?' she asked. 'Be thy mother took poorly agin?'

'Nay, it be not her,' he said, embarrassed. 'I . . . I did want to ask Edith . . . I do hev a problem, loike, and thowt mebbe thy Edith'd help.'

She called behind her down the narrow dark hallway. 'Edith! Young Sam Savage be callin' for 'ee!'

Edith appeared, frowning and rubbing her eyes. By the light of the oil lamp she stood in the doorway; her hands reddened from some labour she had just left, her sleeves rolled back. For an instant he saw her as a grown woman with adult concerns. This was not his foxglove sweetheart but someone older and more serious. He felt not only the surge of love with which his mind and body always greeted her, but a new leap of respect. His only sweetheart would one day be his wife.

'Sam! It be thy same problem agin, I sh'd say?' Edith asked.

Sam blushed. He had not thought through his excuse.

'Nay, niver mind! Mam, canst spare me before it gets dark?'

Mrs Satterthwaite turned away sullenly and went back into the cottage. Sam and Edith set off along Fir Tree Lane towards the hedge that bordered Round Meadow, on whose far side 'their' wood began, with the covert where foxgloves grew. They did not speak or touch each other until they had reached it.

Edith settled herself amid the springy bracken and rolled down her sleeves before taking Sam's hand. In the growing dusk she looked searchingly into his face. 'I see the army'll have thee,' she stated. He could not answer. Under her bare legs she felt the pricking of pine needles or a stinging nettle. She waited for him to speak.

'Aye,' said Sam in a voice that tried to conceal his terror, his excitement and his sense of loss. 'If I c'n pass me medical they will, aye.'

'When?'

'Day after temorry. Then if I pass, they'll let me have four more weeks here. Come September I go.'

'How long shalt be gone for?' Edith rubbed irritably at her legs, which already showed a rash. In the fading light of dusk Sam glimpsed a flannel petticoat and a flash of smooth brown skin at the top of her thighs. He looked away, but the imp stiffened in response.

'Two, mebbe three years.'

Mowgli's throat worked as though the chords in it were being pulled, and his voice seemed to be dragged from it as he answered, 'I will surely come back.'

'Three *years*? Oh, Sam. Thou'd be seventeen, and I sh'd too, before I saw thee agin. Old enough to marry, almost. Dost know where they'll send thee?'

'No. But happen it cud be India.'

In her mind's eye she saw the map that Miss Jamieson used to hook over the top of the blackboard, the bright pink udder of India suspended from the vast multi-coloured continent of Asia, the blood-red drop of Ceylon below it. Between Lower Flexham and India lay the biblical lands of Palestine, the Sea of Galilee, the deserts of Arabia and after those an ocean and half a continent to be crossed. India was so far away it might as well have been the moon.

He turned and met her stricken eyes, saw her love for him, yet could not suppress the treacherous smile that spread across his face.

'Aye,' he said, '*India*! But I'll be back, toime'll pass quick.' His stoic manner broke down. 'Edie, can Oi touch – Oi mean, *look* at 'ee before I go?'

Edith curled her legs under her protectively.

'India be a long way. Thou wudna leave me wi' a babby to rear, a child o' shame?' His head drooped and he looked at his feet in their creased black boots. 'We mun be patient – oh Sam, b'ain't *easy* but three years is a long, long time. Thou mun' change thy mind.'

'Edith, tain't *thee* Oi'm leavin'. I hevta get away from me father. I hate ter leave thee – an' me mam, an' this place. But 'e be boilin' like a kettle, my dad; 'e'll *kill* me soon. I can't stay.'

He felt boyish tears behind his eyes and turned to her for comfort. She held out her arms and Sam nestled against her, feeling the soft rise of her breasts against his cheek.

'Let me touch thee one last time,' he begged.

Edith unbuttoned her blouse. Underneath it she wore a cotton bodice, yellow with age. She looked down at herself, at him, then lifted the bodice up to her chin. Sam leaned across and kissed her on the mouth, then pressed his closed lips against her nipples, each in turn. He felt them harden at his touch, and the imp thickened. He drew back to look at her breasts –

different now – leaned forward again and ran his tongue over the soft pale skin of her chest, tracing its hills and ribcage valleys, licking and circling, astonished at his boldness and pleasure.

'I can't stand it,' she said. 'I can't stop meself. Go on, Sam, if we must.'

Edith's cheeks were dark red in the deepening dusk and he could hear her breathing in and out. Despite herself, she rocked forward on her knees and, leaning yearningly towards him, pulled the bodice over her head with impatient hands.

The Peeping Tom could control himself no longer. From the thicket where he was concealed a few yards away came a harsh volley of grunts, then the crackling of undergrowth as he lumbered off. Instantly, Sam was overcome with shame.

'Edie, someone bin' *watchin'* us!'

Edith covered her eyes and waited for the warmth that suffused her body to subside. She felt a surge of regret. We shudda *done* it! she thought. They sat still, heads averted. Finally she became aware of the itching on her bare leg.

'I've hurt meself,' she said. 'Canst find me a dock leaf, Sam?'

Obediently he stood up, returning with a juicy leaf whose oozing red veins he pressed against the sting, as though that could soothe away years of waiting and yearning.

'Edie,' he said solemnly, 'we got too close. We munn't do that again, or thou'lt be left with a babby.'

'As thou willst, my li'l ol' Sam,' she said, trying to keep the flatness out of her voice.

On a rainy morning at the end of August the vicar's car drove up the lane and stopped outside the Savages' house. Sam's mother embraced him and wept. He picked up the canvas bag containing his belongings and she fell to her knees beside the front door wailing incoherently, repeating over and over again, *Oh Absalom, my son, my son!* The vicar motioned Sam into the back of the car. Sitting in the front, bolt upright, was Jake Roberts. He watched as the vicar went up to the front door and placed his hands firmly on Flora's shoulders to comfort her. Jake turned to Sam and grinned.

'Didst think thou cud go to India *alone*? 'Twas *vicar*'s idea. *Keep an eye on 'im fer me* wor his very words. We're goin' ter go soldiering together, Sam Savage, thee an' me!'

PART TWO

CHAPTER ONE

May 1921

WHILE SAM DOES HIS BASIC TRAINING, LEARNING TO MARCH, stamp his feet and salute in the approved army manner, let us hurry ahead of him to the birthplace of Lakshmi, the little Indian girl who will change his life. If you had started from Lower Flexham and travelled some six thousand miles towards north-east India, you might find yourself in a small village called Budhera, a few miles outside Kanpur. People in the British army cantonment pronounced the town's name *Cawnpore*, with languid English yawning sounds, as in the days of the Mutiny. Only Indians pronounced it in the rapid Indian way, *Kan-pur*. But we'll head for Budhera, a nearby village of some three hundred and fifty inhabitants, and go back in time to the summer of 1921, when Sam was a few months old and Lakshmi about to be born. Can the clock or the globe change direction? Is it so easy to make tomorrow the day after tomorrow's yesterday? Big questions to herald the arrival of a Pariah, of the caste of Untouchables, the child of a sweeper and, worst of all, a baby girl; a lowly, unwanted girl.

At seven o'clock one very warm evening, Sukhia, the young wife of Prem the sweeper, beckoned her husband from the

111

doorway of their hut and whispered, 'My time has come.' Prem spat, frowned and summoned Matin, his mother, who was the village midwife. Already burdened with three daughters, he had prayed fervently to great Kali the Mother and Jara the god of their household that his next child would be a boy. Matin – wrinkled as an old buffalo after forty-two summers – ordered her other daughter-in-law, Parvati, to keep the little girls out of the way and went inside the hut, where she found Sukhia bent double, groaning. Prem rejoined the circle of men sitting on their heels at the end of the day's work and waited to hear if he was the father of a son.

The goddess Kali is mother and destroyer. Propitiated before bat-tles as Kali, bringer of death, her name is invoked before every birth – great mother Kali, may this be a son!

A pregnant woman is vulnerable to a whole host of things. Ghouls, demons and the spirits of people who have committed suicide or died violent deaths are jealous of her unborn child and may try to seize it. To frighten away the evil spirits Matin put a monkey's skull at one end of the bed on which the young mother heaved in labour, as well as a few margosa leaves to placate them. Two of Sukhia's babies had been stillborn but prayers and vigilance warded off the ghosts this time and soon, on this humid summer's night, griping pains signalled the imminent arrival of her next child. If only it turned out to be a son, how joyfully he'd be welcomed! But the newborn possessed the high cleft mound of a girl rather than the tiny elephant's trunk of a boy and Matin, thwarted yet again, went outside to tell her son the bad news.

'Who needs a fourth girl?' she said to Prem. 'I should have smothered her at birth. It's obvious your wife is cursed and will give you nothing but daughters.'

Next morning, sitting in the doorway of his hut, head in hands, shoulders slumped, Prem's attitude proclaimed the sex of the unfortunate child. Still, there were a few omens in the baby's favour. She had been born on a holy day and was given a divine name – Lakshmi, after the lotus goddess, bringer of wealth and prosperity.

A mile to the west of Budhera flowed a tributary of the Ganges called the Pandu. Into it, like a single strand disentangled from a shining plait, ran a tiny stream that local people called the Shoni. These two irrigated the surrounding fields. In hot weather the Shoni soon ran dry and in years when the monsoon was late the Pandu almost dried up too. The villagers were entirely dependent on these two unreliable sources of water, from the highest Brahmin (an amiable fellow cursed with a spendthrift brother and a lazy good-for-nothing arrogant elder son) to the humblest sweeper.

Prem was by no means the humblest of the village sweepers. A decent man, respected by other members of his caste, the fact that his mother was the local midwife brought him further respect. But he and his family were *paraiyars* or Untouchables . . . lowest of the low, scum of the earth, condemned by caste to be *bhangis* (as they were insultingly called): sweepers and cleaners, collectors of muck and all that was foul. *Bhangis*, like all Untouchables, were regarded with contempt because it was their fate to deal with pollution. They contaminated whatever they touched. If the mere shadow of a *bhangi* fell over the food of a higher-caste person, it had to be thrown away. Already, even at three years old, Prem's little daughter Ghashitia was learning to take care where her shadow went, and constantly looked round to check that it was behaving itself. For five thousand years, *bhangis* had suffered insults and humiliation. They and everyone else took it for granted.

Above all, they fear Kali the great Mother, black of face and body, surrounded by a halo of flames and attended by ravens. Her mouth dribbles blood, her long flaming tongue sizzles with the smell of roasted flesh. Her body is charred; she has singed hair and ten arms. Our gaunt, cackling goddesses – Cybele, Sycorax, Hecate – pale beside her powers of destruction.

There are good and bad jobs in any trade and it was Prem's ambition to work in a clean and well-ordered place, above all in the cantonment at Kanpur, a few miles north of the village. Army sweepers were entitled to wear a uniform – only a dingy khaki shirt and long baggy shorts but still, a uniform. Moti – brother-in-law to Bakha, Prem's brother – worked there, walking the eight miles to and from Kanpur once a week to come home, sleep with his wife Maya and play with his little son. The job was highly valued and no wonder: it earned Moti good money and high standing among other *bhangis*. When he died, his son Ramu (still only a baby of two) would inherit the job, as would his son in turn, and *his* son. *Bhangis* hand on their good fortune just like the rich. The circle turns, the oxen plod round the well, money and power pass from one generation to the next.

They believe she intervenes in their mortal lives and placate her to secure her blessing. Kali feels not so much as a candle-flicker of interest. One more birth or murder, what difference does it make? Living for a thousand thousand thousand years, she sees the future as clearly as the past and doesn't think much of either. The centuries follow the millennia like pups stumbling after their mother. Kali is bored.

Moti, Prem and Bakha, together with their wives and inter-linked families, lived in a *bhangi* enclave on the west side of the village, well away from the higher-caste section, beyond the green mango groves and close to swampy, insect-ridden, un-cultivated marshland. Proper houses were built of brick and plaster but *bhangis* made do with squat mud huts surrounded by festering heaps of rubbish on which their children and mangy dogs scavenged. Each morning a sweeper was allowed to enter through the back door of the upper-caste houses to dispose of excrement, sweeping away all trace of his polluting footprints behind him as he went. The other villagers squatted in the open over foetid gutters running alongside the lanes and every day the sweepers cleaned and emptied these drains as well, taking the effluent to fertilize the fields. By long tradition, the wives and mothers of sweepers were midwives, for birth, like defecation and death, was unclean. The hot birth fluids, the animal smells and cries, the raw and pulsing umbilical cord and bloody red bag of the afterbirth polluted all those in attendance. Only the desire to bear a healthy son, the wealth and future of the family line, could permit the Untouchable's touch. The desire for a son was greater than the taboo on contact. Even the Brahmin's spoiled and pale-skinned wife had to submit. Stripped of all pride and dignity, she too exposed her bloated body, panted, heaved, screeched, and delivered her infant into the swarthy, impure, tender hands of a *bhangi* woman.

The food that Prem's mother was given in exchange for her services often saved the family from going hungry, in a village where many of the poorest children starved, especially if they were girls. The newborn Lakshmi was fortunate: 1921 was not a year of drought, plague or pestilence. Bundled in a length of fabric and lashed to her mother's breast, she sucked, joggled and slept her way peacefully through the first dangerous months of her life. But she was cursed with a lifelong deformity. Her eyes looked in two different directions, not squinting but outwards. This would handicap her marriage prospects . . . and being a girl, what other prospects had she? Her future was determined by her sex, caste, the colour of her skin (a gleaming, gunmetal grey) and those eyes – yet Lakshmi and Sam, a couple of puny babies half a world apart, had much in common. They both carried five thousand years of peasant ancestry locked in their genes. Sam had his father's tendency to nightmares and a rare, slow but, when it did erupt, murderous temper. He had his mother's family's nose – the Hopton nose: long and pointed, growing beaky with age, and the Savage chin, eyes and hair. As for Lakshmi, in due course it would become obvious that she had inherited her grandfather's sweet nature as well as his gifts as a storyteller.

All the village children would stop in their tracks at the sound of Dada's voice, hardly breathing, their minds painting the pictures he drew. He told the same stories over and over again, no less dramatic for being predictable, and if he changed so much as a word they made him go back and tell it again. The old tales are handed on, memories and genes pass down the generations, faces reappear decades later. The wheel turns, whether pulled by sway-backed oxen or Suffolk Punches; children grow up to be much the same as their parents were, whether in Budhera or Lower Flexham. That is, if they don't die young.

You can make up theories of genes and wheels but it is Kali the Mother, friend and fiend, beast and breast, who determines whether this miserable infant will be favoured.

Imploring Kali to protect her daughter, invoking their shared motherhood, Sukhia sent up her prayers against the forces of plague, poverty, sun and rain and all the threats that menaced her already unfortunate child. Not that the baby cared. When Lakshmi's belly was full of milk and her mother smiled, she was happy. When leaves shivered patterns on the ground or the women's winnowing made showers of grain and chaff fall from the sky, she was happy. Everyone loved her except her bad-tempered grandmother, who now had six granddaughters and felt keenly the shame of this excessive female tribe. Dada, as everyone called Matin's amiable husband, did his best to console her.

'You'll be the most spoiled and revered grandmother for miles. They'll all grow up to be midwives, forever saying, "Matin did *this* . . ." and "Matin did *that* . . . so this is how it *should* be done." Your memory will live in their praise!'

'*You* like having granddaughters because all men are fools for

116

the wiles of young girls!' she said bitterly. 'You are a vain old man who should have put away his vanity now that you hardly have a tooth left in your head. They climb onto your lap and comb your beard and moustache and stick flowers in the tufts of hair behind your ears . . .'

'It is true. They do.'

'. . . but I have no grandson and that makes me a laughing stock. What does my second son's useless wife bring forth? A hideous girl with crooked eyes. I shall give my body to be torn apart by the crows. Better them than the gossips!'

'If you do I shall rend my beard and rub ash over my naked body and wander the country as a holy man, begging for alms. Without you, what comfort is left to me?'

'You are a thoroughly foolish old man,' Matin said and went inside to fetch a hidden *bidi* for him to smoke.

Lakshmi lay in her mother's lap having her pliant baby body massaged to make sure her limbs grew straight, her head took on a good shape and the invisible organs were correctly positioned. She could see the faded brown and yellow threads in Sukhia's garment and the black gleam of her eyes. Above them the leaves of the jamun tree flickered and dripped the last drops of monsoon rain. Matin's shrill voice cut through the silence:

'Leave her alone. Don't waste your time. Let her fend for herself.'

Lakshmi's left eye tilted as though she were trying to glimpse something just beyond her field of vision. The old woman leaned towards Sukhia, almost choking the baby with her looming body and the smell of her oiled grey plait.

'You're doing it all wrong! If you massage her like that her legs will grow crooked too. Hand her to me.'

Sukhia passed the infant to her mother-in-law, whose curved fingernails dug into the baby flesh like claws. Lakshmi squirmed and was slapped.

'You *close* the eye and *squash* it towards the correct direction with the ball of your thumb. Look, I'm showing you – *look*, stupid girl!'

Sukhia could not bear to watch the horny fingertip pushing the soft jelly deep into her child's head, making her gasp and warble with pain, but she said meekly, 'I will try to do as you say, Matin.' She took back her daughter and sang a lullaby under her breath to console her.

> *'Nini, baba, nini,*
> *Makhan, roti, chini,*
> *Khana, pina, hogaya,*
> *Mera baba sogaya*
> *Nini, baba, nini.'**

Two years later everyone's prayers were answered. Sukhia finally gave birth to a son – a fine, healthy son. Prem strutted round the village and the baby's four sisters realized their rule was at an end. From now on the household would centre on this infant endowed with the one crucial toggle they lacked. In deference to Lord Shiva he was named Shivram.

Sukhia and her baby son sat in the shade opposite their hut with Lakshmi. His doting grandmother lolled on a rope bed beside them. A cloud of black flies buzzed, attracted by the sweet smell of Sukhia's milk.

'Fetch a fan,' Matin ordered. 'Look how the flies swarm around the boy.' Sukhia detached Shivram from her breast and put him in her mother-in-law's arms while she went to get the long fan made of plaited leaves and feathers. Matin's tone became honeyed.

'How fine he is, my little warrior! Who's my princeling – so bold and strong!' An older sister wandered across from

---

*Sleep, baby, sleep/Butter, bread and sugar,/Eating drinking is over,/My baby will sleep/Sleep, baby, sleep.

her game and, picking up Lakshmi, propped her on one tilted hip. 'Who can compare with my big brave fighter?' the grandmother crooned. 'Not that useless creature! She gives me belly-ache. Turn away, Shiv, or she'll put the evil eye on you too.'

Phush, phush, tish-tush, the girl thought; always the same stupid complaints! We all run around doing her bidding and she's never satisfied. She dumped Lakshmi on a bare patch of ground where several village girls were playing hopscotch and the child sat like a squat little Buddha watching as their feet hopped in and out, flicking up sprays of earth.

'Ai, ai, my belly burns, I cannot work!' Matin groaned. 'Sukhia, tell Parvati to help with the winnowing. I haven't the strength today.'

Dada, dozing in the shade beside the hut, heard his wife's fretful voice and his head swayed to and fro. He made funny faces at Lakshmi until she broke into bubbling laughter because when he smiled the dark stumps of his front teeth looked like gaps in a wall. She staggered over towards him. Lifting her onto his lap, Dada intoned, 'In the town of Shamli there once lived a Jat who was greatly harassed by his wife.'

He paused and looked under his eyebrows towards Matin. She was engrossed with Shiv and had not yet noticed the story.

'She would sit idle and nag him all day. She refused even to take food to him in the field where he worked.'

He mimed extravagant horror. No response, unless he detected a certain stiffening in his wife, though she went on smiling at the baby.

'If he ever said anything amiss, even by mistake, she would cry so loudly that all the neighbours came running to see what the matter was.'

His fingers scrabbled like running feet and flicked the folds of his *dhoti* to make flying skirts. Lakshmi's sisters turned to listen, mesmerized by the familiar tale.

'Whenever there was work to do the Jat's wife would complain that she had an upset stomach and was too weak to work.'

He drooped feebly and closed his eyes. Matin tried to suppress a frown.

'One day the Jat thought he would play a trick on his wife . . .'

Beyond the huts, across stretches of darkening green fields and Brahmin fruit groves, the sky turned a deeper rose, then lilac and finally a sheet of limpid blue. Like a circle of hypnotized monkeys, the girls drew closer. Passing children slowed and stopped to listen. The story ended:

'The Jat picked up a stick in order to give his wife a good beating, but she was ready for him and wresting the stick out of his hands she *threw* it into the fire!'

Dada stroked his moustache and slid a private grin at his wife. He knew she had heard; he knew she could not help being what she was and he forgave her.

Dada could sing songs too and had an endless supply of riddles.

'My parents are the sun and sea and they've left me in every house. What am I?'

The little girls bounced up and down shrieking, 'What? What? Tell us, Dada!' The boys herding the bony-hipped oxen in for the night stopped, tried to guess Dada's riddle and failed. When the cattle began to low and shoulder one another impatiently, stamping their feet and flicking their tails, he gave the answer.

'Salt.'

CHAPTER TWO

June 1926

LAKSHMI WAS DAWDLING BY HERSELF THROUGH THE MAGICAL hour she called 'cow-dust time'. She preferred to walk on her own because the other girls often teased her: tipping their heads idiotically sideways or screwing up their faces in imitation of her funny eye. Children are as merciless as chickens towards any deformity. In the sulky, breathless heat of twilight the older boys were leading home the cattle and goats, bouncing sticks on their swaying flanks. The sun's rays, slanting lower through the stirred-up dust, outlined animals and children like quicksilver. A peacock silhouetted in dark green and gold stepped fastidiously along the top of a low wall. Crows bickered for position in the trees. Fifty yards ahead, a group of girls chattered and laughed, darting at one another to pluck or point or slap. They were all heading towards a cluster of mud-walled houses and once the group was far enough ahead to have forgotten about her, Lakshmi turned off the path beside a young tree. She came here to worship Ganesha, the elephant-headed god, remover of impediments, overcomer of obstacles. Lakshmi had chosen him for her own private deity and protector. She had asked him for a friend or a baby goat of her own – either would do – and two good eyes that saw straight. Occasionally she might say she'd like a trunk like his, but this was only to flatter him. Sometimes she made offerings: scrunched-up handfuls of leaves with a peacock's feather nestling in the middle. This time she just muttered the prayers her mother and grandmother used, bowed respectfully and ran off, her skirt flapping round her legs, to catch up with the rest.

As she approached the huts she could smell the pungent, ashy smoke from the burning dung cakes used as cooking fuel. Ahead of her the other children were crouching over something they'd found. Lakshmi ran faster. 'Wait for me!' she shouted. 'Let me see too!' But it was only a dead puppy, still warm. She poked and prodded to see if it would stir but it didn't move except that its paws flopped and a tiny tongue lolled from its mouth. She threw it onto a rubbish heap. Flies rose in a cloud like soot and descended again. Lakshmi hurried on to find her mother.

Kali is the daughter of Agni, god of fire. She is black as charcoal, charred and naked except for a garland of skulls. Lakes of purest rosewater, with shards of ice, would not cool her hands. They tingle as if stung by ants. When fire rises up and hisses, 'Join and be one with me!' she leaps into the flames and her breath scalds like boiling steam.

The women had returned from a day's work in the fields to prepare supper before the men came back. The sound of spices being pounded and the sizzle of oil swirling in a haze above the hot pans poured out of the doorways in a rich miasma, the earthy animal smells in the lane outside mingling with those of cooking. The last child ran indoors.

Squatting beside Matin, Lakshmi tipped gruel into her little brother's gaping mouth. She prayed that the spirits hiding in every home wouldn't pounce on him. You have to be careful about spirits, especially if you are a *bhangi*. They think it's easy to catch you off guard but they're wrong. You have to be very brave when a spirit arrives. You won't see it; you only hear its footsteps, like the sound of little bells, *djang, djang*, when an ox-cart goes by. It goes *han, han*, panting under its breath as if it's craving something. Just let it crave our Shivram! Lakshmi thought: *I'll defend him, even if the spirit takes me instead.*

When the boy had burped and fallen asleep, furled in his grandmother's arms, Lakshmi ate her maize *chapatti* – warm, salty and delicious – and listened to the women's conversation. They were talking about Davadin, the eleven-year-old daughter of another sweeper, who had just returned from her betrothal ceremony. She was not yet a wife, but no longer an unmarried girl. Her extraordinary, god-given beauty made her family cherish high hopes for her. Most *bhangi* women had scowling bullfrog faces but Davadin's was oval, her eyes and hair lustrous, her expression modest yet tender. Being an only child, her limbs were more gracefully rounded than the skinny arms and legs of most girls, half-starved in favour of their brothers. Her parents had kept her at home as long as possible, both for their own comfort and in the hope that news of her beauty might attract a well-to-do and handsome husband.

Lakshmi's big sister Preeti had been betrothed at the same time and was waiting for puberty before leaving to join her husband in another village. Her bridegroom was not nearly as handsome as Davadin's nor from such a well-respected family, so Matin and her daughters-in-law were ridiculing the ambitions of the other girl's parents.

'Who did they think she'd get?' Matin scoffed. 'The son of a maharajah, setting out from his palace on a caparisoned elephant with all his retinue to see for himself if the rumours were true?'

'Perhaps,' suggested Sukhia, 'they hoped a subadar in the army would ride over from Kanpur, his uniform flashing in the sunshine, his mount prancing and jingling, set on fire by rumours of the beauty of a sweeper's girl?'

The women sniggered and Lakshmi, who had been waiting for a story, sighed and snuggled against her mother's soft hip. Her aunt Parvati took up the joke.

'Maybe even a god was supposed to seek her out, coming with ten thousand *devas* to carry her off so that he could caress her on silken sheets to the breeze of a hundred scented fans?'

They cackled as the exaggerations grew wilder, the fantasies coarser. The six little girls of the family – Sukhia's four and Parvati's two – snuggled against their mothers or one another. Caressing of limbs – mingling of perfumes – sweetness of juices – marriage must be like playing games in paradise! Sukhia said, 'High time the *chaudhury* arranged this match. With her looks, it's lucky Davadin hasn't already been taken by force.'

The women's faces in the dingy, cave-like room were lit only by the cooking embers. 'It's true,' Bakha's wife Parvati said wearily. 'Marriage is the only way for a woman. Why else should anyone take a husband?'

'Why is she back home?' asked eight-year-old Ghashitia. 'Today she and Preeti were playing with the other girls just like before. How can they be wives?'

'Before she can live with him she has to become a proper woman.'

'But how will she know?'

Matin chortled. 'She'll know – and so will you, when the time comes.'

Parvati sighed and gathered her two sleepy daughters close to her. 'I am *tired*,' she said for the hundredth time.

One day I shall be married too, Lakshmi thought, and he will stretch out his hand and whisper, 'Come, my dear, let us . . .'

'When will I be married?' she asked, uncurling from her mother's side and looking at her with her good, straight eye, the right one. 'Will it be soon?'

Her sister Mithania (with whom she had quarrelled that morning) scoffed, 'With that face, what man would have you?'

'Plenty of men!' Lakshmi flashed back. 'Many men will be pleased to have me, manymanymany men!'

'Ssshh, children,' Matin soothed, 'you'll wake the boy. Sshh, shh . . .'

Lakshmi burrowed against her mother's body, smelling of sweat and ash, and slept.

The men outside, balanced on their haunches in the warm darkness, were also discussing Davadin's marriage. It was dark; only a sliver of moon hung in the sky. Frogs creaked in the swamps beyond the huts, calling in lovesick voices, *rrark, rrark*. Passing a rolled-up cigarette from hand to hand, its tip glowing like a ruby each time someone drew on it, the men outdid one another with lewd remarks about the bride. Old men, more skeleton than flesh, squatted at the edge of the circle. Their carnal days were over; only bawdy talk was left, the bawdier the better. Several had joined Davadin's father and uncles escorting the girl to her bridegroom's village six miles away, where they had eaten the meal prepared for them and – thanks to her face – been paid a bride price rather than having to bring dowry. Davadin trembled and kept her eyes down throughout the ceremony but Kempa, her betrothed, who had heard rumours of her beauty but not yet seen it for himself, never took his fierce gaze from her veil. She raised it shyly once, and his eyes leaped like a flame.

Sidda laughed coarsely. 'When she lifted her veil, his thing must have swelled up like a stick of sugar cane!'

'He shouldn't waste his syrup,' an old man said from the edge of the group. 'Better to be patient. After a long wait he is more likely to give her a son.'

Prem didn't care for the men's crude remarks. The tender child they joked about could have been Preeti, his own daughter. He changed the subject. 'I hear the bridegroom's father half-starved his wife and daughters to save up enough to buy a bullock as well as their two goats. Why does he need his own bullock?'

Another man answered, 'He could rent it out to plough the fields . . .'

'Plough his daughter-in-law, more likely!' said a mocking voice in the darkness.

'She'd get more pleasure if the bullock did it,' jeered Sidda, an oaf who beat his childless wife until her cries for mercy rang round the huts.

Bakha spat into the darkness behind him. 'Pass the *bidi*.'

'Finished. Have you got another?'

'Only betel.'

'The girl has done well to marry into such a family,' Prem concluded. 'Let's hope he won't starve her, too.'

His own daughter Preeti would soon be at the mercy of her husband and the women of his family: a mother-in-law and two older sisters-in-law. He had watched them sniggering behind their hands and invoked the protection of Jara, goddess of his household, on his child. As an afterthought he added a prayer to Indrani, goddess of the eyes, for Lakshmi, whose deformity would put any man off. Never mind; the expense of her wedding would have beggared him. A fourth daughter can only bring good fortune by staying at home. If she marries, the family is stripped bare. Briefly, Prem invoked the name of Kali.

Kali remains indifferent when her worshippers strive to placate her with garlands of marigolds or crescent bananas. Everyone, from a high-caste priest to the humblest sweeper, tries to better himself. Each thinks, my wealth is good, yours vulgar or ill-gotten; I have earned my good fortune; yours is pure luck. They imagine they propitiate her but a thousand thousand sacrifices would make no difference to Kali the Bored.

One by one the men stretched out on the ground by their huts, rolled cotton shawls across their bodies, pillowed their heads on folded hands and slept. Only Prem lay awake.

An hour later he and his wife, excited by the evening's wedding talk, slipped away to the bushes beside the well. Sukhia prayed not to be made pregnant again but their son Shiv was nearly three. The next child couldn't be delayed much longer.

'Not inside me,' she had begged him urgently. 'Do it the other way!'

Prem, aroused by the sound of another couple making love somewhere nearby, the woman's rising cries and the man's hoarse breathing, could not control himself. Sukhia tried to pull away but her own pleasure was too great. She wound her arms round his hot, naked back and drew him towards her, saying, 'Well then, well then, come, my dear.'

Kali the Mother will swell her womb. What sex shall it be this time? Girl – boy – girl – boy – now he's hurrying – girl, boy, girl, boy, girlboygirlboy – Another boy!

CHAPTER THREE

1926

DAWN: THE CREAKING OF PULLEYS AND BUCKETS AS THE EARLY risers drew water from the wells. By daybreak Sukhia was sweeping the path and lighting the fire, exchanging embers with a neighbour to rekindle the dung cakes to boil water for an early morning drink. Sunrise brought a blast of heat to dispel the night's mist. Lakshmi woke to the tinkle of a cow's tethering chain, birdsong, women's voices, the footsteps and clanking implements of men setting off for the fields. She and her sisters washed their faces, brushed their teeth with a stick dipped in ash, rinsed their mouths, gobbled some breakfast and were off, busy as monkeys. Anything would do for their games – a stone, leaf, petal, smashed egg – anything that could be arranged in a circle, thrown or hopped over. Lakshmi's eye might be crooked but her aim was good and she could land a stone in a square at ten paces. Later on Lakshmi used to think to herself: until I was seven monsoons old my childhood passed as if among the gods on earth. How short it was! I remember Mother telling us, 'Listen, little girls, life's not just songs. You can't play for ever. You have to learn to work or else you're nothing but a greedy mouth and I need a useful pair of hands.'

By the time we were ten summers old we worked almost like grown-ups.

Preeti, since her betrothal, preferred to sit opposite the hut in the shade of a neem tree playing at weddings. She and Davadin tied strips of brightly coloured rags round two bundles of sticks, one for the bride, the other the groom, and sang songs of joy and fecundity, peering at the bundles to see how they liked it. Sukhia called across the lane:

'Don't waste time pretending, silly girl – you'll have the real thing soon enough! Impatience won't bring it a day nearer. Shiv's getting in my way – come and take care of him!'

The boy was sucking the sweetness from a piece of dried mango. Hearing his sister's voice, he lurched towards her and she caught him in her arms. 'Here, Shiv – you be the priest. You have to perform the marriage ceremony. Listen, copy me, say, "*Jaya mangalam . . .*"'

He mumbled, '*Yaya yumyum . . .*' and the girls giggled and nuzzled his smooth fat cheeks.

Every *bhangi* child's first lesson was, avoid contact. Contact sullies. Stay apart. All Pariahs inherited ostracism like their swarthy skin. If Shivram, the beloved princeling, toddled unsteadily towards an upper-caste child, even he would be pulled back and slapped by his mother while the other child was snatched to safety. At first he would jut his lower lip and frown but he soon learned that he was only a prince to his family. To everyone else he was so vile that his touch or even his shadow made them curse and hurry away to bathe. Lakshmi supposed that to be this loathsome she must have done something terrible in a former life. She wished she could remember and be extra careful not to do it again; but she knew that *karma* cannot be denied or avoided. Leave it in the hands of the gods. The cycle of light and dark will turn and come round again, like the moon.

While the girls worked or played Sukhia swept the house,

squatting down to scour the edges and corners until they were as smooth and rounded as the inside of a bird's nest. Finally she wetted the area in front of the hut and, dipping the point of a stick in coloured paste, drew twisting, knotted decorations in the earth to honour the gods and ward off evil spirits. When she had finished, Mithania tiptoed carefully past the fresh patterns and leaned in the doorway, breathless and dusty.

'I'm hot,' she complained. 'I wish the monsoon would hurry. Everything is parched and I'm thirsty.'

'Go and queue at the well for me,' her mother ordered. 'Keep my place. Where's Lakshmi, what's she doing? Tell her to stop it.' She looked up at her second daughter. 'Shame on you, covered with dust and filth! Bring the water and bathe yourself. Plait your hair as well. You look like a road rat. Go on – water – and don't talk to anyone, in that state!'

How do bhangis *endure their lives? No god would stand it. There would be celestial battle – demons, djinns, changings into rats and elephants, trickery and slaughter. But* bhangis *have learned cunning. The world exploits their labour and looks for a chance to rape their women – no wonder they hide what little they possess, shrink into themselves, flatten and fawn like dogs.*

The girls sheltered in a group under a tree when it got too hot to play chase or hopscotch. Lakshmi repeated her grandfather's stories of demons, goddesses and cosmic misunderstandings.

' ". . . The beautiful Rani huddled in a corner of the forest as darkness fell and thought: I shall never see my beloved husband again . . ." ' Lakshmi knew better than anyone else the legends from the Ramayana that the village pundit told, and her light voice went up and down like his to emphasize the drama. She took a deep breath, lowered her voice to a whisper and went on:

' "In the darkness, just as the Rani's tear-soaked eyes were closing and her tired limbs, the colour of burnished gold, grew slack, she heard a voice . . ." '

At lunchtime the girls shared their food so that everyone got something to eat. They sang – they were always singing – or coaxed a fire alight, copying their mothers. This made the boys envious – not the singing but the fire-lighting – and although they were supposed to be minding the cattle they sauntered over and stood around jeering, showing off their male superiority. But they were distracted for too long, and a bullock wandered off and started eating the crops. The farmer ran towards the group like a flying demon and tried to slap everyone with his hard shoe. Funny how the taboo about touching doesn't count if it's a beating. The boys scattered and drove the bullock back to its proper grazing ground.

Moti died, no-one knew how – Moti, the proud sweeper who had the best job of any *bhangi* in the village of Budhera. He set off for the cantonment as usual after a day with his wife, Maya, and their son and never came back. It was probably because of some ugly incident – a fight with another sweeper, a thrashing from a drunken soldier – because the head sweeper came all the way from Kanpur to inform his relatives. Some arrangement must have been reached, money changed hands; no explanation given, none expected. The widowed Maya and her son Ramu were not quite destitute. Ramu had inherited the right to his father's job, a job coveted by every other sweeper, although being only six or seven summers he wasn't old enough to take it on himself. Bakha and Dada discussed the matter and that evening Matin took Maya aside to reassure her. She would not be cast out like some widows; she was a daughter of the household. Parvati and her daughters would move in with Maya, to keep her company.

Next day, Prem came back from the fields while it was still light. He stood at the door of the hut and, beckoning to his wife, whispered urgently, 'Follow me – let Parvati or Maya finish the cooking for once – I have something to tell you that will change our lives! Good fortune has come to us!'

Sukhia's dark eyes lit up with joy and she ran back inside. To her mother-in-law she said humbly, 'Matin, my husband needs me. The maize-flour is milled, the fire is lit, the fuel is warming. May I leave Parvati to prepare the *chapattis* until I get back?' adding to her daughter, 'Ghashi, don't let Shivram near the fire. Take him outside if he needs it and make sure he squats in the proper place. Clean his bottom with a leaf – are you listening, Ghashitia?'

'With a leaf . . .' the girl repeated wearily.

Prem and Sukhia walked in single file towards the fields. A marigold sun seared the horizon. Prem looked round to make sure they would not be overheard, wound his *dhoti* under his legs and settled down by a clump of mango trees, heavy with fruit. She waited. In the silence she invoked the protection of the gods.

As though reading her thoughts, he began, 'Sukhia, the gods have blessed us. But you mustn't tell anyone yet – nobody, do you hear me, nobody! Swear?'

'I swear! Jara, goddess of our household, punish me if I forget my oath. What?'

Feet planted flat on the ground, Prem leaned forward on his haunches and lowered his voice to a whisper, so that she had to crouch even closer to hear.

'My brother Bakha told me *I* can have the sweeper's job at the British Army camp in Kanpur! Yes, it's true. At noon, while the others slept after their meal, Bakha beckoned me away and whispered the news, as I'm whispering now. The job that's vacant because of Moti's death . . . they need someone straight away.'

'Moti was young and strong. How did he die? No-one explained.'

'An accident – a beating – how should I know? The important thing is, they want a man to replace him. Ramu is too young, so Maya offered the job to Bakha.'

'Why didn't he take it?' If this job were such a miracle, she thought, why should it fall to Prem?

'You know what Parvati's like. Ghosts in every corner and demons after nightfall. He daren't leave her alone here. He fears she'd go mad, like a rabid dog. Matin would cast her out and Bakha and the girls would be disgraced.'

Sukhia knew this was true. Her sister-in-law spent half her life huddled on the rope bed, too fearful to work. She was a useless creature.

'What are the conditions?'

'I have to pay Moti's widow fifteen rupees and twelve annas a year and promise to hand the job back when Ramu is old enough.* The British won't take boys younger than fifteen or sixteen summers. That means at least eight years' work for me.'

'You would have to leave us!'

'Not all the time. One day in seven I'd come back here to be with you.'

She knew already that his news was heaven-sent. The British were hard masters but known to be fair. Above all they paid regularly, neither bartering nor finding excuses for keeping back half a man's wages.

'How will you afford fifteen rupees and twelve annas? We have nothing to sell.'

Bakha had already told Prem that the sweepers in the cantonment earned at least sixteen rupees a month but he would not discuss money with a woman, not even his wife, so he merely said, 'My wife, my treasure, I don't know where I shall find the money, only that I must.'

'It's half a day's walk to Kanpur.'

'I shall walk at night. Moti always did. It's cooler. A cart track

* There were sixteen annas to the rupee. The pay of a sweeper in the cantonment in 1935 was sixteen rupees a month, about £1.05.

goes all the way there from Pipargawan, where the market is. Every week I'd be back, outside the hut, calling you, *Phusht-phusht*, before you knew I'd been away.'

At last she smiled.

'You've made up your mind already. I am winded by your certainty.'

'I have. Stand up, my flower. Take my hand. What a firm grip! You are strong, so much stronger than Parvati. She's a frail vessel.'

'Cracked.'

'In more ways than one . . .'

They held on to each other, laughing guiltily that his brother's misfortune should bring them such blessings. She looked up at him and stroked his face.

'What shall I do when I long for you at night?'

'Think impure thoughts . . . as I shall.'

She smiled again and followed him back to the hut.

Lakshmi had been asleep, huddled with her sisters like a nest of puppies. She half woke as her mother came into the hut and murmured, 'Where have you been? What's happened? Is it time to get up?'

'Hush, back to sleep, nothing. Good news. Dadi told me good news.'

'Whisper . . .'

'Sssh, no, Lakshmi, it's a secret.' Sukhia stooped and stroked her daughter's face.

'Come and sleep beside me . . . there . . . good girl. Comfortable?'

Gently, dreamily, the first step had been taken along the road towards Lakshmi's *karma*.

CHAPTER FOUR

1929

THE BAD YEAR CAME WHEN LAKSHMI WAS EIGHT. HER FATHER
had been working as a sweeper for the army for two and a half
years, following the meandering cart track to and from the
cantonment once a week. Prem had borrowed twenty rupees
from Dada to pay Moti's widow Maya for the first year. He was
to repay two rupees a month for those twelve months. With the
money that was left he laid in a small store of grain to tide
Sukhia and their children over in case calamity struck while he
was away. The calamity, when it struck, was not one that the
remaining four rupees and four annas could have averted.

But first they were blessed with good fortune. Several
months after Prem had started work as a sweeper in the soldiers'
barracks in Kanpur, another son was born and they named him
Hari. His sweet-smelling flesh and paddling hands and feet
were some consolation to Sukhia for her husband's week-long
absences. As the days grew longer and hotter she protected the
baby from the unblinking sun with her shawl or, bending over
him, crooned tender lullabies while she worked. Matin, now that
she had two strong and healthy grandsons, began to mellow.
Shivram tried to teach his brother to bang sticks against each

other – using twigs, to suit his miniature hands – so that he could learn to play *gully danda* (the boys' favourite game), but the baby's waving fists couldn't grip except by accident. Even then he was more likely to suck on the twigs to ease his aching gums. He wasn't in the least interested in throwing one up in the air and hitting it with the other, though Shivram showed him how to do it over and over again.

The monsoon came late; very late. A pitiless sun beat down. Hot wind carried grit and dust into every part of every house. It covered the floor and lurked in the folds of clothes, making them itch against scorched skin. The tiny stream of the Shoni had long ago run dry and its insect-infested swamps were as hard as rock and fissured with cracks like Dada's face. The Pandu had dwindled to a shallow stream surrounded by dried mud and the clay gullies carrying water to the surrounding fields were reduced to a mere trickle. Drought was burning up the precious seedlings that would provide next year's food. Even the sacrifice of a bull buffalo to the fierce goddess Mari brought no cooling relief. Skeletal oxen trudged round the well – whose level had sunk lower than anyone could remember – winching up half-full, quarter-full buckets of water. Work under the sun in the open fields was a torment and a waste of effort, since day by day the crops were dying. The farmers cursed and threatened the workers but heat and thirst were relentless. Everyone prayed and waited for rain. Only the kites and jackals thrived, gorged on carrion or half-dead animals too feeble to resist.

Each week Prem walked home through the stifling night to bring his family anything he could save from his own rations. Preeti had reached womanhood and gone to live with her husband, but what little food Prem was able to bring had to be eked out between Sukhia and the children and then shared with the rest of the family. There was never enough. He contrived to give Shivram the biggest portion and Hari was still on the breast. He was smaller than Shivram at his age, but not shrunk and hollow like the four girls.

Ghashitia – always weak – was the first to die. First she became sickly and fretful.

'I am *hungry* . . . I am *thirsty* . . . I am *tired* . . .'

'So am *I*,' Parvati echoed. 'Hungry, thirsty, *tired*.'

'Stop your wailing, daughter-in-law!' snapped Matin. 'Are *our* bellies full? Pray to Jara and be quiet. Soon it'll rain enough to drench you – and then you'll complain about that.'

Within hours, Ghashitia's body was drained of moisture. She collapsed on a heap of rags in one corner of the hut, wailing thinly, too feeble to be cleaned of her own stench.

'Don't waste your prayers on her, or a single anna on the herb man's remedies,' Matin advised Sukhia, hovering over her child's limp form. 'Pick a few leaves from the neem tree and boil them – that's all he does. Above all don't sacrifice to Kali, since we can't spare as much as a rat and the girl's half dead already.' Matin added under her breath, 'Poor creature,' but she dared not show any outward sign of sympathy. Her strength upheld the whole family. Strength was what they needed from her, rather than pity.

Although it was Ghashitia's tenth summer she looked like a wizened child of six. First the diarrhoea shrivelled her body, then her spirit ebbed away.

'May I die instead of you! May I suffer for you!' Sukhia sobbed, while Dada wagged his head outside the door and Matin hurried off to deliver another Brahmin baby. Ghashitia breathed in shallow gasps, her sunken eyes fixed on her mother. Sukhia prayed incoherently to Yama, the god of death. 'Spare her. She's too young to be judged, she's only a little girl, and she'll be so afraid, all by herself . . . She couldn't even watch the bullock being sacrificed because blood frightens her. I swear she's pure.' Ghashitia's eyes dimmed, her jaw slackened and soon her fevered body was an empty heap. Sukhia clasped

Shivram and made him stroke his sister's face in farewell. Within minutes the swarm of flies became unbearable and she summoned Lakshmi to help her clean and arrange the corpse.

Next day Prem returned from the cantonment before sunrise, his throat parched by the dusty trek and the earth's pent-up heat, his mind agitated by the dry storm that often presaged a monsoon, to find Sukhia and Parvati wailing and pulling at their hair. Lakshmi and Mithania sat solemnly beside the swathed bundle, unable to believe their sister would never play with them again.

'Tell the mother of your children not to waste her energy!' Matin said, frowning. 'There's nothing more she can do. The baby needs her and Shiv has been very listless. She should concern herself with her sons! Ai, ai, I have called down the rains a thousand times.'

'But will they come when you call them?' said Dada, eyes reddened with grief.

Turning to Prem he added, 'My son, we must take the child to the Holy Ganges.'

The nearest *ghat* of the sacred river was even further than Kanpur, but the fragile burden of Ghashitia's body, trussed in a sack with a few sweet-smelling herbs, was carried by her father and grandfather through the heat of the day and slipped into the Ganges without flowers or singing or ceremony. The men limped back in the sweltering dusk and humid night, to be greeted by Lakshmi as she emerged from the dark doorway of the hut. She had been listening out for them.

'Is she better?' she asked. 'Do say Ghashitia's better! I talked to Ganesha and he promised to intercede with Yama for her life. I've prayed so hard.'

'She is better, my child, but she sends word that you are not to pine for her, or you will disturb her spirit. Yama has judged her pure and taken her to his kingdom.'

Almost at once, as though the sacrifice needed had been the dead girl rather than the bullock, the rains came. The first warning was a hot, stormy west wind, so strong that kites couldn't soar against it. The wind agitated the dry air, whipping the treetops into a frenzy and the birds with them. The sky reverberated with sheet lightning and a low resonant growl. A few wet drops splashed onto the upturned faces of the villagers, multiplying into a deafening crescendo of water. Water drummed on the rock-hard earth, its pent-up energy exploding in bubbles and turning the lanes into rivers. It drenched the straw roofs of huts and cascaded down their mud walls so hard that some collapsed. But the gods be praised, it was rain not drought. Any households that still had stores of flour, ghee and sugar-cane syrup joyfully fried sweet pancakes to celebrate. None of the *bhangis* had the energy let alone the food to make pancakes.

Sukhia, who was pregnant again, did not ask why the gods had given rain or taken her daughter. It was part of the order of things: sun, rain, water, fire. If I am learning to accept whatever the gods send, she thought, I must be getting old. But a few days after Ghashitia died, Shivram began to sicken, victim of the same flux. His reserves of strength were greater than his sister's and at first no-one believed he would die, though it was obvious that the demon who'd taken her was wrestling with him too. The women reassured each other. Shiv, the bold warrior – of course he would win! They seemed so confident that, lying on a bed of rags, urged on by his mother and grandmother, the boy reproached himself for being a coward. He tried to get to his feet and do battle with the demon but burning liquid trickled down him in a foul stream, his legs buckled, he fell and became delirious. Hearing rain battering against the roof, he thought demons were coming in battalions to attack.

'Ai, ai, they are too many for me!' he cried, waving his arms, frantic with terror. 'I can't fight them all! There are hundreds, thousands, pouring down from the sky.'

'Sshh, my son, it isn't demons, only the rain,' his mother soothed.

Matin scolded, 'Shivram, ai, ai, this is not how a prince should talk!'

Sukhia held medicine to his lips. She had procured it from the herbal man for one rupee and eight annas. It must be good.

'Drink this and it'll give you the strength of ten thousand demons!'

Crouched beside her grandson, holding him in her arms, Matin could feel his strength dwindling. Tears ran down her face and tilting her head against one shoulder she brushed them away. Dada's wet face peered in through the door of the hut.

'Shall I tell you a story, Shiv, to put iron into your muscles and fire in your heart?'

'Drink the medicine,' his mother coaxed. 'Drink, Shivram, it's good. The god of the temple has blessed it.'

Shivram bent his lips towards the bowl but a stream of bile spewed forth and he slumped back. The little girls huddled against the wall of the hut watched fearfully. Lakshmi recognized the expression on his face. This was how Ghashitia had looked. She brushed past and ran out into the rain to intercede with Ganesha. The women leaned over Shivram, blocking the light, while from the doorway Dada intoned steadily, 'There once reigned a king whose chief minister, Ajit Singh, was very wise and able and much in the king's confidence. One day . . .'

Outside, children gathered to listen to the story, wide-eyed and silent under the sodden eaves. Dada reached the end: 'The King's men began to shout, "See, Surajmal goes to heaven riding on a cloud of smoke!" The trip to heaven had indeed started for him, but this time there was no coming back.'

Why such weeping and wailing and gnashing of teeth? Kali might reflect, had she bothered to pay attention to an insignificant bhangi *family. This boy is just one death among millions.*

Lakshmi was sure she would be the next to die. Ghashitia and Shiv had struggled desperately to live. She had heard the pundit's tales of Yama the god of death with his red eyes, green body and blood-red robes and the terror of dying gave her nightmares. She went to explain herself to her god in the tree. Rain dripped onto her bent head as she told Ganesha that all she wanted was to live, and marry, and have children whose eyes looked straight ahead. A small brown bird with brilliant turquoise wing-tips flew up from a branch and Lakshmi, watching the *nilkant* soar, hoped her prayer had been heard.

Lakshmi had grieved for Ghashitia but Shivram's death ended her childhood. At eight years old she realized that all her life she would be walled in by pitiless rules that, until now, she had not stopped to think about. The Brahmin's eldest son, whose behaviour was neither virtuous nor honourable, who was not nearly as brave and beautiful as Shiv had been – *he* wouldn't fall ill and die. Lakshmi tried to console herself by imagining the torments he would endure in the next life as a black beetle, a black rat, no, better still a black-skinned swine grubbing in the gutter with its snout in shit – but this wasn't much comfort when every day she saw him strutting about, fat, lazy and rude, shouting insults at the workers bent double in his fields. He would always have everything, while her life was bounded by nothing and never. Nothing would bring back her brother and sister nor stop her mother weeping. Her sideways eye would never see straight. Even doddery old Dada was losing his place in the stories more often. She would never be carefree again. One thought kept shimmering in her head like a distant figure seen against the sun, too bright to make out: 'Tomorrow is the day after tomorrow's yesterday.' The puzzling, playful words skidded about like light reflected in the ring of water at the bottom of a well. Unperturbed, the oxen plodded round bringing up leather buckets overflowing with water; the streams filled, the crops grew green and summer ended.

No-one knew how much Prem mourned the death of his first son but his former gentleness vanished and he became surly to everyone except his parents, towards whom he continued to show respect. Instead of running to meet him, his daughters were learning to stay out of his way, watching him nervously, trying to judge his mood. Only little Hari still stretched out his arms in welcome. Sukhia, immersed in her own grief, swollen and exhausted by another pregnancy, lacked the will to coax her husband back into their sweet private understanding. When he came home – which was no longer every week – he spent more time talking to the villagers than with his family. The men were avid for news from Kanpur after the wild rumours of unrest they had heard in the market at Pipargawan.

'Mahatma Gandhi goes about the country bringing hope to everyone, especially us in the Pariah castes,' Prem told them. 'He promises an end to bribes. We won't be at the mercy of landlords and bandits any longer . . .'

'One and the same thing!' a mocking voice interrupted.

'. . . or moneylenders or the police. He promises us the vote. We'll be ruled by Indians, even including *bhangis* like us . . .'

'Heard it all before,' scoffed another. 'To hell with the moneylenders!'

Prem went on, 'Gandhi-ji holds meetings in every state and village . . .'

'Hasn't been *here*!' Hawk and spit.

'. . . no, but he will – and they say hearing him speak is like riding on the wind. He inspires huge crowds of people to fight for freedom.'

'My son, *how*? How can we all fight for one cause, when we're so divided?' Dada asked from his usual place under the tree.

'I don't know,' Prem admitted. 'I only know the Mahatma is a great man. Great and good. He promises change for everyone, us included. You know the saying: "Take a ploughman from his plough, wash off his dirt, and he's fit to rule a kingdom"? Well . . .' and he spread his hands as if to say: so why not me?

'Who'll pay our wages?' another voice asked.

'Look, I said I have no answers. I haven't seen him or heard him speak. But the people who *have*, believe him.'

'Why should anything change?' asked Bakha, always a fatalist. 'We inherit our lives from our forefathers. It's the will of the gods.'

Lalla, a gentle fellow, devout in his prayers and offerings to the temple, said, 'Things are as they should be. There has always been pain – why should it end with us? If *bhangis* were happy, the wheel wouldn't turn.'

Bakha went on stolidly, 'That's right. The old order has served us for generations. It gives everyone a task and provides everything the village needs. It *works*.' He looked round the circle of men grappling with the idea of change. 'Take all of us here, Prem. Our fathers' – he inclined his head at Dada – 'taught us what they had learned from their fathers and in time we teach our sons – if the gods grant us sons . . .'

Bakha seems a sensible fellow. Kali has half a mind to give him a son but even she can't do that unless he sleeps with his wife – the laws of biology being even more powerful than those of deities – and he hasn't done that for many a moon. Despite the gods' occasional goodwill, we often miss our chances.

'That's right,' said Dada. 'Nothing will ever change. Remember Amritsar? Hundreds of people put to death in the streets. Unarmed. No guns, no swords, nothing. Everyone talked big after that, swore revenge against the British. Nothing happened. Our lives will go on as they are . . . work or starve and sometimes both. Nobody above us will give up their

143

privileges, doesn't matter what Gandhi says. For *bhangis*? Never!'

Prem did not want to shame his father by contradicting him openly but he was frustrated. What did simple ignorant villagers know of the currents sweeping the big city? He said stubbornly, 'You'll see. Things *will* be different.'

Lalla's voice said, 'Yes – and one day Sidda'll offer round a *bidi*!'

They all laughed and Sidda barged out of the circle without a word.

Mithania was betrothed, aged thirteen. It was high time; she needed protecting from the landlord, who wouldn't scruple to take her by force, given the chance. As soon as she had her first menses she'd go to live in Nagwan, a village close to Kanpur. Twice as large as Budhera, it was more prosperous, surrounded by fertile green fields and less than half a mile from a deep canal that never dried up. Her husband-to-be was the son of another sweeper at the cantonment and Prem hoped the alliance would be useful to him, although the groom seemed a rough fellow. 'He is impatient for marriage,' his father said. 'Hair has sprouted on his upper lip and he's strong enough to do a man's work on the land. He's a fine boy. All he needs is a wife to cool his ardour . . .' and he leered suggestively. Prem let himself be persuaded, despite the boy's hostile gaze and crude manner. It was a good match and might be his daughter's last chance. During the betrothal ceremony Mithania, her slim, henna-painted hands trembling, lifted her veil a fraction; enough to reveal her sooty complexion, close-set eyes and heavy brows. Afterwards Prem overheard the bridegroom saying to a cousin, 'I'd rather fuck an ass!' The other man had replied, 'It'll be a tight fuck whichever ass you pick!' and they laughed raucously. It did not bode well for his gentle, submissive child.

Her sister's union propelled Lakshmi one step further towards her destiny and sealed the fate of eight-year-old Sam in a village on the other side of the world. No man, no island, not even the vast subcontinent of India, is completely self-contained.

For the moment Mithania remained at home. When dusk put a stop to work she and Lakshmi still liked listening to Dada's stories although his mind often wandered. It hardly mattered; the familiar words were like a spell, transporting them to a world of silks and bazaars, wily merchants, cheating husbands and gentle princesses on a quest to find their warrior lover.

'No woman in the three worlds could match the beauty of Chandramala . . .' he would begin; and their busy hands subsided into their laps. 'The handsome Brahma Kanwal, asleep on the bed, seemed like the new moon . . .' His granddaughters sighed. Their minds spun innocent dreams in which acrobatic golden bodies enlaced voluptuously but futilely, like puppies squabbling over a butterfly, all action and no outcome – until Matin came storming out to rebuke his old man's fantasies and chivvy the girls indoors to the stove.

The village pundit's tales were even more enthralling. He made the Mahabharata come alive. He had a highly developed sense of his own importance and vied with other Brahmins for precedence at village ceremonies and on holy days, although they all pretended deference to one another in a charade of condescension. The pundit wore a silver ring on his finger, bathed twice daily, prayed three times, and smeared sacred ash on his forehead. People would gather at dusk outside the door of his house, *bhangis* settling on their haunches at the outer edge of the circle, taking care not to contaminate. As he swept the attentive group with his gaze, their eyes would lock onto his until nothing could be heard but the rustle of leaves and the distant howling of jackals. When every pair of lungs breathed in unison he would murmur so softly that at first they could hardly catch the words:

145

'*Daksha* offered *Rati* in marriage. Her eyebrows were more perfectly arched than *Manmata*'s brow; her breasts were like lotus buds, pointed, with nipples dark as honey bees and so hard that a teardrop falling on them would rebound in a spray. Her thighs, smooth as banana stalks, tapered down to delicate feet, pink-tinted at heel and toe. *Manmata* was overwhelmed with love for *Rati* and married her . . .'* His audience saw the dark blue sky peopled with goddesses or demons, the trees with djinns, the shimmering plain of the Ganges alive with warrior ants that turned into rank upon rank of an advancing army. Afterwards they stumbled away like sleepwalkers, husbands pulling meaningfully on the hands of pliant wives.

Lakshmi and Mithania often discussed the moment after the wedding ceremony when the young pair were left alone together for the first time – the timid bride, the impatient yet tender groom – and their skin would tingle at the thought of such unimaginable joy. When Preeti, who had already left home, returned a year later for the birth of her child – lumbering, distended, serious – her sisters asked breathlessly, 'What's it like when . . . *you* know . . . is it *thrilling*? Are you transported like Rati?'

'You'll have to wait. When you marry you'll find out for your-selves.'

'So *unfair* . . .' they complained. 'You *promised* you wouldn't keep it secret. Ai, Preeti-ji, *tell* us!'

But she withdrew into herself, stroked her rounded belly with dreamy hands and closed her eyes.

'I must rest,' she said. 'It is important to let the child grow and not disturb him. Let me rest.'

The birth of her son displaced even the indignant godling Hari for a week, until her husband and father-in-law arrived to

---

*Adapted from R. K. Narayan, *Gods, Demons and Others*, Vision Books edn, New Delhi, 1965, p. 87.

reclaim her. Just once, Lakshmi contrived to get her sister alone. Preeti was suckling her baby with rapt concentration.

'*What*'s it like?' Lakshmi asked. 'Is it like being veiled in silk and wafted through paradise, the way it is in the stories?'

Preeti lifted her eyes heavily and said, 'Not always, and not at first. But – he *needs* you, like this little prince needs me now. That feels good. The rest . . . let it be. Don't think about it too much.'

By the time she came home for the second birth, Preeti – now fifteen – had grown up and could no longer be cajoled with the whisperings of sisterhood.

Mithania and Lakshmi took it in turns to care for Hari, hooking him on one hip and telling him stories, thoughts, gossip, dreams, in an unending prattle. He would point at Lakshmi's sidelong eye and try to make it look in his direction, but as soon as he succeeded, the good eye focused away from him. This made him chortle with glee and he would hold her chin and swivel her face this way and that, laughing. Lakshmi laughed too, but more soberly.

'Play while you can, my little frog,' she told him. 'The playing will soon have to stop – even for a boy! You're the only son now that your big brother Shivram has been taken by the gods, and the only boy in the family unless Aunty and Uncle have a son. You will be *head* of the family one day. You will be a *wise*, *old* man with a *long*, *white* beard and a *big yellow* moustache like Dada from smoking *bidis* . . .'

The baby pealed with laughter when she imitated his grandfather and bounced up and down to show that he wanted more.

The hunger for more is never satisfied. Pearls as big as pigeon's eggs? Find me rubies as big! Good: and now a diamond. The biggest diamond in the world, the Koh-i-Noor, is worn by a pale and distant Queen, not fit to serve as Kali's humblest handmaid.

Sukhia gave birth to her seventh child in the late autumn; another daughter, born at the side of a field as her mother was harvesting millet. The baby looked more like a monkey than a child, with furry black hair and a curved spine. The drought had taken its toll, even in the womb. Sukhia looked more closely at the spine. It was twisted. As she crouched in a shallow, dusty ditch waiting for the afterbirth, she thought, I could end her life now. A couple of pebbles in her mouth, lay her face-down in the earth, scoop dust and a few more stones over her, scatter some branches, walk away, say she was born dead. Who would argue, or care? The child's clenched purple face worked convulsively and its eyebrows jerked up and down. How ugly it was, ugly, deformed and female. The afterbirth slid out, Sukhia severed the cord and wiped herself and her daughter with the end of her skirt. She sighed as she thought of Matin's imprecations, wound the infant in a shawl and folded it across her breast to suck or sleep, live or die. Then she went back to work; stoop, straighten, trudge, load and bring in the millet. To ward off the attentions of the gods lest they wish any more bad luck on her unfortunate daughter, she named her Kubri, meaning hunchback.

Mithania reached womanhood all too soon. 'Will you go and come back?' Lakshmi asked, laying her head on Mithania's slight shoulders, first one and then the other, feeling the sharp collar-bones beneath her cheek. Both sisters had wept in secret. Marriage was supposed to be the joyful culmination to childhood, not a sad farewell. A slight, heavily draped figure in a borrowed red sari, Mithania was escorted to her husband's village by her father, uncle Bakha and Dada. Lakshmi watched wistfully as they disappeared in billows of grey dust. There was no money for a decorated bullock cart so they would go on foot along the path her father took each time he set off for Kanpur. My turn next, Lakshmi thought, staring after them with her good eye, the other aslant towards her unknown, waiting husband. He will pull on my hand and say, 'Come to me, dear . . .' and shyly, joyfully, I will acquiesce and do as he desires, whatever that may be.

CHAPTER FIVE

1930

PREM HAD BEEN WORKING AT THE CANTONMENT FOR FOUR years and the burden of having to support so many people, as well as pay Maya for the privilege of doing his job, had turned him surly and resentful. Even after two deaths and two marriages his family still numbered eight: his parents, his wife Sukhia, their daughters Lakshmi and Kubri, his widowed sister-in-law Maya along with Ramu, her son – and all of these together meant less to him than his son Hari. He could never provide what they wanted and Kanpur offered better diversions. When he did make the journey home, what drew him was not his wife but his son, the living embodiment of his line and object of all his hopes. Hari was now more than three summers old; the petted godling of the household.

'Hari, come here. Tell me: who is the fastest runner of all?'

'Me!'

'Who is the best tree–climber?'

'Me!'

'Who can skip and turn somersaults and play *kabaddi* with the big boys?'

'Me me me!'

'And *who* sits on the leading bullock at harvest time?'

'Me – memememe*me*!'

Prem thought his son was perfect and Hari thought so too. All day long he hurtled from hut to well to treetops, down the lane into the fields off with a pack of other boys to play *chui chuiyal* – hide-and seek – or *gully danda*, chucking a stick in the air followed by much twisting and throwing and pointing and derisive laughter from the safety of a high perch. If he hurt his leg or banged his head he raced back to the hut howling (but keeping out of other people's way in case they yelled and flailed and made evil faces at him) and after a brief pause to be comforted, raced out again, a small black dervish in perpetual motion. Sukhia watched him, torn between pride and fear. At any moment the tree spirit might drop a branch on his head, a monkey or a rabid dog bite him or the headman aim a warning stone at him all too accurately. He would be carried back with blood pouring from a gash. In her mind's eye a thousand dangers threatened.

'Can you cage a wolf cub?' Matin asked irritably. 'If you do, it grows into a cur, not a wolf. Let Hari go, you'll only crush his spirit. Poor child, it'll happen soon enough.'

Sukhia pounded clothes against a washboard, rinsed them and draped them from the branches of a tree to dry while Matin sat in the shade, instructing her in a shrill, sing-song voice. Pregnant once more, Sukhia was now learning the arts of midwifery. Her mother-in-law resented having to pass on her skills but at her age – at least fifty summers – it was time to rest. She no longer had the energy to stay up all night for a difficult delivery or the strength to wrestle with a breech birth and the babies she delivered were too often born dead. The job should have gone to Parvati, the senior daughter-in-law, but Parvati was too nervous to make a good midwife. Sukhia was altogether steadier. Matin went on:

'Miscarriage can be avoided by looking out for spirits who want to steal from the womb of every pregnant woman. You must learn to foil their wicked ways. They prowl around the lanes after dark, eating any food left lying about and trying to possess people. As soon as they catch the smell of a foetus in a woman's womb they're there, spying, waiting their chance. Will you *listen* or you'll only bring dead children into the world.'

Kali takes them at random, regardless of beauty, prayers or imprecations. Sometimes she carries her cholera jar filled with dark blue oil . . . Cholera: otherwise known as plague, pestilence, havoc, panic, pain, tumour, rumour, black humours, black bile, Black Death . . . Who'll be struck down by her cordial next?

Matin had enjoyed her status as midwife and was reluctant to give it up. The job enabled her to carry herself boldly and she would miss her privileged access to the domestic secrets of every family in the village. When people saw her going purposefully about her business they waited eagerly, since she always had the latest gossip. Higher-caste women, confined by purdah to their own courtyards, could only glimpse the outside world from the flat roofs of their houses, peering through heavy veils into the lane below, but the tops of people's heads are a less than satisfactory guide to what they're getting up to.

She went on irritably, 'Concentrate, my girl: this is important. During labour you tie charms into the woman's hair to ward off the spirits. They'll let you touch their hair, even the Brahmins. They're more afraid of spirits than pollution. After the birth, if all's gone well, you still have to visit often. Infuse leaves of the cow's itch plant and make her drink it three times in case impurities have stayed in the womb.'

'What if the child is born dead, or dies soon after?'

'They're born, they die, it's as if they'd never been. I'm coming to that.'

Sukhia had mourned each of her lost children including the

stillborn. Her mother-in-law was old and her life had been hard, although she'd seen both her sons grow to manhood. Sukhia knew she herself should be kinder to her daughters – Kubri the hunchback, more like a beetle than a child, and poor sweet-natured Lakshmi, whom no man was ever likely to marry – but all her mother love was poured out on Hari. If only Shivram, her beautiful warrior son, were still alive, what fun the two would have had together! Girls from all the villages around would have competed for them. If only her husband were the way he used to be, pulling subtly on her hand to show that he wanted to meet her when the others slept and the white moon rode high above the trees. I long for him, she thought – to touch me, to put out his tongue and lick me, to whisper in my ear as he did when we were alone on the warm earth. He used to fill my body with light. Now when he comes home he's cold and abrupt. I wait at our special place but often he isn't there; or he's drunk on arrack and finds fault and beats me. Even when he does take me, it's different. He seems to have forgotten all our private ways and pleases only himself.

Catching her daughter-in-law's dreamy expression, Matin stopped suddenly. 'Are you listening to me, girl?'

'Yes, Matin, I am listening.'

Sukhia learned fast. The work was taxing but she welcomed it. During the early hours of childbirth, in the intervals between pains ('Quickly, *dai*, it's coming again!') Sukhia found that she and the labouring mother could almost forget the gulf between them and talk like two ordinary women. As midwife, she was the person who knew about the naughty uncles with wandering hands or the aunty who could hardly take her eyes off the shapely back and sturdy thighs of an unmarried nephew. She knew whose husband was unfaithful, whose wife spent too much time with her brother-in-law, 'though always with down-cast eyes and modest manner'. She knew the marriage plans of every family, whose budding daughter was the loveliest, whose sons coveted her. She also knew when a *bhangi* girl was summoned to sweep the headman's house so that he could cup her breasts, thrust his hand ('and worse') between her legs and bury his moustache in her gleaming hair despite the fact that she was unclean (he would bathe afterwards and curse the girl for having polluted him) but these incidents were of no interest. What did a *bhangi* girl's virginity matter? The midwife should not presume to criticize the headman. 'Mind your tongue and know your place!' they would order – until caught by a belt of pain, and then it was 'Quickly, *dai*, quickly!' as they clung to her hand. 'Remember, my daughter,' Sukhia said, turning to Lakshmi. 'Never stop when a man calls. You are still only a girl, but men will try to persuade you to come with them. If an upper-caste man calls, even a Brahmin, don't go. If you're beckoned towards someone's house, don't go. He might make you bend down and lay his hands on you and try to – well, just do as I say.'

Lakshmi thought of her earliest lessons. Avoid contact. Contact sullies.

Once the child was safely born, Sukhia would resume her subservient role. She massaged oil into the woman's aching body, dressed her in a clean sari scented with healing herbs, praised her strength and courage and admired the baby. She saw everyone's joy and sorrow. Boys were welcomed as though a god had descended among them but if the newborn was a girl her mother would examine her with pitying eyes to see how light-skinned she was, wrap her in a shawl and whisper, 'Ai, my daughter, you have come into a hard world!'

'What is more important,' Sukhia would say, 'what matters more to women than children? A woman without a daughter to close her eyes is an unhappy woman. Keep her from sickness so that she can grow strong and marry and give you many grandsons.'

When a birth went badly she had to prepare the hollow-eyed woman to meet Yama, god of death.

'You'll hear him coming,' she would explain, 'with his messengers, all tied to each other with big ropes. You hear them trudging along with heavy steps that go like this: *Ahum! Ahum! Ahum!*' and the suggestible mother would pant too, '*Ahum! Ahum! Ahum!*' If in spite of everything the child was stillborn, Sukhia washed away the blood and mucus with cool, efficient hands and bound the woman tightly, crooning songs of consolation.

Worst of all, Sukhia found, was having to tell a family with several daughters that the dead infant had been male. They would scream abuse, accuse her of witchcraft, blackmail, kidnapping, lying, and refuse to pay her – yet next day she would be back with ointment and herbs to close and purify the orifices, rites to drive away thieving spirits and assurances of another son to come. As time went on and her skills grew with experience, Sukhia learned everyone's domestic secrets. Whereas in the past she had seen upper-caste houses only from the lane, screened by high walls and ornate gateways, now she was familiar with everything that went on inside.

'It's not just one room,' she told Lakshmi, 'but several, all arranged round a shady courtyard with pierced walls that make shadow patterns on the ground. Saris hung up from ropes to dry, fluttering like parrots in the breeze, a rainbow of saris! The colour made my eyes swim. The rooms are high and so *cool*, with holy pictures like the ones in our temple, of Lord Shiva, Ganesha, Vishnu and his consort . . .'

'Lakshmi!'

'That's right, *Lakshmi* – which they drape with garlands of marigolds, and niches in the walls for oil lamps. Precious oil, and they can afford to burn it! They even have wooden furniture so they don't have to squat or lie on the floor.'

'What else do the upper castes have, tell me, tell me?'

'Big stone jars of rice and flour hanging from the ceiling and pots of spices. Even when visitors come, they don't need to share. Everyone can eat as much as they want!'

'As many *chapattis* as they want . . .' Lakshmi murmured incredulously. 'As *many* as you want, Kubri! How many would *you* eat? Four, six, *more*?' Kubri's black eyes grew round. Lakshmi laughed and spread her fingers wide so that Kubri could count up how many *chapattis* she would eat.

'They eat vegetables every day and golden ghee to make their food rich. That's why their skin glows like a bridegroom's anointed with oil. I had to stop myself gasping with astonishment the first time a woman uncovered herself. We're black as crows compared to them. Ai, ai, so fine and delicate . . . and *such* cowards!'

Matin cackled sourly. 'That's true. High-caste women may be light-skinned but I never met one who could endure pain like a *bhangi*. And don't forget' – Matin wagged her head from side to side – 'when their men come at night they all do the same thing, whether they're Brahmin or *bhangi*. When a man's thing swells up he seizes what he wants and tears and thrusts and roars until his pleasure is finished.'

I don't believe her, thought Lakshmi. She is old and she has forgotten. My husband will stroke me gently like a mother dog cleaning her puppies, and then he – and then . . . we shall rise to heaven together in a fiery cloud of bliss.

Sukhia threw a warning glance at Matin.

'We must find a husband for Lakshmi soon,' she said. 'Don't frighten her with your tales.'

'Who tells tales? The father of my children tells tales. I tell the truth. But it is high time we got the *chaudhury* to find her a husband. *If possible*,' Matin hissed under her breath.

Lakshmi at ten was still skinny and flat-chested but even with the sidelong eye her face had a bright, inquisitive look under its tangle of dusty black hair. In spite of her disfigurement she was leader of the village girls, teaching the younger children games and songs and the names of things, always with Kubri propped on her hip, an alert, wizened monkey who clung to her and frowned at everyone else. Lakshmi mothered her with special care, knowing that deformity made you tough on the outside because you were tender inside. She wished she could put off the moment when Kubri realized the hump on her back would never go away. She manipulated her knobbly spine in an effort to force it straight, trying to pretend it was a game, but when Kubri shrieked in surprise, Lakshmi stopped rather than hurt her. Matin was rougher, wrenching the tiny back and ignoring the child's screams. Kubri's twisted bones refused to grow straight.

Lakshmi often missed the old days when she and her big sisters were all together, but Preeti's village was half a day's walk and no girl went far by herself, even if she did have a sideways-looking eye. Mithania's new family lived even further away. When Mitha came home for the birth of her first child, Lakshmi made up her mind to whisper and tease and beg her sister until she gave in and revealed the secret thing that men and women did in marriage.

The work of cooking, sweeping the hut and being at Matin's beck and call now fell to Lakshmi. Dada helped look after Hari (when the boy would stand still for long enough) and Kubri, telling them rambling stories until he got so carried away by his own eloquence that he lost the thread. Then he would make his hands dance like puppets, his rheumy, sagging eyes as bemused as theirs. During the day Lakshmi took over from him as story-teller to the village children. With Kubri curled in her lap, she would choose from her store of tales, wait for the wriggling circle of children to become quiet, and begin:

'Long, long ago there lived a King and Queen. They had one daughter whom they loved dearly. It so happened that the Queen fell very ill and none of the physicians could cure her. When she was about to die she called the King and said . . .'

It was midday. Even the birds were silent; the lizards still; the

157

fields becalmed; the only sound the ratcheting of cicadas. People working in the fields rested in the shade of the trees under a white-blue sky. The village was motionless in the afternoon hush. 'Time to eat!' said Lakshmi suddenly in her normal voice, and the listeners shook their heads and returned like sleepwalkers from a dream-world.

On busy days when the landlord was bad-tempered, marching among the workers with a flail to lash the backs of their legs, the older girls were made to help with the field-work or the harvest, the tiny ones lined up at the edge of the field and told: keep out of the way, sit still, don't move, be good. As the girls and women sifted grain with flat wicker scoops, chaff rose into the air and settled on their dark skin like a dusting of pollen, gilding them like statues.

In the evening a team of bullocks criss-crossed the fields collecting full jars of grain to be carried home on slow, creaking carts followed by the women and a trail of straggling children. On the way they passed a peacock with neck feathers of turquoise and lapis lazuli, its wings glinting green and bronze. Unfurling its train, it strutted for the benefit of an unseen peahen, quivering so that the feathers dazzled like a carillon of little temple bells. The tired women laughed raucously.

'Typical male!'

The sun hung low over the fields, tingeing every blade of grass silver. When the birds had finished searching the fields for grain, they flew up to their perches, a flapping line of Vs silhouetted against a pale mauve horizon. Grasshoppers and frogs crackled and croaked. The sun set and the sky darkened to inky blue.

Fires had been lit and the pans were beginning to sizzle when bad news sped through the lanes. Davadin, the beautiful *bhangi* girl – home after a difficult second pregnancy – had delivered a healthy son but having endured two hard days of labour she was close to death. Kempa, her distraught young husband, his face a grimace of anxiety, came to the door of the hut and whispered urgently. Matin nodded.

'Yes, at once. Bring camphor to placate the gods and sticks and clubs to beat the ground and frighten the demons trying to drag her away. Hurry, don't waste time weeping, are you not a man and the father of a second son?'

She beckoned Sukhia, herself heavily pregnant, and told Lakshmi to finish cooking the *chapattis*. Faces peered from doorways as the two swished through the dusk, their bare feet thudding on the hard ground. Cattle and goats lay ruminating beside the lane, ears and flanks twitching off flies and mosquitoes.

'Why didn't her mother send for us?' Matin asked irritably, not turning her head. 'Vain, stupid woman – she has only one child and yet she thinks she knows better than I do, with two sons, or you who are stuffed with all my wisdom? Kali will punish her for having a daughter who was much too beautiful to be a *bhangi* – ai, ai, poor creature, we have come too late to overcome the demons!'

Davadin's mother was standing in the doorway, alternately beckoning urgently and drawing the veil across her tear-stained face.

'Come, big sister,' Matin said, 'let me see her . . .'

The hut smelled of blood and urine and from inside could be heard the thin cry of a newborn. Sukhia's breasts tingled in response.

'My own child is due very soon,' she said. 'Give the baby to me, perhaps my milk will flow for him.'

She took the dark infant, his face clenched in misery, and put him to her swollen breast. He latched onto the nipple and began to nuzzle, turning his head as it slipped out of his mouth, then gripping fiercely again. Nothing flowed, but he seemed comforted. Matin bent over the dishevelled figure sprawled on a heap of clothes on the hard earthen floor. Davadin looked ten years older than the shy girl who had been escorted to her husband's village four years ago. There was still heat in her body but when Matin lifted her lids the eyes were glazed and unresponsive. She turned to the grieving woman.

'You have a grandson but no longer a daughter. Be gentle to your son-in-law and don't blame him for this death. He was good to her and he too will grieve bitterly.'

The woman threw her shawl across her face and uttered a harsh, ear-splitting wail. In a plangent voice Matin began to sing the ancient incantations to dispel demons and as the sound swirled round the mud walls and was stifled in the straw eaves of the hut, Sukhia felt the gush of her waters breaking.

CHAPTER SIX

1931

IN THE SMOKY GLOOM MATIN CLEANED AND SWADDLED THE
newborn boy and shrouded the corpse. Kempa, Davadin's
husband, stood outside the hut, face contorted with grief, hands
twisting up to the heavens and down again in a gesture of
unconscious appeal. 'I'll take the baby with me,' Sukhia told
him. 'He must have mother's milk or he will die and what use
are two deaths, if one can be saved? My own child will be born
very soon and I have enough milk for them both – for a
while . . .'

Hardly two hours later, in the middle of the night, her
eleventh pregnancy produced another daughter. The birth was
quick – she leaned against the wall of the hut for a few minutes,
panting fast, and the baby slid into the folds of her skirt. She
sighed and glanced towards Davadin's perfect son sleeping on a
pile of rags in one corner of the hut, then looked at her own
infant. It was a girl, healthy and free of deformity. Sukhia felt a
yawning weariness enfold her. She latched the newborn to her
breast and when the nipple began to seep, reached for Davadin's
motherless son and attached him to the other breast. He nuzzled with desperate intensity and began to suck. She wound a

shawl round them both, lay down and fell asleep. In the dim light from the doorway Kubri watched round-eyed.

'Your new sister,' Lakshmi said into her ear.

'*Two* babies,' Kubri corrected.

'No, only one is ours.'

'Want *both*!' Kubri insisted.

'We can't feed them both,' Matin said angrily out of the darkness. 'We can't even feed one. We can't feed *you*.'

Kubri smiled to herself, snuggled against her big sister and slept.

A few days later Kempa, escorted by his father and brother-in-law, signalled respectfully to Sukhia from the doorway of the hut.

'We have beseeched the gods for her safe passage,' he said. 'Now I must take my son home. My mother sends word of a wet-nurse in the village who will suckle him together with her own child. Blessings upon you, may your children always feed bounteously.'

'My daughter has been named Davadin, after the mother of your sons,' Sukhia said. 'In that way she will remember that for the first days of their life she and your boy were wrapped in the same shawl and shared my body.'

The young man looked into her sleeping infant's face.

'May you be as beautiful as the mother of my sons,' he said to the baby, 'and as gentle and dutiful as the goddess for whom she was named.'

Listening to his tender voice, unlike that of any other man she had heard, Lakshmi thought, 'I wish he had married *me*. I want a husband just like him.'

Matin held up the swathed bundle.

'Here, off with you,' she said crisply. 'Take your son and raise him to be a man! Let him remember that the gods took his mother's life in exchange for his. Remind him every day to be worthy of their choice.'

Kempa did not look at her but kept his eyes fixed on his child's tiny dark face.

'Come to me, dear,' he murmured as Matin dumped the baby in his arms. Lakshmi stared at him and, like a child playing grandmother's footsteps, she advanced one more step towards her *karma*.

That night Sukhia lay awake thinking of her new daughter's future, and her own. She knew she was essential to the whole family. Her sister-in-law Parvati spent her days trembling on a rope bed, entwining her fingers in a corner of her sari and shivering at any sudden noise. Her girls ran to their aunt or grandmother if they needed something. Yet Sukhia did not resent her, knowing that she had no choice, it was wished upon her by the gods. Only kindness holds us together, she thought. We have nothing else to offer. I bring babies into a hard and suffocating world and pray that not too many will die. As the rhythmical sucking at her breast continued she recalled the five she had lost . . . Shivram, her princeling; poor sluggish Ghashitia, whose lamp had guttered throughout her short life; the three stillborn whom the demons had got by trickery. Sukhia sighed and her new daughter gave a tiny answering shudder, nibbled at her breast and slept the foetal sleep of a child in the womb. Hari, pressed hotly against her back, scrabbled with his knees as though running. From the other side of the hut Matin snored and Lakshmi and Kubri exhaled gently and in unison. How will we ever get husbands for those two? their mother wondered, falling at last into an exhausted sleep.

Nothing she does makes the slightest difference. Karma will take its course, for good or ill. Kali decides. And, since Kali does not care, her decision is always fair.

Next time Prem came home he was eager to tell the men of the village about the momentous events in Kanpur, some of which he saw at first hand in the cantonment. He hardly glanced at the baby and scolded his wife for naming her after a dead woman.

'Another girl,' he said dismissively, turning to go outside. Kubri tottered after him but Lakshmi scooped her up.

'Not now. He is a *very important man* who must not be bothered.'

Kubri gazed solemnly through the doorway to where a circle of men smoking *bidis* and chewing betel looked up as her father approached. He settled himself comfortably on his haunches and they prepared to listen.

'You heard about the riots?' Prem asked, and one or two nodded. 'The Mahatma is now so powerful they daren't keep him locked up. Since he left prison and led the Salt March, strong feelings have been stirred up against the British. How dare they deny us salt, the stuff of life? It's an insult to us all.' Several men spat red streaks of betel into the dust. 'We've been patient for too long.'

'Too long!' they echoed, shifting on their heels and clenching their teeth.

' "Patience is bitter, but the fruit of it is sweet," ' Prem said, quoting the old proverb. His voice rose. 'Thanks to Gandhi-ji, we'll soon be masters of our own destiny. There've been strikes in half the Kanpur cotton factories. Shops have closed. You can feel it all around, in the air, on the streets – the city is on the boil. Hindu may be against Muslim, Muslim against Hindu, but *everyone* is against the British.'

'The British cheat us less than our landlords and their thieving agents,' Bakha said – Bakha the reasonable, Bakha the moderate – but other voices contradicted him.

'They rule our land and strut like Moghuls in our midst, eyeing our women like dogs on heat, shouldering us aside, insulting us . . .'

'The cantonment is buzzing with rumours like an overturned

hive,' Prem said. 'Armed police are on the streets but it's only show; everyone knows they've lost control. Every day I see the soldiers preparing for action – I'm invisible, for who notices a sweeper going about his work? They're forever drilling, marching, trying to muster up courage to face an angry crowd. Untried boys from a distant country: I can *smell* their fear.'

One or two of his hearers laughed, an ominous rumbling that had nothing to do with humour. Basking in the respect his information commanded, Prem went on: 'Usually when the army is summoned by the civil authorities or the police they only march about as a warning. But now they are always on standby and it's real. There is a rumour . . .' – he lowered his voice and the ring of men swayed towards him like the audience round a snake charmer when the cobra emerges from its basket; like the Bandar-log watching the Dance of the Hunger of Kaa – 'a rumour in the city that there's to be another uprising.'

'We have not forgotten Lucknow and Kanpur in the time of our forefathers,' said Dada. 'Nor have the British.'

'There will be burning of houses, killing and looting,' said Sidda and his eyes glittered. Violence was a drug to him. He liked nothing better than to kick a starving pi-dog to death.

'There will be deaths,' Dada said soberly. 'If what you say is true, *very* many will die – mostly our people.'

In Europe, too, they've begun to march, brandishing the colours of Kali, black and red, along with the svastika, *ancient symbol of prosperity. Violence is on the move – left, right, left, right . . .*

At the end of the evening, excited at having been the centre of attention, filled with a rare sense of pride and importance, Prem walked to the hut and standing beside the door gave the soft summons – '*Phusht-phusht.*' When Sukhia emerged from the darkness he tugged gently at her hand. Her eyelids were heavy with sleep and she was still inflamed from the recent birth but she smiled and nodded. A little later, under an indigo sky, they met in the bushes beside the well. He took her roughly but with a practised ingenuity that was new and different. She realized at once that he had been with other women.

'May you conceive, mother of my daughters,' he murmured as he rolled off her, groaning with relief. 'And may *this* child be another son!'

Sukhia was filled with a sad, subtle anger. Even after many pregnancies, with two daughters married and two grandsons, her husband still gave her pleasure and, as a midwife, she knew better than most women that men's needs had to be satisfied. She should be proud that, at thirty-six summers, he was still lusty. If he must have other women, better they were whores than some village widow around whom gossip and rumour would gather to humiliate her. But the new pain of jealousy weighed her down and tears welled behind her eyes.

'The gods will decide,' she said.

They could hear animals prowling around. Nilghai shivered invisibly in the mango grove and monkeys scuttled along the tops of walls, scavenging and plundering. From nearby rose the howl of a jackal.

'My breasts hurt, I must feed the baby,' Sukhia said. 'If you have just given me another, I am sure he will be a son, a brother for Hari. And if not, Hari is a fine boy – nearly as . . .' She stopped. Two years after Shivram's death she still could not speak his name aloud.

Lakshmi now had two little girls to look after. When her mother first put the new baby into her arms and Lakshmi began to sing the familiar lullaby, '*Nini, baba, nini, Makhan, roti, chini*,' Kubri looked away and spat, then scuttled off and refused to come when called. Later that day, when Matin was cradling the infant, Lakshmi said, 'How small and useless the baby is! She can't do anything at all. She can't talk – can't even laugh or smile. Not like you, little sister, hmm? Now I shall have to call you *big* sister. Will you help me look after that no-good baby?'

Kubri scratched her matted hair and frowned. 'No-good baby looks like a *monkey*.'

'She does.'

'I liked other baby. Boy got taken away.'

'We couldn't keep him – he came from another village. Shall we keep this one instead?'

'Can't throw it *away*,' Kubri said reluctantly. 'On *rubbish* heap, with *flies*. Not down well. Can't do *that* . . .'

'Better keep it then.'

Hari dashed into the hut, whirled round, looked up and down and gabbled, 'Where's Praba? Did he come in here?'

'How can he have done? You can see for yourself there's nobody here.'

'I've looked everywhere! Up in the trees, in the stables, even behind the temple. He's gone up into the sky, like a djinn.'

'Look in no-good baby's shawl?'

Hari stuck his tongue out and rushed off.

'Boys *lucky* . . .' said Kubri, and Lakshmi nodded: 'Boys lucky.'

Kubri had not learned to walk yet, preferring to scurry on all fours, her shoulders tipped sideways by the weight on her back. When she tried to stand up her balance was thrown out by the hump and she often fell – or was pushed by one of the other children. If Lakshmi had given them a chance they would have pelted her with stones like a pi-dog, pulled her hair and prodded the hump to see if it were bone or flesh or perhaps a bundle of stones put there by a demon to punish her for wrong-doing in some other life. But if anyone ill-treated Kubri, Lakshmi refused to tell a story. The others would say, 'Now look what you have done, idiot! Leave the hunchback alone! *Please*, One-Eye, go on, tell us.'

Lakshmi was Sukhia's next problem. Very soon the girl would be eleven; high time to be betrothed. Yet her sideways eye had got worse as she grew older and now stared out of the left side of her head at such an acute angle that she looked like an idiot although she was in fact a clever and resourceful child. She had a sweet speaking voice – unlike the hoarse cawing of many *bhangis*, their throats roughened by dust, ash and chaff – and she could sing all the old songs. Most important of all, Lakshmi had a happy nature. Any boy willing to disregard her deformity would find he had the best of wives. But where could such a boy be found? The flawed eye was an ill omen. What parents-in-law looked for in a bride was lustrous skin, large eyes, and hips that promised to bear many children – every one a son. Without these, only money could smooth her path towards marriage. But they had no money, Prem said; not even a couple of silver bangles. Since she was his favourite grandchild Dada said, 'Leave her a while longer. She is so small, nobody would take her for eleven summers. Besides, you need her in the house and the fields. When she goes away to a husband's hut, who will do the work? Hari is only five and' – he lowered his voice – 'Kubri will never be good for anything.'

Sukhia thought, my husband is putting money away somewhere, I am sure of it. He is paid fifteen rupees a month, I wheedled it out of him once after we had lain together. Yet I work as hard as before, he brings me no gifts, nothing has changed. The money must be hidden. I shall persuade him to offer a dowry for Lakshmi, otherwise no man will take her and an unmarried daughter is a disgrace, especially to me since I'm the midwife. They'll laugh at me. Then she smiled to herself, remembering that Matin used to say exactly the same. Besides, Preeti had two sons and was pregnant again, while Mithania's husband had sent word that she too was with child. It would be hard for her, poor girl. She was very narrow and the first delivery was always the worst. She would soon be home. Perhaps *she* would know of a good man for her sister. An older man, a widower, or maybe someone not quite right in the head. A barren woman is an abomination – and if Lakshmi doesn't marry I'll end up with two barren daughters since Dada is right; no-one will ever marry Kubri.

A few weeks later Prem's prediction came true. Rioting broke out in Kanpur – bigoted, random, murderous. An unprotected ribcage was liable to be pierced from behind by an invisible knife, making the flesh spring apart and blood leap like a deer from its hiding place. One minute a portly Brahmin was trundling down the street at the greatest speed commensurate with dignity; next he was an upturned belly with surprised eyes and a stream of unclean blood drenching his *kurta*. He barely had time for a sharp cry of surprise before breathing his last bubbling sigh.

Ai, the drama! Even Kali is never jaded with death. From the Colosseum to the Crusades, bear-baiting to bull-fighting, from a view-halloo to a body sprawled in a dingy basement – the triumph is in surviving when another lies dead.

By the end of March the civil authorities in Kanpur had lost control. Burning rags soaked in paraffin were hurled from the rooftops until half the city was ablaze. A company left the cantonment in lorries to intervene between Hindus and Muslims milling around cutting fire hoses and smashing up the fire engines, but the murderous mob was in a frenzy, running amok in a bloodlust beyond sense or reason, a high-pitched scream spiralling from each gaping mouth. Madness seized the city. One company on its own had no chance of bringing this rabble under control and the remaining two were summoned. These four hundred men spent twenty-four hours without a break marching about the city dispersing rioters and the next twelve days trying to restore order among a quarter of a million people. The heat was scalding, the temperature soared to 120°. The streets were littered with the decomposing bodies of men, women and children. Babies, even. Indian killed Indian for believing in the wrong religion or politics, for personal revenge or the sheer uncontrollable lust for killing. By the time it was over six hundred people had been slaughtered and thousands wounded – but the army had learned the lesson of Amritsar and not a single British gun was fired. Only the washermen knew how many soldiers had soiled their trousers. Terror loosens the bowels of Hindu, Muslim and Englishman alike.

The next time Prem went back to his village after walking half the night, afraid that a bandit lurked behind every tree waiting to rob him of the annas knotted into his *dhoti*, everyone noticed the change in him. For weeks the riots had been the sole topic of discussion in the cantonment. He had heard and seen so much brutality that it had brutalized him, stifling the last of his old gentleness. He shouted orders at his womenfolk and made Hari stand to attention or march about. (Hari thought marching was a great game and soon had all the other boys doing it.) That evening he drank arrack with his friends and the drunker he became the more vividly he described the blood that had coursed like monsoon water through the gutters of Kanpur, how the old and weak had made for the temples in search of refuge and been hacked down before they got there, how bloodthirsty yells had resounded throughout the city as Muslims slashed at the limbs of Hindus who clubbed the skulls of Muslims, how black smoke had poured through the narrow streets and billowed into the sky; until red blood was smeared over clothes, windows, walls and the faces of cowering mothers and babies as the gods of war and chaos had their day. 'Everything was black and red.'

Kali's colours.

'They summoned sweepers from the cantonment to clean up the city afterwards. We were wading through blood. Our feet and hands and brushes were drenched. Each time I lifted my broom it chucked out a red arc that dripped down the walls like paint after Holi. After we had swept the streets the bloodstains reached halfway up the handles and the bristles were soaked in blood,' Prem said, and his hearers shuddered. 'In the end they diverted water from the Ganges canal to sluice the streets. A thousand sweepers couldn't have cleaned them. And the *stink*!' He held his nose.

'What will happen next?' asked Lalla fearfully. 'Will it spread to the villages?'

'It's over for now. The Muslims have got the upper hand for the time being but we'll show them vengeance!'

'Where is your Gandhi-ji when he's needed?' asked Bakha. 'What's happened to his promises – all that care for the masses, harmony between religions, caste and caste? Where is your peace-loving patriot who was going to expel the British without violence and make us rulers in our own country?'

Prem had no answer. 'You're just pig ignorant,' he retorted. 'Village peasants will never understand politics!' He scowled and spat.

'So we are simple villagers now?' said Dada, his voice steely. 'Tale-tellers under the peepul tree? Humble tillers of the soil? Look at yourself, my son. You don't only shovel your own shit, you shovel the shit of those you despise . . . the British! Guard your tongue and don't set yourself up as better than us. I can tell greater tales of worse killings, yet when the sun sets we are still Pariahs, the feet, the lowest of the low, and evil will follow if we forget it.'

Prem, publicly rebuked, his sense of importance ridiculed, lowered his head and frowned massively. His eyebrows beetled and he tightened his lips. Then he said, 'I bow to your wisdom, my father, for you are older than all of us. But I tell you, there is more bloodshed to come.'

When Mithania came home for the birth of her first child, Lakshmi was shocked at the change in her. She was familiar with the bloated bellies and backward-tilted stance of women in the last days before childbirth but her sister had a cowed, bruised expression and she hardly spoke or even looked at anyone. She sat indoors, ungainly and slack-limbed, and Lakshmi could not persuade her to visit their childhood places or listen to the village gossip.

After a while Matin said, 'So, child, a rotten one?'

The girl looked up, startled, and immediately veiled her eyes.

'You don't have to tell me. He beats you and his mother works you too hard? Yes? I know without being told. *Yes.* Nothing to be done.'

'He is my husband and master,' the girl mumbled. 'I am lower than a pi-dog and must obey him.'

'*Oh God, that bread should be so dear, and flesh and blood so cheap!*' Sukhia recited.

Lakshmi looked at her sister with horror.

'*What* does he do, Mitha? Does he *beat* you? Even carrying his child?'

'Ai, sister, leave me in peace, let me rest . . . I am so tired.'

'Let her rest,' said Sukhia.

The child was born four days later. Mithania groaned and wailed in the throes of labour but her cries were not like the lusty yells of her older sister but the resigned, hopeless cries of someone used to pain. A neglected or half-starved child wails with a passive misery that does not expect comfort and Mithania too seemed to accept that there was no relief for her. The pain of childbirth would be over eventually, but pain without end lay beyond. The newborn was a boy. Mithania rolled dull eyes and breathed, 'May the gods and Mother Kali be thanked, I have borne him a son!' She let herself be cleansed, purified, massaged and securely swaddled in a long bandage. Then she slept, her son asleep beside her.

In the following days, as Sukhia took care of the new baby – only a season younger than her own last child – Mithania lay listlessly on the rope bed inside the hut. The baby fed greedily at Sukhia's breast but when his mother tried to suckle him he moaned querulously, turning his head away as though he got no nourishment. Her lank hair was drenched with sweat, her forehead damp, but the incantations that Matin uttered protected her from the demons and she did not fall ill. After four days of these tender ministrations she began to weep. Having begun, it seemed she would never stop. Her face loosened and tears rained from her eyes, soaking her hair and falling onto the cheeks of her baby, who was crying too. Lakshmi was distraught.

'Oh Mitha, Mitha, what have they done to you?' she beseeched. 'What has happened to my sister, who used to be happy?'

Mithania gulped and swallowed down her tears. She leaned towards Lakshmi, took her hand and looked directly into her face.

'*Listen* to me,' she whispered. 'They keep the secrets of marriage from us because it is *not* paradise. The old tales of rajahs and princesses are a plot to deceive us. There are no silken sheets, no hidden joys, no soft words. It is – believe me, my sister – *the mating of beasts*. Swear that you will never, never marry.'

Lakshmi shook her head. She thought of Kempa, tall, strong and sad, grieving for his beautiful wife. 'I shall marry, whatever anyone says!' she promised herself passionately.

CHAPTER SEVEN

1933–1935

MITHANIA RETURNED TO HER HUSBAND'S VILLAGE AND although she was soon pregnant again, this time she did not come home. The child was a girl; born dead. Mithania's father-in-law assured Prem his daughter was well and he conveyed this news abruptly to Sukhia when he went back. In truth he knew his daughter was ill-treated but could not admit that he had chosen badly. The fault must be hers. She neglected her husband's needs or did not try hard enough to please his mother. She would soon improve. Every young wife had to be taught a few lessons before she learned to adapt.

When he had gone Matin said, 'What would you have? There are good men, and bad ones. She got a bad one.' Dada dozed in a corner, his straggling grey beard stained with betel juice. His wife cackled and added, 'Look at him now – so did I!'

'You are right, mother of my sons, you got a bad bargain when you took this old dog.'

The cantonment returned to normal and Kanpur, in the aftermath of the slaughter, was unusually calm. Prem, a gaunt figure of nearly forty, seldom bothered to walk home any more. His life now centred on the city. In his free time he would leave the precincts of the cantonment, step out into the evening's violet air and, summoning a bicycle rickshaw with a lordly wave, order the driver to take him to the bazaar. There, amid the teeming, huddled booths, each with an elaborate hand-painted signboard and every one illuminated inside by gas or oil lamps, he relaxed and felt at ease. The mass of dark faces, the staccato voices of people arguing and laughing, seemed ablaze with life after the straight lines of the barracks and soldiers marching, parading or barking orders. British speech sounded dull and clipped, '*tish-mish, tish-mish*', compared to the babel of an Indian crowd. The cantonment was grey but in the bazaar every stall and shop clamoured for custom in florid shades of vermilion, yellow, scarlet and green. Noisy groups haggled for sweets – '*Gulab jamans, pairas*, yellow *boondi*; *burfi, rasgulas, ludus, jalebis*!' chanted the vendor – bracelets, cooking utensils, locks, clothes and leather goods. Scores of cotton shirts and trousers hung spreadeagled across a tall trellis, offering themselves for purchase in every possible colour and size. A dwarf seeking a shirt checked in orange and purple would have found one here. Prem's nostrils tingled as he inhaled the dark, pungent smells of meat roasting on skewers over charcoal fires; drains; fresh and decaying vegetables; bright red and orange spices, speckled fruit. Threading his way through the stalls, he lost his accursed status and felt accepted by the jostling, shifting, spitting mass.

It was a relief to shed his uniform and the servile manner he had to assume throughout the rest of the week. He would head for his favourite bar, ease himself between other *bhangis* onto a bench and order lentils and vegetables or rice with tamarind pickle which he ate with his fingers, using a banana leaf as a plate. Then he would settle down to drink. The cheap alcohol inflamed his senses and drove him to the entertainment district where – however much he vowed beforehand to stay away – he visited prostitutes. He rarely left without having spent his wages, or had the money stolen. He knew this would happen but each time he saw them posed provocatively almost in the street, each time he was beckoned by garish, musky women, their eyes blackly outlined, faces thickly painted, draped in diaphanous silks and gorgeous jewels, each time they crooked their hennaed fingers invitingly and smiled their curious little smiles, he found it impossible to refuse. He would sleep off his sore head and sour mouth before creeping back to the barracks at dawn, promising himself that next time he would walk home to his wife.

If Prem had hoped to gain some advantage from his daughter's marriage, he was mistaken. Mithania's father-in-law had been promoted to head sweeper in the cantonment but he did not offer Prem any favours, ease his task or point out the officers who tipped generously. After her next child – also a son – was born and a fourth infant conceived within months he said, 'Good little breeder, your girl. Any more like her at home?'

Prem should have taken the opportunity to say that he knew his daughter was being brutalized; that when she delivered the first son, Sukhia had found her body covered with the scars and bruises of old beatings. He should have answered back, 'Is it that fine lad her husband who beats and kicks her like a half-starved dog, or does your esteemed wife land the blows?' Instead he smirked ingratiatingly and said, 'Yes – her younger sister Lakshmi, although she has a slight cast in one eye . . . but your next son could have her.'

The other sweeper laughed coarsely and retorted, 'She'll be had whether she likes it or not – but not by my lusty son! I'll look for a beauty this time. One skinny, frowning monkey about the place is enough.'

He should have hit the man; drawn back his hand and landed a blow to make him reel. But then he would lose his job – and defiance wouldn't have helped his daughter. Prem held his tongue, bowed his head and picking up the broom, its handle stippled with brown splashes, resumed his sweeping. The stiff, rhythmical strokes scored hard lines in the dust.

Next time he went home he told his wife that Mithania had given her husband a second son and was already with child again. Sukhia sighed heavily.

'Let her come to me for the next delivery . . .'

'Her mother-in-law will take offence. She is a midwife herself,' Prem lied, 'and sends word that it is not necessary.'

'I long to see my sister!' Lakshmi pleaded. 'Ask, please ask if she can visit us. Bring her with you next time you come home – you pass through their village, you said so. She could bring the babies. Matin is anxious to see them too – aren't you, Matin?' But the old woman growled and turned her head away. She had begun to develop opaque cataracts in her eyes and could see less and less.

Prem answered furiously, 'She belongs to her husband and her duty is to him. I wish I could say the same for you!'

Lakshmi was approaching adolescence and her breasts were beginning to bud. Without the sideways eye she might almost have passed for a beauty. Her skin was like a flower at night, blue-black like Lord Krishna. She was no longer a tiny creature with wild hair and a grubby cotton skirt but a young woman who shared her mother's clothes, an ankle-length skirt and long *kurta*, and had learned to draw her scarf modestly across her face when a man approached. This would not protect her from anyone determined to ravish her, and if violated she would be even less marriageable. Sukhia thought: she must be betrothed soon! Lakshmi had been well trained in womanly skills. She mothered all the little ones – Hari, who at six or seven was almost at the end of childhood yet still wild as a tiger cub; the cross and crooked Kubri who trusted no-one else, and Davadin, now an energetic toddler. Other girls of her age were wives and even mothers. A suitable boy must be found; horoscopes compared to make sure they were auspicious. But first the boy must agree to marry her – and however briefly she lifted her veil, the sideways eye would be revealed. The shame of being rejected was unthinkable. There *was* a boy, some fifteen summers old, whose legs had been crushed when he fell under a cart and who now wheeled himself about the village on a wooden trolley, his brawny arms hefting it along, but Lakshmi could surely hope for better than that?

Meanwhile Lakshmi had a secret. At night – the only time she was alone, although surrounded by the sleeping forms of her mother, grandmother and little brother and sisters – she made up stories about Kempa. His tenderness, his grief at the death of his young wife, his deep slow voice and large hands, had moved her for the first time to desire a real man, rather than some figment of her imagination. She no longer dreamed of a young god sweeping her to the clouds on a golden chariot pulled by six galloping silver horses. The earthbound figure of Kempa was preferable. She had heard him utter hardly a dozen words, but they rang in her mind's ear. '*Blessings upon you, may your children always feed bounteously*' . . . such a pure and simple wish, for health and not hunger. Lakshmi had never forgotten the year the monsoon had been late, when her brother and sister had died and Kubri came out of her mother's womb already starved and twisted. Kempa was right – the absence of hunger was the highest blessing anyone could wish for. He was as wise as a god! But he had also said, '*May you be as beautiful as Davadin, the mother of my sons,*' and she, Lakshmi of the sidelong glance, could never claim beauty. Mithania's words came back to her: '*It is the mating of beasts.*' Well, if it had to be, she would mate with Kempa like a beast! She prayed that her *dharma* might be entwined with his like a creeper round a tamarind tree. She brooded on the mysterious words: 'Tomorrow is the day after tomorrow's yesterday.' If that did not mean she could have tomorrow what Davadin had had yesterday, what else could it mean?

The following year, just after the monsoon had started, Sukhia's eldest brother Beera walked twelve miles through the rain from the village where they had both grown up, to report the death of his wife. Beera was now nearly forty summers, stooped after a lifetime of back-breaking work, his hair and beard grey, his remaining teeth ground down to yellow stumps. Sukhia greeted him with loving respect. He had been her hero more years ago than she could count, and behind his gnarled limbs and seamed features she saw the sprinting legs and bright black eyes of the youth he had been when she was a little girl. She remembered sitting round-eyed outside their home as his new wife was brought to the village, shaking with fear. She had been too shy to reassure the girl by saying, 'My brother Beera is a fine, fine man!' That young woman had borne him nine children, of whom six still lived. She had died while pregnant with the tenth.

Now, having comforted him and invoked the care of the gods upon his wife's spirit, Sukhia said, 'Well, my brother, the seasons come and go and children are begotten, born and die. I have two married daughters and now my Lakshmi is of marriageable age but I begin to fear that no boy will ever have her, although she is the best of the girls.'

'What is wrong with her?'

'She has one eye that looks sideways out of her head and one that looks straight. It is her only defect; but people say she has the Evil Eye and young men shun her in case she brings bad luck.'

'I have come to you in search of a wife. My mother-in-law is old. She can't take care of my children and cook for us all. She needs help. My wife has been dead for thirteen days.'

'It is not long.'

'It's the time ordained for mourning and I have observed it.

There is no suitable niece or daughter in the family, except your Lakshmi. Beauty matters less than I once thought. Is she a good girl; would she look after me in my old age and be kind to my wife's children? Six are still at home, though the older boy will soon be married.'

Sukhia clenched her fists unobserved and thought: is my ardent daughter to be an old man's wife and nursemaid to another woman's children? But if no-one else will marry her she is lucky to have this offer. She smiled.

'I promise you, my brother, you could not have a better wife. She is kind and diligent and has a joyful nature. If you sit on the other side from her bad eye you could even think she was a beauty!'

'Which side must I sit?'

'Away from her heart; on the right.'

'She is not yet of an age . . .' he enquired delicately.

'No; but very soon. The signs are starting to show.'

'Is it proper for me to see her?'

'She'll think of you as her uncle rather than as a man – ai, Beera, sorry, I didn't mean to offend you! Let me call her. She's in the fields looking after the little ones – Kubri who's crooked (why did the gods give me two misshapen daughters?) and Davadin and Hari, who's just begun to graze the cattle. He's seven summers.'

Beera saw her face soften and asked, 'Your favourite?'

'He is my favourite now. I had another son but . . .' She turned away.

'My sister, believe me, I know what grief is. May the gods be merciful to him.'

'And to your wife. Yama god of death, spare her the lake of blood.'

Sukhia went to the door and peered towards the fields through the monsoon downpour.

'Wait there, I'll bring her.'

*

Lakshmi's furious opposition to the marriage was entirely unexpected. She began by pleading, 'I love you all! I don't want to leave my sisters! There'll be another one soon – you need me!' Then she tried to reason: 'Dada is old and ill, he needs me; Matin is almost blind, she needs me, too.' When Sukhia took no notice Lakshmi clasped her feet, sobbed and became desperate. This is why girls should be betrothed while they're still young, her mother reflected; before they have begun to think for themselves. If Lakshmi had been betrothed at ten or eleven she'd never have made all this trouble.

'I can't go and live in Kalyanpur!' Lakshmi wept, her dark face streaked with tears, her hair dishevelled. 'It's even further than Kanpur, and it takes Dadi half the night to walk *there*. I shall never see you again. Why do you all hate me and want to get rid of me? Haven't I been good and dutiful, haven't I cared for you enough? Tell me, and I'll do more. I will never play again.'

Sukhia was distressed. 'You'll be with us for a bit longer. You are not yet fully a woman.'

Matin took hold of Lakshmi's arm with her strong sinewy hand and in a voice like the crack of a whip she said, 'How dare you defy your mother? This is madness, girl, and bitter ingratitude. She has found you a good man willing to accept you in spite of your crazy eye. You can jump down the well and drown or do as you're told and be grateful. Do you hear me? Do you? *Answer me, granddaughter.*'

Lakshmi answered, in a voice drained of hope, gaiety and spirit, 'I hear you, Matin. I will obey my mother.'

Two days later she submitted to the formal ceremony of betrothal and began stoically to prepare for her new life.

Matin's order was the last time she exercised power. She was very old and her bones were so brittle that she could no longer walk, yet she tyrannized her husband and family to the end.

One morning, as Sukhia and Lakshmi between them tried to raise her to a sitting position so that they could spoon gruel into her toothless, lipless mouth, she gave a guttural bark of – irritation? reluctance? premonition? – and her light body slumped between their hands. They settled her gently on the earth floor and held their breath as she fought for air in harsh, decelerating gasps. A moment after the death rattle the spirit escaped from her worn-out body, soaring into the morning light. Sukhia almost laughed.

'So she outwitted him in the end! Yama couldn't catch her! Did you feel it, Lakshmi?'

Lakshmi looked up and the brilliance beyond the doorway melted and swam. 'She was so hard on me, said such horrible things, called me Tipanka, cross-eyed and useless creature – but she loved me, I always knew she loved me! And now she's left us. Oh *why* must everything *change*?'

Sukhia thought she heard Yama's messengers dragging their ropes and grunting, *Ahum, ahum, ahum!*

Lakshmi was the last of her group of friends to be betrothed. They had all approached marriage with shy anticipation, looking forward to the privileges of wifehood, the unknown pleasure to be found in a man's arms (which must be overwhelming since women never stopped talking about it), but Lakshmi knew from her sister Mithania that marriage was harsh and from Davadin that birth could kill. Wistfully, she thought of Kempa. She had heard a rumour that he had married again, and fathered another child. Lakshmi sighed. Kempa . . . Beera. One was the husband of her mind's eye, the eye that gazed sideways where no-one could follow; the other the husband of her straight eye, the eye that faced reality. Beera was old and rough-skinned, with a grey moustache and horny black fingernails, but her mother said he was a dear, kind man and she was lucky.

In a dream she moved towards her *karma*, tugged by forces

beyond her control, relentless. She had no choice, any more than Sam, who, having crossed the globe towards her, was now only a few miles, a few months away.

CHAPTER EIGHT

Summer 1936

LAKSHMI PARKED KUBRI IN THE SHADE OF A NEARBY CLUMP OF trees and gave her a pile of stones to build. There was not a breath of wind. The monsoon was due and the hot air stung like ants. She hoisted Davadin onto her back with difficulty. The little girl was nearly five but it was not safe to leave her alone with Kubri, who was so jealous and bad-tempered that she would lash out at her sister if she got the chance. Heavily laden, Lakshmi joined the row of women bent double in the fields, their bodies black against the grey earth. After a while, a sensation, so slight that she had ignored it, became more distinct, as though a soft funnel inside her belly had parted and a trickle of warm liquid was seeping out. She slipped a hand between the folds of her skirt and it came away smeared with blood. This, she knew, signified that she was now a woman and it was time to go and live with her husband. She was late; both her sisters had left home much younger. Lakshmi straightened up and the parched earth sent a gust of heat between her legs like a yawn. The trickle meandered down her thigh. She unhooked Davadin, put her down and arched her aching back. Kubri was still propped against the trees. The glare from the empty sky was blinding. Not a leaf shivered.

'Hai, cross-eyes!' shouted the overseer. 'Don't stand there dreaming of your lover, get back to work, idle bitch!'

Sukhia frowned towards her daughter who shrugged back and gave a complicit downwards glance. Intuitively, her mother guessed what had happened. Now this one will leave me as well, she thought, and I shall only have Hari, who will soon be a man, Dada, who is old and gaga, Kubri, twisted as a rabid dog, and Davadin. Of a full clutch of children, three will be left, and a husband I hardly see. From the corner of her eye she could see Kubri putting stones in her mouth to soothe her thirst. She called out, 'Sorry, master, sorry, master!' and, hurrying over, made the child spit them out. Kubri clawed and scratched but her mother hoisted her up into an ungainly piggyback and went on with her work. This one has nothing but stones to put in her belly and before the year is out Lakshmi will be with child. Why do the gods give us children but not the means to feed them? – ai, Mother Kali, it was not I but a spirit in my head who thought that!

Too late to regret that thought, for Kali overheard it and will bring disaster upon her. Too late, old woman, to gabble invocations.

Sukhia, aged thirty-seven summers, had silver and white hair pulled into a knot at the back of her head. Her fingers looked like bones charred in a fire. Only Hari could still make her smile – or her husband, had he bothered to try. But Prem rarely came home and since her last pregnancy – which had ended in a late miscarriage and a great gush of blood – she refused to sleep with him. For this he beat her. Sukhia, who had heard the birth cries of half the women in the village, would not cry out. A woman has a duty to relieve her husband's urges, otherwise what can she expect?

That evening Lakshmi performed her first ritual purification – for menstruation pollutes even the unclean Pariahs. Her mother stirred lentils into a rich broth and while Lakshmi ate it – watched enviously by Kubri – Sukhia told her about the dangers lying in wait for menstruating women.

'Drink this; you'll need extra strength to face your new life. And remember, your smell at the moment attracts evil spirits.'

'More evil spirits? What will this lot do?'

'Don't joke about it – I'm warning you. They'll try to creep into your womb. If that happens, you can't conceive and then you won't give your husband sons or make grandsons for me.'

'You've got grandsons already. Four.'

'Not enough. Your father and I can never have enough for our old age. What would have happened to Matin and Dada if they hadn't had sons to look after them? Believe me, my girl, I rely on you to give me grandsons! There's nothing to be afraid of. I'll be there when you give birth. I'll ease your baby into the world so gently you won't even notice.'

Her mother's behaviour towards her had changed now that she was about to be married. Fearfully, in a low voice, Lakshmi said, 'Mithania told me terrible things about what a husband does to you . . .'

'Why does she talk such nonsense? She should let you find out for yourself. What did she say?'

'She said, *it is the mating of beasts*.'

'My poor child. She's right, in a way. You've seen a bull mount a cow, or pi-dogs hopping after each other. You know what they do, and your husband'll do the same. At first you may not like it, it may hurt. But – look at me, Lakshmi – I swear on Mother Kali, in time you will get pleasure from it. Quite soon you'll long to be alone with your husband so that he can do it to you. There are all sorts of secrets hidden in your hairy flower. You're smiling – you don't believe me, but it's true. Your sister was unlucky. It doesn't have to be like that.'

Kali has seen the millennia come and go, and knows that

civilization is scarcely a veneer. Men must spread their seed and they don't care how or where. Sometimes they woo with sweet words and a foxglove, with temple sculpture or sonnets – but a hand clamped over the mouth and a dozen thrusts will do the job just as efficiently. It's all one to Kali, goddess of birth.

'What am I supposed to do?' Lakshmi asked. 'Say soft words? What sort of words?' *Come to me, dear.*

'Words don't matter. Obey him, and don't think of any other man. Don't provoke him by disagreeing.'

'But Matin often disagreed with Dada and called him rude names.'

'Oh, Matin . . . !'

'He didn't seem to mind. He laughed at her.'

'See, you are disagreeing with me. You can't do that from now on. Beera is your master and you must coax him as if he were a god. Tell him those stories you're so good at. If you please him, he'll love you and treat you kindly – just as he did me when I was a little girl. He played and did silly things to make me laugh. Now it's your turn to do it for him. I tell you, my daughter, I'm happy that Beera is to be your husband. Better him than the legless boy.'

'You *didn't* . . . ?'

'No, of course not.'

Word of Lakshmi's womanhood was sent to Beera's village. In six weeks' time she would follow with her dowry, escorted by her father and uncle Bakha. Prem happened to return home a few days later, trudging slowly through a night of scorching heat along a track that burned the soles of his feet. He had managed to hold on to part of his wages – nearly twenty-five rupees – and was anxious to hide the money safely under a certain stone behind the hut. Maya's boy Ramu was sixteen summers old and would very soon be taking over the sweeper's job. Perhaps the English would let Prem stay on; perhaps he could bribe the head sweeper, but his best years were nearly at an end and he would have to work in the fields again or starve. He greeted the news of his brother-in-law's offer to Lakshmi with relief.

'About time! I've been feeding that Tipanka long enough. Better still, let her take Kubri with her.' Prem laughed harshly.

'Once upon a time there was a beautiful dark goddess named Tipanka,' Dada started to mumble. 'She had one attendant whose name was Kubri, and together the two set out on a long, long journey . . .'

'He's not half as mad as he makes out,' Lakshmi whispered to Kubri. 'Ssh, don't interrupt; maybe he'll tell us a story.'

'About her dowry. Your daughter needs things to bring to her marriage,' Sukhia said curtly. 'She can't go to her husband empty-handed. It would shame us and her village.'

It would shame *me*, Lakshmi thought.

'He's getting someone to mind his children and warm his bed,' Prem retorted. 'She'll earn her keep. Why should I pay for a dowry as well?'

'You have money,' Sukhia said stubbornly. 'You're the richest sweeper in the village now. What else have you been saving for, if not so your daughter can hold her head high and we can be proud when she goes to her husband?'

'Why?' Prem asked sullenly. 'It's a second marriage, it'll be done without ceremony. You're trying to pile up my money for your brother. He has grown-up children, the household has everything it needs. I'll pay for a new sari and a plate or pitcher and we'll bring our own food with us, so he doesn't have to provide. That's enough.'

'She *needs*,' Sukhia said, and for once her voice was steely, 'a fine wedding sari, with an underskirt, shawl and blouse; another sari for feast days; a stud for her nose and two for her ears, and glass bangles for each arm. Her husband has clay pots and dishes already but she will bring a *brass* pitcher, as a sign of her skill in the kitchen.' She lowered her voice. 'Your other daughters left the house like paupers but this one is going to have her due. It's little enough, so don't complain.'

Prem complained. He protested that he had no money; would have to borrow; the moneylender's interest rates were exorbitant . . . all this, for a daughter who couldn't even see straight?

Sukhia said in an undertone that only he could hear, 'Go and borrow from the hole in the back of the house then, for if you don't, I swear to you that I will!'

The weather was abnormal that summer, and menacing. A violent dust storm plunged Lucknow into darkness and all but destroyed the mango crop. Two days later an earthquake shook the city so severely that buildings were damaged. That was in May. The following month was exceptionally hot. In Kanpur the thermometer rose to 111° – a temperature barely endurable, even by the black and hardened frame of a labouring *bhangi* – and for weeks on end it never dropped below the eighties, even in the small hours of the night. The unrelenting heat drove people half out of their minds while their bodies sagged with lethargy. It was not allowed to affect the labourers of Budhera, although some got sunstroke, black as they were, and everyone was thirsty. Still they laboured on. In the middle of June came a partial eclipse of the sun – an ill omen. At the end of the month a pack of ravenous hyenas began seizing small children from beside the fields where their mothers worked. One woman whose baby was sleeping a few yards away, alerted by its screams, managed to grab it from the jaws of a hyena which she hacked to death with her scythe. The animal, half-starved like herself, almost matched her in size and weight and she was horribly mauled, but her baby survived.

Kali the omniscient: the baby died a year or two later. Malaria.

But it's true, that story. Mother love, the great universal impulse.

The monsoon was heralded by looming skies and massed black rain clouds; then distant thunder, vivid lightning, and an agitation that swept through the body as intensely as relief flooded the mind. The sky darkened. It groaned and cracked and its waters broke. The earth, baked hard by weeks of unrelenting heat, did not turn to mud straight away. Every path and road became a fast-flowing river, surging with warm rain. Overnight the temperature dropped by twenty degrees. The gods be praised for the monsoon!

Lakshmi had begged her mother to let her visit her sister in the short time left before marriage took her out of reach. Mithania's village was halfway to Kanpur, on her father's route to the cantonment.

'Once I'm married she'll be too far away and my husband won't let me go,' Lakshmi pleaded. 'I have to see her one last time! I must find out how she is, her and the little boys.'

Next time Prem came home (bringing the bridal jewellery with him: half a dozen plastic bangles, a pair of glass earrings and a red glass nose-stud) his wife urged him to take Lakshmi as far as Nagwan, where Mithania lived.

'You'll be her escort on the way there and if Hari goes too, he can look after her on the way back. She's almost a married woman now,' Sukhia pointed out. 'Anyone seeing them would take Lakshmi for a wife and Hari her son. She'll never see her sister again otherwise. She'd only go for a day, two at most.'

He agreed in the end with a show of reluctance; secretly, he hardly cared. His job at the cantonment would finish soon and he faced a hard future, the end of regular wages and a lowering of his status in the village. Bakha was pressing him to hand over to Ramu as soon as possible; the boy had waited long enough. It would happen within a few weeks. He should have saved more money – but then he would never have known the hotly scented embraces of the prostitutes.

Prem and his two children left Budhera late in the afternoon, well before sundown. It was warm and humid but the heat was no longer unbearable. After more than ten days the monsoon had not diminished. It rained in a hard, unrelenting downpour.

'I'll be back very soon!' Lakshmi called to her mother from the end of the path and Sukhia held Davadin up to wave. Kubri skulked furiously inside the hut. Warm rain sprayed their shining skin and as Lakshmi passed the tree she had talked to as a little girl, she breathed a prayer to Ganesha for their safety on the journey. She followed her father round the edge of the fields where she had run and danced, told stories and worked all through her girlhood. On the outskirts of the village she looked back at the distant huddle of dark shapes, like upturned cooking pots. They made a wavy line against the horizon, from the pointed dome of the Brahmin temple, the flat roofs of the *pukka* houses and terraces with clay flowerpots on both sides, to the muddle of thatched huts in the *bhangi* quarter. Ahead strode her brother's lithe brown body, rivulets of rain sliding down his back. He was looking forward to being her protector. How I love my family! Lakshmi thought, swelling with tenderness. She wanted to tell Dadi but he hadn't used affectionate words since she was a tiny child and she didn't know how to frame them now. Suddenly girlish, she broke into a run and as her feet came pounding up behind him, Hari sprinted ahead. They ran like fawns, ecstatic under the hard rain.

It was the evening of the eleventh day of the monsoon. Three inches of rain. The following day nearly four inches fell. Lakshmi is playing grandmother's footsteps and can't resist hurrying at the end. One pace, two paces, almost there now, you can practically lean out and touch . . . no, not yet.

The brief summer twilight was followed by a swift darkness. After walking for two hours Lakshmi was tired but she kept her eyes on the ground and followed her father's grey heels and

191

sinewy black ankles as he strode steadily onwards. Rain sluiced off him, hit the ground at his feet and bounced up again. She sensed that Hari was tired as well, but too proud to admit it. Occasionally they passed other figures moving through the night, veiled and shrouded, and would draw aside and stand at the edge of the path so as not to contaminate.

A wise dog would have smelled the threshold and run away, Lakshmi thought as she entered the smoky hut where her sister lived. Mithania cried out joyfully when she heard their voices. Her mother-in-law lumbered to her feet from the rope bed on which she had been lying and peered at them through the gloom. Lakshmi could hear other people breathing. A child shifted and moaned. 'So,' the old woman said, 'this is the ugly cross-eyed girl my fine son was supposed to marry? Lucky escape he had.' Lakshmi placed her palms together and greeted her respectfully, then laid her head on her sister's shoulders, each in turn. Mithania became rigid, her head bowed and voice subdued, but Lakshmi knew it was because she was trying not to cry. Two small boys nestled beside their grandmother; Mithania cradled another baby in her arms. She was about to light a lamp but the woman said, 'Don't waste good oil. It'll be light soon enough!' Lakshmi whispered, 'We'll talk in the morning, my sister . . .' Her father and Hari stretched out for the night under a dripping tree, having been offered a pitcher of water but nothing to eat after their long walk. Lakshmi crouched on the earth floor of the hut, laid her head on her folded arms and plummeted into sleep.

Next day Prem set off for the cantonment, his head and shoulders bowed under the downpour. The mother-in-law, as though fearful of the secrets that might be revealed, made it hard for the sisters to be alone together. She found end-less tasks for Mithania – scouring the pots with ash, scouring them again because she claimed they weren't clean enough, picking nits out of her hair, scrubbing the boys' teeth with the splayed end of a twig and checking their ears, besides the usual daily jobs: milking the buffalo, fetching water from the well and sweeping the floor. 'In a minute she'll mix together one measure of rice and one of lentils and tell you to sort them!' Lakshmi whispered and her sister smiled wanly. Her two little boys ran in and out of the rain, splashing about in the puddles and watching Hari, their uncle, show them how to make boats out of leaves and sticks. They at least were happy.

Finally the old woman was called away. Casting a sour glance at Mithania she said to Lakshmi, 'Don't eat us out of house and home and don't believe everything she tells you!'

Lakshmi exhaled deeply. 'Is it all right to talk now?' she asked. 'Where is your husband?'

'Didn't Dadi tell you? His father got him a sweeper's job in the cantonment. He's there now but he often comes home – it's only about two hours' walk. Oh *Lakshmi*, I am glad to see you! Look – isn't my daughter beautiful? The boys are bold and rough but this little one is a gentle baby.'

Lakshmi leaned forward and gazed into the dark, folded face of the sleeping infant. 'She looks like you, my sister.'

Outside, rain drummed harder on the roof. It had rained heavily in the night and the path was transformed into a torrent of water swerving between the *bhangi* huts. Wind lashed the side of the hut and rain cascaded off it in a muddy stream, joining the bubbles that eddied along the path. The boys were sailing a frail leaf-boat which rocked unsteadily. After two weeks of moderate rainfall the temperature had dropped suddenly – a portent of heavier rain to come – and the sodden sky was dark and lowering. Lakshmi shivered.

'I hope your mother-in-law will let me stay for a day or two. I don't want me and Hari to walk back in this.'

'I hope so too. My sister-in-law has gone back home to have

her first baby, may the gods give her a son, so we'd have a chance to talk. Be very humble to my mother-in-law and praise her cooking and her grandsons. Don't mention the girl; she didn't want me to have a daughter. Lakshmi, you're going to marry Uncle Beera! Is he very old? Do you like the look of him? Are you keen on this marriage or did our mother and Matin insist? Did Matin have a good death or did she die cursing you – the way she had all her life!'

'So many questions! I never really minded Matin. I miss her. She held everyone steady. But I can tell you that in front of . . . quick, first, are you all right?'

'No – yes – no. I am happy to have children but . . . my husband likes to play the role of master and I mustn't just be obedient, I have to cringe like a dog, whine and wag. My mother-in-law reports on me when he gets home and however hard I try to please her, he always beats me . . .'

'*Mitha* – my poor sister –'

'The old woman laughs and says every wife has to take her punishment. But it *hurts*, ai, Lakshmi, it really hurts! I get terrible headaches and – I shouldn't tell you this but no-one ever speaks gently to me and it's comforting to talk to you; I have *missed* you so much! – his beatings draw blood on my back and I can't lie down for days.'

'And his sons? Does he hit them, too?'

'No . . . though already they copy the way he talks to me. They're learning to despise me.'

'*She*'s unkind too.'

'Not to them. But they belong to this household, not to me. I am a prisoner for the rest of my life. Already I am with child again. It has to be a son. He thinks daughters are proof that he is not manly.'

Lakshmi lowered her voice. 'At night . . . you said . . . do you remember . . . ?'

'*It is the mating of beasts!*'

194

'Our mother said it takes time but eventually one gets great pleasure.'

'*You* might. I don't. He makes me go on my hands and knees like ... no, Lakshmi, I can't tell you. I am ashamed. Look, now I've woken the baby. I'll feed her.' Modestly she attached the infant to her breast, but not before Lakshmi had glimpsed a ring of white scars around the nipple like tooth-marks, not caused by a baby's soft gnawing but a deliberate, savage attack.

Mithania's mother-in-law came in from the rain soaking wet, her long plait sodden, drops of water winding through her wrinkles and running down her arms. The girl jumped up and fetched a clean sari with which she rubbed her dry.

'Where are my grandsons?' the old woman asked irritably. 'You're neglecting them. Your sister is more important, I suppose. Have you been filling her ears with poisonous gossip?'

'They are fine, brave boys,' Lakshmi soothed. 'We tried to keep them with us but no, they had to go and play with their new uncle. They're real *men* already.'

'They take after the son of my husband. *And* his father,' the woman said.

Ganesha, Lakshmi's special protector, squats behind his trunk, wise, benevolent and plump. He will not intervene. She must fulfil her own dharma.

That afternoon the storm intensified, inundating the fields and threatening to wash away the crops. The brimming canal, only four furlongs away, was about to overflow its banks and flood the village. Rain fell remorselessly, drumming on the hammock backs of cattle, bending trees and making their branches groan in the gale, saturating the thatched roofs and collecting in pools on every flat surface.

Mithania's hut was fragile. Its mud walls were not as thick as they should have been since the men of the family worked outside the village and the job of plastering them with fresh mud had been done by the women for the last two years. The side that took the full force of the wind was battered relentlessly until mud streamed down it in a dark, ominous torrent. Mithania was sent outside every half hour to inspect it and she and Lakshmi tried to paste handfuls of twigs and leaves into the deeper dents, although the rain immediately washed them out. Little bundles like birds' nests swirled downstream between the huts for a few seconds before disintegrating, like the children's boats an hour or two earlier. Everyone cowered indoors, leaving the village deserted. Mithania's small sons began to wail fearfully and Lakshmi launched into a story to distract them.

'Once upon a time there was an old woman who lived in the jungle. Her son, who lived with her, used to graze cattle. One day the woman shouted loudly, "Son! Come home quickly, a hurricane is coming!"'

'What's a hurricane, Aunty?' the older boy asked.

'It's a sort of rushy, roary, windy, grabby thing,' Lakshmi replied. 'Now listen, and let the story explain . . .'

The sky grew louder and darker. Mithania's mother-in-law became hysterical, shrieking that Lakshmi's arrival had brought the storm; she was ill-omened, her crooked eye had brought evil upon them, she must leave them in peace, go away, no matter where . . . Lakshmi, fearing yet another beating for her sister, ducked outside where at least the air was sweet after the foetid, ashy smell of the hut. She checked the mud wall that was taking the brunt of the storm. It was on the point of collapse, water coursing down and revealing the thin plaiting of rushes at its core. The whole side of the hut would soon be washed away, and if that happened her sister's home would be reduced to a muddy heap. Her heart pounded as she ran back inside.

'Forgive me, Matin,' she gabbled, 'forgive me, one side of the hut is about to fall down! We must take shelter or get help before everything is swept away, you, the children, all your possessions!'

The old woman wailed and cursed, knocking her hands against her head and swaying.

'Where shall I go, who should I ask for help?' Mithania said, shaking her mother-in-law's arm. 'Think, Matin, I beg of you, *think*, who will shelter us?'

'Nobody, nobody, they are all envious . . . they talk spitefully against me, they are jealous – no-one, ai, ai, my husband, father of my sons, I am dying!' She threw the shawl over her head and rocked to and fro cursing futilely.

'Lakshmi,' Mithania said calmly, 'you'll have to go and fetch Dadi and my husband.'

'*Me?* I can't. How?'

'Walk to the cantonment.'

'By myself? I don't know the way.'

'A cart track goes straight there. I can show you where to pick it up and then you just follow it. It's about two hours' walk.'

'I've never been anywhere alone.'

'You won't meet anyone in this downpour. I know: take Hari. *You*'ll go with her, my brother, won't you?'

'Yes,' said Hari bravely. 'I'll take care of her.'

Lakshmi smiled. 'You and me together? What an adventure! *Course* we'll go. But Mitha, how will I find them once I get there?'

'Everybody must know them. Say you want Prem the sweeper. Be very respectful.'

Matin stopped wailing for a moment and said in a muffled voice, 'What will happen to me?'

'My brother and sister are going to get help,' Mithania said. 'We'll wait here for the men and hope the wall doesn't fall down before they come. What else can we do?' She would have liked to add, 'If you weren't so cantankerous and your son didn't beat me so viciously we might have found shelter. As it is, no-one will risk taking us in.' She squeezed Lakshmi's hand and said, 'Go in safety, my sister. May Jara our family god and your own god Ganesha watch over you.'

'Get that she-devil out of my sight,' the old woman muttered.

Mithania gave them some cold *chapattis* to sustain them on the way and, wrapping her baby tightly in a corner of her shawl, took Lakshmi and Hari to the eastern side of the village where she pointed to the cart track along which they had walked with Dadi less than twenty-four hours previously. It was still light, although the sky was almost blotted out by rain. The two girls embraced, clasping hands and laying their wet cheeks together, and Mithania touched her forehead to Hari, a mark of respect that he solemnly returned. He had become very silent and serious now that he was responsible for both his sisters. Mithania pointed northwards. 'Just keep going in that direction!' she shouted against the lashing of the rain. 'There's a bridge soon, over the canal, and then you go straight . . . I think.' She resisted the desire to add, 'And *hurry*!' They waved and turned and set off together along the muddy track in the direction of her tense, pointing arm.

They had gone less than half a mile when the banks of the canal loomed up ahead through the rain. The bridge creaked and groaned like a boat straining at its moorings.

'Do you think it's safe?' Hari asked.

'We have to go over it,' Lakshmi answered, 'and the sooner the better.'

The wet planks were slippery underfoot and below them, terrifyingly close, the waters of the canal rushed past carrying a swirling broken mass of debris, branches, leaves and the sodden corpses of animals. 'Don't look down!' Lakshmi shouted. 'Hold on tight!' They clung to the rickety wooden rail with both hands and hauled themselves step by step across the torrent. As they reached the other side a peal of thunder split the sky, followed several seconds later by a whiplash of lightning that showed a huddle of huts ahead on their left and a clump of bending trees on the right. 'The storm's still a long way off,' said Hari and at the same instant Lakshmi said, 'We'll be all right now. The bridge was the worst bit.' She took his wet hand in hers and they walked side by side through the deep waterlogged ruts of the track. After a while Hari let out his breath in something between a nervous laugh and a sigh of relief. 'Ai, ai, I don't ever want to do *that* again!' 'Nor me,' said Lakshmi.

She had meant to tell Hari stories to keep his spirits up, but the effort of shouting against the wind was too great. Save my breath for the journey, she thought. She held his hand tightly and braced herself to lean into the storm. Her mind was as electric as the lightning, ideas whirling like djinns. Memories flashed up from her childhood: Shiv her brother, so confident and happy, who had been dead for seven summers. Poor thin drooping Ghashitia, who never had much energy and had slipped through life without a trace, leaving only a faint image in Lakshmi's mind. Kempa, strong, tender Kempa, who had wished them prosperity. She heard his voice saying to her mother, 'Blessings upon you, may your children always feed bounteously.' They had fed, not often bounteously, but none of them had starved. If only both her eyes had faced in the same direction, Kempa might have been her husband and then she would have been happy all her life long, and every night would have been . . .

'Look where you're going!' Hari said nervously. 'You nearly fell over.' His hand clutched harder at hers and Lakshmi thought: I must concentrate, not dream.

They were both as wet as if they had been swimming in the Shoni, splashing about on a sunny afternoon, soaking their hair and clothes and shrieking with laughter, throwing transparent sheets of water across one another, glittering with joy. The thunderclaps were receding now, the lightning moving away. Through the gloom they saw two or three figures ahead holding up black umbrellas like bats' wings. Lakshmi flinched and slowed down. 'Don't be afraid, you've got me,' said Hari, and he stood up straight so as to look taller. They followed the group for a while, reassured by the presence of other human beings in the flooded landscape, until the three turned aside at a crossroads and disappeared into the rain. Lakshmi and Hari trudged wearily on. 'I wonder how much longer it is?' he asked and she said in a cheerful voice, 'Not long at all.'

'Tomorrow is the day after tomorrow's yesterday.' Time snaked backwards and forwards like the loops of the stream in which she had paddled as a little girl. She knew it was important; something about time and repetition. It meant that nothing lasted for ever and everything would diminish when seen down the long perspective of a lifetime. But she was still young and every day imprinted itself clearly on her mind. Their four feet, walking through the muddy channels of the track, kicking up dark splashes that mottled her legs, the squelching of mud between her toes – she wouldn't forget this. The way Mithania's half-starved body and milky breasts had pressed against her for a moment as they embraced – the grip of Hari's slippery fingers in her own, the rhythm of his walk as his shoulders bounced up and down beside her, the diagonal sheets of hard rain that fell and fell and fell as though they would never stop . . . Lakshmi surrendered to the bodily ecstasy of walking, her head high, the good eye gazing forward through the murky light, the other sideways towards a life that might have been. She saw with vaulting clarity that tomorrow *is* the day after tomorrow's yesterday; all will be well and we shall find my father and he will know what to do and the old woman will have to be nice to Mitha and this is my *karma*, to walk through the rain with my brother and rescue my unhappy sister and do something so good that people will talk about it yesterday and tomorrow, for ever. Nothing matters except being alive.

'Do you remember that song I used to sing when you were

little?' she asked Hari suddenly. 'Our mother sang it to Shiv, who you hardly knew, and I sang it to you and Kubri and Davadin.'

'Which one? There were lots of songs.'

'Oh you know, the nonsense song . . .' and she began softly, almost to herself:

> *'Nini, baba, nini,*
> *Makhan, roti, chini . . .'*

'Course I know it,' he said, picking up the baby words: *'Khana, pina, hogaya.'*

Together they ended, loudly:

> *'Mera baba sogaya*
> *Nini, baba, nini.'*

They walked along singing at the tops of their voices to the featureless black sky, the obliterated landscape and endlessly falling rain:

> *'Nini, baba, nini,*
> *Makhan, roti, chini,*
> *Khana, pina, hogaya . . .'*

until finally they were marching, stamping, swinging their arms and bawling:

> *'Mera baba sogaya*
> *Nini, baba, nini!'*

They had to stop in the end because they were laughing so much, bending double in the rain, clutching their aching bellies, water pouring down their open, laughing faces.

They calmed down and walked for another hour or more, in tune with each other and the ground underfoot and the black sky above their heads, not needing to laugh or sing or speak any more because they both knew this shared experience would link them for the rest of their lives. Mithania had been right; the path was easy to follow. Ahead they could see two double lines of wide iron track that gleamed like liquorice in the rain. Here the path seemed to peter out. There didn't seem to be a bridge over the lines so they walked across, picking their feet up high and making their way delicately through a network of wooden sleepers and shiny metal rails to the far side. Beyond lay a wide smooth road, empty because of the hour and the rain. A few steps later a large noticeboard appeared, on which was written in letters that neither could read:

BRITISH ARMY CANTONMENT
NO ENTRY EXCEPT ON OFFICIAL BUSINESS
REPORT TO MAIN GATE
←RIFLE RANGES
GENERAL PARADE GROUND↑
←BARRACKS (OTHER RANKS)
SUJATGANJ→

Lakshmi and Hari stared at the rainswept board until she said, 'This must be the place where Dadi is to be found so let's go and look for him.' They were confronted by a high fence. Hari climbed it first, finding invisible footholds till he could hook one arm over the top. He leaned down and offered Lakshmi his hand to pull her up. On the other side, like a glistening sheet of water, extended a vast flat area – the parade ground – ringed for as far as they could see by large and small buildings. Hari gazed, awe-struck. 'It must be a palace!' he said.

'Walk until you find someone and then ask for Dadi-ji,' Lakshmi said, since she had to say something and Hari looked frightened. 'I'll find out if he lives in there.' To their left was a series of long low blocks, dormitory buildings for soldiers. Not a soul was to be seen. 'As soon as one of us finds him we'll meet by *this* thing,' and she pointed to a noticeboard on which was written:

AIR LANDING STRIP➔
RIFLE RANGES➔
←DORMITORIES

'Quick as you can, Mitha must be getting worried!' Obediently, Hari broke into a weary run. He disappeared into the sheeting rain and Lakshmi headed towards the first of several bleak, grey two-storey buildings with a verandah at one end. Now that Hari had gone her shoulders slumped and she heaved a sigh of utter exhaustion. The light was dwindling; the rain was not. It would soon be dark.

The scene is set. Lakshmi walks on-stage. Orchestra: a drumroll, nice and slow, and perhaps some softly plucked strings. A subliminal patter of applause like rain on a tin roof as the audience waits for the next act. Menace or bliss: which is it to be for Lakshmi? Kali won't stay to find out.

But we will. The globe has been circumnavigated, Sam and Lakshmi are about to meet, propelled towards each other by Abel's anger and the monsoon's torrent. From Lower Flexham to Kanpur, by car, train, troopship, train again and finally on foot, forwards and backwards, their moment has come. Both arc ready, yet unaware. Brave and scared, Lakshmi watches as a wooden door creaks open and light floods across the tarmac.

FIRST INTERMISSION

The mid-1980s

WALTER AT THE BRITISH LEGION HAD ASSURED HIM THEY wouldn't be a bother. They were making a programme about soldiering abroad; he'd only to answer a few questions and they'd be gone in half an hour. As soon as the television crew arrived it was obvious it wasn't going to be that simple. For a start, Sam's tidy front parlour had to be rearranged.

A brightly smiling girl from the television crew said, 'Hello, Mr Savage, I'm Lorna! Lovely room you've got here. So *cosy*. Mmm! You don't mind, do you, if we sort of dress the set a bit?'

He had no idea what she meant, but he nodded. Two of the men started moving his furniture around, pulling Edith's armchair away from the fireplace, taking down some of the ornaments on the mantelpiece and putting them on the nest of tables beside him. Lorna said again, 'You don't mind?' before placing his and Edith's wedding photograph against a blank bit of wallpaper for the cameraman to film. 'Don't worry,' she said with another reassuring smile, 'we'll put everything back exactly where it was. By the time we leave you won't know we've been here!'

Sam had planned to begin by describing the landing in Bombay, then Deolali, his first impressions of India, and perhaps something about the train journey to Cawnpore. After that – the regimental band, what sort of music they'd played; whether he'd seen action, done a second tour of duty in India – it would depend what they asked. A young chap in a black T-shirt and black jeans who seemed to be in charge came over to him.

'I'm Tom Martineau – call me Tom – the thing is, you see, Mr, erm, Savage . . . OK, we just want you to talk us through your time in India. We don't have any special, you know, agenda – it's your personal memories we're after.'

'Best start at the beginning, how they landed us in Bombay and took us on up to Deolali for two or three days and then on to Cawnpore. I wor band boy there, '35 to nearly end of '36. One year.'

'Cawnpore!' the chap said. 'You were *there*? Excellent. Perfect. We've done some location filming already – not much of the old cantonment left now.'

'I wuddn't know,' Sam answered. 'I niver went back.'

'We shot in the British cemetery as well – lovely moody stuff – anything you can remember about that or the memorial church . . .'

'The regimental band used to play there on special occasions, like the anniversary of those poor ladies and their children massacred in the Mutiny. We'd end with the Last Post for Major-General Wheeler and his men. That wor the beginning of the end for Empire. Owd Kipling would turn in 'is grave.'

'Don't start yet,' Tom Martineau said hurriedly. 'Wait till the camera's running or we'll lose the spontaneity. Be with you in a tick.' He moved aside to let the cameraman hold a round metal instrument against Sam's face.

'Light meter,' he said as he took a reading. 'Not a Geiger counter. Five point six. Marco, swivel the reflector a touch, would you? To me, to me . . . *stop*.'

'We filmed in Deolali too,' one of the young assistants told Sam while the director and cameraman conferred in a corner of the room. 'Amazing place. Great shots of the plain. Fantastic. Bloody hot. Hotel air-conditioned of course, but even so . . .'

'It's eighteen hundred feet above sea level,' Sam told him. 'Not half as hot as Cawnpore.'

'Yeah, and what a dump *that* was!' the man said. 'Arsehole of the world bar none. Hang on, I'm needed.'

A young woman holding a powder compact came over to Sam and began to dab his nose and forehead. He flinched.

'Don't want you too shiny,' she said. 'Now, touch of colour for those cheeks . . .'

'No!' Sam said with unexpected vehemence, and she stepped back.

'You don't *have* to,' she said, 'but most people do. Sort of cheers the face up.'

'If I wunta look cheerful Oi'll smile.'

She left him alone.

Sam looked round. His familiar room had been transformed into an olde worlde parlour. The traycloth was draped over the back of Edith's chair like an antimacassar, their wedding photograph had been propped on the table next to him and his trumpet lay along the mantelpiece, flanked by a pair of Toby jugs. At each end they had placed a couple of framed photographs, one taken at the prize-giving day of a pretty, uniformed schoolgirl and another showing him and Edith surrounded by grinning schoolchildren. They were never short of the company of children: quite apart from those she taught they'd got more than a dozen nieces and nephews. Edith had been meticulous about listing all their dates of birth in a special Birthday Book and making sure each child always got a card and present.

The chap in charge said, 'Super. Love it.' He motioned Sam to sit in his own chair, which had been put by itself on one side of the fireplace; then crouched down beside him and said in a low, confiding voice, 'What's so *fascinating* is that you must have seen it through the eyes of a child, as it were . . .'

'I wor fourteen and 'alf when I went out. No child. Not in them days. Bin workin' on land five years.'

'No, of course, I didn't exactly mean a *child* – more like, innocent. You were *innocent*, weren't you? Then?'

'Lork, aye. Oi were innocent. Babe in arms.'

'That's what I mean!' Tom Martineau said excitedly. 'It's that *freshness* of vision we want. To capture India through *your* eyes, OK? – your impressions, the local people – women, perhaps – yes, how did you feel about the *women*? Did you find them attractive? Did you get to know any Indian girls? Maybe even have a sweetheart? *That* sort of thing.'

He turned to the waiting crew – 'OK, everyone, ready to roll?' – and back to Sam. 'Now *relax*. Don't look at the camera. Forget the audience of millions and imagine you're talking to *me*. Anything you're not happy about, we'll stop and do it again.'

Sam nodded unhappily. Tom Martineau sat in front of him and took a spiral notebook from his pocket.

'*Quiet*, everyone . . .' he said.

'Sound running . . .'

'Speed . . .'

A young fellow from the crew held out a clapper-board and intoned, '*Lest We Forget*, 59, Take One.'

They allowed him to ramble on about his arrival, letting him get used to the noise of the camera, the strangers crammed into his small front room, the pace of the interview. After several minutes Tom Martineau called out, 'Cut!' The camera stopped and everyone stood patiently while he talked to Sam again.

'Mr Savage, we've got lots of sync already about the journey to Bombay, the troopship, arriving, the transit camp—'

'Deolali, yes, I remember it very clearly. I could tell you more about Deolali,' Sam said. 'The lectures they gave us, about' – he lowered his voice – '*diseases* . . .'

'Well, *great*, terrific, only what I'm trying to say is that we've *got* that already. Your friend, sorry, name escapes me—'

'Ivor? Albert?'

'Probably – maybe – anyhow, he sort of half mentioned an incident in the barracks involving a girl, an Indian girl, but then he stopped and couldn't remember the rest. I wondered if *you* might know?'

Sam lowered his eyes before the man's sudden penetrating gaze. Thoughts flew about his mind in an uncoordinated, panicky fashion. He shook his head as though to clear it and Martineau assumed he was trying to recall the past. He prompted, 'Was she someone's girlfriend? Do you remember her name? I wondered if perhaps one of the lads was disciplined for having, you know, a relationship that crossed the, erm, race barrier?'

'I dunnt remember narthen like that,' Sam mumbled, but the colour was rising in his cheeks and mottling his neck. Tom Martineau noticed and pressed on.

'It's all water under the bridge *now*, of course. There'd be no comeback, not after all these years.'

No comeback? thought Sam. There'd been a comeback all right. He shook his head and met Tom Martineau's sharp gaze.

'Narthen comes back to me. Thou'd best ask me mate Ivor, or mebbe Albert, though pore ol' boy don't make too much sense nowadays, gone addled in his wits, they say it's Michael Parkinson's disease.'

The crew sniggered and Sam thought, phew, that was close!

The director stood up.

'OK, right, thanks, Mr Savage; terrific stuff, you've been a great help. Let me sleep on it in case there's anything we need to add. If I think of something I'll give you a buzz in the morning. That OK by you?'

Anything to get rid of the probing questions, the intrusive strangers crowding his and Edith's cosy little room, the memories they brought back.

'That'd be no bother.'

'Probably won't be necessary.'

'It 'ud be no bother,' he repeated.

They fiddled about a bit, filmed him pretending to listen to Tom Martineau, took pictures of his ornaments, his tray with one cup of tea on it, and then packed up. They were as good as their word. By the time they'd finished moving his furniture and put the ornaments and framed photographs back you couldn't tell they'd ever been disturbed.

'How c'n you remember 'tall?' Sam asked the young woman, Lorna.

'I write everything down,' she said, showing him the pad on her clipboard, 'and you can usually tell from the dents in the carpet where things are used to standing.' She'd done a little sketch of his mantelpiece as it was when they arrived, every ornament in the right place. It hadn't been a casual chat at all, Sam realized, but a well-planned, smooth-running operation. She offered him fifty pounds, just for answering those few questions. He tried to decline it but she said everyone got the same, and stood in front of him holding it out and smiling. It was a crisp, new note. He'd never seen one before. That was more than a week's pension money.

He said, 'Sorry, miss, I bin no good to 'ee. Keep the fifty pun'. I ain't earned it.'

'Course you have! You were *great*.'

She was very persistent, but he still didn't accept.

As they walked away down his narrow brick front path she turned round and twinkled her fingers at Sam, who was watching them through the window. To Tom, walking beside her and waving too, she said, 'He wouldn't take the money.'

'I saw. That proves it. Blood money, he thinks. That little chap's got a helluva story to tell and tomorrow we're coming back to get it. He may think it's over but it's not.'

PART THREE

CHAPTER ONE

July–November 1935

IN YEARS TO COME SAM OFTEN THOUGHT: IF I COULD HAVE THE choice all over again, the morning when I was about to sign me name in front of the recruiting sergeant in Ipswich, I'd summon up me courage and say, 'I'm wholly sorry, vicar, but I've changed me mind.' No matter how much the sergeant tried to bully me or how surprised the reverend was, nothing would budge me. If I could 'a' known what was gonna happen, that's what I'd 'a' done. But life's not like that story Miss Jamieson read aloud (the class so quiet you cud hear every shuffle and sniff) – the one called *The Time Machine*. Time dunnt stand still, much less run backwards.

Sam was borne forward on the ever-rolling stream. He passed his medical, small and skinny as he was. During the hard but halcyon days of the last summer of their boyhood he and Jake worked on the harvest for a month, gleaning, threshing and stacking the warm spiky corn into golden stooks, singing the field songs they had always sung. In the long evenings Sam and Edith Satterthwaite met in secret, storing up memories to last two or three years. At home, as usual, he did his best to avoid his father's eye and his blows. Then he was off, after a final tryst with Edith and a distracted hug from his mother. He did six weeks' hard basic training and travelled by train with his platoon to Southampton, where the new recruits, lined up on the dockside in stiff new uniforms, gazed at the immensity of sheds, cranes, bollards, ships and oily grey water. Even Jake Roberts, who had swaggered and bullied his way through the first weeks, was awed by the size of the ship. Sam thought of his mother, tried not to think of Edith, left right, left right, mounted the gangplank like an automaton, kitbag swinging from his hand; heard the boom of the foghorn and was carried on the outgoing tide of the English Channel towards India.

Sam, who had never seen the sea before, now found himself trapped on a whole ocean of it. His eyes ached for green and gold and muddy brown. The troops swung in hammocks in the lower decks, packed head to tail like sardines. The only ventilation came down canvas wind-chutes from the upper deck. They rattled or drummed hollowly, according to the direction of the wind. Confined by night to these dark narrow quarters, by day they were subjected to a rigid timetable of physical training and lectures, captain's rounds, boxing tournaments, games and sports and concerts. Sam grew and ripened in the sun. Once the Bay of Biscay was behind them he stopped being seasick. Shipboard rations – more nourishing than anything he'd eaten at home – filled him out. At fourteen and a half he was a good two years younger than most recruits but during the voyage he grew two inches. His arms and legs became thicker, his back broader and his blanched English face turned first pink and then a painful deep crimson before taking on the colour of a hazelnut. But even after the Straits of Gibraltar, when the tossing sea became a sheet of cobalt blue and the Mediterranean air was soft and warm on his skin, he would willingly have exchanged it all for a black and white winter's day in Lower Flexham or a back-breaking summer one in the golden Suffolk fields.

After six weeks at sea the ship made a brief stop at Port Said to take on fuel and provisions and the men were marched round the city to stretch their legs. From Aden onwards, for the rest of the voyage there was nothing except water as far as the horizon and nothing to read except what they had brought in their kit-bags: in Sam's case, *The Jungle Books*, his Bible and a book Miss Jamieson had given him called *The Thirty-Nine Steps*. There was also a booklet issued to each man on board called *Some Hints for the Use of Soldiers Proceeding to India*. This set out basic facts about the country in which they were to spend the next three years, with tips on how to behave towards the natives. *Mutual trust and good understanding will surely turn the scale in the close struggle between civilisation and savagery*, Sam read. *National honour demands that each of us should do his little best towards that great end.* He wondered whether Mowgli was a savage and came to the conclusion that he probably was – though a lucky and enviable savage; a savage with whom Sam, the supposedly civilized one, would gladly have changed places.

The air grew hotter, the sky whiter. Fishing boats with raking masts manned by wiry little figures in loincloths signalled the approach of Bombay. The first building Sam could pick out was the Gateway to India, a marble archway beneath which the Viceroy greeted distinguished visitors. The next thing he noticed (heart swelling with pride) was that the British flag fluttered above the harbour-master's building, proclaiming the port, the city and the land of India British. What an adventure, Sam thought, this whole huge country made civilized and decent under British rule! And now I'm part of it.

He thought he had got used to the heat but, as the ocean breeze receded, it became even hotter. Hawks swooped overhead and round about as the ship made its stately approach towards Ballard Pier; great dark birds, not at all like the shrieking white seagulls they had left behind at Southampton. Circling above the town itself were vultures. Sam had never seen a vulture before but he recognized their long bald necks, black heads and sinister appearance. As the ship came alongside, the troops were mustered on deck. Not even Kipling had prepared him for the seething mass below. Since the British were so important and necessary to India he had expected every third or fourth face to be white but the people crowding the dockside were overwhelmingly dark, their skins every shade from swarthy black to a colour that shone like brass. Their hair was black, glinting dark blue or silver in the sun. As the ship edged towards the disembarkation area he could see mutilated beggars with opaque upturned eyes sitting cross-legged or squatting in front of a bowl for coins. Their limbs were bones covered in skin, ending in stumps where they should have had hands or feet. Tiny women held up maimed babies with huge, black-ringed eyes. The ship tied up at the dock. Over the cacophony Sam heard shouted orders as, stepping mechanically down the gangplank, he set foot on the sacred ground of India. From the crowd, someone spat and a long red stain landed at his feet. 'Filthy niggers!' muttered the man behind him. At the order to march the troops lifted their heads high, shouldered their kitbags and strode past the watching crowd.

It is frightening, horrifying to our civilized eyes, but yet marvellous too, he wrote in a hurried letter to Edith. Cooped up in stifling troop-sheds while their equipment was unloaded and checked at the dockside, the men had been told to let their loved ones know of their safe arrival. They sat at wooden tables and were issued with letter forms and pencils. The post would be carried back when the troopship set sail on its return voyage, so his letter would take less than seven weeks. Sam wrote, *I haven't seen any animals yet except for lots of dogs, very thin, but I musta seen more people in one day than my whole life before. Dear, you can't imagine how they crowded round, like the feeding of the five thousand. They all look as if they could do with a good meal. The women are little as children, their skins all colours from nigger black to a pretty pale gold like you after you've been in the sun awhile.* Sam paused and thought of the feel of Edith's skin beneath his stroking fingers.

'Five minutes!' shouted the sergeant. 'Xs for kisses, leave out the rest, stick down the regulation envelope, *put the address on –* we haven't got second sight – and hand 'em in.'

Hurriedly Sam resumed: *I shan't never be able to tell you properly what it's like, my head's reeling and not just from the sun. I miss you ever so much and think of you dear a lot. Give my best to your mother, you know what I want to say to you only words can't express it, forever your loving sweetheart, Sam.* Jake Roberts loomed beside him but Sam, knowing Jake could hardly read, did not bother to cover up his letter.

'Thou be writing to thy sweetheart,' stated Jake. 'Tell 'er, pass on word to me mither I be well.'

P.S. Jake Roberts be here too but mostly leave me in peace, Sam added. *He tell a whole nest of lies about thee but I know my dear they be not true. He says tell his mother he be well, which he be, more's the pity.*

They finally boarded a train that left Ballard Pier at noon. It was sunset as the train climbed the Western Ghats and pitch dark by the time they got to their temporary quarters at Deolali. Perched high on the Deccan plateau, this was the transit camp for troops arriving at or leaving Bombay. Next morning, as they marched to breakfast through the rising heat, Sam gazed across a wide expanse of dusty plain. It looked like the steppes of the American West in one of the Tom Mix cowboy films they'd watched during the voyage. Yet in his imagination the flat-topped rocks dotting the plain could have been the Council Rock where the pack of wolves gathered round Akela, their leader, as Mowgli challenged Shere Khan the tiger with a blazing firebrand.

At Deolali the platoon was issued with groundsheets, blue rugs and Indian kitbags. In the three days before they boarded the troop train for the last stage of the journey they had to sit through more lectures about discipline, especially regarding the native population. One old sergeant-major, an experienced

India hand, said categorically: 'You'll soon get a feeling for what's right and proper here and discover that native women are scheming, dirty, lecherous and best left alone. No matter how they beckon and smile, give 'em a wide berth. Most of you have sweethearts at home. Think of your duty to them, and keep yourselves pure in word and deed. Some things just aren't done and going with native women is top o' the list. Remember, you are white men. It's up to you to set an example and behave decently. And finally, every last one of you, are you listening to me? – *finally* – never forget that the Indian, like all dark races, is a savage under the skin. Your native-wallah has a capacity for violence that you forget at your peril. They'll hack each other – or their womenfolk – to death over a trivial slight. Given half a chance, they'll do it to you. Never trust 'em. That clear? *Good.*'

Apart from listening to lectures, eating unpalatable meals and playing housey-housey there was nothing to do and nowhere to go. The dry heat was stifling, especially in the middle of the day. Sam felt listless and exhausted. Time-expired men waiting for the return voyage grinned knowingly. 'This is only November; cold weather time. Wait till the *summer*!'

At eight o'clock on their third morning in India they finally boarded the military train that travelled along the Great Indian Peninsula Railway from Deolali to Jhansi and on from there to Cawnpore. The journey would take at least twenty-four hours, with several meal stops on the way. Each compartment had slatted wooden seats and folding wooden bunks. The windows had three separate sashes: glass to keep out dust, wire mesh to keep out insects and a wooden one that, when drawn down, kept out the sun if not the unrelenting heat. Sam was sharing a compartment with three Suffolk lads who had all joined up together. One asked Sam how old he was and when he answered, 'Fourteen and eight months,' said: ''Ow cum th'art in army? Th'art too young.' Sam explained about bell-ringing, though not about his father, and said he had been accepted as a musician to train for the regimental band. He returned the question.

'Me ooncle 'Arry were in army durin' Great War an' me mither's that proud of 'im, I thought I'd give it a try. I'm 'oping it'll learn me to drive trucks. Me name's Wordley, Ivor Wordley. Thou'rt?'

'Savage . . . Sam.'

'Savage Sam, eh? These 'ere's me pals Sidney Hale an' Albert Fitch. Sidney an' Albert – meet Sam.'

Albert said, 'Me father died in war. I niver seen 'im.'

'I came to India hopin' it wor like *Jungle Book*,' Sam told them eagerly.

Sidney, it turned out, had read Kipling as well. 'Mother teaches at school,' he said, 'an' she worn't gunna have me on land; said I wor too good fer that, I deserved proper chance. I wor curious – more'n curious – I wor *burstin'* ter see world. Niver been further than Cambridge.'

Sam had never even been that far yet here they were, the four of them, rumbling across the undulating grey landscape of India. He grinned hugely at the very idea and the three opposite, assuming he was grinning at them, grinned back. Behind the noisy bravado, unfamiliar uniforms and occasional bad language they were decent lads whose company might provide some protection against Jake's bullying. Sam leaned back and let himself relax.

Ivor, Sidney and Albert were nearly seventeen. They had left school with little hope of finding work. After two years as agri-cultural labourers, half-starved on meagre pay, they joined up the moment they were old enough. The army offered a wage, a trade and a chance to escape. All three were passionate supporters of Grimsby Town Football Club but although it was in the first division, they thought their team didn't stand a chance for the Cup. Sam knew little about football but was an ardent Grimsby supporter too. He nodded and said, ''Ere's 'opin' anyway!'

The plains of India stretched and wheeled away from the

line. Plodding bullock carts stirred up dust along the roads. Once Sam saw an elephant lifting logs with its trunk: a huge, wrinkled beast, it looked willing and intelligent, with none of the jungle madness of Hathi and his sons. Once the train stopped to let the sticky, sweating men wash and cool themselves in a river. An Indian appeared out of nowhere with half a dozen young girls – some, by the look of them, hardly fourteen years old. For a few annas they would go with a man into the scrubby bushes bordering the river. Sam was shocked and embarrassed when, back on the train, Jake boasted that he'd had one. ''Tis like sticking a wooden spoon into a jar of honey. Not that thee'd know, Edith tells me!' Sam turned away and went back to his new friends.

Darkness fell and at last the temperature cooled a little. Hours later the train slowed down, drew into a station and came to a halt. The engine sighed and clattered and hissed. The stationmaster, an old man in a green turban and silver-rimmed spectacles, saluted and, inclining his head, invited the officer in charge to take tea. The officer declined. The men got down, stretched their legs, and were served sweet tea and biscuits on the platform. They were immediately pestered by dozens of people, evidently convinced that any sahib must be rich. Have they no shame? Sam thought. Gas lamps burned above the platform and insects circled the light, each one a miniature solar system. Men wearing nothing but loincloths proffered goatskins of water and jars of milk. Despite two cups of tea and the bottled water he had drunk on the train Sam was thirsty, but he remembered the words of the booklet: *Drinking impure water is the commonest cause of illness and to be on the safe side it must be boiled. Hundreds of cases of enteric have been traced to drinking dirty liquids, and probably thousands more to drinking bazaar milk.* However did the Indians manage?

''Ow can they drink it and not get ill but we b'ain't allowed to?' he asked.

Albert pointed to a miserable figure crouching beside the

track a few yards away, just beyond the main circle of light. 'See? They can't,' he said shortly.

Perhaps it was true, Sam reflected, that Indians were savages. Their toilet habits were very public. Next morning, as the train steamed alongside fields and villages, he saw men squatting everywhere, a modest half-turn away from the next person but in full view of the travellers.

'Don't they 'ave privy?'

'Most of 'em probably don't 'ave *roof* over heads, never mind privy!' Sidney said.

Next day they reached Jhansi where the train was shunted into a siding and they ate goat stew and rice pudding for lunch. An hour later the coach was attached to the Lucknow Mail for the final stage of their journey. It steamed across the Ganges plain for six more hours until at last, weary, cramped and hot, the men arrived at Cawnpore Central. Sam hopped down onto the platform, stretched his legs and looked round. He had left home nearly three months ago, trained for six weeks, travelled for nine, and finally reached his destination. The recruiting sergeant in Ipswich had said, 'The regiment's stationed in India, near Cawnpore. Might post you out there with the next draft to join the regimental band.' Now he was here and it was unlike anything he could possibly have imagined.

Punkah fans whirled rhythmically overhead. Beneath a corrugated iron roof, pigeons fluttered through the dusty air. The tiled floor was spattered with the red marks of betel juice. As the men formed up on the platform Sam glimpsed shrouded, sleeping figures, one arm flung over their faces for darkness and privacy. Beggarwomen cradling tiny dark infants stretched insistent, plucking hands towards him. Shoe-shine boys sat cross-legged behind tins of Cherry Blossom polish, brushes and shoelaces, shouting appeals at the passers-by. Men pushing handcarts threaded their way along the platform offering food, drink, fruit, nuts, tobacco, ready-rolled *bidis*, flowers, newspapers, garish magazines and self-help books. Stout Indians in long white shirts and trousers strode through the crowd followed by porters balancing one, sometimes two suitcases on their heads. Sam saw a cripple on two crutches, like scissors walking. Somehow they all made way for each other and nobody collided. Next to one of the cast-iron columns supporting the roof sat a white-haired blind man, his face tilted towards a little girl, only about three or four years old, who crouched beside him wiping gum from his eyelids with careful fingers.

It was seven o'clock and dusk had fallen but the men, having been cooped up for three days, were ordered to march to the cantonment. It would give them some exercise and, more important, display their discipline and numbers. A truck followed with baggage and equipment. They emerged from the station with uniforms, belts and boots gleaming, chins jutting. Warm air clung to Sam's skin. Heat, noise and light surged from stalls spilling across the pavement, illuminated by scores of Tilley lamps.

His nostrils flared to a rich mix of smells: something acrid, like a burnt-out bonfire; something rotten, like old meat; something spicy in the smoke that billowed from street braziers; something sour, like marigolds, and an underlying stench of ordure. They marched down the centre of the road past slow-moving cows, men pulling rickshaws and uniformed Indian policemen with guns slung over their shoulders. People stood back but their expressions were not friendly. Women in jewel-coloured draperies averted their eyes and veiled their faces as the soldiers approached, some extending a rigid palm as though to ward off their gaze. Sam had read about this: *Women veil their faces and run away from Englishmen because if they do anything that could arouse their husbands' suspicion, they will be beaten.* Not so very different from his own father, then.

By the time they entered the cantonment after more than half an hour's march, Sam was dizzy. The lumbering cows, fearful women, strutting policemen and limbless beggars – how could this happen, why was it allowed, under British rule? He could not reconcile what he had seen with the pictures in the Mowgli stories that lit up his mind's eye. He would have liked to share his wonder and bewilderment with Edith – or Mr Persimmons – or even his teacher, Miss Jamieson – but they were thousands of miles away. He wanted India to be as he had imagined and not as it was. Swarming right up to the cast-iron gates of the cantonment, piling up behind its perimeter wall, out there in the dark, the real India was noisy, smelly, teeming, chaotic and – Sam finally admitted to himself – frightening.

CHAPTER TWO

November–December 1935

SAM WAS IN DORMITORY 'D', THE ONE NEAREST TO THE WALL surrounding the cantonment. It was a single-storey building with a high roof and outside, at the far end away from the door, stood a square brick structure that housed the camp incinerator. Its fire rarely went out. The smoke had the same acrid, grainy smell that Sam had caught from the street braziers. Under the corrugated metal roof of this long bare dormitory they would sleep and clean their kit and pass the time not spent drilling, parading or – in Sam's case – rehearsing and making music with the regimental band. Ranged down both sides were two rows of cast-iron beds with canvas mattresses, lightly covered with blankets. Beside each one stood a bedside table with a small cupboard for their personal possessions. It had no lock but this didn't matter since Sam had no personal possessions. On top were two bottles of water. Sam was thirsty after the march and he was about to unscrew one when the sergeant bellowed an order and the whole platoon stood to attention. They bent over their kitbags and began to stow things away in the cupboard or in neat piles on the slatted table at the foot of every bed. When they had finished he bellowed again:

'Canteen – know where it is? Course you don't! Will by to-morrow, *won't yer?*'

Sixty parched throats shouted as one, '*Yes, sarge!*'

'And then there's the wet canteen. Who knows what a wet canteen is? Yes – you?'

'Where you can buy beer and . . .?'

'Wonder how *he* knows? Dare say I'll find out soon enough. Right, the wet canteen caters for yer drinkin' habits. Couple of snooker tables and an Indian behind the bar. Treat him with respect and don't call him a nigger or he'll spit in your beer.'

Uncertain whether this was true, the recruits laughed nervously.

'I'll be back in half an hour to show you the way. Till then, *one* bottle of water – the other is for when you wake up *'owlin'* for yer mothers in the night – *and* you will – now, *on* your beds, *lie down!*'

'Yes, *sarge!*'

Thankfully, Sam lay down.

Next morning they were told they would have the honour of being addressed by the colonel. As they marched through the cantonment behind their sergeant-major, Sam noticed dozens of Indian sweepers in tattered khaki shirts and grimy trousers. Some leaned on their brooms grinning through discoloured teeth at the arriving recruits. One or two called out a greeting. When the sergeant-major had halted his platoon outside the assembly hall, he said, 'You will 'ave observed a number of native sweepers. The Hindustani word for 'em is *mehtar*. It's their job – not yours, lucky bleeders – this is India – *their* job to keep the place orderly and clean out the latrines. It naturally follows from the above that they are *low-caste*, *dirty*, not to be trusted wi' money – that's to say, greedy and grasping, like every other Indian – and inclined to toady. On the other 'and they can also be loyal and tractable. *No man is to 'ave anything to do with them.* Got that?'

'*Yes, sarge!*'

Rows of wooden chairs were lined up inside the hall and the troops shuffled along until each man was standing in front of one. The colonel entered, climbed the steps of a small dais and stood beside a blackboard, flanked by a gleaming adjutant. Everyone saluted.

After some opening remarks of welcome and warning, the colonel said, 'Sit down! Now! You are *here*!'

The adjutant's pointer flew to the map and tapped a black dot marked Cawnpore.

The colonel continued, 'Eighty years ago, the greatest catastrophe in the history of India began *here*!' The pointer slid an inch or two to rest on another dot. Lucknow.

'The Indian Mutiny. Innocent British women and children – *white* women and children, *infants* – were brutally murdered. Here, in this very city, within the area of this cantonment. *It could happen again!* In the past four years this city has been torn apart by rioting. The whole country is in a state of dangerous unrest. Nationalism is rife. That little fellow Gandhi travels from north to south' – the pointer flickered up and down – 'east to west' – side to side – 'fomenting trouble, stirring up the natives. His Excellency the Commander-in-Chief, Head of the British Army in India, Field Marshal Sir Philip Chetwode, contends that the British armed forces *alone* stand between order and anarchy! That means *you*.' The adjutant turned and swung the pointer towards the seated recruits. Its tip made a wavelike motion along the rows of newly arrived soldiers.

'And do you know how many troops there are in India like yourselves? Who knows?' The pointer flickered interrogatively. Nobody moved.

'Sixty thousand! *Sixty thousand*, to control this vast nation of three hundred million people! *That* is the responsibility you bear!'

His fierce eyes travelled along the lines of young men – boys, really. He looked at Sam, seated between Ivor and Sidney, his small face intent and awed. Good God, he thought, they send us children and expect us to govern savages! Sam's back became even more rigid under the colonel's gaze. The colonel's own spine stiffened fractionally as he concluded, 'The danger of disorder is ever-present in India. The population is inflammable. Jealousy and ill feeling are rife, made worse by rumbling, empty stomachs. This can, *and does*, lead to riot and public disturbances. Nowhere in the world is there more need for courageous and prompt action, and nowhere is the penalty for hesitation and weakness greater. The army could do with many more troops. There are, I repeat, sixty thousand, and our job – your job – the job of His Majesty's troops in India – is to prevent internal disorder if or when the police should fail at this task, and if necessary to quell it. This means that each and every one of you may find himself facing a lawless and violent mob driven by frenzy. Steel yourselves, every last man' – he looked at Sam again – 'and boy, to do your duty for King and Empire!'

The adjutant's pointer flicked upwards as the colonel prepared to leave. Sixty recruits snapped to their feet, the colonel wheeled, descended the three steps from the platform and marched out of the hall, leaving sixty sober and thoughtful new India hands in his wake.

The adjutant spoke for the first time.

'Your sergeant-major will now take you to the parade ground for half an hour's drill. I hope its importance has been made clear to you all. Perpetual readiness is our best defence. After that you will go to the canteen for lunch. After lunch you will lie on your beds for an hour. This is not because you need to rest but for your own protection, since the heat in the middle of the day is insupportable to Europeans. At four o'clock you will reassemble here, when I myself will give you the benefit of my knowledge of the flora, fauna and native population of the United Provinces.' The pointer flickered briefly towards the top right-hand corner of the map. When the adjutant turned back from the board, the sergeant-major had materialized on the dais beside him.

'Sergeant-major,' he said, and the two exchanged a salute before the adjutant, stiff-legged in his polished boots, stepped down from the dais and vanished into the brilliance beyond the door.

It was supposed to be the cool season, but the heat at noon was stifling. The cantonment was vast, some two miles by three, but well laid out and orderly after the confusion of the city. It was systematically arranged with bungalows, mess buildings and parade grounds linked by wide avenues bordered with trees. There were polo fields, a race course, tennis and badminton courts. There were tree-shaded clubs for officers with wide verandahs, reclining chairs and rattan tables at which they could lounge, cooling their thirst with ice-filled drinks and smoking du Maurier or Sullivan & Powell cigarettes like the English gentlemen they were back home. They lived in white villas in rooms where punkahs moved the air languorously to and fro. Their wives strolled in spacious gardens and had Indian women to mind their babies; other Indians to cook and garden and wash and press their clothes, leaving the wives to droop with boredom. There was no club for other ranks, just the regimental canteen and bar, with squat bungalows for the older, married NCOs. A memorial church and a Methodist chapel catered for their spiritual welfare. There were dormitory blocks, each one guarded by a sergeant's bungalow; and every one of these buildings had an overhanging roof shading a wide verandah; every opening was covered with slatted blinds, in an effort to cool the rooms and keep out the hot gritty dust.

Jake Roberts, for the first time in his swaggering seventeen years, found himself ill at ease. He had never wanted to come to this heathen country or even to join the army. His chief motive had been to spite Sam Savage; the long-hated Sam Savage

whose cleverness, decency and even smallness rebuked everything he was himself. In the recesses of his mind clanged the
hated words, ''E *dusna* know *narthen*.'

Jake had harboured the desire to get the better of Sam for so
long that it had become his main reason for living. Because of
his size, strength and viciousness Jake had easily dominated his
classmates and the smaller boys below him, but he had no
friends; only hangers-on who preferred his protection to his
bullying. The people worth impressing – Miss Jamieson, the
vicar and his wife, even, curse her, skinny Edith Satterthwaite –
turned away from him, grimacing in exasperation. He longed to
hear his teacher say, '*Good*, Jake!' or the vicar exclaim with surprise, 'Well *done*, Roberts!' the way Sam and Edith were praised
all the time. It did not occur to him or anyone else that he
missed his real father – whoever he might have been – and hated
the stepfather who had usurped his place in his mother's warm
bed. Lizzie and Rose, his sisters, blended into one doting figure
but once they married and started to have children of their own,
they had become more and more remote.

Jake had noticed how, out here in India, Sam's eyes were
everywhere, seeming to make sense of the bewildering horde of
animals, people, transport and chaos that unnerved Jake. He
had not lied when he said he had bought the body of a slender
Indian girl, but her alien smell and utter passivity had repelled
him and her dark skin seemed more like that of a cow than a
human being. Secretly, Jake had been disgusted by the girl, and
by himself, and enraged by his failure to raise a glimmer of envy
or admiration in Sam. Some of the other recruits were already
ganging up around him, finding in his brute strength and foul
language the only kind of manliness they understood. He would
work on them and plant lies about Sam that would make him
the outcast of the barracks. He would plot some retaliation that
would have Sam on his knees, begging for mercy. And when
that happened . . . maybe he would relent, maybe not.

Later that afternoon the men reassembled for the adjutant's lecture. On the blackboard hung a fraying roll of illustrated oil-cloth. It had begun to uncurl and the words *Animals and Birds of* could be seen on the top page. Below it, on the bottom of the first two sheets, animals' feet were visible . . . a tiger's paws, an elephant's horny toes and the curl of its wrinkled trunk. Shere Khan, thought Sam; Hathi, and probably Bagheera, Baloo and the Bandar-log as well!

The adjutant mounted the platform and surveyed the lines of recruits.

'Good afternoon, men.'

'G'afternoon, *sir*!'

'Sit down.'

With his pointer he smoothed down the front page of the roll to reveal its complete title: *Animals and Birds of the Upper Provinces with some notes on habitat*. He flipped it deftly over the top of the blackboard. On the next sheet stood a ponderous elephant flanked by diminutive natives and a palm tree.

'Who knows the name of this animal?'

Sixty hands shot up. With the pointer he indicated Jake.

'Elephant, *sir*!'

'Good man. Elephant. You won't see many of them in this part of India. The friend and servant of man, also sacred to the god of rain. As you will soon learn, just about every animal in this country is sacred to some god or other.'

They tittered sycophantically.

'Better remember which. Hurt their feelings by insulting their gods and you could find yourself with a knife through your ribs.' He turned the sheet over to reveal the next page. A magnificent tiger shouldered through long grass towards a hunter perched on top of an elephant, gun at the ready. In the background two dead tigers were stretched out in front of a semicircle of solar-topeed hunters.

'Anyone *not* know the name of this animal?'

A couple of foolish hands were raised and, after a few seconds' sniggering, lowered. The pointer swung towards one.

'Sir, tiger, sir.'

'*Tiger*. Average length, eight feet from nose to tail. Bag yourself a twelve-footer and you're close to a record. No good to eat but very good to kill. Next!'

A colony of monkeys perched in the treetops. 'These?'

Hands shot up. The pointer quivered towards Sam.

'Monkeys, sir! Bandar-log!'

'Band o' *what*?'

In a less confident voice Sam repeated, '*Bandar-log*, sir. That's what Mowgli called them. I mean in *The Jungle Books*, sir.'

The others shifted nervously, not sure whether Sam was doing well or making a fool of himself. The adjutant, who had not read *The Jungle Books* but knew of their author, said, 'When I want Mr Kipling's advice I'll ask him for it. Name?'

'Savage, sir.'

'Savage by name and savage by nature, I dare say.' Bolder titters. The adjutant swivelled back to the illustration and repeated, '*Monkeys*. Bloody nuisance. Steal your food, throw things at you, infest the villages and temples, natives won't touch 'em. Why?'

A dozen hands.

'Is it because they're sacred, sir?'

'*Because they're sacred*. To a god called Hanuman. Plenty more reasons for leaving them alone. In the first place they're no use if you do bag one – can't skin it, can't eat it, can't stick its head on the wall – and in the second, a wounded monkey looks altogether too much like a human infant. So you ignore them. Next.' A picture of a herd of blue-black deer – *nilghai*, thought Sam, but didn't say so – another of a different, smaller variety: *chinkara* or ravine deer, then a pack of wolves.

'The wolf. A savage, unreliable brute, one up from the hyena or jackal for low cunning and reckless killing.' Sam winced at the injustice of this description. 'Still find plenty around the banks of the Ganges. Dangerous to man if cornered, and to the natives if hungry or with young.'

The lecture continued. Sam did his best to listen although the heat and stillness of the stuffy hall made him drowsy.

'All these are, or were until recently, found in this part of India. Apart from monkeys and the odd deer you probably won't see any of 'em. The only animals *you*'re likely to come across are cattle and they're sacred for Hindus, which is why the perishers wander all over the place getting in everyone's way. The bull is holy because they believe the god Shiva rides on one. The cow is their symbol of bounteous Mother Nature.'

Picture of cow with calf. Picture of goat. Picture of wild pig. Picture of domestic pig rooting in ordure. Warning about Muslims, pig untouchable to, not because holy but because filth-carrier, same cautions apply. Next, snakes.

'Snakes are also thought to possess supernatural powers so don't let a Hindu see you kill one or he'll get over-excited. Cobras are specially holy and specially poisonous, particularly when their hoods are raised like this' – picture of cobra with raised hood – 'so leave them strictly alone. Snake-charmers, for the use of, *only*. And if you ever come across one of *these*' – he flipped over to the next picture showing a python – 'give him a very wide berth indeed because this fellow can *hug* you to death.'

The familiar words rang in Sam's memory: *Kaa was not a poison-snake – in fact he rather despised poison-snakes as cowards – but his strength lay in his hug, and when he had once lapped his huge coils round anybody there was no more to be said.* The adjutant droned on . . . porcupine (Ikki, Sam supplied automatically) . . . hare, fox . . . Sam and several others dozed, but unluckily for Sam his was the only name the adjutant knew.

'Savage! Am I boring you?'

'No, sir! Sorry, sir . . .'

He was saved, literally, by the bell. The church clock across the compound tolled its deep, curiously English note. Five times. Five o'clock. The adjutant unhooked the roll from the top of the blackboard and tucked it under his arm along with the pointer. The drowsy recruits jumped to their feet and the lesson was over.

A few days later, like all newly arrived men, they were marched to the British cemetery and All Souls Memorial Church. Here they were lectured about the events of the Indian Mutiny and shown the tablets to those who had died, each with its pathetic inscription. *Memorial in Memory of an Excellent Son, erected by his Afflicted Parents, who while gallantly fulfilling his duties was treacherously killed by the mutineers in the boats at Cawnpore, 27 June 1857, in his 18th year. Respected and beloved by all who knew him . . . Lieutenant Philip Hayes Jackson and Jane Amelia his wife and her brother Ralph Blythe Cooke, all massacred by the rebels at Cawnpore, 27 June 1857.* The concluding admonition rang in Sam's ears: *Vengeance is mine, saith the Lord; I will repay!* In the nearby cemetery a dozen Indian gardeners walked between the tidy graves, sprinkling them from a hose connected to a huge waterdrum on stilts, keeping the graves and the memories green. Sam thought their memories should be left in peace before they led to more killing, but he didn't risk saying so. He couldn't even put his thoughts on paper in case outgoing letters were read and besides, he was not at all sure that Edith would agree.

CHAPTER THREE

January–June 1936

Take up the White Man's Burden –
And reap his old reward:
The blame of those ye better,
The hate of those ye guard.
Rudyard Kipling, 'The White Man's Burden'

CHRISTMAS CAME AND WENT, MARKED BY PAPER CHAINS, FAKE holly and a fake Christmas tree in the regimental bar. Christmas lunch – dry turkey with tinned sprouts followed by tinned plum pudding doused in brandy with blue flames flickering round the base – was paraded round the canteen by a grinning but baffled Indian cookboy. They pulled crackers and wore paper hats. After they had risen to their feet for the loyal toast the presiding captain uttered the traditional words, 'You may now smoke!' and every hand reached into a top pocket for Players' Navy Cut. At one rupee for twenty, even those who had not been smokers when they arrived in India were now – except Sam. He had tried once or twice but disliked the sooty aftertaste that clogged his mouth and nostrils.

For the last two months he had put up with mockery and horseplay. As the butt of Jake's gang he suffered in silence when they threw his kit about the barracks, forcing him to stoop, retrieve and clean it all again. Their idea of a joke was leaving greasy fingermarks on his trumpet, or matches and cigarette ends stuffed down it. He guessed that some of the others were sympathetic but nobody wanted to incur Jake Roberts's wrath ... better to let some other poor devil be the victim. His three friends could do little to help, beyond telling him to give Jake a wide berth. ''E be dangerous; Oi know 'is sort,' Ivor said darkly. 'Oi seen 'em on farm, takkin' pot-shots at cats and birds with catapult or chuckin' paraffin over kittens 'n' settin' fire to 'em. 'Im'll go after thee for fun o' hearin' thou squeal.'

'Then 'e'll be waitin' when Doomsday strikes,' Sam had replied stoutly, 'fer I won't niver squeal.'

New Year 1936 was welcomed in with scenes of revelry and drunkenness. The regimental band had played for the officers during their dinner and been cheered, ending with a ceremonial march round the candlelit mess. It went on to play jollier tunes for the NCOs. Sam had been released, but he did not care to sit alone in the dormitory so instead he lolled in the depths of a rattan armchair in the canteen, watching the goings-on. He was pressed to join in the fun and foaming beer glasses were pushed towards him, but he had promised Edith not to touch strong liquor. To please the vicar's wife, who campaigned strenuously against drunkenness, he had also taken the pledge. He grinned and shook his head.

It was nearly midnight. The sergeant-major and a couple of NCOs were about to make their genial way towards the bar to chivvy the lads to bed. Drinking hours and lights out had both been extended by special dispensation to mark New Year's Eve and by now plenty of men had been drinking steadily for three or four hours. The place was in a state of pleasant male uproar. Hand and eye were too unreliable for snooker but several card games were in raucous dispute and much pay had been gambled and lost. Sam and his mates bent towards one another in a nostalgic quartet, crooning the remembered songs. Suddenly, Jake and some of his gang loomed over them. Jake prodded Sam.

''Ee dun't drink, 'ee dunt smoke, 'ee dunt even cuss – what'd 'ee join army fer?' Jake sneered.

'Play trumpet,' Sam answered.

'Aye – an' 'ee dunt do that neither!' Jake made a lewd gesture, one finger plucking at loosened lips, the other at his crutch. ''Is bint 'ad ter come to me fer a bit o' touchin' up . . .'

Jake turned away and half lurched, half strutted towards the bar. Sam got to his feet, his father's rage finally surfacing. 'I wuz so mad,' he told Albert afterwards, 'you cudda boiled a kittle on me.' Hardly knowing what he was about to do, Sam took a flying leap at Jake from behind. Wrapping his legs tightly round his tormentor's body, he leaned forward and jabbed both thumbs hard into his eyes. Taken utterly by surprise, unable to see from whom the attack came, Jake roared with pain. With huge brawny fists he tore Sam's hands away and extending his own wide, held both their arms apart. Sam, clinging like a jockey on a rearing horse, drummed his heel into Jake's groin. 'Ride 'im, cowboy!' whooped one of the onlookers. 'Yee-hah!' yodelled another. Jake fell to his knees in agony and, finding his assailant still on top of him, rolled over and tried to crush him. Sam was forced to relax the grip of his legs and Jake, one hand cupped protectively over his balls, leaped to his feet. Yelling with pain and rage, he was about to launch a volley of kicks when he found himself yanked backwards by both elbows. Sam scrambled up and his elbows too were gripped. In front of them, dangerously immobile, stood the sergeant-major.

'Take 'em to the main guard room,' he ordered the NCOs holding the pair. 'Lock 'em up. Roberts! Savage! You'll both go in front of the CO tomorrow. *And may God have mercy on you . . .*'

Bearing in mind the fact that it was New Year's Eve and Savage – although the instigator of the scrap – was said by witnesses not to have touched a drop of alcohol while Roberts was paralytic; bearing in mind the fact that they both came from the same village and thus, the CO guessed, a long history lay behind this particular attack; but above all because he was a wise, experienced and humane man who knew the effect India could have on young soldiers a long way from home, he let them off lightly. After reading the charge he lifted his head and looked at them. Through swollen lids and bloodshot eyes, Jake stared sullenly back.

'Attention!' rapped the sergeant-major and the two, already rigid, stiffened further.

'Because there are no bones broken, no outsiders were present and no damage was done to army property, I shall exercise my prerogative and go easy on you both. Twenty-four hours' solitary confinement. After that – Roberts: barred from the wet canteen – Savage: barred from band rehearsals – for a week. But if anything like this ever happens again, believe me, you'll both have cause to regret it. Dismiss!'

Sam was not put out by solitary confinement, or by Jake's harsh whispered threats. All he had to show for the fight were two vivid red circles round his wrists where Jake had wrenched away his fiercely jabbing fingers, and bruises all over his body from the weight of his enemy as they rolled on the floor. He would have endured far worse for the sake of the huge grin he could not suppress whenever he thought of Jake's public humiliation. Sam had proved, in front of the entire company, that he was not a coward. If only he'd had pen and paper to write and tell Edith about it he would have been almost happy.

When they were released next day, Jake's eyes looked like scarlet ping-pong balls and he could hardly see. He was marched off to the doctor for ointment. Sam hoped it stung. After this their beds were separated. Jake was moved down to the bed beside the door while Sam slept at the far end, in the bed next to Albert. For a while the taunting ceased but Jake brooded heavily on revenge. The hated words whispered in his head:

'*Sam, listen to me: "He does not know anything." Now you say it.*'

'*'E* dusna *know* narthen.'

He would kill Sam if he got the chance; and he didn't care if he swung for it. In due course his eyes turned from red to purple, then a murky green, eventually fading to yellow. Sam's bruises did the same.

One evening in the canteen Sam was reading the *Daily Mirror* when he came across a piece of news that made him sit up and read it twice. The paragraph said: *Yesterday, 18 January 1936, the popular author Rudyard Kipling died of a perforated stomach ulcer, aged 70. His wife and daughter were with him. It was snowing outside. Kipling, author of* Kim *and* Puck of Pook's Hill, *was one of our greatest writers and his chronicles of life in India are among the most vivid ever written.* Moved by the words, *It was snowing outside*, Sam gazed unseeingly at the punkah fans stirring the stale air, picturing Lower Flexham and the flat fields around it blanketed in snow . . . clean, white snow, pure and cold and crisp. He understood for the first time why some people hated India.

He was unmoved by the death of George V two days later but the news threw the regiment into a frenzy of patriotism. Patriotism meant polishing, practising, playing in the band, marching and more marching. They made garrison marches through the city, ostensibly in mourning for the late King, in fact to demonstrate the continuity of British rule; and marched again to mark the accession of the new one. *Deep Gloom All*

Over India, proclaimed a headline in the *Times of India*, but it wasn't true. Not since Queen Victoria had the King-Emperor meant much to the Indian people. The marching did not prevent a flurry of rioting throughout Cawnpore. As Sam strode through the city, a brilliant sky reflected in the highly polished brass of his trumpet, he could see beyond it the scowling faces of the crowds at the side of the road. He felt their resentment and dislike as if it were a sound, a low growl passing from throat to wrathful throat. We are not the rulers here, he realized; we are barely even tolerated. They are biding their time, like Jake.

Weeks passed and the weather grew steadily hotter. By April the temperature was high enough to count as a heatwave in East Anglia. Just walking from the barracks to canteen, church or parade ground made Sam break out in a prickly sweat. He felt listless and confused. Like everyone else in 'D' dormitory, he spent as much time as possible lying on his bed watching through half-closed eyes as the punkah flapped lazily. The sergeant-major did his best to keep discipline up to scratch, shouting orders and castigating the latecomer, the straggler, the insufficiently highly polished. The bored and drooping men under his command tried feebly to comply. Once, Sam tried speaking normally to Jake: 'Lork, what'd I give to be back 'ome under a nice shower o' rain!' Jake turned his head swiftly and spat into the grey dust. Right, Sam thought, I bin warned. No quarter.

Edith, too, had warned him about Jake. Troubled by his account of their fight, her answering letter – three months later – said: *Do look out for him, my dear. I know Jake Roberts and he is a slow burner. He will keep a grudge like a ferret under his coat and bring it out when you don't expect it. I am that proud of thee for standing up to him but you aren't any good to me dead. Mark my words, he isn't to be trusted.*

Spring had been bad enough. Early summer was worse. May was an exceptionally hot month even by Cawnpore standards, the temperature around 110° in the shade – what shade there was – day after day. Families living in the cantonment began to disappear to the hills. Some of the younger officers were also allowed a break, a fortnight at a time. For the ordinary soldiers there was nothing. They had to stay and suffer the heat. 'Like it or lump it, lads,' said their sergeant-major, running a finger inside the damp collar of his summer-issue shirt and jacket. Everyone's armpits were stained and darkened by sweat but each morning the camp washermen produced fresh, starched, ironed, spotless shirts. No soldier in India, however lowly, cleaned anything except his own kit. Every other task – scrubbing out the barracks, preparing vegetables, washing up or other fatigues – was done by Indian servants.

Regular food had filled Sam out and regular exercise had added another couple of inches to his height since they first landed in Bombay, yet he remained very much a boy. He was more thoughtful than most lads of his age but he was still an innocent, sweet-natured boy. The arrival of the post was the high spot of the month and he pored over Edith's letters. She wrote every two weeks and, despite the time-lapse between his writing and her reply, they had established a rhythm of correspondence. Her news evoked the green and golden landscape of Lower Flexham, its familiar people and their special way of talking. The shy, affectionate words with which she closed every letter made him yearn to be back with her. The latest one had concluded: *I miss thee, my li'l old Sam, and sometimes wonder if we was silly not to make the most of our time together.* Could this possibly mean what he thought it meant?

One evening, remembering that it would soon be her birthday, Sam made up his mind to go to the native bazaar at Sati-Chowra, on the banks of the river near the Memorial Cross, to choose a present for Edith. This bazaar was not out of bounds, being within the cantonment area, and its vendors were supposed to be honest. He asked his three friends to come with him for support. He knew better than to risk going alone – and knew that Jake, rather than the natives, posed the greater threat.

The four set off together, Sam clutching ten rupees saved from last month's pay. The sun had set but heat still brooded in the air. The moon hung, soft and brilliant, above the cantonment trees and the dust in the atmosphere made it shine with a curious powdery radiance. A tatty parade of stalls, festooned with canvas awnings and cheap advertisements, was lit by Tilley lamps that hissed softly. Like all native areas, it smelled of roasting corn, sweetmeats and spices from the braziers, which could not mask the underlying stink of dirt and excrement. Stallholders darted forward trying to attract custom, shouting at one another, grasping the sleeves of passers-by, shoving up close, wafting hot breath into their faces. One dark-skinned fellow even smaller than Sam himself wheedled, 'Sahib, sahib, this way, soldier-sahib . . . very good prices!'

Sam said, as he heard others say, '*Jao, jao*' – go away – and '*Jaldi karo!*' – be quick! This unleashed a volley of Hindustani, flowing through the man's lips in a rapid sing-song chatter. Sam shook him off, saying to Albert, 'This blinking market-wallah wun't leave me alone!'

Ivor said, 'They dunnt want to leave their stall far be'ind. Keep on walkin', ignore 'im. *Sur ka bacha!*' he hissed at the man, who dropped back with a furious look and spat into the dust.

'What'd thou say to 'im?' Sam asked admiringly.

'I dunno, but it's some kinda curse these fellers dunt like. Gets rid o' 'em!'

Sickly-looking dogs skulked behind the stalls, worrying at flaking patches of skin, snapping at fleas or turning in wild circles. Rabies, thought Sam fearfully; the dreaded hydrophobia that drives a man mad before it kills him.

Old women with plaited grey hair and stringy limbs hobbled

past. Lively black-eyed children darted in and out of the mayhem. There were even a few native women in brilliantly coloured saris but they averted their eyes, showing proper respect, unlike the men who stared insolently and made bold, beckoning gestures. At the edge of the darkness behind the stalls, Sam saw two men fall upon a youth, knock him down and start to beat and kick his defenceless body. It's true what they tell us, he thought bitterly. Mowgli is a story for children. These people are wholly savages.

He speeded up past the covered stalls. He had the sudden feeling that anything could be bought here . . . some forbidden substance like opium or whatever it was they smoked through long hubble-bubble pipes, something whose sweet, complicated odour coiled between other, sharper smells. His rupees would buy him a snake or a monkey; the body of a woman or a child; the death of a man; or just the innocent trinket he sought. The bazaar was a place of danger and wickedness. 'I dunnt like it 'ere,' he said suddenly to Sidney. 'Us shud be on our way.'

'But thee ain't got no present for thy best girl,' Sidney said. 'Look – 'ere be pretty things. Find summat 'ere and then us'll go back.'

A gleaming array of gold ornaments was laid out on a piece of red velvet cloth. There were gold or glass bangles such as all Indian women wore jingling at their wrists; twisting gold necklaces, pendants set with brightly coloured stones, rings for the fingers, ears or nose, flashing and enticing. On a dark blue velvet tray at the back lay a number of silver rings with duller stones. They looked more real, less garishly native. Sam indicated these and the man lifted the tray eagerly and, bowing, tilted it up beside the light to show it off.

'Tip-top, soldier-sahib, all very tip-top!' he said.

One filigree silver ring was set with three opaque blue stones, uncut turquoise, the middle one deeper blue than the others and irregularly shaped. Sam pointed at it.

'Very excellent choice, tophole!' said the man. 'Only twenty rupees for the sahib.'

Sam turned to his friends. 'Oi cunn't afford that. Oi only got ten.'

'Bargain with 'im, go on. 'E'll tak' seven. Offer 'im foive.'

Sam fidgeted in his pocket where he had been clutching the coins in his fist for safety and extracted five. He held them up to the man, who shook his head.

'Think 'e'll tak ten?' Sam muttered.

'It's far too much!' whispered Sidney. ''T'ain't worth five.'

'It be,' Sam said stubbornly. Sidney turned as if to go and fearing all three would leave, the man beckoned to Sam, took his five rupees and dropped the ring into a little paper bag.

'Check it, make sure 'e 'asn't cheated thee,' Ivor advised.

Sam looked. There it was, his ring for Edith. He couldn't resist giving the stallholder a radiant smile and, equally radiant, the man smiled back.

After seven months in India, Sam had made other friends in the dormitory besides Sidney, Ivor and Albert. He was welcomed into the camaraderie of the band, which included men of all ages, not just young recruits. He had become proficient on the trumpet and loved the full-throated sound of the band in full swing, its stamping rhythms and rousing crescendos. He liked the feeling of being one among many, contributing his small but necessary sound. He especially liked guest nights on Fridays in the officers' mess, the formality and decorum, the hierarchy of crisp white uniforms, the elegant progress of the meal, enlivened by the music they played . . . Gilbert and Sullivan, Rossini, Offenbach, sometimes Elgar . . . rousing, sparkling, charming tunes from another continent.

Jake was jealous of this too, but Jake was as patient as a farm cat crouching beside a mousehole. He seemed to take no notice of Sam and never spoke to him, but the weight of his brooding revenge was an ever-present threat. San had learned long ago that being forewarned was the best way to avoid his father's beatings and he watched Jake covertly until he could anticipate his movements and habits. He always knew where Jake was, in a room, in the canteen, on the parade ground. Only when Jake vanished into the cantonment bazaar in the evenings – as he frequently did – was Sam uneasy.

It was probably on one of these sorties that Jake picked up his first bout of malaria. The MO had instructed them on arrival in precautions they must not fail to observe – sleeves rolled down to the wrists, especially in the evenings, when mosquitoes were most common; mosquito nets draped securely over the beds in summer – but Jake swaggered through the bazaar with rolled-up sleeves as though he were immune, slapping impatiently at his bare forearm from time to time. One night in the dormitory he began to complain of a chill. The others laughed disbelievingly, being themselves clammy with heat, but soon afterwards Jake's teeth began to chatter. Despite the chill, his temperature soared. Then he leaned over the side of his bed and vomited. At this point, although it was half-past two in the morning, Sidney Hale cursed, pulled on his shorts and went to fetch the sergeant. He took one look at Jake and had him transferred to the sickbay, where the MO diagnosed malaria. Jake was liberally dosed with Dr Collis-Browne's Chlorodyne, sponged with ice-cold water every few hours and ordered to rest completely. After less than a week he was back in the dormitory; pale, listless and temporarily chastened. After this he wore his shirt-cuffs buttoned but the malaria parasite had taken hold and he suffered recurring though progressively less serious episodes of headache, fever and drenching sweats. These intervals were the only times throughout his service in India when Sam was free of the feeling of menace that otherwise dogged him.

One hot evening in the canteen Sam was drinking ice-cold lemonade while glancing through the papers and magazines scattered about. To his surprise he found an article about Grimsby Town Football Club in the *Times of India*. He looked around for his friends. Ivor and Sidney were drooping over the billiard table, glasses of iced beer beside them. Sam beckoned excitedly and they came across. Sam pointed to the headline and Sidney held up the paper and began to read aloud. Soon other men gathered round, avid to hear news of their club. It had ended the season sixth from the bottom of the first division. On the far side of the room, Jake wound up the gramophone, put a record on the turntable and bellowed along with the cocky little song, '*Who's afraid of the big bad wolf?*' His pals joined in, guffawing and clapping one another on the back. After this brief raucous outburst the bar subsided into lethargy.

By early June, after a fortnight of baking winds and intense heat, the city and the cantonment steamed like a cauldron under pressure. Leprosy was rife in the slums and streets; agitators were at work and several cotton mills went on strike. The garrison was often called out to parade a show of strength it did not really possess. 'Co-operation with Britain should be your watchword!' the outgoing Viceroy declared in his final message to the Indian people, but the words rang hollow. Unrest – dignified by Gandhi's followers as Civil Disobedience – unrest was everywhere, spreading like bindweed, rooted deep in the country's past.

The Upper Provinces that summer didn't only suffer from political upheavals. There was a series of natural convulsions bad enough to unnerve the British and fill the native population with panic. At the end of May Lucknow had been shaken by a violent earth tremor. Crops shivered as though a mighty wind had rushed over them; the ground moved and shook the trees, making the birds and monkeys perched along their branches cry out in alarm. Fragile buildings in the centre of the city wobbled and many collapsed. The streets swarmed with terrified people on the verge of anarchy. Two weeks later, shielding their eyes, they stared at a partial eclipse of the sun, muttering that it was a portent; it boded ill. The air grew thicker and dustier, rasping the skin and parching the throat. The heat was abnormal; the fierce, dry wind almost unbearable. There was no sign of an early monsoon.

Sam adapted to the heat better than most. His skin turned nut-brown rather than burning. Jake, because of his bulk, was particularly unsuited to it. His face and hands swelled up, becoming inflamed and shiny like a blood sausage, and he suffered blinding headaches. Sidney overheard one of Jake's cronies saying to another, 'He's that mad, there'll be murder done before summer's out . . .' and although Sam tried to laugh it off, the threat quivered in his mind like a scorpion. The dormitory was divided into pro- and anti-Jake factions though if it came to blows not everyone would join in. Sam did his best never to be caught on his own, walking from barracks to canteen flanked by his mates, making sure he was with one or two others when he went to rehearsals and back. He did not dream of making a complaint and besides, what was there to complain of? It was nearly six months since their fight yet Jake had not laid a finger on Sam; hardly even looked at him. He was biding his time.

CHAPTER FOUR

June–July 1936

The pools are shrunk – the streams are dry,
And we be playmates, thou and I,
Till yonder cloud – Good Hunting! – loose
The rain that breaks our Water Truce.
Rudyard Kipling, 'How Fear Came'

THE MONSOON FINALLY BROKE ON A MONDAY TOWARDS THE end of June. More than two inches of rain fell on the first day. First a few, then a volley of large drops fell to the ground; then an explosion of bouncing bubbles, until water spiralled from every tree, roof, verandah and umbrella. Parched flowers released a gust of scent before being battered to the ground. After weeks of scorching heat the rain was a blissful relief. Everything that had been dry was wet; everything dusty became shiny. As the downpour increased it was followed by a weird agitation in the atmosphere that seemed to disturb people's balance and churn up their minds. The empty skies darkened with black clouds, then were torn by sheet lightning and deafening thunderclaps. Everyone's clothes were sodden and

247

clinging. 'Us look like drowned rats,' said Ivor. Monsoon rain was like no other rain Sam had known. 'Rainin' stair-rods,' his mother used to say of a heavy downpour in Suffolk, but this rain was an unstoppable force of nature. Solid blocks of water hammered the ground, pounding the tiled roof of the barracks and sending a river of mud through the cantonment.

The rain made little difference to the rehearsing, marching and parading – the only activities left to the garrison – but since the parade ground was washed out, all exercise had to be taken in one of the steamy corrugated iron-roofed drill halls. Birds swooped and twittered in the rafters while underneath the men marched and swung their arms, wheeled, turned, peeled off like a line of stamps torn along the perforations, re-formed and marched perfectly on. Drill gave them a workout and was supposed to be good for morale but the cooped-up soldiers, seeing the same faces day in and day out, needed better distraction to take their minds off the boredom of their routine. Forty minutes' hard drill left them dripping with sweat but no less discontented. Weapons were guarded twenty-four hours a day, rifles oiled and checked and polished, stores delivered, orders issued, anniversaries marked with a display of pomp.

On the new King-Emperor's birthday, Sam marched at the head of the regimental band through the cantonment's tall wrought-iron gates and paraded round the city delivering the national anthem to a drenched and shifty audience corralled behind lines of white-uniformed local policemen with menacing bamboo sticks. It was all show and little substance. What chance had a blond, blue-eyed King thousands of miles away against the small stooped brown man who travelled everywhere and was seen uttering impassioned appeals to conscience, pride and justice? Gandhi's talk of truth and non-violence was honest and straightforward, his moral certainties overwhelming. Yet one peaceable figure swathed in homespun cotton could not prevent the threat of anarchy. Sixty thousand fearful, dispirited British servicemen longing for cool English weather and home cooking would not keep the lid on India's hissing kettle for much longer.

By now Sam had seen enough of India to suspect that their presence in Cawnpore was futile. He sensed the panic behind the army's rigid ceremonial and discipline. During their frequent patrols through the city he saw poverty, disease and starvation. The cantonment servants were as obsequious as ever but the faces in the streets were not friendly. Only the children grinned and danced, only little boys swung their arms and marched briefly alongside the band before being hauled back by a scowling parent. Menace choked the air. *It is Fear, Little Brother, it is Fear!*

The annual parade to commemorate the siege and slaughter of 1857 was one of the main events in their calendar. Rage at the massacre still burned among both British and Indians. Sam knew only one side of the story: that the few survivors of the six-week siege of Cawnpore had been promised safe passage but within moments of setting off, helpless and unarmed, in open boats down the Ganges they were fired on from the bank. Few recognizable bodies were left for burial and by the time the relieving forces arrived there was little left to bury. The place where they died was marked by a cross on the bank near where the cantonment bazaar now swarmed. The memorial week was preceded by days of rehearsal. The effort of thumping and blowing in the stifling humidity made several band members faint, whereupon the bandmaster would march furiously over to the fallen man, slap his cheeks to revive him, jerk him to his feet and yell into his face, 'Can't stick a bit of heat? Think it was any different for them? *They* stuck it but *you* keel over like a bleedin' schoolgirl! Pull yourself together, man, *play*!' and the rehearsal would continue. On the day of the memorial parade the band, with Sam in the front row, led the soaking wet regiment in paying its respects, ending at the church where the dead were commemorated in elaborate Gothic lettering. Burdened with an overactive imagination, Sam hated these places, hated them more each time he was forced to go there, rootle-toot-tooting in memory of those poor ladies and their dead infants. He agreed with the inscription below the memorial tablet: it was up to the Lord to take revenge. *I* will repay, saith the Lord. Sam grimaced to himself and thought: wish someone 'ud tell Jake.

'What's us 'ere for?' Sidney grumbled. 'Eight months an' I've 'ad enough. Oi'm chockful of India. Big country, dirty people, weather's a washout – might as well go 'ome. No point in loafing about or marchin' up 'n' down in straight lines to exercise sergeant-major's lungs. Not gunna learn to talk the lingo; not gunna pick a fight. Wastin' our time.'

Sam heartily agreed. The wild world of Mowgli and his companions was a fantasy, fit only for small boys. Now that he was among men he had learned the harshness of communal life, its crude appetites and foul language. 'I've had a bellyful too,' he said, 'an' ter tell thee truth, 'and on 'eart, I'm in a blue funk about Jake Roberts. 'T'ain't natural fer 'im to 've bin this quiet this long. 'E's got to blow soon. 'E'll go on the rampage, smash things up, an' me with 'em.'

Not even the rain dampened Jake's hot blood: if anything, it made him worse.

The dormitory divided into men who toadied up to Jake and those who were disgusted by his brutish, scowling manner and blatant depravity. In the evenings, Jake and his cronies would break off their card schools to slip into the dark recesses of the cantonment with little Indian boys who supplied sex for a few annas. As they grew more confident they sought out forbidden brothels where for a rupee they could do what they liked to the body of a slim Indian girl. After these encounters they would swagger back into the bar or dormitory, grinning and boastful.

The coarse sexual talk in the dormitory no longer passed over

Sam's head. To his shame, occasionally he found himself stirring and rising in response. He had become an adolescent, if not yet a man, and was disturbed by vivid dreams. Sometimes they were about Edith but lately they had conjured up the slight dark bodies of little Indian girls. No bigger than children, they already had dark buds on their ribcages and would look at him with sidelong, wheedling glances, crooking their slender fingers invitingly . . . Sam would wake with a start and a stifled cry in a sticky puddle, confused and mortified.

The monsoon became exceptionally, freakishly heavy. Water levels recorded by the rain-gauges outside each barracks were higher than they had been for years. A few more days of this, and vast swathes of the Upper Provinces would be inundated. By the first week in July the Gumti, the river that flowed through Lucknow and irrigated scores of villages beyond it, was in flood. If it burst its banks, the city and most of the villages bordering it would be drowned. The Indian Army and police moved in to evacuate people but they refused to leave unless their cattle, grain and possessions were carried with them to safety. Since this was impossible they were left to their fate. Posters were put up proclaiming: *Strong bamboo poles supported by thick ropes have been suspended from the arches of all the bridges in the city so that anyone swept away by the strong current may find support and be saved from drowning*, but those in most danger were illiterate and the posters went unread. Only the cows paused to nibble at the ropes as they lumbered over the bridges, wet flanks gleaming.

Accidents happen, people live or die, whether they call it *karma*, destiny or bloody bad luck. A British soldier – Lance-Corporal Totten – drowned in the Gumti despite frantic efforts by his comrades to save him, when his mule went into deep water and he slipped off. They found his body floating in the swollen river next day. Early in July a certain Captain Hills, who weighed eighteen stone, was impaled on his shooting stick while umpiring a cricket match. He was rushed to hospital but the army surgeon couldn't save him. Finally, invisibly, the monsoon sparked a series of chain reactions that linked Sam and Jake to Lakshmi. Jake's slow-burning anger against Sam was the fuse. Sam's tense, impartial waiting – would he murder Jake, would Jake murder him, or would they hop at each other's wedding? – was the wire. Lakshmi's decision to fetch help for her sister was the detonator. Each would have been unscathed without the others. Jake might have gone through life guilty of little more than cruelty to animals and a few drunken brawls. Sam might have enthralled his children with stories about India – stories, perhaps, owing more to Kipling than to his personal experience. Lakshmi might have had her moment of heroism and been pointed out for ever afterwards as an unusually brave girl, even if she did have a funny eye. But the three were being drawn closer every time she placed one foot in front of the other, left, right, left, right. Tomorrow is the day after tomorrow's yesterday . . .

It was a Thursday, the low point of the week. The men had been cooped up for most of the day, unable to do anything in such torrential rain except check and polish their equipment. They had eaten stew and sponge pudding for supper, played darts and had a few drinks in the bar. Now they lay steamily on their beds, smoking and bickering. They listened to the rain drumming on the roof and took bets as to whether it would exceed Wednesday's record of 3.1 inches. The last time anyone checked the rain-gauge outside their quarters it had just topped three inches. 'Go'n' 'ave another look, Roberts, you're nearest!' shouted one man, and Jake Roberts levered himself off the iron bedstead and walked to the door. He peered through the mesh grille, looked again disbelievingly, then turned and said with a whistle of astonishment, 'Our luck's in, lads! There's a girl out there and she's coming our way!'

A dozen men leaped off their beds simultaneously but Jake motioned them back. 'Don't do that, you'll scare 'er. Leave this to me. *I* know 'ow to talk to 'em . . .' He opened the verandah door and light flooded across the tarmac.

Jake leaned over the railing and smiled encouragingly. Lakshmi halted; but when he beckoned she began to walk uncertainly towards him. Jake came slowly, slowly – *Softlee softlee catchee monkey* – down the verandah steps and, holding out his hand, spoke in a low voice to reassure her. 'Ain't thou a *duzzy* cross-eyed monkey?' he observed pleasantly. 'Where's thy tail? Want some nuts? Follow me then . . .' Lakshmi smiled uncertainly, her smile widening as Jake uttered the only Hindustani sentence he knew, picked up from the wheedling women outside the brothels of Cawnpore: 'Come to me, dear . . .'

The distance between them narrowed; she was almost within his grasp; he could have touched her; he did. He touched, not took, her hand and indicated the dry verandah. He pointed to the door at the top of the steps, hoping the men would stay back. Lakshmi could see nothing inside. Was this where her father was? She looked at him enquiringly, and Jake smiled and nodded. Easily, without the least resistance, he escorted her up the steps, through the door and into the long bright expanse of the dormitory. When she walked in she was still smiling.

Jake slammed the inner door and, since it had no lock, banged his kit table hard up against it. He straightened, turned and said triumphantly, 'OK, lads, look what Jake Roberts has brought yer all! *Now* for some fun . . .'

Lakshmi was slow to realize what had happened. She had never been inside such a large space in her life before. She had never seen a white man, let alone more than fifty at once. She had never seen a cast-iron bed, let alone two rows of them. And on each bed sat a man, upright or leaning towards her, seeming as astonished as she was. Several had not yet noticed her and were still lounging, reading or half asleep. For a few seconds she stood and stared.

Then Jake laughed hoarsely and said, 'Right, girl, Jake goes first and second *and* third and *when* 'e's finished the rest gets their turn. Let's git yer clothes off.' He pulled her towards him, ripped off her bodice and skirt and dropped them in a sodden heap on the floor. She was naked underneath. She crouched down, crossing her arms over her body, shivering. She tried to call out for her father or Hari, but although she opened her mouth no sound emerged, only a hot exhalation of breath. Lakshmi panted, her ribs moving up and down frantically, her mouth and belly heaving deep dry gasps like a fish out of water. Jake stood above her, grinning in expectation, pulling at his fly buttons.

'Kali, great Mother goddess, help me; Ganesha, my own god, help me! Dadi, where are you, come quickly, save me from these manymanymany men! Kali, mighty Mother, help me,' Lakshmi prayed.

Sidney got off his bed and walked deliberately down the centre of the dormitory. Jake turned towards him like a dog guarding a bone.

'Fuck off,' he growled. '*I*'m 'avin' first go at 'er.'

'Leave off, Roberts,' Sidney said. 'It's only a little kid – look at it, poor thing's terrified. Leave it alone, there's a good chap.'

'Ain't no kid. Issa a *girl* – look!' and Jake yanked her upright, pulling the protective arm away from her chest. Thrown off balance, Lakshmi fell sideways revealing two small breasts, their dark nipples shrivelled in terror. She curled into a tight ball, grovelling, panting faster. *'Kali Kali Kali, help me, help me, help me, quick – or it's too late!'* Rain drummed overhead.

'Whatever it is, leave 'er be,' Sidney urged. 'You can see she ain't no whore.'

'All the better for us! Won't catch no nasty disease off 'er. Now fuck off, I told yer – wait yer fuckin' turn.'

Three other men leaped off their beds and strode towards the group. One was Albert Fitch, but since his bed was at the top end of the dormitory, furthest from the door, he was last to arrive. The other two – Fred Steemer and Jim Argent – were cronies of Jake's; big strong men, already bright-eyed with anticipation. Argent shoved Sidney aside. 'Yeah, fuck off, Hale, mind yer own fuckin' business, can't yer? Y'eard what the man said. 'E got 'er in; 'e goes in first. An' *Oi'm next,*' he added.

Jake lifted Lakshmi and carried her the few steps to his bed. He threw her across it, pulled his trousers open and forced himself inside her. '*Hari, Dadi-ji, quickly, Matin, save me from the mating of beasts! Ai, the pain, I am torn apart . . .*' At last Lakshmi cried out, a high thin wail. At the sound, Sidney and Albert tried to drag Jake away but his mates threw them off. Outnumbered by men who were thoroughly aroused, the two stood no chance if it came to a fight. Sidney turned towards the door to raise the alarm – the sergeant's house was only yards away – but another of Jake's faction was there already, knees flexed and arms spread-eagled.

'No yer fuckin' don't, 'Ale, yer fuckin' bastard. Stay where yer are or I'll bash yer bloody brains out.'

'*Too late. Dadi, Hari, stay away. The cruelty of men. My sisters, how you suffered. Wolves are tearing me apart.*'

The dormitory filled with roaring, panting, incoherent sounds. Rain drummed on the roof, louder than ever. Tonight the rain-gauge would break all records. Jake glanced along the room to where Sam was hunched on his bed, hands over his eyes, apparently gabbling to himself. 'Oi'm comin' to *yew* in a minute, li'l ol' Sam!' he shouted above the noise but Sam didn't seem to hear. 'We'll see who *dusna know narthen* now.'

Several men wanted nothing to do with her. Others would have intervened if they could, but no-one got past the thugs taking turns to stand guard and give warning should the sergeant approach. Five minutes' door duty, then back to watch.

'My turn! 'Ere, mate, you've 'ad 'er long enough!'

''E's no good, 'e can't get it oop!'

Roars of derisory laughter.

'Look 'ere, Oi'll show yer – yer gets it out an' yer shoves it in 'ard – see? Back or front, don't make no difference. Back's tighter but 't'ain't clean nor Christian.'

''Ere, Roberts, bring it over 'ere. I bin keepin' a lookout by door. Ta, mate . . . fuck me, what's 'appened to it? It's gone all floppy. Dead meat's no fun.'

'Chuck 'er on this bed 'ere . . .'

'Give us another go, Oi cum too quick.'

Lakshmi's keening had stopped. '*Kali, grind me into little pieces. Scatter my blood like rain. I will not be reborn . . .*' Her body became limp and motionless. Her eyes rolled upwards in her head. Blood and semen mottled her thighs. The air stank, like stagnant water or rotting flowers.

Sam tried to shrink into himself, to become invisible. He curled up tightly, hugging his knees, protecting his privates, making incoherent animal noises of terror and drawing harsh breaths from the pit of his lungs. Teeth chattering, eyes screwed up tight, he tried to think about Edith, to conjure up a vision of her lying in the long grass twining strands of hair round her fingers, then jumping up to pick blackberries. The thudding and panting ceased and he heard footsteps approaching, left, right, left, right. Jake stood over him, grinning.

'Sam Savage, Oi've waited a long toime fer this. On yer feet!'

'Shove off, Roberts, mind yer own business,' Sam said, trying to steady his voice.

'Oi *said*, on yer bleedin' feet! Come on, you 'eard.'

Revenge. It was good to take revenge, long-delayed, wholly satisfying revenge for the lifelong echo in his head . . .

Jake chanted out loud, 'Poor li'l babby – 'e dusna know narthen, narthen, *narthen*.'

Two men reached forward and yanked Sam off his bed. He would have sunk to the floor on boneless legs but they propped him up and dragged him to where Lakshmi sprawled, quite motionless, her knees and feet dangling over one side of the bed. She could almost have been asleep, except that her mouth was oddly swollen and distorted. Her hair spread round her head and her hands curled, palms upward, like a baby's. One dishevelled strand was trapped between her fingers.

The dark skin of her breasts was smooth and glossy, their indigo tips like ripe blackberries. Sam felt the rising of an erection and shrank away.

'Get 'is trousers down,' ordered Jake. 'Let's see if our bubba can act loike a man.'

'Yeah,' cried the sycophants. 'Let's see if he's a man!'

A pause, then a roar of laughter.

''E's a man all right, look at 'im. It may be little, but it's standin' to tenshun.'

He heard Sidney's voice.

'Yer a filthy sod, Roberts. Oi 'ope ye burn in hell.'

Several hands shoved Sam towards the bed and, as he toppled forward, pulled down his trousers. His bare thighs fell onto those of a naked female. Fumbling for his stiff little penis he pushed it between her dripping legs. As he did so he lifted his head and howled like an animal, *Uhwowwowwowaah* . . . Behind him he heard the stamping of feet, ironic applause and Jake's yell of triumph.

'Got yer, Savage! Ye'll niver live *that* down.'

SECOND INTERMISSION

The mid-1980s

'NOW *RELAX*. DON'T LOOK AT THE CAMERA. FORGET THE
audience of millions. Just imagine you're talking to *me* in your
own words. If there's anything you're not happy about we'll
stop and do it again.'

Sam nodded miserably. That was what he'd said yesterday.
The very same words. He said it to everyone. Sam now understood that, far from being friendly, this man was interrogating
him. Smiling in a relaxed sort of way, Tom Martineau sat down
in front of him and took yesterday's spiral-bound notebook out
of his pocket.

'Ready to roll, quiet please, everyone . . .'

'Sound running . . .'

'Speed . . .'

The young chap from the crew held out a clapper-board:

'*Lest We Forget*, 60, Take One.'

'Turn over.'

Perhaps he had been worrying about nothing for Tom
Martineau merely asked, 'What did the barracks look like
inside?'

Sam told him about trying to keep it cool, the steps up to the verandah and inside, the two rows of canvas beds. He described the kit boxes, the punkah – they seemed amazed when he told them about the punkah-wallah who sat outside flipping his big toe up and down to make the punkah sheets billow and keep the air moving. Tom asked about the dormitory routine and Sam described the barber who came before they were even awake to give them a shave.

'He wer called a *nappie* an' 'e wud come round in th'early hours o' mornin', say, 'alf-past four, five, an' shave us all. Every man in the barracks. While they wor still asleep. So say there wor sixty of us, less meself – I didn't get a shave for some reason or other – well, th'reason was because I 'adn't started needin' ter shave . . .'

He told the old story that always got a laugh, about the man who, on their first morning, finding an Indian bending over him with a cut-throat razor, thought he was about to have his throat slit and leaped out of bed yelling blue murder. They'd laughed, the television people, but he sensed it still wasn't what they were after. Tom Martineau wanted to know what they talked about in the dormitory, what they found most exciting. Sam thought back. They'd talked about home, and football, and the sergeant-major; they'd sat on their beds smoking endless cigarettes and playing cards, but all that was obvious. He told them anyway.

'Uh-huh,' Tom said.

There was a pause while the crew murmured among themselves and then they started again. 'Sound running . . . speed . . . 60. Take Two.'

Tom Martineau said lightly, 'All those men cooped up together – where did they go for sex?'

Why was the telly always on about *sex*, Sam wondered, but he tried to give an honest answer.

'Even goin' out on the boat we wor warned what cud happen.

They told us VD wor a risk and, well, y'know, you'd all be better off if you'd do without all that.'

'So what did men in Cawnpore do for girls? They must have wanted them.'

'Well, they didn't. Er, they didn't have girls.'

'Not at *all*? Young men of seventeen, nineteen and so on – they're usually gagging for it! Did they put bromide in your tea or what?'

'Well, Oi dunno . . . Oi wer wholly young. Like y'said, just a li'l ol' boy.'

Tom Martineau nodded energetically, meaning, go on, go on. Sam glanced at the young woman, Lorna. It didn't seem right to talk like this in front of her. But she wasn't listening; she was looking down and writing on her clipboard. He lowered his voice and went on reluctantly, 'There used to be dirty little nigger boys who came into camp—'

Tom interrupted: 'Sorry, Sam, could you just do that again but say "native boys"? Would you mind?'

Sam began again patiently, 'There used to be *native* boys who came into camp. Worn't supposed to, 'twere forbidden, but fr'a reward, say, a rupee a time, they'd do it fer a chap, y'know, wi' their mouth, you see. Oi niver 'ad it. I 'ad me sweetheart at 'ome, Edith. I wor still young then. We got married before war.'

'Yes . . .' Tom said; but Sam could tell he didn't want to hear about Edith. 'So what else did they do for sex?' he persisted.

'Or a man, y'know, 'e did . . . they used ter call it *the five-fingered widow*.' He smirked bashfully. What must that Lorna be thinking?

'And *sex* – proper *sex*?' Tom persisted.

'If it wor *that*, it 'ad ter be with people that were brought in or strayed in . . .' He stopped. Not that.

But Tom sat forward eagerly and locked his eyes onto Sam's. 'Yes? Did *that* happen often?'

'There wer this one case when someone came in – *girl* really, she wor, just a li'l ol' bint, girlie . . .' His voice trailed away.

'*One* case . . . ?'

'Aye, an' she, well . . .'

'*Yes?* Go on. What happened to her, hmm?'

'Well, she wor passed from man to man an' from bed to bed an' . . . an' then . . . an' she finished up as a dead body on th' incinerator next mornin'. *That*'s the sort of thing they warned us against. Oi knew then, what they meant, goin' on at us. Oi 'adn't understood before. Because there wor allus, you know, the bad egg in the box, that give 'em all a bad name.'

'Give *who* a bad name?'

'Us. Men in our barracks. Th'unit.'

Imperceptibly, the director nodded at the cameraman, who tightened his framing until all he could see through the lens was Sam Savage's face in huge close-up.

Tom prompted softly, 'Tell me more about the one who died, how did it happen?'

Sam thought, thank heaven Edith can't hear me, she couldn't have stood it all coming out. They crowd round me and that camera whirrs away and after they've gone to all that bother, all those lights and stuff – *I* can't tell 'em, off ye go, pack up, that's it. But I never meant to talk about *this*. Still, like the bloke on *Mastermind* says, *I've started so I'll finish . . .*

He went on doggedly, 'Well, this er – *girl* – 'ad strayed into the unit lines, and it started off with one of the fellers an' it got goin', y'see, the men got 'eated, an' she was passed from one to anither. Quite a number. Oi suppose, what, dunno, twenty-five, thirty fellers went with 'er, you see. Mebbe more. Cudda bin a lot more. Oi cuddn' look. An' she died doin' it – or 'avin' it done to 'er. Next morning, 'er body was found on th'incinerator. She wor dead.'

'She died in the dormitory? Or was she still alive by the end?'

'In the dormitory, that's right. We – they stopped 'cos she wor dead. Dead meat, one of 'em said.'

'She'd just appeared in the barracks and then she died?'

'S'pose so,' Sam said unhappily.

'Did anybody ever find out who she was?'

'No, I dun't think they did. Jes' an ordinary girl. Probably, Oi mean, there must've bin people that missed her from their side, but none of us knew who she was. A stray who'd come in, maybe looking for money or looking for men or – or what . . . *We* didn't know. She worn't nobody's bint. Not an Indian girl. You wuddn't, see. She wor took away by one of the sweepers.'

'Sweepers?'

'The ones as swept up rubbish an' dirt an' latrines. *They* removed 'er body. It hadn't burned on th' incinerator, you see, because there wor too much rain that night. The monsoon wor that heavy.'

'What happened next?'

'Th' sergeant an' two others held an enquiry next day, asked questions, talked to people . . .'

'You too?'

'. . . not all of us, but they couldn't pin it onto any one person, so it sorta died a natural death. That wor it, as far as we were concerned. We were guil— they were – they were all guilty, but I mean, you couldn't pinpoint any one – one that – who was to blame for the actual *death*.'

'What sort of punishment did you get?'

'*Punishment?*'

'Yes. Were you confined to barracks –?'

'We was that anyway.'

'– made to do drill or forced marches or something?'

'Narthen' loike that. We wor punished enough already.'

'You mean, by feeling guilty for what you'd done?'

'Well, they . . . we – we thought it pretty disgusting, the unit responsible. We wor ashamed t'wor *our* unit.'

'What upset you most?'

'We'd besmirched the good name of the unit.'

'Not the woman . . . girl . . . whatever she was?'

'Well, she shuddn't 'ave been there in the first place, shudda? If she 'adn't bin there it cuddn'ave 'appened. She just appeared and that was it. She made a big mistake there. Pore li'l ol' thing.'

'Did the men feel *besmirched* by what had happened to her?'

'Some of 'em. Oh yes.'

'Did *you* . . . ?'

'Oh yes. Wholly. Oh aye.'

'Why? Had you done anything?'

'What?'

'Had sex with her?'

'I wor just a boy. Only jest fifteen.'

'Yes, of course. But . . . ?'

Sam Savage looked through unblinking eyes at Tom Martineau who, after a pause, straightened up, turned to the cameraman and said, 'OK, cut! Quick two-shot, few cutaways and it's a wrap.'

They put the furniture back as efficiently as the day before while Lorna chatted to Sam. She took out a printed form and said, 'Can I have your autograph?'

'Famous already, am I?'

She gave him a grin – she had nice white teeth – and said, 'You are to me! No, actually it's just that I need you to sign this release form to say it was OK us coming and you didn't mind being filmed. Just the standard stuff.' She clipped the form to her board to steady it and handed it to Sam. At the foot of the first page of her notes he glimpsed the words, *Won't cry*, and below that, *Wrap, 12.35*. He scribbled his name on the form, handing over copyright to the television company and authorizing them to transmit anything he had said during the interview without further reference to or permission from him.

Sam stood at the window of his front parlour watching them

leave. Tom Martineau turned to give him a last wave as he went down the path. They had offered a larger fee – seventy-five pounds this time – but again he had refused. They'd invited him to join them for lunch at the Golden Lion but it wasn't his kind of place. '*Do* come,' Lorna had urged. 'We'll book you a car home afterwards' – as though he weren't capable of walking a couple of miles on his own two feet. She must have thought anyone in their sixties was antediluvian.

They'd stirred things up. Stuff he preferred not to think about had come floating up from memory. Edith had always said, 'No use thinking about it – what's done is done. It only upsets you. Let it be. God knows, we've been punished enough.' He'd almost given himself away when he mentioned the bad egg, but they hadn't noticed. *Jake.* What would he have said if they'd asked him about Jake Roberts? 'We lost touch.' Someone must have told them about the girl in the barracks – they were already primed before they got to him. Must've been Ivor Wordley; he'd become a tattler in his old age – tongue never stopped wagging, poor old boy – but whoever it was had forgotten about the feud between him and Jake Roberts. Old scores. Nobody knew how it had ended; not even Edith, though Edith had known everything else.

PART FOUR

CHAPTER ONE

July–November 1936

THE UNKNOWN GIRL FOUND ON THE INCINERATOR FAILED TO burn because of a record 3.8 inches of rainfall the previous day. One of the camp sweepers disposed of the body, nobody enquired how or where, and was paid off with forty rupees to stop him spreading rumours and disaffection. He was sent home to his village, along with a bedraggled small boy found wandering round the cantonment. His place was swiftly taken by Ramu, Moti's son, impatient to step into his father's shoes. Prem resumed his former life in Budhera and the gap Lakshmi left in the family soon closed, almost as if she had married Beera and gone to live with him and his six motherless children. Only Sukhia mourned her daughter's mysterious death. Kubri the hunchback became spitting, spiteful and uncontrollable. In the end the *chaudhury* declared her possessed by devils and she was driven out of the village.

Back in the regiment there was a brief internal enquiry. Men were invited to come forward and give their own version of what had occurred during the night of heavy rain. When there were no volunteers, eight were picked at random and brought in one by one to give evidence in front of their sergeant, the company sergeant-major and a captain from another unit. These eight included Albert and Sidney but not, as it happened, either Sam or Jake. The enquiry took up most of the following morning, reconvening at five o'clock to consider what action, if any, should be taken. The witnesses had not named a ringleader and no single man seemed more guilty than the rest. It would have been unfair to dole out specific blame or punishment, beyond a general reprimand. The sergeant-major, remembering the New Year's Eve affair, gave his opinion that Roberts was the most likely culprit, being a brute and a bully quite capable of intimidating potential witnesses. When it was pointed out that Bandboy Savage had been involved in the same incident, the general feeling among the tribunal – if it could be called that – was that while a small group of men might initially have been responsible, others in the dormitory had also taken advantage of the girl and no one person should be made a scapegoat. The death was an unfortunate accident but the bint had largely brought it on herself.

The enquiry reprimanded soldiers from 'D' dormitory for sullying the good name of their unit and the honour of the regiment but no punishment was deemed necessary, beyond a warning that such incidents would not be tolerated in future. No official record was made of the deliberations and proceedings concluded at six o'clock sharp. With no official enquiry, record or punishment, the unfortunate business of the little Indian girl would soon be forgotten. The sergeant – having had an ear-bashing from his company sergeant-major – told the lads their superiors took a pretty dim view. A few chastened looks; matter closed.

The rape was not reported in the newspapers either. A genial note from the adjutant to the editor of the *Times of India* ensured that the paper was fulsome in its praise for the resourcefulness of the officers and men who laboured in appalling conditions to strengthen the bridges over the Gumti river, which rose five inches in twenty-four hours due to exceptionally heavy monsoon floods. The paper also reported the demise – 'the sad demise' – of Mrs Margaret Smith aged eighty-two, last survivor of the Indian Mutiny. She had been smuggled out of Lucknow as a toddler by her ayah who, displaying great loyalty and resourcefulness, had darkened the hands and faces of her small charges and their mother and led them through the siege lines to safety, enabling all three to escape. And after all, why should the regimental records or the *Times of India* concern themselves with the death of an unknown, unmarried, Untouchable cross-eyed girl?

That evening in the officers' mess there was some desultory talk about the case among those who had remained in Cawnpore while their families were in the hills. 'Always more of a risk chaps'll go on the rampage during monsoon,' commented one old hand. 'Roberts spotted the girl and saw red. Young lads, cooped up . . . Could have been worse. Cheaper than if they'd smashed the place to pieces.'

'Must have been a tart,' said someone else. 'Camp follower, I dare say. Not to put too fine a point on it, there to be used.'

'Got more than she bargained for,' sniggered a man in his cups.

A young officer, recently at Sandhurst, recalled an evening when a group of them had gone up to London to investigate the pleasures of the West End. They'd had too much to drink and it had ended in a buggerhunt, terrifying one poor bloody pansy so much that he – well, be that as it may, things had rather got out of control. 'Some fellow runs amok . . . too much to drink, can't perform – and trouble starts. Someone's bound to get hurt – in this case the bint. Can't blame young chaps. Human nature and all that.'

'Seems to have been a Pariah. Thank God it wasn't an ordinary girl or the family might have kicked up a bit of a stink,' concluded the old hand.

The padre, listening in a corner of the mess, thought to himself: so the lads turned on the poor girl who was, so to speak, doing them all a favour? All the same, surely they needn't have killed her. Out loud he said, 'There could be many reasons. One can never legislate for evil – and what they did *was* evil – or comprehend why human beings do this, that or the other extreme thing. We can only pray God to forgive the young fellows who were led astray – and pray for her as well, poor heathen creature.'

That closed the subject. The regimental medical officer made a mental note to call a sick parade and check for infectious diseases. Another draft was imminent; some of the lads were due to go home and an epidemic of VD would be frowned upon. The men crossed their legs, shook out and refolded their newspapers, drained their glasses, drew on their pipes and clicked their fingers at the barman for another peg.

Lakshmi's misguided venture inside the cantonment left no more mark than a pebble chucked up by a cartwheel, but a few days later the barracks was rearranged. Jake's gang was dispersed between several dormitories. Jake himself had gone down with another bout of malaria, more virulent than the others. High time he was packed off home with the draft, thought the medical officer, sooner the better.

The rape had left its mark on Sam. He could not efface the image of the slight dark body he had violated. For a time he wanted to die himself. He went alone to the bazaar, half hoping to be attacked and left for dead. At dusk when the mosquitoes were most active, he deliberately rolled up his sleeves and let them settle on his bare reddish-brown arm. He would watch the insect wandering briefly through his light hairs – that to it must seem like tall grasses in a meadow – before plunging its sting into his arm. The mosquito would quiver sensuously for a few seconds, then take off. But although this happened a number of times and he came up in several itchy red bumps, he seemed immune to malaria. When he heard that a new draft was expected, he wrote to Edith saying he hoped to be back home soon. After much heart-searching he added that he felt unworthy of her love, should never have asked her to marry him, and she need not feel bound by her promise. Edith wrote back saying he should tell her this again when he got home as she wanted him to hear her answer.

Sam, Jake and Ivor Wordley were among those sent back to England. Jake, not yet fully recovered from malaria, could still be a potential trouble-maker while Sam had lost his touch and was playing erratically. A new trumpeter was due shortly. In the case of Ivor, the medical officer suspected the onset of neurasthenia. All three were discharged. Sidney Hale and Albert Fitch had given a good account of themselves at the enquiry, claiming convincingly (and truthfully) to have taken no part in the rape except by trying to intervene and stop it. They stayed on, marked down as future NCO material; Albert for his steadiness and Sidney because he was thought to display leadership qualities.

After disembarking at Southampton Docks, Sam, Jake and Ivor travelled up to Waterloo and made their way by Underground railway to Liverpool Street station for the last stage of their journey, the train to Ipswich. They used their travel warrants to get tickets and when the train drew in, after some hesitation all three got into the same compartment. Jake shivered and chain-smoked and stared out of the window. Sam had bought a magazine from a news-stand in Liverpool Street because the headline promised *Adventure Stories for Every Man Who's Still a Boy at Heart*. After half an hour's reading, he decided he didn't fit that category. He'd soon be sixteen and Jake was eighteen and a half. The army had made men of them both, in its way.

Ivor Wordley, always the quiet one, had been even more taciturn since the night of the rape. He couldn't forget the girl's terrified eyes when she realized she was trapped, or her battered mouth after what they had made her do, or the way her feet splayed when they gripped her under the arms and dragged her across the floor. Somehow the image of her hardened soles and toes, the earthy colour of field mushrooms, bothered him very much. It wasn't so bad in England where at least people wore shoes, but every time Jake lolled on the opposite seat, stretching his legs so that the underside of his army boots formed a wide V, Ivor tucked his own feet behind him, ankles crossed, folded his arms and buried his hands deep in the crook of his khaki sleeves to hide their uncontrollable tremors. He left the train at Ipswich after muttering a brief goodbye to Sam.

'Oi'll keep in touch,' Sam said, but he doubted whether they would meet again.

When the train had steamed out of the station and begun to gather speed, Jake stared directly at Sam for the first time. More than a year had passed since they had set off on their journey to India. Sam stared back. Feeling as he had when he attacked Jake on New Year's Eve, he leaned across and said recklessly, 'I'm gunna punish thee when I git the chance. Whether it be war or peace, 'ome or abroad, mark my words, Jake Roberts, Oi swear it. Dunn't thou forget. An' keep thy polluted 'ands off Edith Satterthwaite.'

Jake shrugged. 'Thy 'ands be polluted too, Sam Savage,' he said. He felt neither triumphant nor threatened by Sam's words; just very, very tired. He leaned back and gazed out of the window as the train chuffed across the cold Suffolk fields, wondering if his mother would meet him at Woodbridge and trying to remember what she looked like.

She was there, Jake's mother, warmly wrapped up against the harsh November wind. She and her son greeted each other stoically.

'Th'art back, then.'

'Th'art here.'

'Look loike a darkie, thou dost.'

'India wor hot.'

'Get in car then. Stow thy kit in back.'

She turned to Sam.

'Sam Savage. 'Ow be'st thou plannin' to git hoam?'

'Walkin', Mrs Debney.'

'Not wi' that blurry great kitbag. 'Op in car.'

'Oi be strong, Mrs Debney.'

''Op in car, I said, or Oi'll tie thee to mudguard like tin can at weddin'.'

They drove in silence through the familiar lanes, unimaginably green although it would soon be midwinter. Cows stayed behind hedges and fences where they belonged; children kept their hands to themselves and every pinched grey face was muffled in thick wool. As the car slowed at the approach to the village, people peered curiously at Sam's and Jake's funny-coloured complections. Mrs Debney stopped at the end of Sam's lane.

'I'll drop thee 'ere. It be too narrow to turn.'

''Twor very kind . . .' Sam said awkwardly. 'Oi'll be goin' then.' He hesitated, not knowing whether to say goodbye to Jake.

As if reading his thoughts, Jake growled, 'Don't bother, Sam Savage, Oi'll see thee soon enough!'

'Aye,' said Sam. He climbed out of the car, shouldered his kitbag and trudged down the lane towards his parents.

CHAPTER TWO

November 1936–June 1946

HE HAD PICTURED THE FIRST MEETING WITH EDITH A hundred, maybe a thousand times. The reality was very far from that rapturous soldier's return.

'Thou'rt grown, Sam Savage, taller'n me now!'

Thou'rt pretty, Edith Satterthwaite, prettier than ever before, he thought; but he said, 'Army fed us up. Three meals a day, niver less.'

Thou'rt a man now, Sam Savage, my sweet boy's gone for good. What happened to change thee so?

'More than thy poor mither could give 'ee.'

Edith, Edith, there's things I need to tell 'ee that be knockin' at my teeth to get out, but I daren't let 'em past my tongue.

'Oi be frorne, in this cold. Hast been well, Edith, year past?'

Pining, Sam, pining for thee with every nerve in my body . . .

'Aye, well enough . . . same as thee, I reckon.'

Tell me, tell me!

'Art really still the same?'

'Oi be. Thou'lt see. Give it time.' (Shyly.) 'Didst think of me, Sam?'

'Chance times,' was all he could bring himself to say.

274

All the time. Not a day passed. Now I am here with you, and bitterly ashamed.

Sam's father barred his son from the house, cuffing his wife when she tried to plead for him. She had got no further than 'Abel, 'ave pity, 'e be still a lad . . .' before her head spun from the impact of her husband's hard flat palm.

''E med 'is choice one year gone. Pride must abide – can't come skulkin' back 'oam now loike narthen 'appened. Let 'im earn 'is oon bread! Tek thisself out abroad!' Abel shouted, flinging his arm towards the back door where Sam had crouched six years ago watching his father beat Tom to a pulp. With a brief backward glance at his mother, Sam hoisted the kitbag on his back and lurched into the yard.

He went first to his sister Matty, hoping to find shelter with her, but Matty – married for four years to Jim Collett, now promoted to head groom at the big house (*only* groom as it happened, but the designation stuck) – had two little boys to preoccupy her. Taking pity on his exhaustion, she let him sleep in the parlour for a few nights but warned him he'd soon have to go somewhere else: they had not the space or the money to harbour him. His other sister Joan lived under Lady Manning's roof and *she* couldn't take him in, that was 'sartin-sure'. His brother Ezra had not been seen since his disappearance two years earlier, though Joan had heard a rumour that he was living over at Woodbridge, and courting. Sam was left with three choices: Edith, Miss Jamieson or the vicar.

The vicar welcomed him at once. 'Huge house, too many empty bedrooms – we could do with a strong pair of arms and the gentlemen of the road never stay long – and leave with full pockets, too!' he said. In fact, Mr Persimmons felt responsible for Sam. The army had been his idea but one look told him something had happened during the year in India; something into which he should not pry, that had marked the first lines on Sam's boyish face and left a darkness behind his eyes. Sam followed him upstairs to an attic room at treetop height. It was full of dusty furniture and old books that he read by candlelight until he fell asleep. In the mornings he listened to the wood pigeons' cooing, washed at the basin and went down to help Mrs Persimmons by clearing out the grate in the morning room where visitors warmed their hands by the fire, stumbling through their troubles or pouring out grievances. Sam chopped logs, filled the wood-baskets, stacked more logs beside the stove that fired the cooker and in return was given two good meals a day and his bed. His yellow skin resumed its normal Suffolk pallor. The healing of his mind took longer.

After he had been back for a few weeks he tried to confide in the vicar – not going into detail beyond saying there had been 'a ruckus' in the barracks one night and Jake had publicly humiliated him.

'Sam, old boy, that's all part and parcel of army life! It was the same when I was at school – ragging in the dorm – boys ganging up in the classroom after the lesson was over . . . you young chaps are like that! You mustn't take it to heart. Want me to have a word with him, see if I can persuade him to shake hands and make up?'

Sam recoiled. 'No, vicar, no – dun' do *that*!'

'Well now, you see, you're harbouring the grudge too. Forgive and forget, my boy – it's the only way. Ring out the old, ring in the new, like the New Year bells. Forgive us our trespasses, as we forgive them that trespass against us.'

Sam thought: I don't want to forgive Jake, I want to kill him.

He resumed the bell-ringing, worked in the frozen fields for eight shillings a week – he still only counted as a boy, not yet a lad – saw the soft greening of spring and was accepted as Edith's sweetheart. They were both sixteen; not an unusual age to be betrothed. He no longer had to pretend to her mother that he had come on some errand. At the sight of his face in the doorway she would call out, 'Edie! Thy young fellow be 'ere!'

Often the two would be wringing out heavy calico and cotton sheets or standing with outstretched arms to fold them lengthways, pacing towards each other for the final square. Mrs Satterthwaite would say, 'Finished thy work already, young Sam? It be all right for they men, b'ain't it, Edie?'

In the glorious summer of 1937, unaware that the world rocked on its axis, the only event that touched them was the crowning of King George VI. The little Princesses looked like children at a fancy-dress party, Edith thought, with tinsel coronets and rabbit fur round their necks, but Sam shushed her.

'He be thy undoubted King,' he said. 'Thou munnt talk as if they were real people!'

Sam avoided the subject of marriage and Edith did not mention it, although there was plenty of room for them to share the house with her mother. Her father was never coming back – 'scarpered, Oi dunno where, an' good riddance to 'im!' – and Mrs Satterthwaite would have been glad of Sam's help. But he was comfortable in the vicarage. The Persimmonses' calm kindness helped the raging in his dreams to become less frequent. He had wondered at first whether Jake Roberts would blazon the story of the rape all round the village but there seemed to be a conspiracy of silence between them. Sam's hatred of Jake did not diminish but he could encounter Jake (as he occasionally did) without breaking into a thudding heat of fury. He no longer spent half the night plotting how to kill him – though he never weakened in the certainty that one day he would. At Easter, moved by a sermon on the text *Father, forgive them, they know not what they do*, Sam tried once more to talk to the vicar but Mr Persimmons shook his head.

'If it was true for Our Lord it goes for you as well, Sammy: you must forgive him, for he knew not what he did! Let your stubborn heart soften. You and Jake Roberts shared grand experiences – no other lad in the village has had that luck – you two should be friends, not enemies.'

The trouble was, the more Sam tried to banish thoughts of Jake, the more the Indian girl came into the forefront of his imagination. She grew like a dark angelic presence, shimmering with rain. He couldn't recall exactly how she had looked beyond the fact that she was black-eyed and black-haired. The white-winged angels that hovered above the stable in Bible storybooks and soared over the stained glass window behind the altar were her bright familiars. Then he seemed to hear his mother's voice: *Men love darkness rather than light because their deeds are evil.* Sometimes when he thought about Edith, the dark figure of the Indian girl would intervene with outspread arms and floating hair, as though surrounding and protecting her. Sam, in his attic bedroom, would curl up, tuck his hands into the crook of his elbows and try to sleep.

Edith was troubled by a tingling in her limbs and a stirring of imagination. The seeds of future life zinged and thrummed through her body like the wind through telephone wires, making her tingle and throb. She was sure Sam must feel the same, but something within him had shifted. His face often crumpled as though he had troubled thoughts but he looked so grim that she was afraid to ask. Then, as in the old days, they would spend a blissful Sunday afternoon drifting through the lanes, drunk with languor, and she told herself she was imagining things; it was all right; everything was all right.

Jake strutted and preened, making lewd suggestions to the pretty girls, the buxom girls and in the end the horse-plain girls, but a year later he was still not courting. Something about him warned them off, or maybe they listened to their mothers for once. With his heavy hobnailed boots, trousers tight to bursting and a wiry thatch of black hair, Jake looked as dangerous as a young bull. He had learned to drive and would borrow his mother's car to go into Ipswich on Saturday evenings, returning drunk and lustful. Eighteen months after coming home from India he went to see his sister Rose, the one person in whom he could confide.

Rose, married for six years and already suckling her third child, saw through her brother's boastful remarks and knew he was lonely.

'Thou'rt not duzzy, Jakey, thou'rt a fine strappin' man. Why hast'ee no sweetheart?'

'Plenty willin'.'

'Is't pride that holds thee back? You'll niver make a man in the world unless you say good morning to folk.'

'Nay, I be not proud – nor mewl-hearted, neither. It be the lasses. Mawthers, all o' 'em.'

'What's wrong wi' Dorcas Spring, Beddy's sister? She be a good 'un – not courtin', neither.'

'Ol' Beddy wor niver a mate o' mine,' Jake said sullenly.

'Our village be full o' girls lookin' for a li'l ol' sweetheart . . . Dot Croker, she wor spiteful but she's grown up whoolly bonny. Hast asked Dot to step out?'

'Naw I hanna,' he muttered, 'nor willna.'

''Tis as I thort. Pride. Marriage is what you need, John Jakoby. This wonderful thing. But you can't break a colt with roughness, nor bragging neither, not if you want it to tek the bridle willingly.'

Jake looked away discreetly as Rose unlatched the baby from her breast, covered herself up and hooked him over her shoulder to rub his rounded back until he burped. 'Hold him fer me while I look out a napkin,' she said, handing the swaddled grub to her brother.

'Thou be a roight li'l ol' boy . . .' Jake crooned to his nephew. 'Foine babby!'

When Rose came back the child was already asleep in his uncle's arms. He grumbled and stirred as she put a clean nappy on him, then laid him gently in his wooden cradle before sitting down opposite her brother, rocking the cradle with her foot.

'Be there sumthin' you ain't tellin' me? Sat there like a scaly old bull givin' away narthen. Mebbe thou'st a secret on thy conscience?'

What keeps a man silent, when his mind resounds with a confession aching to be heard? Pride, the desire to be thought well of by the world and his sister? Shame, since he was not entirely devoid of conscience? Or did Jake simply lack words to express the thoughts clogging his actions? He loved Rose and knew that nothing he might say could alter her sisterly love for him; but confronted with the opportunity, he reddened to the roots of his hair and said, 'Secrets? Oi've narthen to hide! 'Tis duzzy girls that keep hidin' from me!'

Rose's clear blue eyes gazed steadily at her brother. Tick-tock, tick-tock, went the clock in the corner of the room. The sleeping child breathed in and out, tiny milk bubbles popping through his moist pursed lips. A car jolted over potholes and the chatter of children running home from school could be heard from the lane.

'Well in that case thou'lt allus be eatin' other people's weddin' cake, Jake Roberts, an' niver thy own!'

War loomed, overshadowing the glorious summer of 1939. For more than a year Edith had been helping out at school with the younger children, becoming a full-time assistant teacher in all but name. Although nothing had been officially sanctioned, Marjorie Jamieson paid her seven shillings a week from her own pocket. Sam at eighteen earned ten shillings, four bob extra if he worked Saturdays and Sundays, so the bell-ringing had had to stop. If they married he would be offered a tied cottage and the farmer would raise his wages. There might even be time for a baby before he was called up to fight.

In the evenings they strolled in the slanting summer light or settled in their foxglove glade. Edith would lie back, pillowing her head on the soft triangle of her arms while they discussed the future, though Sam preferred to talk about the past. He loved telling stories about India and the cantonment – 'big as our whole village: nay, bigger!' – conjuring the scene until she saw as vividly as he did the swaying cows and mangy dogs, the tiny dark-skinned women balancing pots on their heads, stalls heaped with rainbows of gold-embroidered fabric; smelled the hot spicy smells and heard the foreign chatter, shouted warnings and the klaxon of the rickshaw men. But why don't we kiss and caress as ardently as we used to before he went away? Edith thought. We were far more daring then. I want much more than this soft meeting of lips and touching of hands. Maybe there's too much talk at the vicarage about lechery and temptation. Finally she took the initiative.

'Sam,' she asked, 'when be us goin' to get wed?'

They were married six weeks later in Lower Flexham church, the bell-ringers performing a special change in their honour, the beautiful and complicated Stedman's Double. It was the last time it was ever rung. Soon afterwards the bells were silenced for the duration of the war and by the time that was over there weren't enough ringers left who were able to follow its intricate mathematical pattern. As he stood at the top of the aisle, Sam found himself so busy counting, mentally waiting for his turn to pull the sally, that when the service began he could hardly concentrate on the familiar words: 'First, it was ordained for the procreation of children . . .' The vicar smiled as he said, 'Repeat after me: *I, Samuel Henry, do take thee, Edith Alice, to my wedded wife, to have and to hold from this day forward . . .*' Sam repeated it clearly enough for everyone to hear. '*With this ring I thee wed, with my body I thee worship . . .*' His mother stood in the front pew, a garland of wild flowers round her neck, loudly following the vicar's exhortations and raising her voice to match his in the final duet: *Those whom God hath joined together, let no man put asunder!*

They started married life in the Satterthwaites' rickety old cottage whose stairs, floorboards and bedsprings creaked and groaned with every movement. Every night they climbed the steps and latched the bedroom door. He would watch her undress (she was not too modest to watch him, too) and look at the curves of her back and hips as she splashed cold water into her face and armpits from the bowl in the corner. He longed for and dreaded the moment when she turned towards him in the high wooden bed. Her gentle exploring hand, the soft intake of breath when he cupped her breasts, would make his penis quiver and rise – and then the dark image of the Indian girl sprawled across an iron bed would take shape and his penis would waver and droop. Edith had hoped that marriage would change everything but however much they cuddled and stroked each other at night, Sam was too embarrassed to go any further. He imagined her mother telling the neighbours – 'Sheet wor that stained, you'da thought li'l 'ol pig 'ud bin killed!' or maybe, 'My poor Edie cried out so, I thort he wor murderin' her!' He might disgust or hurt her, do it wrong or, worse still, not manage to do it at all. She knew instinctively not to ask him what was the matter. He must grapple with his own demons. They still gave one another pleasure, yet her body moved with a new tension rather than the drowsiness of the contented young wife, while Sam's smooth forehead was often furrowed.

He was called up a few months later, in April 1940, to leave the wooden room and creaking bed, put on a uniform and travel to a training depot with a parade ground where – being nineteen years old and no longer a little bandboy – he must learn to fight. Edith couldn't watch the train draw out but walked away with head high, eyes closed and tears trickling down her face. She was nineteen too, they'd been married for nearly six months and she was still a virgin.

She was a virgin when he returned from the war five and a half years later. She and her mother had been employed as laundry-workers on the American air force base at Martlesham Heath, collected by bus each morning at eight and driven to and from their long day's labour. Here, far from having to immerse their arms up to the elbows in scalding water, using lime and carbolic soap that inflamed the hands and stung the skin, they simply loaded clothes and linen into huge stainless-steel drums and pressed buttons to switch them on. The machine did the rest, rubbing and rinsing and tumbling. The dry laundry was laid across a flat surface and a steam-press cranked down for a hissing second, after which sheets and uniforms emerged crisply ironed, needing only to be folded. The Americans paid even better wages than the local munitions factory. Their boys were large, friendly and homesick. There were dances on Saturday evenings to the sound of big-band swing or swooning melancholy tunes. The Americans showed them new dance steps with unfamiliar names – jitterbug and bebop – clicking their fingers to the swirling, jaunty rhythms, and the local girls soon got the hang of them. At the end of the evening the music would become slow and romantic. Edith often had to reject an invitation to 'step outside into the fresh air for a minute and look at the stars, Mrs Savage, ma'am?' but the young airmen usually seemed just as happy to tell her about their best girl back home.

By 1945 Edith Savage had learned to love jazz and to like Americans. She picked up some of their breezy manner and slang expressions – 'Betcha life!' and 'radio' for 'wulless', 'teenager' instead of 'mawther' – along with air force jargon like 'recce' and 'Wilco'. She lost much of the deference imposed by the rigid village hierarchy and was no longer in awe of Lady Manning (who had been domineering but less than efficient in her wartime role as head of the local WVS). In the post-war election Edith voted Labour. She was officially appointed to teach at Lower Flexham Junior School at a salary of three pounds ten shillings a week and, encouraged by Marjorie Jamieson, joined the teachers' union. Married for six years, Edith had spent only six months of that time with her husband. Now she waited for him to come home, thankful that he had survived. The war must have made a man of him.

In November, six months after the war ended, Sam returned to Lower Flexham wearing his demob suit, carrying his kitbag and trying to smile. Their eyes locked as he took the last few paces towards Edith and she folded him in her arms. He trembled and his teeth chattered. She thought his knees would buckle under him. The hand-painted poster proclaiming WELCOME HOME SAM seemed to mock what he must have been through. She guided him into the kitchen and he sat down in a chair under the pulley from which the usual clean white laundry hung, waiting to be ironed. A dry, peppery smell filled his nostrils. Edith stood beside him cradling his head against her waist, stroking his hair and listening to the racking breaths that rose from the pit of his lungs as he struggled against tears. Mrs Satterthwaite turned her back and concentrated on the kettle and teapot.

''Ere, 'ave a drink o' this,' she said finally. 'I made it good 'n' strong, three lumps.'

'Tea,' Sam said. 'Tea. Oi'm not used to going first. It'll burn me tongue. I'll wait my turn. Edith?'

'I'm here,' Edith said. 'Drink the tea. It'll do thee good. Thanks, Mam.'

The table had been ready laid with a starched cloth and a little stack of Spam sandwiches, but he ignored it. He asked no questions, just rested his head against her. After a while he muttered, 'Niver knew I cud be this tired.'

'Shouldst go to bed?' Edith suggested. 'I mean – sleep?'

'Mebbe later.' He lifted his head and looked round. 'Nothing's changed. Two and a half years since I sat 'ere on leave and not a cup's moved.' He sighed deeply.

'Not a cup,' Edith confirmed.

Beyond the kitchen window a dog barked and a child shouted to its mother, who shouted back. Mrs Satterthwaite bent down to straighten the edge of the rug where it had flipped over. Lord, what was the matter with them both? He'd come back in one piece, hadn't he?

'That's better. Sit down, Edie, why dunna?'

'In a minute.'

Sam looked up at her. 'I brought thee a souvenir from Belgium.' He repeated ironically. '*Souvenir from Belgium.*'

'Later, not now . . .'

'Woman offered it me in the street. I gave 'er ten fags and stowed it in my pocket. Pretty thing.'

Some earrings or a brooch that had belonged to a dead person? Edie thought; hope not . . . that would spook me. She said again, 'Later. Drink thy tea fust.'

This was not the homecoming she had imagined.

In bed for the first few nights she let him weep, feeling sure that tears were better than no tears. His body was rigid and he clutched her so tightly that it hurt. He tried to explain, to tell her things, but nothing came out except incoherent, gulping sounds.

'Yes, yes,' she soothed, '*I* know. Never mind. All over now . . .' as if comforting a heartbroken child in the playground. After a week he took off his pyjamas and made her pull the nightdress over her head but he didn't try to make love, just pressed his thin, shaking body against her warm softness. He was cold, in spite of the bedclothes piled on top of them, and she felt as if she were breathing life into a corpse. What could he have seen to bring him back more mad than sane, more dead than alive?

The gift turned out to be a little china cradle with a sprigged china blanket covering a tiny china baby. It was beautifully fashioned, each individual bar a fine porcelain twig, the miniature face painted with closed eyes and tiny lashes on its rosy cheeks. It wore a white bonnet with holes pricked in it to look like lace.

'It be a pretty li'l ol' thing,' she said admiringly. 'Where didst get it?'

'The woman I gave ten ciggies to,' he said. 'She wor' 'oldin' it out in street.'

Edith couldn't imagine how a woman could give away a treasured family heirloom for one day's smoking but she said, 'It's beautiful, Sam. I s'll put it on mantelpiece.'

As winter intensified and snow swept down from the north, a young stray cat hung about the house, miaowing to be let in. Edith's mother shooed it away with the broom but Sam felt sorry for the shivering thing. He fed it surreptitiously and, roused from his usual torpor, pleaded with her to relent.

'It's a boy,' Mrs Satterthwaite said. 'It'll do its dirty business all over my clean house, makin' a smell. Shoo it abroad, Sam, let someone else tek care of it.'

To her astonishment, however, he caught the cat, put it in a box and carried it to the vet, who castrated it for half a guinea. After this the cat was allowed indoors where it spent much of its time purring on Sam's lap. He liked its cosy, anchoring weight and named it Pushy because it had pushed its way in.

Gradually Sam seemed to get a bit better. He mastered his shaking and night-time sobs, managed to walk through the village and greet the neighbours civilly, though he grimaced and shook his head if anyone called him a hero. Spring came and everyone shed their utility winter coats, exchanging them for tweed jackets with leather buttons and elbow patches: garments made to last. Edith's pupils picked primroses and catkins – 'lambs' tails' – for her. She stuck them in a jug and put it on their bedside table. New life was everywhere, newly swollen bellies in the village and at market; shaky new lambs in the fields pulling urgently at the teat. At night when he was away, Sam had recalled every detail of Edith's nakedness; the shadowed ovals of her breasts and buttocks; the convex scoop of her belly that must carry his child one day. Now he was back he couldn't bring himself to touch her. They no longer even enjoyed the hot fumblings of childhood, living chastely side by side, flinching every time Mrs Satterthwaite asked crossly when they were going to get round to giving her grandchildren.

One Sunday afternoon Marjorie Jamieson came to tea. Edith pooled their butter ration for the week to make a Victoria sponge. She had already confided some of Sam's problems; not the night-time ones but the lassitude, apathy, his seeming inability to summon the energy to look for work. When Marjorie walked into the room and Sam stood up from his arm-chair to greet her she was shocked. This was not the bright-eyed lad she had recommended to the army when he was fourteen but a broken man, cowed and bitter. Oh God, she thought, why must wars take our straight young men away and send them home twisted – if they return at all?

They sat in the parlour round an oak gate-legged table and ate off the best china. Pushy wove round their legs looking up at them hopefully. Edith's mother declined to join them but took her slice of cake out to the kitchen, wondering if the schoolmistress understood her son-in-law any better than she did. Marjorie sipped her tea, praised the cake, reminisced about Sam's friends from school and asked after his sisters, Joan and Matty. Finally she said, 'Well, Sam, you've been home nearly six months now. Any plans?'

'I'd hardly thort, Miss Jamieson,' he said. 'I do whoolly live for th' day.'

She supposed he meant he was lucky to be alive at all. 'Plenty of people could do with a willing pair of hands, and yours as I remember were always willing.'

'I'd rather not work on land agin,' he said. 'Need to git me strength up a bit fust.' He leaned down to stroke the cat and at once it jumped onto his lap.

'Oh, I think we can do better than labouring for you, Sam. You were always a clever lad. Would you mind if I made a few enquiries?'

'Don't aim too high. I cun spell and I cun count, that's all.'

They looked at each other and Marjorie thought, how he's changed, poor Sam Savage! All nervy, his face more like a man of forty than – how old must he be now: twenty-five, twenty-six? Sam returned the gaze thinking, she's getting old – but I allus thought her old. Musta bin young when she put me next to Jake Roberts, sharing the same desk. That was the start of all me troubles.

'We'll see about that!' said Marjorie Jamieson.

CHAPTER THREE

July 1946–Christmas 1949

JAKE ROBERTS, NICKNAMED OX, TWENTY-EIGHT YEARS OLD AND strong as an ox, had avoided being conscripted because he was still subject to bouts of malaria. The army may also have taken into account that, as an agricultural labourer, he contributed to the war effort. He ate well throughout the war and the rationing years and never wore uniform; not so much as a regulation-issue gas mask. He never experienced exhaustion, other than ordinary tiredness after a day's work, let alone fear, pain, hunger, cold or the head-sunk-in-hands, broken-backed grief and guilt of losing a comrade-in-arms. Nobody pointed a weapon at him, he wasn't forced to hide in a hedge or cellar or run panic-stricken from grenades, explosions or fire. The earth never shook beneath his feet; instead he turned the gleaming, familiar sods under the harrow and in due course they yielded their usual crops. No-one threw their arms around him in a long, tearful goodbye and nobody welcomed him rapturously back when the war ended. He had never been away. He waved, shouted and brandished the Victory V-sign but Jake knew he hadn't much right to share in the celebrations. He had spent five years producing vital, indeed desperately needed food, but agricultural work was for old men, pacifists, Land Girls and those unfit to fight by reason of extreme physical or mental disability. Billy Debney – his stepfather – had been forty-two when war was declared, exempted on grounds of age and because he was needed to run the farm; yet Billy had done everything in his power to enlist and been furious each time he was rejected.

The past five years had intensified the rivalry between Maggie's second husband and her son. They sparred and snarled constantly – over the first slice on the outside of the Sunday joint or the last roast potato in the dish, over who should sit in the chair nearest the fire or get up to open the door when the chimney smoked – shouldering each other out of the way and competing for warmth, comfort, food and Maggie's attention. She was more than sixty and their demands tired her.

'Stop yer blarin, do!' she'd complain. 'Allus scrappin' like pups in a litter. Leave me in peace or ye'll soon be cookin' yer own dinners.'

Jake was always on the lookout for signs of favouritism. He was afraid Billy would persuade her to leave the farm to *him* when she died rather than to himself, her son, to whom it rightfully belonged. If that happened, Jake would be out on his ear, with a thankless future labouring on someone else's land. When he tried to please his mother with clumsy offers of help or a bunch of meadow flowers for the kitchen table she looked at him in a baffled way and twitched off his gestures of affection. His sister Rose, now with five children, had little time for him. Lizzie's two daughters had grown into cheeky, long-limbed young creatures but he had nothing to say to them and felt unwelcome in Lizzie's household, though he could not have said why. He had no circle of mates. The closest he came to friendship was with the roarers in the pub on Saturday night, farmhands or itinerant workers who got fighting drunk on ale and yelled bawdy songs and stories or boasted of their exploits with girls or in the Forces. Jake was in the prime of youth, strong, healthy, ruddy, the soil of Suffolk embedded in the skills of his hands and the soles of his boots, unencumbered by wife, child or friends. He made up his mind to leave Lower Flexham and look for work somewhere else – Ipswich, Stowmarket, even as far away as Colchester. Then perhaps his mother would come to her senses and regret having preferred her husband over her own flesh and blood. His sisters would miss him and be sorry they hadn't paid him more attention. He would be like the Prodigal Son: only appreciated once he'd gone. He kept his ears open in the pub, hoping to hear about any jobs going.

In due course he did hear. The communal slaughterhouse, used by half a dozen villages, needed a man and the money was good, if you had the stomach for the work. Jake borrowed his mother's car and eventually found the place, though he drove around for half an hour before realizing he was within a hundred yards of the entrance. It was discreetly signposted in small lettering, but Jake's reading skill had deteriorated since his days in Miss Jamieson's classroom. No matter; the stocky, compact foreman summed up Jake's size and strength at a glance and took him on. He told Jake about a room for rent in the nearby village. Jake took a look at the room and the land-lady and said he'd come back next day and move in with his things.

Next morning after breakfast, when Billy was already in the cab of his tractor several fields away, Jake said, 'I'll be off abroad then, Mam. Leave ye in peace. An' *him*.'

'Git awa' wi' thy nonsense.'

''T'ain't nonsense. Oi be leavin' hoom. Not before time.'

'Suit thisself. Thou'lt be back soon enough.'

'Naw, I won't. He driven me awa'.'

'Th'art a man, whoolly grown. Mek up thy own mind.' She looked at her son, his half-defiant, half-pleading stance, and softened. 'Canst stay, John Jakoby, if thou wilt. I'll talk to Billy, tell him he's bin too 'ard on thee. Oi'm that sick of thy scrappin' 'n' snarlin' but thou'rt still my lad – Lord knows, th'art no-one else's.'

He could have broken down in tears then, clung to her for comfort, agreed to stay and make peace with her husband – but at that moment the radio struck up the perky theme tune from her favourite programme and she said, 'Oi mun lissen to this – never miss it! Mek up thine own mind, but dunna say thy mam threw thee out for I havna.'

As the tune faded and the announcer's crisp tones reminded listeners of the previous episode, Jake picked up the bundle containing a towel, his razor, clothes, underwear and a spare pair of boots and strode out of the door. Hidden at the bottom of the bag was a nightdress belonging to his mother. At the last moment, on an impulse, he had taken it from the washing line. He had also taken his wartime gas mask.

Once Jake had left Lower Flexham, he and Sam seldom ran into each other and their feud remained secret. The episode was ten years ago and although Jake too thought about the little Indian girl occasionally, to him she had never seemed human, more like a wild animal that had tried to escape its pursuers and was finally cornered, wild-eyed, heart beating frantically. Animals knew when death was imminent and he'd often seen hares and rabbits like that at harvest-time, when the last circle of corn was cut. A calf about to be slaughtered had eyes like hers. Jake didn't know why he should feel remorse – she was a native bint who shouldn't have been there in the first place – yet her crouching figure was engraved on his inner eye as if by a lightning flash. She lodged brilliantly in his mind and trembled.

Sam found himself a job as a postman, starting work directly after the timely retirement of old Jimmy Ince, Postman Ince, who had delivered his letters to Edith, and to everyone else in Lower Flexham and the outlying hamlets. Sam was spared the anguish of having to bring wartime telegrams and all the other bad news that men far away from home heap upon their loved ones, though there were still sometimes telegrams and even in peacetime their news was not always joyful. The job got him out of bed early – which was his natural inclination – to gather up the sacks dropped off by the Royal Mail van and sort them first into villages, then lanes and streets and finally house numbers. He worked alone, making as much or as little conversation as he chose. Everyone welcomed him – 'Marnin', postie!' – because he wasn't nosey and never commented on their postcards or Pools coupons. He learned the postman's tricks of always being optimistic about the weather and not waiting while people opened their telegrams. Good news or bad, it wasn't *his* news and he didn't want to be blamed . . . or be made to stay and celebrate either. It was a healthy life, cycling, emptying pillar boxes, striding up people's garden paths, remounting the bike and cycling on. His complexion grew ruddy with fresh air and he regained the weight he had lost in the last months of the war. He enjoyed cycling between villages along deep lanes overhung by greenery, their borders banked up high on either side. Every field name and bird's note had been familiar since he was a boy. Pheasants scuttled into the hedge, tramps waved as he passed. He didn't mind if it rained; his dark blue peaked cap was water-proof and he had a cape to put over his shoulders with armholes through which he thrust his hands to grip the handlebars. The round covered more than fifteen miles and if there were telegrams to deliver he cycled it twice a day. It gave him time to think and he let the bad thoughts come to the surface, finding that the images of rain and fire and terrified people could be effaced by lifting his eyes and gazing at the peaceful country-side. Sometimes when the wind blew from the north-east he could smell the sea; at other times it would be manure, diesel, hay or rain. This was the air he had been born into, the sur-names on the letters he carried were those of the children he had grown up with; the names he saw in church on memorial tablets or tombstones. This was England, safe England, where he belonged.

The job's only drawback was that it kept him in contact with Jake. Although he could only just read, Jake got a number of letters – one a month from his mother and also some in plain brown envelopes; even occasionally a package. Usually his land-lady took them in but from time to time it would be Jake himself.

'Still gunna kill me, Sam Savage?' Jake once asked mockingly.

'Dunna jest about it,' Sam replied, 'for I swear by God I shall.'

Jake laughed, knowing he could knock Sam out cold with a single swing of his fist; but as Sam bicycled along the lanes on his peaceful round, he brooded and plotted, searching for a means or an opportunity. Could he deliver a package containing explosives that would blow up in Jake's face? No, that would probably only maim him. Could he somehow contrive to give him poison? Hardly, since they never took a drink together and Sam had never been inside the house; besides, the landlady might take it by mistake. A shooting accident? Sam didn't possess a gun. In a hand-to-hand fight he wouldn't stand a chance. Murder was difficult. He would grit his teeth and clench his knuckles so hard that the front wheel wobbled. He couldn't kill Jake in an obvious way – that would result in him being imprisoned, perhaps hanged, and he would never put Edith through such an ordeal . . . Jake had to be killed silently, invisibly; yet for true revenge he must die knowing that Sam had fulfilled his vow. Outwardly the cheery postman, inwardly Sam seethed with slow-banked rage, the rage that had fired his Savage ancestors.

By the time the heatwave summer came in 1947, two years after the war ended, Sam and Edith had settled back into their peacetime lives and would have been content if only they had had a child. Each evening after the nine o'clock news Sam would stretch and yawn, and say, 'A postman's work starts early . . . Oi'd best be goin' to bed!' Edith would look up from her mending, her book or the exercises she was correcting to say, 'Good night, dear. Sleep tight! I'm coming soon . . .' and they would smile fondly, perhaps mime a kiss, before he closed the kitchen door behind him. In bed they no longer touched each other, as they had in the first weeks of their marriage, let alone shared the fevered explorations of adolescence. They never talked about these barren nights. A wall of passionate, unspoken words rose between them. *What sort of marriage is this?* and *Why can't you be a man?* and *Something stops me, I feel hard but I stay soft* and *I'm no use to thee, Edie* – but above all, *Help me – I can't help myself – I'm sorry!* In spite of everything they loved each other and, afraid of what might happen once the wall was breached, neither wanted to be the first to speak.

Edith turned twenty-six longing ever more urgently for motherhood. She was full-breasted and healthy, her periods regular as clockwork, and this obvious, wasted fertility was a mockery and an ordeal. The affection Sam lavished upon Pushy showed how much he too yearned for a child. Finally, after a bitter and stupid row about something quite different and entirely unimportant (though their red faces and angry voices belied its triviality), she persuaded him to go with her to the doctor.

Old Dr Roffey was overdue for retirement but, although the practice had been advertised, in the post-war shortage there were no applications and he was forced to stay on, looking after the people he had delivered as babies, some of whom now complained of stiff joints and arthritic hands. He had not delivered Sam but he remembered his violent father Abel – recently dead after a stroke – and Flora, his mother, a religious maniac of the first order.

He saw Edith first, spending half an hour with her; then sent her out and summoned her husband. He looked up as Sam came in, thinking: something's gone very wrong here. I'm baffled by this one.

'Sit down,' he said gruffly. 'Well, young Savage. I think you know very well why your missus hasn't had a baby. Eh? Eh? Am I right? Tell me?'

'I . . . ain't ye gunna examine me, doctor?'

'Don't need to. Ye look healthy enough. Fit as a fiddle. So what's her trouble, eh? You tell me.'

'Oi dunno, doctor. We 'oped ye'd find out.'

'Don't beat about the bush. Your wife is *virgo intacta*. Know what that means? Course ye do. It means she's never been penetrated by the male organ. Why's that? How do you expect her to give ye a child?'

Sam's first reaction was one of relief that she had been true to him during the long years apart. Then his face became suffused with blood until it was dark red. The veins in his throat tensed and tightened. He lowered his gaze.

'Get up on the couch then, let's examine you. Not that I need to, but just in case. Take your trousers off first, man.'

Sam turned his back, bent over and unhooked the belt of his trousers. Half-naked, he clambered onto the examination couch. Dr Roffey covered his lower half with a light blanket while he listened to Sam's heart and lungs and took his blood pressure. He shone a blinding light into Sam's eyes and down his throat. It had become a habit. He did it even if the patient complained of corns.

'Nothing wrong there. Let's have a look at yer nether parts.'

He rolled back the blanket and handled Sam's privates, parting his legs and gently palpating his testicles.

'Sit up. Get your trousers on. Don't do yer fly buttons up yet.'

Sam did as he was told and perched on the edge of the couch. The doctor sat down behind his desk.

'Right. First. Do you know how the act of intercourse is performed?'

'Course I do,' Sam muttered, frowning.

'Ye'd be surprised how many don't. I've had couples here who think it goes in via the belly button.'

Sam grinned.

'Aye, they do. Rural ignorance is a bottomless well. Second. When you attempt relations with your wife, do you achieve an erection?'

After a pause Sam said, 'No.'

'As I thought. Third. Have ye had relations with any other woman?'

Sam twisted his hands in his unbuttoned lap and said nothing. After a minute the doctor barked impatiently, 'Come along, man, your secrets are safe with me! Nothing goes beyond the door of this surgery or I'd never have lasted fifty years. Have you had other women?'

'Once.'

'Was the act successfully performed?'

A dozen possible answers ran through Sam's head but he simply said, 'Aye.'

'By this I take it you mean an erection and full penetration. Did pregnancy result?'

Sam was beginning to shake and he clasped his hands tightly together. 'No,' he whispered, and then again, much louder, '*No!*'

'How can ye be sure?'

'She – because she – the girl – died.'

Dr Roffey, a model of the old-fashioned GP, was not without compassion and he had heard of and even dipped into the works of Sigmund Freud, although by and large he thought they had about as much to do with his patients as a milking machine has to do with chickens. His expression softened as he looked at Sam, whose legs dangled over the side of the couch, toes clenching and unclenching.

'Listen to me awhile. I am going to assume that this experience occurred during your army service . . . ?' – Sam nodded – 'And that you have since regretted it. But cannot put it behind you. I'll not bother you with the jargon, but such incidents can leave a lifelong mark. If your wife is to conceive – and physically I see no obvious reason why she should not – you are going to have to overcome this memory. Do you understand?'

''Ow can I do that?'

'The previous incident may be what's rendering you impotent. Stops you sustaining an erection with your wife. If you can get over that and become hard – I make myself clear? – full marital relations should follow in the natural course of events. Ye're both young, vigorous, healthy – and, I take it, fond of each other. Ye don't find her repulsive?'

'*No*, doctor!'

'Right.' He glanced at his watch. 'Do you masturbate?'

Sam's face reddened. 'Do what? . . . *Oh*. Aye. Chance times.'

'And is that successful?'

How could what he did be called successful, Sam wondered. In lonely disgust, far from Edith's loving, willing body, standing in the cold dark privy – successful?

'No.'

'Ye don't reach orgasm?'

'I *cum*, doctor, if that be yer meaning,' Sam said with unexpected aggression.

'That is what I mean, yes. Good. There's hope, then. Now, my advice to you, if ye want a family, is this. Teach your wife to masturbate you – she may not even find it unpleasant – until you're erect. Hard. If she won't you'll have to do it for yourself. It may take several attempts, but if you love each other, there's no shame in it. Have the two of ye tried this method already?'

Sam shook his head without looking directly at the doctor.

'Mr Savage, I'm trying to talk to you man to man. Spare me your embarrassment. So . . . let me suggest that you may find it helpful to use magazines – you know the sort of thing: *Men Only*, *Health and Efficiency* – or she can start by talking to you, using the so-called dirty words. Then, when . . .'

Sam slipped off the couch, buttoned his trousers and looked at the doctor angrily.

'I cudna do it, doctor. I cudna shame her so, nor meself. Thank you for yer time. Good day.'

'*Mr Savage*,' Dr Roffey began, wondering how on earth other GPs handled these matters, but Sam had already crossed the room.

'I'll hand the ten bob to yer receptionist.' He closed the door silently behind him, thinking: cheaper than cutting the balls off a cat.

Sam overcame his silence sufficiently to tell Edith that their barrenness (he always substituted the word 'difficulty') was his fault. Physically, *she* was perfectly healthy and normal. I know that already, she thought. *He* was not, though it seemed that his trouble was in here (he pointed to his head) rather than down there (jabbing a thumb towards his privates). It was unlikely to change, or be cured.

The full impact of bad news rarely strikes all at once. It takes a while to sink in. Not having a child was just something they must learn to live with and Edith's first response was to console her husband. After all, they had lots of nephews and nieces and she spent her days surrounded by children. It'd be nice to have their freedom and a bit of extra money to spare. Yet she began to resent the casually pregnant mothers who arrived at the school gates in the mornings with a clutch of children in tow, a sticky-faced toddler sitting up in the pram and a swollen belly. They often asked her, 'When art plannin' to start th'own family, then, Edie?'

'I've enough children to deal with at school all day,' she would joke. 'Don't want to be coming home to a whole lot more!' It was accepted: some couples just never had children, whether by choice or bad luck.

But as the reality of lifelong childlessness – and virginity as well – sank in, Edith became overwhelmed with secret anger. The years of wasted menstrual blood, the futility of her youth and health, her nun-like ignorance of sex, dominated her thoughts. She and Sam had always spoken kindly and considerately to each other but now she imagined violent rows during which she hurled cruel accusations. She began to wonder whether, far from loving Sam, she didn't in fact hate him. Unless she talked to someone soon she would explode – if not at him then perhaps at one of her pupils. She'd stopped reading them *The Ballad of Young Lochinvar* – though they relished the dramatic scene in which the young lover gallops up the aisle at the very moment when the bride is about to make her marriage vows – because it was too close to her own fantasy. The foolish romantic side of her longed to be spirited away, thrown onto a rough bed covered with the pelt of wolf or bear and initiated into carnal pleasure. There seemed no-one to whom she could confide such a private matter, until she thought of Marjorie Jamieson. She and Marjorie had taught together for years and by now, although not exactly friends, they had become close. After all, Edith thought, her colleague was childless too, and quite probably a virgin.

Edith stayed behind one winter's afternoon, waylaid her as she prepared to cycle home and said there was something she needed to ask. Marjorie hid her surprise – normally their conversations took place in the deserted classroom after the last of the children had finally left, as the two of them straightened desks, tidied away textbooks, wiped the blackboard and restored the chalk and rubber to their slot below it. She took the hint and said, 'Come and have tea! One of the mothers gave me a pot of raspberry jam – as well she might, the hours I've spent with her Isaac.'

Pedalling side by side along the recently tarmacked lane, they gossiped about school affairs until they reached the cottage where Marjorie had lived for nearly thirty years. It was dark and silent – not so much as a cat or a canary to welcome her, Edith reflected; she must get lonely – but once the lights and kettle were on, the place sprang to life. Marjorie fiddled with the knobs on the wireless and the kitchen filled with the sound of a classical symphony, achingly sweet, precise, yet human. 'I never listen to proper music,' Edith admitted. 'Mam has the Light Programme and Sam the Home Service, so it's allus one or t'other. He loikes quizzes like *The Brains Trust* or *Animal, Vegetable, Mineral*.'

'Well, *this* is Mozart,' Marjorie said, 'but it isn't all music on this wavelength. There's lots of interesting talks. It's like having a really clever person keen to tell you things or play you their favourite music. I have it on all the time except when I'm asleep. The only thing I can't listen to is the science programmes. I ought to keep up with the latest discoveries but I really can't make head or tail of them. Now then, kettle's boiling – India or China?'

'Pardon?' said Edith.

'What kind of tea do you like?'

'Ty-phoo – Lyons – anything.'

'Lyons – bread and breadknife; butter and jam in larder – tea-spoons, cups and saucers (sorry, when you live alone you get into this dreadful habit of talking to yourself) – tray beside cup-board – table napkins . . .'

'It's the same now that Mam's gettin' old and forgetful: Mam, hast remembered the knives an' forks, Mam, hast tha scrubbed the potatoes? Put kettle on to boil? In the end you think heck, might as well do it meself, less bother.'

'And Sam . . . how's he?'

The music reached its perfectly rounded conclusion, the final chords lingering in silence for a few moments before applause broke like a rain shower. Edith's eyes roamed about as though wondering where to begin, or perhaps looking for a way to escape.

'Come through and sit down,' Marjorie invited.

In her sitting room the gas fire had already been lit and the side-lights were reflected in the glass of the watercolours on the opposite wall. Edith sat in a chintz-covered armchair, solid and comfortable. Marjorie poured two cups of tea and sawed energetically at the Hovis.

'How is Sam?' she repeated. 'Or should I be asking how *you* are?'

'Oi shudna be tellin' you this,' Edith began in a rush, 'but if I dunt tell someone my 'ead'll crack open and all the bad words'll fly out.' She drew a deep, strained breath. 'Sam 'n' me went to see doctor, round June it musta bin. Turns out Sam can't niver be a father. We ain't niver gunna have children. Oh and I *do* want a babby so!'

'My *dear* . . .'

''T'ain't my fault, doctor said. There be narthen wrong wi' *me*. It be sumthin' Sam did when 'e wor in army, it's upset 'im inside 'is 'ead. Oi dunno what.'

'You know, these conditions can often be helped nowadays.'

'Not this'n.'

'What makes you so sure? Medical science has taken huge strides.'

'Not for this,' Edith repeated. She took a bite of her jam sandwich but her eyes and even her mouth filled with tears and she had to take the bread out of her mouth and put it soggily on the side of her plate.

'I'm iver so sorry,' she muttered, rubbing at her eyes and nose. '*Manners* . . .'

'Couldn't matter less. Would you like a handkerchief?'

'Thing is, Miss Jamieson, um . . .'

'*Marjorie.*'

'. . . Marjorie, Oi dunno 'ow to say this but we've bin married eight years an' we've *niver done it*.'

For a moment Marjorie thought, never done *what*? but seeing

Edith's face, dark with shame and modesty, she understood.

'You're a virgin, you mean. And Sam – is he too?'

'Aye. No. No, I don't think so.'

The account emerged in fits and starts over two teapots and four cups of tea each. At half-past six, Marjorie suggested a glass of sherry. The treacly-sharp liquor went straight to Edith's head and she began to giggle. The release of tension made her cry again. Finally Marjorie asked:

'Edith: what matters to you most – a) that you're still a virgin, b) that you can't have a baby or c) that for the moment you feel you don't love your husband?'

'*All three!*'

'Have another glass of sherry.'

Emboldened by the intimacy their conversation had created as well as by the sherry, Edith asked, 'How about thee, Miss – *Marjorie*? Thou'st niver had a child? Or a man?'

'No. Yes.'

Not, in fact, a virgin after all, it turned out. During the war Marjorie had had an affair with an American airman. It wasn't quite her first physical encounter, but the only time it had happened several times with the same person. Yes, he had been married. No, she didn't regret it. Nor did she miss him, feel guilty or begrudge his wife in America his daily company.

'He was a nice chap – a sweet man, really, homesick like the rest of them – but I wouldn't have wanted to be with him all the time.'

Before Edith left, quite tiddly after two glasses of sherry, she asked, 'What's it loike . . . the act of intercourse? Is it like all the books say? *Is* it whoolly wonderful?'

'Perhaps it was my fault – or the men's,' Marjorie answered, 'but if you ask me, it's overrated. I don't suppose it's very different from what animals feel when *they* mate. It's a necessary physical act and by no means repulsive. Vigorous, energetic, healthy, nothing to be ashamed of. But not *divine* . . . not like *Mozart* is divine.'

'In that case I must get me own radio!'

Some months later, worried by Edith's withdrawal and formality since their visit to the doctor, Sam decided he must do what he had always dreaded: tell her about the little Indian girl. Their erstwhile knolls and coppices were now the secret places for younger courting couples and what he had to say needed privacy. They walked along the lanes at dusk one spring Sunday, startling rabbits into the hedgerows. A solitary bell tolled. It was nearly seven o'clock and Evening Prayer had just finished. Sam caught sight of Mr Persimmons walking back to the vicarage and wondered if anyone had attended the service.

'We mun go to church more often, you 'n' me,' he remarked to Edith. 'Vicar wor ever so good to me when I wor a lad.'

'Dost believe in God, Sam?' she asked.

Sam was surprised. He hadn't thought about *believing* in God. They had gone to church as children because Flora Savage had insisted on it. He had been christened and confirmed and as a man he had kept up the habit of going to church because, as his mother always used to say, *The devil, as a roaring lion, walketh about seeking whom he may devour*. But did he *believe*? What a question. They walked down the flagged pathway towards the church, past leaning tombstones, their inscriptions blurred by lichen – *Dearly beloved wife of* . . . *Peter John Hardie, aged six months and four days* . . . *Rest in Peace*. He realized that he no more believed in God than in *The Jungle Books*. He liked hearing the old stories with their familiar language and phrases and he would go on coming to church because its rituals ordered his life, marking its seasonal progress towards the day when a gravestone would bear his name: *Samuel Henry Savage, born 27 March 1921, died* . . . when?

'Oi dun' know. Oi loike prayin', and hearin' vicar preach,

an' Collect for the Day. Loike singin' th' old hymns.'

'Aye, but art thou worshippin' Him?'

'Isn't that how it's done?'

... and that of Alice his Second Wife, born 3 January 1803, died in childbirth 5 May 1842, and her Little Son Thomas, nine days old ...

'Mebbe it's harder'n that.'

'Me poor mither, weeping an' wailin' an' gnashing of teeth. If that's worshippin' God I'll not go along wi' it.'

The day thou gavest, Lord, has ended ... take into thy safe-keeping Ellen Mary ...

'Thou'd rather have an easy God?'

They looked at each other.

'Loife be hard enough . . .' he said.

They sat on a worn seat beside a yew tree in the churchyard. Swifts darted round the square church tower, wheeling in pursuit of insects. Sam took a deep breath. 'Edie, *this* be hard.' He paused to gather his words together, hoping she wouldn't look at him. Edith gazed ahead into the gathering dusk, waiting.

'Remember before we were wed, Oi tol' thee I'd not been true to thee in India?'

'Remember I forgave thee?'

Another silence.

'But I canna forgive *myself*.'

'Sam, Sam—'

'Nay, listen. Give me toime. 'T'ain't easy.'

Edith's hair had come undone from the loose hank tucked at the nape of her neck. She gathered it up to twist it into a fresh knot. A winding strand lay along her bare shoulder. She leaned back against the seat, twining her arms above her head and stretching her legs to show that she was in no hurry. The vision of the little Indian girl flooded Sam's mind; her dark slender body and coils of thick black hair; the smell of sweat and semen . . .

He shuddered convulsively.

'Edie, thou'rt only girl Oi ever loved nor ever will – thou know'st that?'

'Oi know that, I believe thee,' she said. He reached for her brown hand, raised it to his lips and kissed it.

'I hafta tell thee what happened that night in barracks, because doctor thought that be causing our – *my* difficulty.' He paused to gather his thoughts, wondering how much he had to tell her. Everything.

'It wor monsoon that night. It rained like no rain thou'st iver seen, as if heaven wor gushin' a thousand Niagara Falls. Ye cud hear it drummin' on roof. Us lads, nigh sixty on' us, wor cooped up and bored wi' ourselves. Jake Roberts had bed nearest door. He got up and went to check rain-gauge, cos we wor takin' bets whether it'd bruk all records. So Jake walks to door . . . an' then, an' then, an' then . . .'

He stopped and she waited, unconsciously twisting a loose curl.

'An' then, an' then – *Edie, dunt touch thy hair!*'

Startled, she jerked upright and turned to him with a tiny cry of pain. One strand was caught between her fingers, pulled out by the sudden movement. She shook it off convulsively and both hands dropped to her knees, palms upwards. 'Sorry,' he said, and she leaned back again. In the silence there was a rustle and a pounce from somewhere behind them and a tiny, strangled squeak. A couple of cars drove past, returning from a day out. Their headlights illuminated the yew hedge round the churchyard, flickering between its interlocked branches.

'It wor a girl, a little Indian girl he'd tricked summow to come in. He did it to her first, Jake; an' then everyone did. Till she wor dead.'

'Did – what? Clobbered 'er?'

'Nay, 'e worn't violent. 'Tworn't necessary, she wor that little. Jake 'ad 'is will of 'er. 'E tuk 'er first. Oi mean . . . oh Edie, thou dunnt even know th'word!'

'Th'art sayin' everyone *fucked* 'er?'

He was shocked.

'Aye,' he mumbled. 'Mebbe not quite everyone, but nigh all of 'em. She wor layin' over bed wi' no clothes on, only a li'l ol' girl, an' – Oi'd forgotten this till now – she 'ad one long black curl caught in her fingers . . . Oh *Edie* . . . !' Sam swallowed several times, his Adam's apple rising and falling, the sinews in his jaw flexing. He struggled to control his breathing because until he did, no words would emerge. 'Edie, *I did it too.* I wor the very last. Jake made me. It ain't no excuse, I ain't escapin' blame – I wor on my bed coverin' my eyes an' havin' narthen to do wi' it. But Jake cum along wi' 'is mates, big lads, pulled me off bed, dragged me over to 'er an' tuk down me trousers . . .'

In a dry voice she said, 'An thou didst to her what hast niver done to me, Sam? Fucked 'er good 'n' proper?'

He took her hand and she let it lie passively.

'Oi did. God forgive me. Oi'll not ask, but Oi pray thou canst forgive me too, for Oi love thee so. Without thee Oi've narthen and no reason for bein' on this earth, Oi swear it, Edie.'

Her hand tightened against his.

'What happened then, Sam, to the poor li'l girlie?'

'She wor dead. After they, all of us, after mebbe *I* killed her – two or three o' Jake's cronies tuk her out in th' rain an chucked her on incinerator, to burn along o' rubbish. Only 'cos the rainfall bruk all records, she wor still there next marnin'. Otherwise no-one 'ud iver 'ave known. My difficulty be punishment for what I did that night. Oi know now, I shud niver 'ave married thee.'

Edith cut her hair soon afterwards. Not at once, but two or three weeks later she complained that the weight on the nape of her neck was unbearable and, borrowing her mother's dressmaking scissors, cut off the thick hank that had hung down her back all her life. It changed her gipsyish looks, turning her into a little Bohemian, a Dorelia John with a wiry geometric bob. She looked older, more serious, but there was no longer any risk of a long curling strand getting caught between her fingers. Sam lamented the loss of her beautiful heavy hair but Edith never let it grow again.

Edith and Sam could fill the house with nephews and nieces whenever they wanted: their four sisters had nine children between them and Sam's brother Ezra, too, had married a local girl after the war, though in a register office, not a church. (This unsanctified union meant, to Ezra's mother, that the young pair were living in sin and she refused to visit them, even when their first baby boy came along.)

Starting with sixteen-year-old Hester, Matty's eldest, there were Anna and Bobby and Mick; Stan and Abel and little Davie and finally Joan's late-born twins, Flora (Florrie) after her mother and Giorgio (Georgie), named after the distant father of her husband Pino, an Italian prisoner-of-war who had stayed on after the war ended and released Joan at the age of thirty-eight from a long unwanted spinsterhood. Italians liked big women, she said, and Pino appreciated her hearty cooking, though he'd laughed his head off the first time she offered him macaroni pudding. At Christmas Edith and Sam had plenty of presents to buy and wrap – doll's house furniture, glass or china animals, puzzles and jigsaws, storybooks and, as the children got older, poetry anthologies or dictionaries. Childless people often make the best aunts and uncles and whenever they could afford it, they took the big ones to the circus or pantomime in Ipswich or Bury. They might have tried again for their own child once Dr Roffey finally retired and a younger, more enlightened GP took over the practice, but by then a long silence had closed over the subject. Sam remained a demonstrative and loving husband; Edith an affectionate wife. A life without lovemaking (*fucking*, in her mind: call a spade a spade) or children was the price she paid for the death of an unknown girl almost exactly the same age as herself. Had that girl lived, by now they would surely both have been mothers.

CHAPTER FOUR

Spring 1950–6 February 1952

EDITH CARRIED HER SHOPPING BASKET THROUGH THE FRONT door, worn out after a long day's teaching. From the kitchen where he was reading the *Daily Mirror*, Sam called out a loving greeting and put the kettle on. She hung her raincoat on a peg in the hall and bent to undo her cycle clips. As she came in and started putting things away in the larder he asked, 'Do they still put their name and address on the front of their books and then England – The World – The Universe – Space?'

'Aye, they do.'

'They do when they write and thank their gran for a half crown postal order or sumthin'. I 'ad one today: *Mrs Clarry, 14 Undermeadow Lane, Lower Flexham, Suffolk, England, The World, The Universe, Space.*' He laughed. 'Lucky the kid put *Universe* or I mighta 'ad to send it back: address unknown.'

She smiled. 'Children don't change much. It's their way of tryin' to understand infinity. Space is hard for 'em to grasp, but funnily enough they dunnt have no problem with *for ever*. They think *everythin*'s for ever.'

'Biccy?' he offered.

'No, ta.'

'There's some nice choccy ones left from Sunday . . .'

'No, love, ta.'

'Oi tuk a letter to Jake Roberts today,' Sam said. ''E dun't git many proper ones, just some in brown envelopes and 'is Pools coupon. Oi'm surprised 'e cun fill it in, 'e dun't know narthen about numbers.'

'Didst see 'im?'

'Aye,' Sam said. ''E opened front door just as I wor about to put it through letter box. 'E said, "It be thee," and Oi said, "Aye," an' 'e said, "How'rt doin'?" an' I said, "Capital," an' Oi give 'im letter direct into 'is 'and and he tuk it and off 'e went.'

'He ain't married yet?'

'No, he b'ain't.'

''E bin punished too, Sam.'

'*Not enough!*'

They sipped the hot tea in silence.

'Where be Mam?' Edith asked.

'Gone out, visitin' Mrs Winterton, she said.'

'They'll be blatherin' for hours, then.'

There was a pause, a long pause; then Sam said, 'We cud adopt a babby, easy.'

'Why should we do that? You niver know what you'll git.'

'But Edie, lovey, you just said children don't change much.'

'*Blood tells* . . . I want me own blood, an' thine. Not some stranger – some mucky girl who cud give away a chance child even though it be her own flesh 'n' blood.'

'She mighta bin – *taken* – against 'er will . . .'

'An' *we*'re to bring up the child of a man who cud do that? *No!*'

Edith bought herself a Roberts radio and listened to it in the seldom-used parlour while marking the children's exercise books. Like Marjorie, she was not fussy about which pro-grammes she heard. Since everything was new, it hardly mattered whether the music was by Scriabin or Shostakovich.

Her mother, cooking supper in the kitchen while listening to her own 'wulless', would call out, 'Turn off that row, Edie – it's drownin' my *Archers*!' and Edith would adjust the volume as she scrutinized her pupils' curling rows of a, b and c, apple, baby and cat, adding *Well done!* and a gold or silver star at the foot of especially careful work. She listened to talks entitled 'The Modern Novel – Galsworthy to Greene' or 'Fan Vaulting from Durham Cathedral to Christ Church Hall'. The former prompted her to borrow books from Marjorie; the latter to take a train to Ely one summer Sunday and look at the cathedral's Lady Chapel, flooded with mysterious pale green light.

Outwardly she and Sam were a devoted couple but both knew their marriage had suffered. Once upon a time, everything had been open and light and there was nothing they couldn't talk about. Now they both nursed dark areas of reticence, anger and disappointment. The forest had grown up dense and tall since their courting days and they chose to tread safe well-worn paths rather than risk venturing into unknown territory. At quiet times of day – making the bed, changing its unstained sheets, ironing Sam's white work shirts – Edith brooded about the unknown girl whose name she didn't even know. How old would she have been? What did she look like? Pretty? What was she doing there? 'She musta bin a loose sort o' woman?' Edith had once said to Sam. Remembering the sodden, cowering creature scarcely out of childhood who had trembled at Jake's feet, he felt sure she was no tart but a terrified little girl who had strayed into the wrong place. Sam decided to go in search of Ivor Wordley, in case he remembered more.

Ivor was easily located through the Royal Mail records and one spring afternoon, when he had finished his rounds for the day, Sam cycled through the familiar villages, out of his own territory, leaving behind the sharp smell of the sea and heading inland towards Ipswich. Ivor's house was a newly built bungalow on the outskirts. A corrugated iron garage stood beside it. The door was opened by a young woman.

'Mrs . . . Wordley?' Sam asked uncertainly.

'Aye,' she said, puzzled.

'Oi be a friend of Ivor . . . well, I wor, it's a while ago now. We wor in India, him 'n' me.'

'Oh, aye. He ain't back yet. Wilt tha come in?'

A pair of children appeared at the end of the hall and stared at Sam.

'Oi'll wait outside, if that's all right. He'll not be long?'

'Half an hour at most. Be'est thou *Sam*?'

'Aye, that's me!' he said with relief. 'Sam. Sam Savage. Ivor's told thee about me, then?'

'Chance times. An' Albert, an' Sidney, an' that brute, Jake Roberts. '*E* wor a nasty piece of work! Art sure thou'lt not come in?'

'No, missus, thanks. Oi'll wait outside till 'e gits back. Oi'll not bother thee.'

'It's no bother . . .' she said; but when he still didn't step forward she smiled and closed the door gently.

Sam waited near the bus stop on the other side of the road, reflecting that Ivor Wordley had certainly not told his wife about the rape or she would never have invited him into her home, or uttered Jake's name so innocently. Nor, obviously, did Ivor share his own difficulty; the children were proof of that. Ivor had been able to bury his memories of the incident and keep his mouth shut. Honesty was not the best policy, he knew that now. He should never have told Edith what had happened on the night of the monsoon. After half an hour a car drove up and Ivor steered it into the garage and emerged. He looked taller and older, much older; the fresh contours of his boyhood face overlaid by the sharper angles of a man. He unlocked the front door, entered, and a few moments later stuck his head out and looked up and down the road. Sam stepped forward and waved.

The two of them walked to the pub, Sam wheeling his bike. They sat in a corner and Sam bought two glasses of beer.

'Thou'rt a drinkin' man now?' Ivor enquired. 'Thou wast tee-total in India.'

'Aye. 'Twere war that did it. I cudna 'ave gone through the war wi'out me beer.'

They exchanged small talk and Ivor bought another two pints.

'Here's to the good old days . . .' he said, lifting the glass. Sam was astonished.

'*Good?*'

'Aye – we 'ad good times, didn' we?'

What had happened to his memories? How had he managed to efface them so completely that the nervous figure shivering convulsively on the train back to Ipswich was now a happy, confident family man?

'Not allus . . .' Sam said.

Ivor frowned. 'The bint who came into dormitory that night?'

'Aye,' Sam said almost eagerly. 'Thou hasn't forgotten 'er?'

'She wor tart,' Ivor said dismissively. 'Shudna've bin there in first place. Deserved all she got. Mucky little nigger.'

'She wor no *tart*!' Sam protested. 'She wor just li'l ol' girlie who lost her way!'

'What wor she doin' then, comin' into dormitory? She'd niver 'a' dun that if she wor good girl!'

'Jake Roberts – *Jake Roberts* med 'er come in! Dusna thou remember?'

'No,' said Ivor firmly and pressed his lips together to put an end to the subject.

Sam leaned forward over the marble-topped table to focus Ivor's concentration.

'That girlie be causin' me such difficulty!' he began.

'Didst catch disease off o' 'er? That proves it, see!'

'*No!*' said Sam. 'No, Oi didna, but . . .' his voice trailed away.

Ivor was baffled. 'Hast cycled all this way, Sam Savage, to ask me about that night? It wor fifteen years ago. Ferget it!'

'Thirteen and a half,' said Sam.

'Oi dun' want to speak about it. Oi've shut me mind to it.'

'Ivor, old mate, thou dusna know my trouble. Oi come to ask if canst remember anythin' about the girlie. Please. *Anything!*'

'She wor wet.'

'Aye . . .'

'An' little; very little an' skinny. All the darkies wor littler 'n' us.'

'Aye. Dost remember her name?'

'She niver told us 'er *name.*'

'Narthen else?'

'Sam, the missis'll be waitin' wi' my tea. Wilt come hoam along o' me fer a bite?' Ivor asked civilly, but Sam knew he was ill at ease.

'Dost see Jake Roberts iver? Or Sidney, or Albert?' Sam said.

'Sidney got killed in war, pore old boy,' Ivor told him. 'An' Oi wudna give toime o' day to Jake Roberts if 'e wor last man on earth.'

They parted then, Ivor to go home to his wife and children, Sam to swing his leg over the bike and pedal wearily back to Lower Flexham and tea with two women, a radio and a welcoming cat.

Sam's rage against Jake grew like a tumour that summer. He began to suffer blinding headaches. These were so bad that sometimes he had to take a day off sick, since the pressure of bright sunlight on his throbbing temples and watering eyes made it hard for him to read addresses or ride the bike steadily. Fearing he might lose his job, he made an appointment to see the new doctor.

Dr Fellows's predecessor had scribbled on Sam's case notes

the words, '*Reason for visit: wife's failure to conceive; incident during army service has > partial impotence. Genitalia normal; patient healthy; resisted suggns of mut. mast. No prescripn. 10/07/47.*'

The young doctor looked up as Sam came in.

'Ah, morning, postman!' he said, and Sam smiled wanly. 'What seems to be the trouble?'

'I bin havin' such headaches I 'ave to cry off me round.'

'Any idea what's causing them?'

'They comes 'n' goes.'

Dr Fellows shone a light into Sam's eyes.

'Anything on your mind?'

'Oi be cheerful, usually. But sometimes, aye, my thoughts be whoolly black.'

'What sort of thoughts?'

'This 'n' that. Past.'

The doctor let the silence lengthen but Sam did not add anything.

'How're things at home?'

'Narthen's changed.'

'Your wife . . . Edith, isn't it?'

'Aye, that's right. Foine, she be foine.'

'Children?'

'No, doctor.'

Not much to be got out of this one, the young doctor thought. What's the point in coming to see me and shutting up like a clam?

'Oi just want sumthin' for the headaches, then I cun leave thee in peace.'

'Pills only mask the symptoms. I could recommend something a bit more radical that would put a stop to them for good.'

'What be that?'

'Have you heard of ECT?'

'No.'

'Stands for electro-convulsive treatment. It sounds alarming but—'

Sam had already recoiled.

'Oi've heard o' *that*, doctor, it's electric shocks, innit? No thanks very much, I'll not 'ave that, no, no, I'd rather stick with me 'eadaches.'

'Steady on, Mr Savage, it's not as bad as it sounds. Let me explain . . .'

Sam was adamant. No therapy, above all no electric shocks. He'd come for some pills stronger than aspirin and if the doctor wouldn't prescribe them he'd double his aspirin dose. Dr Fellows managed to establish that Sam's headaches were not migraines, scribbled a prescription and watched his patient make a hasty departure. To Sam's record he added: *Patient complaining of severe headaches, ? due continuing marital/sexual complicns; refuses ECT; paracetamol prescribed, 12/08/50.*

The obsession with Jake grew in the cavern behind his eyes, narrowing his field of vision and eclipsing the red and golden autumn days. He said nothing about it to Edith and continued to do his best to talk and behave normally, but heavy-footed thoughts trudged round and round his brain to the beat of the name of his enemy. It never occurred to Sam that he was hated with equal force.

As far as Jake was concerned, they'd both been involved years ago in something that had got out of hand but as no-one knew about it besides him, Sam and Sam's three mates – who'd vanished into thin air, likely killed in the war – what did it matter? If it hadn't been for Sam's proximity, Jake would have forgotten all about it. There was no longer any quarrel between them. But Sam's threat persisted in his mind – an odd threat from such a tiddler: *I'm gunna punish thee when I git the chance. Whether it be war or peace, 'ome or abroad, mark my words, Jake Roberts, Oi swear it.* Jake couldn't forget the time Sam had leaped on him from behind in the canteen, hanging on for dear life, jabbing viciously at his eyes. Jake was not a man capable of much speculation but those two moments – one of icy calm, the other of raving fury – nagged persistently. He knew from the slaughterhouse that it took one solid blow to transfix a beast, a second to catapult it from life into death. He didn't want it happening to him. What if Sam carried a cudgel under his navy-blue postman's cape or in his saddlebag? Face to face, Jake was more than a match for him, but surprised from behind, felled, clubbed till blood poured from his head and the soft skull splintered to a mass of red and grey jelly . . . ? He shivered and thought, 'Me mam wudda said, *A goose walked over yer grave.*'

All his life Jake had taken for granted that when he grew up he would marry and farm his mother's eighty acres. They had been Roberts land for several generations; the house in which he grew up was called Roberts Farm House; behind him stretched a line of men bearing his name, John Roberts, who had shared his ancestral feeling for those particular fields and trees, the medieval boundaries locked in by those lanes and hedges, the gentle undulations of that horizon. *Roberts* land; his by right. Even as a boy of eight Jake's boastful conceit sprang from the knowledge that he was better than a labourer's son. He worked alongside other boys at the same tasks with the same tools but they were hired hands whereas he owned – or would own – the earth from which he picked out stones, hurling them at birds or rabbits rather than piling them up beside the road like the rest. What was a halfpenny per pail to John Jacob Roberts, whose belly was never empty? Now, at the age of thirty-two, he lived in a rented room and worked for a boss amid the steaming bodies of terrified animals.

Yet the job of slaughterer suited his choleric temperament. Its frenzy, panic and suddenness, the beasts whose bodies crashed to the ground in a buckling of hooves, a bouncing and gushing of blood, satisfied his craving for violence and cruelty.

His other needs were less easily satisfied. Girls didn't care for slaughterhouse men. However carefully Jake bathed, Bryl-creemed his black hair and dressed up on Saturday nights, the smell lingered – a hot, visceral smell carrying with it the foam-flecked terror of his daily life. His coarse features and swaggering manner put off the girls he wanted to attract: girls increasingly younger than himself, since women of his age were mostly married now, with little girls of their own. In the pub or village hall Jake would loom, pint of beer in one hand, Players' Navy Cut in the other, shouting and showing his big white teeth and strong throat. When the music struck up he would seize a girl and clump about, trying to get closer to her reluctant soft body, but at the end of the evening he hardly ever achieved more than a kiss, from which the girl would struggle free. His offer of a trip to the cinema ('Oi'll tek 'ee to pictures – it be *Kind 'Earts an' Cornets* next Friday . . .') was nearly always rejected. Girls warned one another about Jake Roberts and even those who did agree to go out with him never accepted a second date. His daily life and the lack of a woman's influence combined to make him even cruder than his nature dictated; yet beneath the large, loud movements he was lonely and craved tenderness. The most he got was an occasional grapple with his landlady, a tight-lipped widow given new vigour by the brown paper bags of fresh meat that Jake filched from the slaughter-house and stuffed down the pockets of his blood-stained overalls. Perhaps she craved tenderness too.

Sam's life seemed the opposite of his own. Jake was a man of the field, forced to slaughter the beasts he would rather have reared and nurtured. Sam was a plain man but he had a home and a wife – as neat and clean as a little cat – furthermore a schoolteacher wife who earned good money and was known and respected by everyone in the village. Even as a girl, Edith's rapid thoughts had been reflected in her clever, dancing eyes. Now Sam had the daily solace of her company at supper and in his bed. What had Sam done that he, Jake, had not done? Sam was no better than him – even puny, timid Sam had mauled the Indian bint; could have been the one who killed her – he'd done it to her last. That would make him a murderer. Jake envied Sam and was jealous of everything he possessed, even though he himself had – soon would have – much more.

Towards the end of 1950 Jake's mother fell ill. Maggie Debney, now in her mid-sixties, looked a decade older and it was some time before Lizzie and Rose, her daughters, let alone Billy her husband, realized that her greyish skin and hollow frame signalled more than ordinary midwinter pallor. Not that it would have made any difference; her aversion to doctors and hospitals was so great that she refused to go near either. January was a cold, cheerless month. By the time they finally summoned Dr Fellows Maggie was spending all day huddled by a roaring fire despite the fuel shortage, moaning and trembling with pain. The doctor carried her up to her bedroom where he examined her, rolled back her eyelids, patted her shoulder gently and said, 'You'll feel a little better when you've taken some of these pills. Shouldn't have waited so long to call me, you know, bad girl! We'll book you in at the hospital for some tests and . . .'

'No 'ospital, no tests, thank you all the same, doctor. Oi know what Oi've got, just as thou dost.'

She would not be persuaded.

In the farmhouse kitchen afterwards he broke the news to her daughter Rose.

'There's nothing I or anyone else can do, your mother's condition is too far advanced. I can't think how she stood the pain this long, and it's going to get worse. I shall have to go against her wishes and get her into hospital.'

'She'll niver go to hospital, doctor. She'd die rather than do that!'

'I am afraid she'll die either way. Can you nurse her at home? It won't be easy. I'll give her something for the pain and have the district nurse look in but . . .'

'Me 'n' Lizzie'll look after 'er between us,' Rose said, thinking: an' who'll get the children to school? How'll I do the house 'n' feed 'em, if I'm here? She asked, 'How long is she gunna . . . ?'

'Weeks. Not months.'

Maggie took three weeks to die. At her request, Jake was summoned just before the end. His mother lay on the bed from which he had been evicted as a little boy, more than thirty years ago. Rose, who had warned him before she led him upstairs, watched from the doorway as he approached the bed. How could that wraith-like body, scarcely rucking up the blankets, have produced this swarthy male, harsh and quarrelsome as a rook, whose florid face and hands seemed engorged with blood?

'I'm gunna die now, Jakey,' she said; and when he protested, 'Dun' talk nonsense. No time. Billy in 'ere?'

'No, Mam.'

She looked at her son with infinite resignation. People were who they were born to be and could not always govern what they did.

'Hast guessed, mebbe. Th'art no Roberts, son – too much of a savage fer that. John Roberts wor a gentle soul but thou wert allus full o' spleen and fury.'

'What art saying, Mam? What art *tellin'* me?' he asked angrily.

She struggled for breath, each phrase uttered between gasps. 'Work it out, John Jacob, but don't – blame – thy *savage* – nature on 'im. An' govern thisself, or thou'lt end in jail.' Her eyes had sunk, the bony nose jutting sharply between their sockets. She had no lips or teeth, only a cavity inside which her dry tongue laboured.

Jake bent over the bed and tried to speak softly. 'Oi'll leave thee in peace now, Mam . . . thou mun rest. Git thy strength back.'

Her eyelids were strings of gristle, her eyes watery slits.

'Things 'appen, durin' war, that – niver wud – in normal times. After my John went 'n' died I did me best fer thee. Billy wore me down, till – I got that sick of 'im rantin', I jes' wanted – peace 'n' quiet.'

'Thou'st left farm to 'im.'

'Aye.'

He stepped back from the bedside clenching his fists and swearing.

'God damn and blind 'im! Fuck the bastard! Fuck 'im! 'Twer *mine* to inherit, not *'is*! *Roberts* Farm! *Years* Oi bin' waitin', five years in slaughter'ouse, blood 'n' guts 'n' shit 'n' stink, an' now . . . 'Tain't what my father wudda wanted.'

She sighed and lifted her hand a fraction as though to ward off his anger.

'Thou niver 'as listened, John Jacob. Allus fightin', niver words.'

Jake Roberts thumped heavily on the end of the brass bedstead and strode out of the room. Lizzie and Rose were waiting outside. Rose extended a comforting hand but he jerked his shoulder violently, swung away from her touch and stormed off.

That night Maggie Debney, Roberts that was, born Margaret Wright, murmured something inaudible to her daughters before moving beyond consciousness. She died next morning in the small hours, rain sheeting down behind drawn curtains. Old Tom, the big church bell, tolled the sixty-six years of her life. Three days later her family trudged in procession past respectful villagers, black umbrellas dripping shiny streaks down the best coats of Rose's two youngest, following the slow black hearse that carried her coffin. Jake and Billy were chief pallbearers, the strong furious men Maggie had nurtured and loved, whose rivalry – the only tribute they could pay her – was undiminished. Lizzie and Rose's faces were wet with rain and tears and their blue-eyed daughters alternately snivelled and giggled but her son and husband were tearless.

Sam's mother Flora sat at the back of the church, rocking and wailing random scraps from the Bible – '*They were as fed horses in the morning*' – muttering the words of the Service for the Burial of the Dead as well as strange chants, imprecations and laments: '*Behold, and see if there be any sorrow like unto my sorrow.*' Jake, scowling in the front row, turned round and hissed, 'Shut thy gob, daft old bat!' but she answered in a loud, clear voice, '*He is like a lamb or an ox that is brought to the slaughter.*' When the vicar discoursed on the dead woman's attributes, Flora muttered, '*Aye, but my brother is a hairy man and I am a smooth man.*' Others in the congregation turned to frown reprovingly but even then she would not be quiet.

The coffin was lowered into the muddy earth and strewn with a handful of soil from a Roberts field. As soon as they got outside the church gate, Jake and Billy squared up to each other and began a quarrel that almost ended in blows. Jake roared off on his new motorbike, never again to enter the house in which he had been born or set foot on the land that all his life he had looked forward to owning; now the property of Billy Debney. His mother had left him two hundred and fifty pounds ... enough to buy a small cottage beside a stream on the wide flat marshes bordering the Deben estuary, almost within sight of the sea. From his front door he could smell the damp ozone and even, when an east wind blew, feel its salty droplets sting his face.

A year later almost to the day, King George VI, by the Grace of God ruler of all the pink bits on the schoolroom map, also died in the small hours of a chill February morning. Big Ben tolled the fifty-six years of his life.

CHAPTER FIVE

Friday 30 January–Sunday 1 February 1953

1953 WAS CORONATION YEAR AND FRIDAY 30 JANUARY ITS FIRST really good day, the warmest for two months. The weather report singled out the eastern counties for special comment: 'East Anglia enjoyed hours of sunshine with temperatures in the mid-fifties,' said the BBC announcer in his plummy voice. Sam made his deliveries in the wintry sunlight, saying cheerily, 'Lovely day! – yes, lovely day! – About time too!' wherever he went. There was a package for Jake from – curiosity got the better of Sam and he examined the postmark – London WC1. That didn't tell him much. He propped his bike against Jake's rickety fence wondering why the man didn't bestir himself to mend it, and rang the front doorbell. No answer. Jake must have gone to work. Sam rang the bell a second time to be on the safe side but there was still no answer, so he tucked the packet securely between the inside wall of the overgrown porch and a compartmented basket for milk bottles, noticing that Jake didn't rinse out his empties, let alone scald them hygienically, as Edith did. Who'd have thought strapping Jake Roberts would still be a bachelor at the age of thirty-five, with not so much as the rumour of a bastard child let alone a lawful family to carry on the Roberts line? Yet his own predicament was worse. Sam knew every inch of his wife's body, dressed or undressed, but at night he was unable to show his love for her. He longed to stroke her smooth flesh but was too ashamed to reach out his hand, so imprisoned by guilt and habit that he could not even kiss her. Impotence had made a mockery of their marriage and the sense of failure tortured him.

Once or twice he had wondered if Jake knew. 'Tell thy schoolmarm wife, if she wunts a babby o' her own, Jake Roberts'll be 'appy to oblige . . .' he had leered once, when Sam delivered a couple of Christmas parcels. Could Edith be so desperate that she'd let his sworn enemy . . . ? He refused to speculate about whether she was true to him. In the last year or so she had moved with a new physical confidence. She even held her head in a different way, arching her chin so as to display her beautiful neck. It made her more desirable than ever and when they went to the flicks on Saturday nights she attracted lots of admiring glances. Such thoughts released a swarm of demons in Sam's imagination, black and spiky like flying cockchafers. If he didn't control his fantasies they would drive him mad. She was his wife, for better for worse; she'd never look at another man, just as he himself averted his eyes from the women who sometimes answered the door in their nighties, hillocks of plump blue-veined flesh rising like dough, making him thicken and swell . . . Sam gritted his teeth, seized his bike, clasped the handlebars, hooked his leg over the saddle and pedalled along the lane beside the stream.

His life had been cursed because of one dreadful act. Jake had forced him to commit the rape that had disgraced and unmanned him. Sam was manacled by the leaden, terrible weight of his guilt over the death of the little Indian girl. She had been so small and trusting when she came into the dormitory, staring in wonder at them all. When Jake tore off her sopping wet rags her body had looked pitifully thin and frail, with tiny limbs and hands – oh, her hands! The way she had threaded her fingers through her hair still made him recoil with pity. She must have had a family but they probably never found out what happened to her. She was not a prostitute, he was sure of that; just a little girl who had strayed from her proper destination. It was up to him to avenge her death although he didn't even know her name. He had seen plenty of wounded, starving or abandoned children during the war, but the Indian girl's plight touched him more deeply than any of them. Old Dr Roffey had been right – only when he had freed himself from this obsession would he become a man. His mother's religious fervour and his father's ungovernable rage came together in his determination to avenge her.

Sam brooded on safe ways to murder Jake. There weren't many. Poison could be traced back to the chemist and ultimately to himself. Killing at close quarters was out of the question. Jake's work in the slaughterhouse had doubled his strength. All day he lugged huge carcasses of bullocks and pigs, heaving them onto his back – broad and solid as an oak table – and loading them onto butchers' lorries. Sam, though he had developed strong calf muscles and wiry biceps, was puny by comparison. One thing was in his favour. Jake's cottage was several hundred yards from the next house . . . odd that he should have picked somewhere so isolated, but it meant Sam could linger unobserved. His first idea had been to disable the brakes on Jake's car by tampering with the rods, but Sam worried that the first time Jake jammed his foot down hard he would notice something wrong. A better way might be to pollute the water supply. The old well in Jake's garden had been capped, which must mean he had a water tank in the attic. The back door was loose; Sam could prise it open without difficulty, nip up there, remove the lid of the tank – probably just a few dusty planks – and drop in the corpses of a couple of dead birds, maybe a rat as well. Jake would gradually sicken. With no-one to watch over his health, he might neglect the symptoms long enough to die of stomach poisoning. It was worth a try. The lane ended, Sam rejoined the main road, settled his shoulders, speeded up and whistled cheerfully. The mild day seemed a portent of better things, a foretaste of spring in midwinter, despite the leafless trees.

Even in temperate England the weather can unleash surprises. That gentle Friday was the day before a storm that the papers would call the worst catastrophe since the Great Plague of 1665, though newspapers often exaggerate. Already, though neither Sam nor anyone else in Lower Flexham was aware of it, unusually strong winds were driving water from the Atlantic towards the shallower North Sea, funnelling the spring tide south into the bottleneck between Scotland and Norway. At the same time – fatal combination – a depression was moving from Iceland towards northern Scotland. The weather boffins christened it Low Z in a friendly way, marking it on their diagrammatic charts with a neat oval. With hindsight they would call it 'an unprecedented rogue depression' but for the time being they chose not to upset everyone's expectations of a pleasant, unseasonably mild weekend. By midnight on Friday a tidal surge was building up, added to which tremendous gales were lashing the Hebrides with freak winds of more than a hundred miles an hour. Still the experts issued only cursory warnings, a form of words that implied, 'Nothing to worry about.'

Next morning, as the storm hurled itself from the Orkneys down towards the Highlands with winds of more than a hundred and twenty-five miles an hour, tall Scottish pines were uprooted and thousands of acres of forest laid waste. At noon on Saturday the duty officer in the central weather-forecasting department in Dunstable did mention, in his usual six-hourly bulletin, that exceptionally strong north-west to northerly gale-force winds were settling in over the North Sea. To those who understood these matters, this gave notice of serious trouble on the way but it seemed premature to set off public anxiety. It was Saturday lunchtime, people were relaxing . . . why spoil things on the off chance? Strong winds and high tides were normal in January. The storm might veer, subside, even fade away altogether. And if not, the sea defences would surely hold.

Out at sea, the depression changed course. Up till now Low Z had been north-westerly. Suddenly it swung round like a sea-monster and lunged south-eastwards, shoving a wall of water ahead of itself. The waves boiled and thrashed and even hardened seamen swore afterwards they'd never seen a storm like it. At about two o'clock that Saturday afternoon a fishing trawler, the *Michael Griffiths*, sank in the Outer Hebrides, drowning her crew of fifteen. At the same time a car ferry in the Irish Sea bound for Larne from Stranraer was overwhelmed by mountainous waves, listed heavily to starboard and sank. The captain stayed on the bridge and saluted as his ship went down – or so the papers reported. Perhaps he really did. 1953 was a very patriotic year. A hundred and thirty-three passengers and crew were drowned, leaving forty-four battered and dazed survivors.

Further south, where the catastrophe would strike hardest, as late as two o'clock in the afternoon no-one yet took the storm seriously. All afternoon the sea whipped itself up to greater heights and more power, gathering force as it headed down the east coast towards the Wash and the towns, villages, bungalows and beach huts clustered along its happy family coastline. News travelled slowly and although the six o'clock bulletin on the Home Service mentioned the sinking of the Irish car ferry, nothing was said about freak tides or waves ten feet high. These were now only a couple of hours away.

The evening before a disaster is like any other. In their snug kitchen Edith and Sam were mashing up Mrs Satterthwaite's supper. All over Suffolk, couples were getting ready to go out to the pictures (Charles Laughton in *The Private Life of Henry*

VIII, Jean Simmons and Robert Mitchum in *Angel Face* or, showing prophetically at the Ritz in Felixstowe, *A Night without Sleep*). Others were enjoying a gentle bridge foursome, breaking off from time to time to say, 'Wind's gettin' up!' and smile at one another before concentrating on their cards again. There was even a dance in progress on Southend Pier, despite high waves lashing the struts and a howling wind that made the music difficult to hear. The usual Saturday night dance in Ipswich had been cancelled the day before – to Jake's annoyance, since he'd planned to go. Now he faced a solitary evening with the radio. At the Floral Hall in Great Yarmouth, thirty miles further up the coast, another dance was underway. No-one noticed the floodwater lapping and creeping up the steps. At eight o'clock, by which time the dance was in full swing, the River Yare began to overflow.

Later, people would say it was the extraordinary suddenness with which the water rose that was most terrifying of all. At ten, when high tide reached Great Yarmouth, the river broke its banks and a double curve of water like the bow wave of a ship parted on either side of the concrete central support of Haven Bridge. The phone lines went down and soon afterwards the electricity failed, making the swirling water and incoherent cries all the more sinister in the lilting darkness, beneath a bright full moon.

The Irish ferry tragedy, reported in more detail on the nine o'clock news that evening, shocked everyone – 133 drowned! – obscuring the fact that an even greater disaster was imminent. The weather bulletins were still talking in general terms of gales and heavy seas. Over the next hour the sea broke through all along the coast from Great Yarmouth and tidal waves eight, sometimes ten, occasionally as much as fourteen feet high smashed the hopelessly inadequate sea defences. Water surged across fields, along streets and into houses, often right up to ceiling level, and the church bells started ringing frantically to rouse the sleeping populace to the danger. One man, enjoying a peaceful evening with his wife and dog, caught sight of a glimmer of light through the curtains and thought it must be snow. Opening his front door to admire the virgin whiteness, he was almost knocked off his feet by a wall of water. He and his wife managed to reach higher ground but they had to leave their terrified dog behind. (The dog was found alive twenty-four hours later, floating on the kitchen table.) An eight-year-old boy was woken in the middle of the night by a cracking sound and ran to his bedroom window just in time to watch as the sea wall fell down and a surge of water poured through the breach. His father, with manic energy and unusual presence of mind, ripped up the floorboards in the hall so that the sea water rushed down to the cellar rather than up to ceiling level. Elsewhere a woman heard a dripping tap and got up to turn it off . . . only to find her kitchen under several feet of sea. At first people tried to bale the water out, but the tide rose too quickly and they were forced to take refuge in upstairs rooms, eventually climbing through windows onto the roof, dragging children after them. Others battered holes in their bedroom ceiling, clambered into the attic and using anything they could find – bricks, planks, chair legs – smashed through the tiles. They huddled on the roof clutching cat, dog or teddy bear, a sheet or towel hoisted as a distress signal, teeth chattering with cold and shock as they waited to be rescued. 'My poor home!' one woman cried over and over again; 'Oh, my poor home!' Families spent the night wrapped in sodden blankets, wind, rain and salt spray stinging their ice-cold faces, parents trying to comfort their shivering children and secretly believing their last hour had come. Rain fell remorselessly, the torrent swirled past their gumboots, the world turned to water.

All night long the tide sped down streets and into houses and gardens, ripping out furniture, fences, gates, rabbit hutches, dog kennels, drowning the animals trapped inside and surging on with its load of fish barrels, tables, armchairs, prams. Some prams had a child inside and some of those children survived. A young woman cradling her newborn baby waded in pitch darkness towards the safety of her neighbour's house a dozen yards away. The swirling waters knocked her off balance, she tripped, fell, and the baby was snatched from her arms. Struggling to her feet, she peered desperately into the black sheeting rain but the baby had gone.

At Aldeburgh, a few miles from Jake's house, the sea easily demolished the fragile wall separating it from the river Alde, flooding the reclaimed land for more than four miles. It rolled towards the grazing marshes of Deben in exuberant flood, uprooting everything in its path. Terrified animals were swept off their feet and swam towards high ground, only to be inundated again. Sheep, whose fleece quickly became water-logged, were the first to drown. Rabbits got stuck in the forked branches of trees, marooned beside sodden partridges and pheasants. The Deben estuary was transformed into a mighty river, its swollen tributaries bouncing and bubbling. Beside one of them stood Jake's house.

Jake Roberts was alone. He had cooked himself baked beans and sausages for supper and opened a tin of treacle pudding. Afterwards, making sure that the curtains were securely drawn, he studied the contents of his parcel: a handbook on knots, two reels of strong nylon cord and a selection of barbed, needle-sharp fish hooks. He scrutinized them approvingly and ran the cord between his fingers before locking them away in the cupboard under the stairs, the one in which he also kept his mother's nightgown, a six-foot length of brass chain, two or three padlocks and a selection of pretty, flimsy undergarments folded and wrapped in tissue paper. Buried in the centre of all this was his old gas mask; also a razor-sharp penknife, the sort with several blades, a corkscrew, and a thing for taking stones out of horses' hooves. Jake went back to *Saturday Night on the*

Light, twiddling the volume dial so that he could hear above the roar of wind and rain. Like everyone else, he was slow to grasp that this was no ordinary storm.

A few miles away in Lower Flexham, Edith settled her querulous mother in bed and came downstairs to join Sam, who was listening to the Saturday evening play, *The Troublemakers*. All evening Pushy had been restless, refusing to sit on their laps, jumping onto furniture and tables, miaowing fretfully. Finally he managed to leap up onto the mantelpiece, dislodging the porcelain baby in its cradle. It dropped on the tiles in front of the fire, shattering into jagged white-painted twigs balanced on rockers and a head that, like the swaddled body, turned out to be hollow. Sam, genuinely upset, apologized several times – Pushy was his cat, so in a way the accident was his fault. Edith said briskly, 'What's done is done and can't be mended, and nor can this.'

She cursed the cat, grabbed it by one leg from where it cowered under the sofa and threw it out of the back door into the howling night, returning with a dustpan and brush to sweep up the shards.

'It be blown' up a turrible tempest out there,' she said. 'The wind's blorin' as if Owd Hinery an' all the devils was let out o' hell.'

Sam glanced at the clock on the mantelpiece. 'Nearly ten,' he said. 'Us best go to bed. Can't 'ardly 'ear th'wulless. Foul ol' night.'

He lingered to heat milk and water for their bedtime hot chocolate. Pushy was pressed up against the kitchen window, his black fur soaked, and Sam unlatched the back door to let him in. Scooping up the cat, he rubbed its fur with a towel, whispering, 'Shush, do 'ee be quiet or Mum'll throw 'ee out agin!' When its shivering had settled down to a vibrating purr Sam poured a saucer of milk and set it down beside the cat basket. Then he carried the two mugs upstairs.

Edith was sitting up in bed in her pyjamas, a book propped on her knees to catch the bedside light. He handed her a mug.

'Didst let Pushy in?' she asked.

'Aye,' Sam admitted shamefacedly. 'He wor outside window, beggin' . . .'

'Good. So *I* needna get out my warm bed.'

A quarter of an hour later, Sam listened to the wind lashing the trees and thought: Now. *Now* is the time. Now's the time when I might do it. Tonight I can kill him. I've waited seventeen years for this moment. As soon as she's asleep, I'll go. He was wide awake, brimming with energy. A sliver of moonlight shone through the bedroom curtains. It'll be bright outside and anyhow I know my way, know it backwards. There'll never be a better moment. He could hardly bear to lie still, but he had to be sure Edith was asleep. Her breathing became slow and deep. In, out, regular as clockwork, inhaling and exhaling sweetly. I'll give it five more minutes, Sam thought, and then . . .

He slid out of bed softly as a shadow and gathered up his folded clothes from the chair. He pressed the door handle down, pushed the door against the frame first to silence it, then pulled it towards him. Not a sound. He melted through the open gap, closed the door noiselessly and, using the inside edge of the stairs against the wall where it was quietest, tiptoed down to the kitchen.

I shall need something hot to keep me going, he thought as he got dressed; maybe a thermos. Although he could hardly control his impatience, he forced himself to boil a kettle, added three spoonfuls of sugar to the teapot and sipped a few scalding mouthfuls from a cup, feeling it slide down his gullet and heat his belly, which was fluttering with excitement. He filled the thermos flask and screwed the stopper in firmly. Now, warm clothes. Sam put on his plaid jacket and tied a woollen scarf round his throat. From his gumboots he took a pair of thick socks and stuck his feet into those; then eased on the boots.

Over the jacket he wore an oilskin. Finally, unhooking the sou'wester, he tied it securely under his chin. Now he would stay warm and dry and, seen from a distance, wouldn't look like Sam the postman. Pulling on his gloves, he wheeled his bicycle out of the porch into the lashing rain. Pushy yawned, tucked his nose between his paws and went back to sleep.

The noise and the wind were like nothing Sam had ever known. Trees bent and creaked, their branches whipping back and forth. The wet road glistened and arcs of water splashed his boots as he rode through puddles. The verges were slippery with rain and it was hard to keep his balance against the force of the wind. He mustn't fall. A brilliant moon sailed in and out of scudding clouds and when his eyes adjusted he found the darkness almost as bright as day.

Controlled and unhurried, Sam rode past houses where not a soul was awake and others where every window shone with golden light. He met no-one on the road – who'd choose to be out? The kitchen clock had said ten past eleven as he left. It normally took no more than half an hour to get to Jake's house but on such a night as this it could be an hour; maybe more. He mustn't tire himself out, just cycle as if it were an ordinary postal round. He was a messenger, delivering a long-delayed message; that was all. He gritted his teeth, put his head down to keep the rain off his face and rode on through the storm. In some places the water was more than a foot deep and it was all he could do to force the bike through it. At times he had to dismount and push, water swirling round the top of his boots, its weight impeding his progress. Good thing I've had plenty of practice, Sam thought; my legs 'ud niver hold out otherwise. I haven't seen rain like this since that monsoon night. If I can get through this I'll be a man again.

By now the sea had risen ten feet or more, inundating fields four miles inland. Jake's house was entirely surrounded by water. The pretty stream that normally gurgled beside it had merged into a sheet of water stretching as far as the eye could see, the tops of trees showing here and there through its surface. Water had reached the eaves of the house, threatening to sweep it off its foundations. Jake, sitting on the topmost point of the roof, could feel it shuddering and straining under him like a boat tugging at its moorings. 'Help!' he called into the roaring night. '*Help*, someone, help me, *help*!'

He had been woken at midnight by strange rushing sounds that seemed to be part of his nightmare. It was several minutes before he got up and drew back the curtains, to find water lapping at the windowsill. Jake, slow-witted and half asleep, was on the point of going back to bed when water began seeping under the window-frame. When it trickled down the wall and he touched it with his fingers and found them wet, he knew it was no dream. He blundered about the bedroom, grabbing a heavy pullover and the eiderdown from his bed, moaning under his breath in an incoherent stream of curses that invoked God, the devil and his mother and blamed all three. Clutching the eiderdown, he forced the window open, struggled through it and heaved himself upright on the sill. He leaned forward, spreadeagled over the tiles, and inched his way up the roof, hanging on with one hand and stretching out towards the next hold with the other, until he was sitting astride the topmost row of ridge tiles, panting hard. After several minutes he reached down for the quilt and sat in the rain sucking it, as a baby sucks on a blanket for comfort. He began to cry.

Half an hour later, soaked through and terrified, still calling out, 'Help, help!' from time to time, he spotted a small boat in the distance. Someone was rowing it, clumsily, inexpertly, so that the boat rocked from side to side. Hope shot like lightning through Jake's arteries. He clambered to his feet and, swaying precariously on the ridge tiles, flapped the sodden eiderdown and shouted as loudly as he could, 'Help! I'm here! Save me! Help, help, he-elp!' The wind lashed against him and he almost lost his balance. Crouching down again and holding on, Jake shouted at the advancing boat, 'Help me! I'm drowning! Help!'

Sam had no sense of his own danger. He did not feel the rain or hear the wind. He seemed to be rowing serenely through a landscape of scintillating colours. A blue sky like that in the Bible illustrations sparkled around him. The olive trees and cypresses of long ago were iridescent green. The clouds were pink and orange-tipped, sailing majestically through a turquoise heaven. This is the Sea of Galilee, he thought, and this is my fishing boat. I am a fisher of men. That man over there is the one I am after, but I mustn't make too much haste or he may get away. And listen, a storm is starting up. The wind is moaning in my ears and rain makes circles in the water. I will row steadily and fear not.

With clenched fists he pushed the oars rhythmically ahead, with elbows bent he pulled them towards his chest. The boat tipped and bobbed through the howling storm and, as it approached, Jake's voice came faintly over the water: 'Help! I'm all in, help me!' Sam shouted back, 'I'm coming . . .' This is where it ends, he thought. One of us will die, and it has to be Jake. My life against his. If I don't kill him I shall be killed.

The scene changed, as though the epidiascope had clicked onto a new exotic picture. Lands of the Bible had become Our Indian Friends. A little Indian girl stood in a doorway gazing at her English friends. Her dark eyes widened in amazement at their pale faces . . . yes! thought Sam, yes, *now* I remember: she was squint-eyed! How could I have forgotten? When she came in she didn't look straight at us. One eye pointed sideways, of course. The little girl walked slowly into the room, awed as though it had been a church. Very slowly, the figures of many men rose to their feet and they welcomed her gravely. She turned from side to side, acknowledging them with a gentle smile. Then there was the sound of a door slamming and the scene splintered into chaos. Men jumped up and ran towards her; the girl shuddered in terror and sank to her knees. One man stood over her laughing. He shouted triumphantly, 'Mine – she's mine! Oi'll 'ave 'er first!' Bending over the crouching girl he said, 'Jake goes first and then Sam 'as a turn. Let's git yer clothes off.'

The scene slowed down again and Sam watched as the girl's clothes, their bright colours darkened by rain, were pulled from her body. Her skin shone like mahogany. Long black hair undulated over her shoulders in glorious abundant tresses. She was dazzlingly beautiful, perfectly shaped, miniature. Sam gazed in holy adoration.

'Sam! Our Sam! I knew thou wudsna let me down!' shouted Jake as Sam rowed the last few yards towards the house, now almost submerged, on whose rooftop Jake wobbled dangerously, clutching the sodden quilt. 'Sam Savage, me ol' mate! What a hero!'

A *hero*? Sam thought. He must know I've come to kill him. Then I will be shriven. 'Dusn'a know *narthen*?' he shouted. 'I be 'ere to *kill* thee, loike Oi promised. Thou murdered that girl, 'twasna me, but Oi've bin punished!' His throat rasped from the efforts of the last hour and it hurt to roar against the wind.

Jake heard, and now he was afraid. The boat was rocking unsteadily against the wall of the house. Sam stood up and flexed his knees, struggling to keep his balance. For a moment Jake had the advantage. He slithered down the roof tiles towards the boat and leaned out to grab one of the rowlocks. As he did so, Sam lifted an oar and smote him over the head, once, twice, thrice, until the blood ran through his matted black hair. He lifted the oar time after time, smashing it down on Jake's clutch-ing fingers, Jake's outstretched arm, his broad shoulders. Finally he stopped and the body bobbed and eddied in the black water before floating off slowly and with great solemnity. Sam watched it for twenty yards or so, then turned his little boat round and began to row away.

The wind was behind him now but Sam had no idea where he had left his bicycle. If the tide began to turn, he thought, it might drag him towards the sea and he was already exhausted. He'd never be able to row against it. He glanced back to try to orientate himself by the stars but they were obscured by scudding clouds. The moon, then. How much time had passed; how far would the moon have swung in its nightly circle? It hung in the sky, apparently motionless, shedding light over a flickering sheet of water broken here and there by the tops of trees. No sign of Jake. Just glide, he thought, and let the elements do the work. He shipped the oars and as the waves carried him steadily along, he began to pray. *Our Father which art in heaven, Hallowed be thy name. Thy kingdom come. Thy will be done on earth, as it is in heaven. Give us this day our daily bread. And forgive us our trespasses* ... Will God forgive me my trespasses? I took the Indian girl by force and now I've killed Jake. Seventeen years I've waited. But seventeen years in prison would be longer than a life sentence ... *forgive us our trespasses as we forgive those that trespass against us. For thine is the kingdom, the power and the glory, for ever and ever. Amen.* The boat dipped and swayed at the mercy of the wind and rain.

The trees were growing taller now; the tops of bushes began to emerge and not long afterwards, prodding with an oar, he felt muddy ground. The little boat rocked and scraped and abruptly beached itself beside a waterlogged path. Peering through the rain along the bordering trees, Sam could see something gleaming. Settling the oars tidily side by side under his seat, he clambered out of the boat and began to splash through deep puddles towards his bicycle.

I'm looking forward to my warm bed, he thought; I shall sleep well tonight. And when all this is over, I shall find out if my trespasses have been forgiven.

AFTERWORD

THE LAWS OF MANU – THE CLASSIC CODE OF INDIAN SACRED law, written around the third century AD – set out the rules of the caste system as they relate to Untouchables. Most enforce their permanent subjection. For example:

The dwellings of the *candala* (Untouchables) should be outside the village; they must use discarded bowls and dogs and donkeys should be their wealth. Their clothing should be the clothes of the dead and their food should be in broken dishes.

They should not walk about in villages and city by night. They may move by day to do their work, recognizable by distinctive marks.

If a man has touched an Untouchable, he can be cleansed by a bath.

Those who are . . . born of degradation should make their living by their innate activities,* which are reviled by the higher castes.

---

* In other words, dealing with everything associated with waste, filth, blood, birth and death.

341

'Young women are unusually vulnerable here [in the south Indian state of Kerala], as an almost incredible story in the *New Indian Express* brought home to me. Three years ago a schoolgirl was raped by forty-one men. The accused, whose names have long been known, have not yet been brought to trial. Meanwhile the victim and her family are objects of derision. A woman police officer sent to guard the girl threw water over the disgraced family's dry firewood. When the mother complained, the policewoman asked why, if she was so particular about guarding her firewood, she had failed to guard her daughter.'

Brenda Maddox, 'A Marxist Paradise for Women',
New Statesman, 14 June 1999

ACKNOWLEDGEMENTS

THIS NOVEL WAS INSPIRED BY A TELEVISION SERIES CALLED *Ruling Passions*, produced by Anton Gill and shown on BBC2 in March 1995. Specifically, it was prompted by a brief interview in the second episode. I am grateful to Roger Bolton Productions, Amanda Seely the programme researcher and in particular to David Wilson the director, for allowing me to draw on that series.

Rudyard Kipling's *Mowgli Stories* were the genesis of my love and respect for India. I first read them at the age of nine and must have reread them dozens of times and to this day I know bits of them by heart.

I began my research for this novel in a fog of ignorance that gradually lifted thanks to the many people who shared their knowledge and information. Some mistakes are bound to remain – all mine – but I am grateful to all those listed below.

In Mumbai, Professor Nilufer Bharucha, Ph.D., from the Department of English at the University of Mumbai, my first informant and constant guide; and also some of her students with whom I had interesting conversations; John Edmundson, director of the British Council in Mumbai, and Havovi

Kolsawallah, for inviting me to a seminar at the university in 1996; Mrs Sathya Saran, my friend and the editor of *Femina*, for letting me stay with her in Mumbai and glimpse the nature and traditions of Indian family life; Dr Firdaus Gandavia, for answering many ignorant questions.

In Kanpur, Mr R. N. Misra, former Professor and Head of the Department of Sociology at V.S.S.D. College Kanpur, shared his knowledge of the villages of Uttar Pradesh, escorted me to one in particular and introduced me to many people living there. He also allowed me to consult a thesis submitted in 1962 by his former student, Chandra Pal Singh Bhadauria. My thanks are due also to Professor Hem Lata Swarup, former Vice-Chancellor of Kanpur University. Dr Munishwar Nigam, unofficial historian of Kanpur, provided much information and access to a quite invaluable map of the town in the 1930s.

In Lucknow, Begum Habibullah was kind, helpful and extremely interesting on the subject of the British Army in India.

In Delhi, we enjoyed the hospitality and helpfulness of David and Jenny Housego. Mark Tully and Gillian Wright also talked to Tony Price during his research and Gillian generously checked the book for errors in typescript.

In London, thanks are due to my neighbour Martin Rowlands, whose knowledge of the railway systems and timetables of the world, especially India, is inexhaustible; to Peter Scott, whose military expertise and willingness to share it know no bounds; and to Ian Jack, who read an early draft of Part Two.

In Suffolk, I am grateful to the Suffolk Records Office at Ipswich, especially Angela Plumb. Nick Farnes checked the relevant chapters for Suffolk detail and pronounced most of it correct. Thanks for spotting the bits that weren't.

While researching this novel I consulted more than sixty books about Suffolk and India – and then tried to forget most of what I had read, since mine is a work of fiction. The village of Lower Flexham, like all its inhabitants, is entirely imaginary. Budhera, near Kanpur, is based on a real village but I have changed its name and location. Its inhabitants too are invented.

I owe special thanks to Lindsay Jones for correcting the sections on bell-ringing and to Dr Peter Jones for faxing instant replies to my questions. My agent, Caradoc King, a king among agents and a paragon among friends, had more than his usual creative influence upon this book. Peter Snow encouraged me with boisterous enthusiasm at a stage when I felt I would never finish it. My children Carolyn Butler, Johnnie Lambert and Marianne Vizinczey-Lambert read each successive draft and made lucid, scathing and helpful criticisms.

Tony Price acted as my researcher in India for six gruelling weeks and my guide during a further week there in 1999, and was the patient first and last reader of every paragraph in every draft. His hard work and perceptive comments helped, as always, to make this book what it is – whatever that may be.

Angela Lambert
Groléjac
April 1995–November 2000

SELECT BIBLIOGRAPHY

India

Allen, Charles (ed.), *Plain Tales from the Raj, Images of British India in the Twentieth Century*, André Deutsch/BBC, 1975

Anand, Mulk Raj, *Coolie*, 1936

Anand, Mulk Raj, *Untouchable*, with an introduction by E. M. Forster, 1935

Bhadauria, Chandra Pal Singh, *Agrarian Reforms and the Rural Community: A Sociological Study of the Impact of Post-Independence Agrarian Reforms on Amiliha in the District of Kanpur*, field report submitted for the MA degree of Kanpur University, 1962

Kipling, Rudyard, *The Complete Verse*, Kyle Cathie, 1996

Kipling, Rudyard, *The Mowgli Stories*, Pan Books, 1948, taken from *The Jungle Book*, 1894, and *The Second Jungle Book*, 1895

Narayan, R. K., *The Bachelor of Arts*, Nelson, 1937

Narayan, R. K., *Gods, Demons and Others*, Heinemann, 1964

Nehru, Jawaharlal, *The Discovery of India* (especially 'The Theory and Practice of Caste'), written in prison 1945, Asia Publishing House, 1961

SELECT BIBLIOGRAPHY

Oatts, Lt Col L. B., *Proud Heritage: The Story of the 74th Highland Light Infantry* Part IV 1919–1959, House of Grant Ltd, Glasgow, 1963

Srinivas, M. N., *The Remembered Village*, OUP, 1976

Stuart, Lt Col A. G., *The Indian Empire: A Short Review and Some Hints for the Use of Soldiers Proceeding to India*, HMSO, 1920

Times of India archive: newspapers from 1936

Viramma, Racine, Josiane, and Racine, Jean-Luc, *Viramma: Life of an Untouchable*, Verso, 1997

Wiser, William, and Wiser, Charlotte, *Behind Mud Walls 1930–1960*, University of California Press, 1963

Suffolk

Blythe, Ronald, *Akenfield*, Allen Lane the Penguin Press, 1969

East Anglian Daily Times archives for January/February 1953

Evans, George Ewart, *Ask the Fellows Who Cut the Hay*, Faber & Faber, 1956

Evans, George Ewart, *The Crooked Scythe: An Anthology of Oral History*, Faber & Faber, 1993

Evans, George Ewart, *The Pattern under the Plough: Aspects of the Folk Life of East Anglia*, Faber & Faber, 1966

Malster, Robert, *The Mardler's Companion: A Dictionary of East Anglian Dialect*, Malthouse Press, Suffolk, 1999

Summers, Dorothy, *The East Coast Floods*, David & Charles, 1978

Wilson, Angus (ed.), *East Anglia in Verse*, Penguin, 1984